D0030260

# CALLING
## THE **DEAD**

DISCARDED

# What Reviewers Say About Bold Strokes Books

"With its expected unexpected twists, vivid characters and healthy dose of humor, *Blind Curves* is a very fun read that will keep you guessing." – *Bay Windows*

"In a succinct film style narrative, with scenes that move, a character-driven plot, and crisp dialogue worthy of a screenplay ... the Richfield and Rivers novels are ... an engaging Hollywood mystery ... series." – *Midwest Book Review*

*Force of Nature* "...is filled with nonstop, fast paced action. Tornadoes, raging fire blazes, heroic and daring rescues... Baldwin does a fine job of describing the fast-paced scenes and inspiring the reader to keep on turning the pages." – *L-word.comLiterature*

In the Jude Devine mystery series the "...characters seem fully capable of walking away from the particulars of whodunit and engaging the reader in other aspects of their lives." – *Lambda Book Report*

*Mine* "...weaves a tale of yearning, love, lust, and conflict resolution ... a believable plot, with strong characters in a charming setting." – *JustAboutWrite*

"While these two women struggle with their issues, there is some very, very hot sex. If you enjoy complex characters and passionate sex scenes, you'll love *Wild Abandon*." – *MegaScene*

"*Course of Action* is a romance ... populated with a host of captivating and amiable characters. The glimpses into the lifestyles of the rich and beautiful people are rather like guilty pleasures ... a most satisfying and entertaining reading experience." – *Midwest Book Review*

*The Clinic* is "...a spellbinding novel." – *JustAboutWrite*

"*Unexpected Sparks* lived up to its promise and was thoroughly enjoyable ... Dartt did a lovely job at building the relationship between Kate and Nikki." – *Lambda Book Report*

"*Sequestered Hearts* ... is everything a romance should be. It is teeming with longing, heartbreak, and of course, love. As pure romances go, it is one of the best in print today." – *L-word.comLiterature*

"*The Exile and the Sorcerer* is a mesmerizing read, a tour-de-force packed with adventure, ordeals, complex twists and turns, and the internal introspection of appealing characters." – *Midwest Book Review*

*The Spanish Pearl* is "...both science fiction and romance in this adventurous tale ... A most entertaining read, with a sequel already in the works. Hot, hot, hot!" – *Minnesota Literature*

"A deliciously sexy thriller ... *Dark Valentine* is funny, scary, and very realistic. The story is tightly written and keeps the reader gripped to the exciting end." – *JustAbout Write*

"*Punk Like Me* ... is different. It is engaging. It is life-affirming. Frankly, it is genius. This is a rare book in that it has a soul; one that is laid bare for all to see." – *JustAboutWrite*

"*Chance* is not a novel about the music industry; it is about a woman discovering herself as she muddles through all the trappings of fame." – *Midwest Book Review*

*Sweet Creek* "... is sublimely in tune with the times." – *Q-Syndicate*

"*Forever Found* ... neatly combines hot sex scenes, humor, engaging characters, and an exciting story." – *MegaScene*

*Shield of Justice* is a "...well-plotted...lovely romance...I couldn't turn the pages fast enough!" – Ann Bannon, author of *The Beebo Brinker Chronicles*

*The 100th Generation* is "...filled with ancient myths, Egyptian gods and goddesses, legends, and, most wonderfully, it contains the lesbian equivalent of Indiana Jones living and working in modern Egypt." – *Just About Write*

*Sword of the Guardian* is "...a terrific adventure, coming of age story, a romance, and tale of courtly intrigue, attempted assassination, and gender confusion ... a rollicking fun book and a must-read for those who enjoy courtly light fantasy in a medieval-seeming time." – *Midwest Book Review*

"*Of Drag Kings and the Wheel of Fate*'s lush rush of a romance incorporates reincarnation, a grounded transman and his peppy daughter, and the dark moods of a troubled witch—wonderful homage to Leslie Feinberg's classic gender-bending novel, *Stone Butch Blues*." – *Q-Syndicate*

In *Running with the Wind* "...the discussions of the nature of sex, love, power, and sexuality are insightful and represent a welcome voice from the view of late-20-something characters today." – *Midwest Book Review*

"Rich in character portrayal, *The Devil Inside* is an unusual, unpredictable, and thought-provoking love story that will have the reader questioning the definition of right and wrong long after she finishes the book." – *JustAboutWrite*

*Wall of Silence* "...is perfectly plotted and has a very real voice and consistently accurate tone, which is not always the case with lesbian mysteries." – *Midwest Book Review*

Visit us at www.boldstrokesbooks.com

## By the Author

Carly's Sound

Second Season

Calling the Dead

<u>The Cain Casey Saga</u>

The Devil Inside

The Devil Unleashed

Deal with the Devil

# CALLING
# THE DEAD

*by*

Ali Vali

2008

Prescott Valley Public Library

**CALLING THE DEAD**
© 2008 BY ALI VALI. ALL RIGHTS RESERVED.

ISBN 10: 1-60282-037-6
ISBN 13: 978-1-60282-037-1

THIS TRADE PAPERBACK ORIGINAL IS PUBLISHED BY
BOLD STROKES BOOKS, INC.
P.O. BOX 249
VALLEY FALLS, NY 12185

FIRST EDITION: NOVEMBER 2008

THIS IS A WORK OF FICTION. NAMES, CHARACTERS, PLACES, AND
INCIDENTS ARE THE PRODUCT OF THE AUTHOR'S IMAGINATION OR
ARE USED FICTITIOUSLY. ANY RESEMBLANCE TO ACTUAL PERSONS,
LIVING OR DEAD, BUSINESS ESTABLISHMENTS, EVENTS, OR LOCALES
IS ENTIRELY COINCIDENTAL.

THIS BOOK, OR PARTS THEREOF, MAY NOT BE REPRODUCED IN ANY
FORM WITHOUT PERMISSION.

**CREDITS**
EDITOR: SHELLEY THRASHER AND STACIA SEAMAN
PRODUCTION DESIGN: STACIA SEAMAN
COVER DESIGN BY SHERI (GRAPHICARTIST2020@HOTMAIL.COM)

# Acknowledgments

My thanks to Radclyffe for her continued belief and support in me and the stories. There is no better publisher, cheerleader, and advocate in this business, and I feel fortunate to be a part of the BSB family.

Thank you to my editor Shelley Thrasher for her input and continued support, and to Stacia Seaman for her eagle eye and ideas to make the book better.

To my beta readers Kathi Isserman and Connie Ward, I appreciate all your hard work and suggestions as the book came together. Also, thank you both for all you do for me and everyone at BSB.

The start of a new series is a daunting task, and this one more so since it starts in post-Katrina New Orleans. That storm changed not only the city but the citizens like C and me who love it. We know now that there isn't anything we can't survive as long as eventually there's air-conditioning.

For C—my partner, editor, and biggest supporter, thank you for sharing your life and yourself with me and giving me the strength to rebuild.

And finally, thanks to you, the reader, for your encouragement and your thirst for more.

# Dedication

For C
my partner
and
best friend

# CHAPTER ONE

S ave my baby." Noel Benko sounded frantic just before she disappeared into the brown, murky water. "Please, Sept," she pled again when her head popped up briefly, farther away, before the flood swallowed her, leaving no trace of her or her five-year-old daughter Sophie.

A few feet away Sept gulped air before plunging under again, trying desperately to find them both. The water had started out clear, so she could see Noel flailing against the current, her movements panicked, like she was fighting to get her head above the surface. Knowing her sister Noel had never learned to swim, Sept struggled harder to get to her. Only Sophie and her safety would have made Noel jump in at all.

No matter how hard Sept kicked, she couldn't get any closer, and her lungs felt tight from being submerged so long. She kicked for the surface, and as she sucked in a breath she heard Sophie's voice in the direction opposite from where Noel had disappeared.

"Come get me, Aunt Sept," Sophie screamed, her little hands slapping the surface of the water. "I'm scared. Please, come get me."

"Hold on, Sophie," Sept said as loud as she could. She felt like she'd been treading water for hours, but she wasn't any closer to Noel or Sophie.

"We're here, Sept," Noel said. Her voice sounded weak. "Why won't you help us? I can't do this by myself."

Sept dove, trying to forget the ache in her chest, and finally almost reached her loved ones. They were floating peacefully, holding hands and smiling at her. They didn't need to fight anymore, but Sept kept swimming so she could touch them.

Noel shook her head and lifted her free hand—not to stop her, but to wave good-bye. Just before Sept reached them, the serene picture of mother and child changed into one of grotesque bloated bodies that stared at her in disgust before they vanished into the water that had killed them.

Lieutenant Sept Savoie woke up in a sweat, bile in the back of her throat. The recurring nightmare was no easier to accept with time. Almost four months had passed since Noel and Sophie had died during Hurricane Katrina, but the pain of losing them was still fresh and heavy in her chest.

"Fuck," Sept said as she poured two fingers of vodka from the bottle she kept in her freezer. She'd fallen asleep on the couch again, thinking the change of scenery would change her nightly sojourns to hell. The nightmare's only reality was that Sophie and Noel had died alone, and no wishes or dreams would change that fact.

The smooth liquor left a warm trail from her throat to her stomach. She poured a splash more before she returned the bottle, not wanting to endure another lecture from her mama about how Grey Goose wasn't a cure-all.

"You drinking yourself to death ain't going to bring her back," Sept said, imitating Camille Savoie. She finger-combed her white hair back impatiently, noting that she needed to get it cut.

The red numbers on the clock in her bedroom changed to 5:00 when she dropped her gun, badge, and cuffs on the bed. She tossed her shirt and pants into the hamper in the closet before she stepped into the shower. She wouldn't be able to sleep. Work was the only place she could escape the dreams.

She ignored the suits that hung on the left side of the closet. The dress code had relaxed since *that day*, and because no one had said anything about her khakis and leather jacket, she pulled the next pair of pressed pants off the hanger.

Most New Orleanians referred to August twenty-ninth as *that day*, probably to keep from cursing or crying—depending on what they'd lost, or who. Hurricane Katrina had changed everything, from the old neighborhoods to the people whose lives she'd wrecked when the levees broke. As Sept drove through the French Quarter, she likened it to ordering gumbo and being served hot water. Katrina had scattered the ingredients that made New Orleans unique.

Some characters were already out at this hour. It'd take time before the Big Easy shook off her beating and returned to the business of being simply New Orleans.

"What the hell you doing back here already?" Royce Belanger, French Quarter Bureau Chief of Detectives, asked Sept as she dropped into her office chair. A twenty-two-year veteran of the force, he displayed the stress of the job in his hair and his waistline. The small potbelly had more to do with his love of food than beer, and his light brown hair now resembled a laurel wreath, but Royce's smile hadn't changed much.

"Couldn't sleep." She flipped through her messages, sorting them into two piles. "What's your excuse?"

"I got tired of my wife bitchin' about the mold on the walls I haven't gotten around to ripping out yet." Royce sat down next to her desk and scratched his stomach. "It's not like I've fucking forgotten there's mold on the walls. Hell, some of it's so colorful I think I'll leave it as a conversation piece."

"You ought to get the place gutted as soon as possible." Sept finished categorizing her messages and sat back. "If you have to live in that FEMA trailer too much longer, one of you isn't going to make it."

"I complain a lot about my wife, but I wouldn't lay a hand on her."

"Who the hell said anything about you? My money's on her," Sept said, and laughed. Royce looked at her with what she'd describe as nostalgia. Laughing wasn't something she did much anymore.

"Sept, heads up, you got a visitor," the cop at the desk yelled. Their precinct house was one of the few not working out of a trailer, so nothing much had changed except that the equipment wasn't all up and running, including the intercom system. The place hadn't flooded, but the old roof had let a lot of rainwater redecorate the walls and the wiring.

Sept pressed her fingernails into her palm, her habitual reaction whenever she saw Damien Benko now.

She had attended the academy with Damien, and after a year of riding a beat with more seasoned cops, they'd even partnered together. Not long after that she'd taken him home for Sunday dinner because her family wanted to meet her partner, so Sept had finally given in.

Damien hadn't noticed Sept's mama's cooking as much as her sister Noel, with her easy charm. After that he became a fixture at the

Savoie table on more than just Sunday afternoons. He kept coming around until Noel agreed to marry him, continuing a Savoie family tradition of either becoming a cop or marrying one.

When Sept got her gold shield, she left Damien behind, but that was okay with him. He was happy patrolling the streets and going home to Noel and Sophie every afternoon. He had decided for Noel and Sophie not to evacuate. He'd told them to stay put so he wouldn't worry about them, using the same rationale that so many in the city had.

"Our house didn't flood during Betsy," Sept could hear him saying when she asked where he'd sent Noel to ride out the storm. Hurricane Betsy—the storm that had hit New Orleans in the mid-sixties—had forever become the marker for so many, including a lot who weren't even alive when Betsy came ashore. The false assumption that if a house hadn't flooded then it wouldn't flood now had caused the tragedy the rest of the country watched on television.

Damien's decision had cost them all dearly. The day the levees broke, Sept and her brothers Gustave and Joel made it to their sister's house by boat and discovered only the hole that Noel had cut so she and Sophie could climb out of the attic and onto the roof. When they didn't find them, they thought a more zealous rescuer had beaten them there. Their sense of dread blossomed when they spotted the neighbors huddled together on the next roof.

The man who had gotten his family to safety on his rooftop told them that, after sitting next to her mother for hours, Sophie had wandered to the edge, and their shouts had woken Noel from the light sleep she had succumbed to. Noel and her neighbor had jumped in after Sophie, but he lost both of them in the strong current of the floodwaters.

Sept and her family didn't blame Damien for what happened, but he tested Sept's patience every time she had to see or deal with him. She hadn't yet forgiven him as fully as her parents had. Her head knew Damien would change what had happened if he could, but the loss of her sister had left a void in her heart, and for that she fully blamed Damien.

The door into the bullpen buzzed, and Damien shambled around and moved slowly toward her desk. His once-handsome face appeared haggard and wan, and his clothes and hair were disheveled. As Sept stared at him she thought about the lecture Noel would have given him for appearing in public like this.

"What you doing out this early?" Royce asked him.

"Just walking," Damien said, so low they had to strain to hear him. "I couldn't sleep."

"You're not taking the pills the doctor sent you?" Sept asked.

"I start taking pills and they won't let me go back to work," he said, louder. "And I want to come back. If I have to stare at the walls of that trailer much longer, I'm going to lose it."

Sept and Royce glanced at each other briefly but kept quiet. It'd be a while before Damien would be cleared for duty. The house, his wife, and his daughter were gone, and no amount of gutting and cleaning were going to make his life whole again. When Sept and her brothers had gotten back from the flooded house without Noel and Sophie, Damien had snapped.

After that he had been on leave until he could demonstrate some level of stability. Everyone handled grief differently, and while Sept had thrown herself into work to forget, Damien had locked himself away in the trailer the government had given him and stared at the hole in his roof for hours on end. These rare visits occurred when he could no longer take the loneliness.

"If you want to get out more, that means you're getting better," Sept finally said. She wanted to avoid him, but thought about what Noel would've wanted. "Why don't you accept the department's counseling offer? Talking about it can only speed up the process."

"You think the guys would ever take me seriously again if I go see some shrink?"

"Most of the guys on duty are in counseling, and they've just lost their houses. You've got a bigger load than that." Sept's words only made him shake his head, and she didn't see any sense in pushing him and making it worse. "Come on then, let me take you home."

"I don't need your help," Damien said, sounding frustrated. "Sorry, didn't mean to yell. I just wanted to stop by, but I want to walk some more."

"Let me drive you. You know Mama wouldn't want you to get hurt."

"I'll walk." Damien got up and bunched his coat together in front and lifted his hand in a brief wave before he hurried out, as if he was afraid Sept would try to stop him.

"He's not getting any better," Royce said.

"He refuses any help from any of us no matter how often we try, and my mama's tried harder than anyone."

"Camille's a good woman," Royce said, and pointed to the picture on Sept's desk. The Savoies were almost legendary. "That's the way she's wired. She can't help but worry and want to help—you and your dad and brothers have made it so."

Their history had begun with Eulin Savoie patrolling the streets in the 1940s, when he was kept busy with organized crime and the less classy remnants of the famous red-light district of Storyville with its multitude of brothels.

His son Sebastian followed him into a patrol car in the 1960s, when the city was electrified with the hunt for John F. Kennedy's assassin. Sebastian married into another cop family, and he and Camille Falgout raised their seven children while Sebastian's career in the police department took off until he became the chief of detectives.

With five sons and their youngest daughter, Sept, on the job, Camille had plenty to worry about. The only one who hadn't gone into law enforcement was Noel, but she'd married a cop and followed her mother's path.

"Mama just needs something to take her mind off all the stuff she doesn't want to face," Sept said. "She can't fix Damien or what happened with a pot of gumbo, but she tries, bless her heart, so she doesn't have to think about how empty her kitchen is now that Noel's no longer around."

"Are you sure she isn't the only one who doesn't want to forget about what happened?" Royce asked. "Why don't you take the advice you gave Damien?"

"You saying I need therapy?" Sept laughed at the absurd notion. "What I need is a new partner."

"Just think about it." Royce stood and put his hand on her shoulder. "And I've got a lead on a partner. Your pop reassigned some kid named Nathan Blackman off patrol. Sebastian thought he's got potential and you'd be a good trainer."

"I'm getting someone green?"

"I'm green, but I'm eager," Nathan said from the door, then flashed a smile that Sept figured most women fell for, when you added his blond hair and green eyes into the mix. "Everyone has to start somewhere, right?"

Royce laughed but Sept didn't crack a smile. The storm had driven a lot of cops, including her old partner, to quit for a multitude of reasons. He'd turned in his badge for a sledgehammer and started a business gutting houses.

Sept's phone rang and she started taking notes as she listened to the person on the other end. "Okay, just make sure you rope off the area until we get there."

"Catch something?" Royce asked.

"Patrol found some guy laid out behind the Dumpster at Blanchard's bleeding from a few holes in his chest. The order came from downtown for us to take it."

"Take Blackman with you," Royce said, and rapped his knuckles on her desk before he stood up. "No time like now to get used to each other. Keep me in the loop. The chief is riding our ass about preventing crime, since the world's watching us. And if they've already gotten word on this, they'll want it wrapped up by noon."

"No pressure, then," Sept said.

# CHAPTER TWO

I said get back behind the tape," Officer Lourdes Garcia ordered the news-sniffing media. "If I have to say it again, I'm arresting whoever I get my hands on first."

"Does that go for me too?" Sept asked softly as she lifted the yellow crime scene tape. Scenes like this weren't so common after the hurricane. Fewer people meant less crime, especially since so many citizens, including the criminals, had evacuated to other parts of the country. Now places like Houston were dealing with their killers and drug pushers.

"Anytime you want to get up close and personal with my handcuffs, Detective, feel free to call," Lourdes whispered back. Sept made no secret of or excuses for her lesbian lifestyle, so some of the female cops flirted whether they were straight or not.

"Tempting," Sept said with a smile. "Tell me what you've got."

"Male, about forty, shot in the chest a few times from the looks of it, and his pockets were turned inside out," Lourdes said. "Simple robbery gone bad, if you ask me."

"What's the big fuss, then?" Sept took her pad from the inside pocket of her leather jacket and headed toward the Dumpster. She waved to Nathan, who was walking too slowly.

"You're kidding, right?" Lourdes laughed. "Somebody gets popped behind Blanchard's," she said slowly, as if Sept would catch on. "This is Della Blanchard we're talking about. Her family is like the royal family of New Orleans cuisine. They own this place, Della's, uptown, and the Le Coquille D'Huître in the Quarter."

"I know who the Blanchards are. I just don't see why this is a major case."

A woman standing by the restaurant's back door interrupted them. "Because the guy we found this morning is our pastry chef, and it upset my grandmother. According to her, his raspberry tart soufflé was to die for. We just didn't take her that seriously." Her arms were crossed, her thick red hair pulled into a tight ponytail, and her pressed chef's uniform was pristinely white. "Della Blanchard is a hard worker, but hardly royalty, Officer," she informed Lourdes.

"That's her granddaughter, Keegan," Lourdes whispered, and pointed stealthily.

"Who found him?" Sept asked.

"One of our cleaning crew this morning." Even though Sept had addressed Lourdes, Keegan answered and kept her eyes on Sept the entire time. "And you are?"

"Detective Sept Savoie, Ms. Blanchard." Sept nodded in Keegan's direction. "If you could wait inside until we're done, I'm sure I'll have some more questions later." Keegan didn't move at first but gave in as Sept opened her mouth to say something else.

"Tell me what you see, Nathan." Sept took a step back, carefully placing her feet so as not to compromise any evidence. Her father had used this method to teach her, and it was a good way to judge Nathan's potential.

"He stepped out here to smoke, some guy shot him, then emptied his pockets. Lourdes was right, it's a robbery gone bad."

"Did you offer to wash my father's car for the rest of his life in exchange for this job?" She held her hand up to keep him from moving. "If that's all the effort you're planning to put in, I suggest you go sit in the car and plan your return to patrol."

"What am I missing?"

Sept squatted by the body and used the end of her pen as a pointer. "He was stabbed, not shot, since the hole, not holes, in his chest shows no sign of a gunshot but rather a long, even cut. There aren't any cigarettes anywhere near him or on him, so we can assume he was out here for something else."

"The killer could've taken his pack."

"He was killed for his pack of cigarettes?" Sept phrased it so Nathan would understand what an idiot she thought he was.

"What's your theory?"

"Step over here." She walked to the area behind the restaurant and away from the cameras, but in view of the kitchen's windows. "How close do I have to be to you to stab you in the chest? Remember, one stab most probably hit his heart, from the position of the wound."

Nathan stepped within arm's length of her, and she slowly put away her pen and notebook. "About this close, if you have to swing hard enough to sink it in that deep."

"Think you'd let someone you don't know this close if you're just outside for a smoke?" She inched nearer, to the distance she thought she'd need to be.

"No," Nathan said hesitantly.

"Uh-huh." Sept glanced toward the back of the restaurant and noticed Keegan Blanchard watching her. With enough speed to make the blow more of a surprise than anything, she punched Nathan in the chest so hard he doubled over. She punched him in the jaw next, dropping him to his knees. "If I'd had a knife in my hand you'd be dead from the first blow."

"Then what the fuck was the second shot for?" Nathan spit out a good amount of blood.

"For going into a crime scene with your eyes on Lourdes's ass instead of what they're supposed to be on." She held her hand out to help him up. "Want to walk the scene again, or you ready to hit the beat?"

"You gonna clobber me again?"

"Depends on how slow a learner you are," Sept said, already walking away from him. "Come on, Watson, we're wasting time."

"Does that make you Sherlock?"

"Let me teach you a few things and you be the judge." She stopped three feet from the body. "Start at the most obvious thing and work your way out."

"How about you use this one as a tutorial?"

"The dead guy is the most obvious thing," she said as she reached for her pad again. "As I just demonstrated, he probably knew who killed him, since he let him or her into his comfort zone. Whoever it was stabbed him in the heat of the moment, then two things probably happened."

"What?" Nathan asked.

"Panic and regret."

"How the hell do you know that?"

"So skeptical already?" Sept laughed, then squatted closer to the body. "I could just say human nature. Wouldn't you panic if you'd just fatally stabbed someone? Wouldn't you regret that?" She pointed to the guy's chest.

"I've never killed someone, but yeah, I think I'd feel bad."

"Most people never contemplate murder and don't consider it a normal way to handle a situation."

Nathan stepped closer. "Are you saying it is for some people?"

"A handful has a driving need to kill. I call them hunters." Sept pointed to the right side of the body. "But in a robbery it's all about speed. They do the deed and want to get out before anyone sees anything."

"Is that what happened here?"

"The victim allowed the person close enough to kill him. That's the main thing. There was minimal struggle, he got stabbed and died where he landed, since I can't see any blood trace anywhere else. But have forensics go through here carefully."

"Sure thing," Nathan said as he took notes. "What else?"

With her pen Sept pointed to the blood pool. "This is what doesn't fit with the true murder-for-robbery scenario."

"If he's been out here all night, it's not weird that he's got all that blood around him."

The victim looked like he'd lain down, then someone had poured a can of blood over him and it had run three feet to the left side of his torso. "The blood isn't what's out of place. It's that." Sept pointed to the two indentations in the blood pool opposite them. The spot was on the side closest to the building and obscured from the street because of the three Dumpsters and some newly planted shrubbery. "He was stabbed and fell here, then whoever did it knelt next to the body. The low temperatures last night made the blood congeal faster, but still it didn't happen instantly. And with only one wound for the blood to drain from, it took quite a while for that pool to form."

"Why'd the killer do that?"

"A good question." Sept waved over the department photographer who'd just arrived. "Unfortunately, I don't know, since the killer didn't leave a note with the details of the how and why."

"What's your best guess?"

Sept stood and stepped back. "What's your guess?" Nathan stayed quiet the whole time the forensic team went through their procedures, and Sept assumed he was thinking through his answer.

"From what you said, they were probably sorry they did it. Maybe they knelt there for a long time because they were in shock."

The answer surprised her, but revealed some of why her father had given Nathan a chance. "That's good, but take it one step further."

"A step further?"

"Whoever perpetrated this knelt here long enough to leave evidence that they were here. Who does that?" Sept asked as she kept her eyes on the windows of the kitchen that faced the side where they were standing. Only one person was interested in what they were doing, and Keegan Blanchard locked eyes with her.

"Someone who knew him?" This time Nathan answered with much more authority. "That makes sense, doesn't it? He killed the poor bastard and felt bad about it."

"There's hope for you, Blackman. Come on, let's go find our killer."

"Wait." He grabbed her by the sleeve and let go when she turned around and stared at him before she dropped her eyes to his hand and he removed it. "You think someone who works here killed him?"

"Do you know if he's married or seeing someone?" Sept was still, but her attention was again on Keegan, who stood at the window.

"I haven't even gotten his name yet."

"It doesn't matter." She pointed to the large pool of blood. "People who have something to be passionate about carry out crimes of passion, and we end up with a poor bastard next to a trash pile. In this case I'm guessing it was someone in there." When Sept cocked her head toward the building, Keegan disappeared.

As Sept and Nathan stepped through the door, Keegan drove a large chef's knife into the breast of a duck. She sliced through it so easily she seemed to be cutting soft butter.

"Ms. Blanchard," Sept said, to keep her distance. "Today's special?" She indicated the duck.

"One of them." Keegan cut the duck up and moved to the next one. "I don't usually get to do this, but the storm scattered our staff, so we're all having to kick in to keep the restaurants at the level people expect."

"Having a dead guy outside doesn't throw you off your game just a little?"

"His name was Donovan Bisland, Detective, and even though we'll miss him, the business has to go on." Keegan wiped her hands on a towel, then laid them on the stainless steel surface not covered in poultry. "Are you finished?"

Sept concentrated on Keegan's hands and noticed the bandage on each of her knuckles on her right hand. "We've almost finished outside, but we have some questions for you. Can someone take over for you?" Sept asked, meaning the ducks.

"You can ask me whatever you like right here."

"Okay." Sept dragged out the word. "How long have you been sleeping with the victim?"

"What?" Keegan screamed, clearly outraged. "I was *not* sleeping with him," she hissed, before she stormed out through the swinging doors that led to the first-floor dining room.

"Is your nickname Subtle Savoie?" Nathan asked as he studied more carefully the knife Keegan had left behind.

"Is that your way of begging me to pop you in the face again?"

Keegan was sitting at the center table, tapping her foot. "Did you think of some less stupid questions?"

Before Sept answered, she unclipped her phone from her belt and answered it. "Savoie." She wrote a few things in her pad. "What's your best guess on the time?"

Sept hung up, then asked Keegan, "Where were you last night between ten and midnight?"

"I was having dinner with my grandmother, mother, sister, and our business advisor at Le Coquille D'Huîte in the Quarter. We had dinner at eight, then talked about business until eleven thirty." Keegan fell silent for a moment, then scowled. "You think I had something to do with this?"

Sept figured she could play Keegan one of two ways, and if she picked wrong, the Blanchard family would quickly put a team of attorneys around Keegan that the Pentagon couldn't break through. If that happened, the next time she'd see Keegan was in court wearing a designer suit and a smug smile, but only if she was lucky enough to build a case against her.

"I didn't say that, Ms. Blanchard. We eliminate people until we find someone we can't."

"I suggest you start canvassing the neighborhood, then, because no one here is the killer."

"Don't worry, we'll do our jobs." Sept flipped to a new page in her pad. "Could you tell me why Mr. Bisland was here so late? Granted, it was Wednesday night, but it was still kind of late."

"Do you moonlight as a chef?"

The question made Sept smile. "If I did that, I'd have more than one lawsuit pending." The words made Keegan visibly relax. "I'm not trying to be flip or disrespectful, Ms. Blanchard, but I need to find out what happened."

"Donovan liked to stay late and try out new recipes, and late nights are the only time he had the kitchen to himself. We're famous for our bread-pudding soufflé, and he always wanted to find something to top it."

"Did anyone ever stay with him?" Sept figured that giving Keegan the upper hand was working, so now she just had to ask short questions to keep Keegan talking.

"After a long day most of the staff is ready to go home," Keegan said as she shook her head. The mask of control was staring to slip as her eyes filled with tears. "Usually the only one who volunteered to stay was me."

"Can you tell me what happened to your hand?" Sept kept her eyes on the fingers with the Band-Aids. Keegan started to flex her hand but stopped halfway to making a fist. Probably because it hurt.

"It's an occupational hazard. You work with food that makes your hands wet and slippery, and sometimes the knife slips. But don't worry. My cuts are well covered and won't affect my cooking ability."

Keegan had given an answer, but not the one Sept was looking for. *"I was cutting a duck like you just saw me do and the knife slipped."* That was the difference between answering directly and answering in a nondescript way. "Does it hurt much?"

"No." Keegan answered as if words were at a premium.

"Were you and Mr. Bisland seeing each other socially?"

"Donovan was a creative genius in the kitchen, Detective, and he was a wonderful person to be around. That doesn't always translate into wanting to sleep with someone."

If Keegan had gotten close to breaking down, Sept realized that moment was gone. "I didn't ask if you were sleeping with him, ma'am. We covered that in the kitchen. There's a difference between sex and seeing someone socially, like in the occasional date."

"The way you keep harping on it makes me think otherwise."

"When did you cut yourself?" Sept changed tactics again, which made her sound like she suffered from ADHD, but questions out of sequence sometimes garnered more truthful and forthcoming answers than an interviewee intended.

"Yesterday morning."

"Anything else you want to share with me about Mr. Bisland?"

"He was my friend and someone viciously killed him. Stop wasting your time on me and go find whoever did. You owe him that." Keegan pushed away from the table and stood, then stalked out and slammed her way into the kitchen.

"That went well," Nathan said, his eyes on the still-swinging doors. "What now?"

"Now you ask the rest of the people in the kitchen the same questions I just asked Martha Stewart on steroids."

"Why me?"

"Because Ms. Blanchard is busy telling everyone in there what a bitch I am, so it's up to you to find the disgruntled cook wannabe to give us the real story on her." She shook her hand at him when he took a deep breath and opened his mouth to speak. "Trust me, someone in the place is always ready to roll on the boss. Also it'll show Keegan she's the only person I picked to talk to. People get nervous if the lead detective breaks them away from the herd."

"How come she won't think I'm not the lead detective?"

Sept couldn't help but laugh. "Mainly because she's not an idiot and she watched me punch you earlier. The fact that you stood there whining like a girl defined the chain of command for her."

# CHAPTER THREE

W hen Sept stepped back outside, she had to zip up her jacket because of the strengthening winds and the overcast sky. The crime scene tape was still up, but now that the body had been removed, the media had thinned out. Sept watched the two forensics guys examine the area.

George Falgout was twirling a print brush along the front of the Dumpster closest to where the body had lain, and his assistant Alex Perlis was taking pictures of the crime scene from every angle possible. The killer had most likely put his hand on the square George was checking to get back on his feet.

Still in his crouched position, George said, "Don't tell me you're going to run me ragged again, Sept? I've been enjoying the lull."

"I'll see what I can do. Find anything?"

"A lot of blood in this one spot, and not one fingerprint except on top of this damn thing." George expanded the area he was dusting. "Did you check these Dumpsters out?"

The question made Sept look at the three large metal boxes. Wiring coming out the back of each one was attached to an electric-appearing box. "What are the power stations for?"

"They're refrigerated," George said. "Like a big icebox full of bad food, and someone comes out here regularly and wipes the outside down."

"I guess the exorbitant prices for an entrée inside means no take-away from the Blanchards' dining experience."

"If you'd ever met Della Blanchard, kid, you'd understand the attention to detail." George finished his fingerprint search and began taking blood samples.

"Did she pass that along to her granddaughter, you think?" Sept ignored George for the moment and tried to imagine what the area looked like at night, because in the light, the place seemed fairly wide open. "It would take someone with a tremendous capacity for detail to not leave a trace of themselves at a scene like this. You know what Pop always says, Uncle George." The way Camille's brother stared at Sept reminded her of her mom when she was concentrating hard on something.

"There are monsters in the world, but no such thing as ghosts."

"Damn right." Sept continued to scrutinize every foot. "Only a ghost can come and go as he pleases and not leave a trace." The only thing that didn't make sense to her was the evidence that the killer knelt next to the body. Aside from the two indentations, none of the other blood was out of place. "Hey, Alex. Did you find any blood trace coming this way?" Sept was still standing by the door to the kitchen.

"No, but there isn't a drop in any other direction either." Alex removed the flash assembly from the camera and carefully placed it into its case.

"Keep at it. Nobody kneels in blood and doesn't leave a clue as to where they're headed next." She carefully made her way to George and patted him on the shoulder. "See you and Aunt Valerie Sunday."

George placed his hand over hers and repeated the mantra Sept's father had originated. "Remember to keep your head down."

She spent the rest of the afternoon going door to door in a two-block radius, hoping to find someone who saw or heard anything out of the ordinary. In a post-Katrina world, at least four out of ten homes were empty. The owners were either waiting for federal aid, battling their insurance companies, or seeing if the levees would be shored up.

"Any luck?" Sept asked Nathan when she got back and found him sitting on the front of the car.

"Keegan Blanchard was a bitch to you, but everyone else loves her. Not one disgruntled cook wannabe in there." Nathan flipped through his notes. "One of the dishwashers was the last person who saw Donovan alive. Like Keegan told us, this guy said Donovan was pulling ingredients out to work on something when he said good night. And everyone agreed that Keegan wasn't here because of that business dinner."

"Anyone strike you as hinky?" Sept turned the key in the ignition and put the car in reverse, but got only two feet before Keegan slammed her hands on the trunk. "What the hell?"

When Sept got out, Keegan said, "If you're leaving, take all this crap with you."

"What crap, Ms. Blanchard?"

"The yellow tape and the people trampling through my yard."

Sept followed the rigid finger in the direction Keegan pointed. "Sorry, the tape and the tramplers are staying until I release the crime scene."

"Which is when?"

"Around ten tonight."

"What?" The way Keegan shrieked made Sept press her fingers to the side of her head. "That's totally unacceptable."

"You asked me to do my job, didn't you? That's what I'm trying to do, so back off, lady." She raised her hand and Keegan clenched hers as if she wasn't intimidated at all.

"If you think you've heard the last of this, you're crazy."

Sept's father had told her she had an intuitive ability to read faces. She could detect the subtle signs that people tried to hide, but that in reality revealed the essence of who they were. And the truth of what and who they were bubbled up in a flash that they could no more deny than their name. The set of Keegan's mouth and the way she narrowed her eyes gave Sept what the crime scene could not.

Here was a woman whose passion probably made her great at her job, but could that be twisted to give her the ability to take a life? The way she didn't flinch made Sept think that Keegan was more than capable of driving a knife through Donovan's chest just as easily as a duck's.

"I'm sure your family knows everyone from the mayor on down, and a few phone calls could make my job more difficult," Sept said, trying to sound reasonable. "But you'd just delay us finding who did this. Do that and I have to ask myself why."

"Get out of here, and try to stay out of the way. Our lunch crowd will be here in a couple of hours, and it's hard enough to make a living without people being afraid they're in danger if they come in."

"We'll do our best, ma'am."

❖

For the rest of the afternoon Sept studied her notes and started her report, with Royce Belanger screaming at her for even thinking that Keegan could in any way be involved. Both he and the French Quarter district chief had given her their version of a talking-to, which meant Keegan hadn't kept her word.

"Where you going?" Royce asked when she reached for her jacket.

"To arrest Keegan Blanchard."

"The fuck you are."

The way the veins in Royce's neck and forehead stuck out made Sept laugh. "Crank it down a notch, sir." She took her gun from the top drawer of her desk and slipped it into her shoulder holster before slapping Royce on the back so hard he stumbled a step forward. "I'm on my way to Blanchard's, but it's to give the duck Nazi what she wants."

"What the hell are you talking about?"

"I'm going to release the crime scene."

"You call Della Blanchard's granddaughter the duck Nazi to her face, and I'm feeding you to the screaming assholes downtown who've been chewing on my ass all day." Royce shook his finger at her the entire time he was talking. "And get your ass home and get some sleep."

Alone, Sept drove back to the restaurant and parked a block away. In her career she'd worked a lot of murders, and living someplace like New Orleans meant she would never have a shortage of work.

She stood in the backyard of Blanchard's and glanced at her watch periodically.

The door would open every twenty minutes or so, and two guys would empty the kitchen's garbage cans into the Dumpsters. Sept had a good view of not only the restaurant but the street. If this had been a random crime, the perpetrator might take his chances again.

At ten, the traffic in the entire area slowed down until the last trip to the Dumpster was made and the door closed, and in the quiet Sept heard the dead bolt click into place. With most of the restaurant's lights off, this was the scene that Donovan had faced the night before.

Now the area was barely lit from the kitchen lights, because the streetlights were one of the storm's victims. She stood at the cusp of where the pool of blood had been and slowly surveyed the area again. The darkness made it hard to see the gate and the street beyond.

"If you want to scream at me some more I'll be happy to consent, but first give me ten minutes to think." Sept turned and faced a surprised Keegan, who leaned against the Dumpster and crossed her arms over her chest.

"How'd you know it was me?"

"A mixture of your perfume and spices," Sept said. The white chef's top added light to the area. "Or maybe it's that endless supply of sarcasm that just oozes off you. It's hard to tell."

"Do you have some sort of social disorder?" Keegan never moved.

"My mother thinks I'm the best thing since sliced French bread."

Keegan laughed so quickly it came out as a snort. "Even Son of Sam's mother loved him. That's not exactly a ringing endorsement."

"At least I don't go crying to her when someone wasn't willing to treat me like a princess." Sept tried her best to push Keegan's temper points to see the reaction.

"You think I called my mother and told on you?" The question still bore traces of sarcasm, but also a bit of humor.

"Maybe it was just my turn to have a bad day at work." Sept recalled the position of the body. If Keegan or someone else had come out of the kitchen, the argument had to have escalated to the point that the killer paced around Donovan. Judging from the way Donovan fell, he was facing the gate, not the door, because the wound he sustained was fatal. He hadn't fought at all. "Are you used to always getting your own way?"

"What the hell do you know about me?"

*Come on*, Sept mentally chanted. "You seem easy enough to read. If the world doesn't go your way, you change the world."

Keegan's fists clenched in front of her body, and even in the low light her heaving chest was visible. "You're an idiot if you think I did this, and that's what you believe, isn't it?"

"No, it's not, Ms. Blanchard. Please accept my apologies for being rude." Sept could see that Keegan had a temper but was also a control freak about keeping herself in check. Keegan would kill someone only if her own life was in danger, and according to everyone, including Keegan, Donovan was merely a threat to sugary treats.

"Not so fast." Keegan moved to face her. "Are you bipolar or something?"

"You liked it better when I considered you a suspect?" Sept said with a laugh. "You didn't do it, Ms. Blanchard, just accept it."

"Who did, then? Or do you not care?" Keegan acted like a balloon with a slow leak.

"I care about every case I work, ma'am. I wouldn't be here otherwise. Was your friend a smoker?"

"No, Donovan's only vice was sugar. That's what made him such a great pastry chef. He wasn't a violent person and didn't deserve such a horrible ending."

"No one does." Sept had to discover what he'd been doing out there in order to reconfigure her theory of the crime. "If you can, could you describe his routine when he stayed late?"

"He experimented, cooked, and cleaned up. He wanted to work here so he could try new things."

"What was he working on last night?"

"Why's that important? It's not why someone robbed him."

Keegan was obviously still angry because she was frustrated. "Investigating is like following a recipe, Ms. Blanchard, only in reverse. The result always has a reason. We simply have to find the ingredients that brought it about."

"It's December so it was probably something to do with pecans. We buy directly from certain farmers so our selections reflect our area, and the crop was late this year so we just started making pecan-based dishes." Keegan stared at the door as if trying to remember something. "The dirty pots were out this morning, which wasn't like Donovan."

"What was the dish?"

"The cleaning crew had a hard time getting out a hard coat of caramel at the bottom of his favorite pot. His pots were special, that one especially, since my grandmother gave it to him. He would have left it like that only because he was dead."

"I guess you have to cook to understand what you just said, because I don't get excited about pots."

"The dirty pot belonged to my great-great-grandmother. If your expertise is candy or desserts, you can't cook anything else in your pots. If you do, any impurities or spices in the pot end up where you don't want them."

"Good to know, if I have a sudden urge to whip up something sweet that I don't want to taste like fish. Find any caramel-pecan anything in there?" Sept pointed to the kitchen.

"Just the pot."

Sept shook her head and opened the top of the Dumpster Donovan was closest to when he died. She handed her jacket to Keegan and jumped in. Of course it had to be the one the busboys had used all night.

"Shouldn't you have done this earlier?"

"We did, but I was looking for one of those great knives you were using this morning, not sweets." Sept raised her voice as she moved bags around. With her small flashlight in her mouth she found what she was searching for in the front corner. Donovan had scraped his concoction into a piece of foil and tossed it in. "This look like something?"

"I didn't see the pot this morning, but that's how he got rid of anything he wasn't happy with. What does that prove?"

Sept pulled herself out and brushed her pants off, grimacing when she touched something cold and gooey. "Nothing yet, but now I know why he was out here."

"And?"

"Can I walk you to your car, Ms. Blanchard?"

"You're done talking to me?" Keegan gave Sept her coat and crossed her arms again.

"When I have something I'll let you know—you have my word. Can I give you that escort? I don't want you out here alone this late."

Keegan nodded and led Sept to the parking lot out back. She stopped next to the Mercedes coupe, and Sept wiped her hand before opening the door for her.

"Don't forget to keep me updated or I *will* call my mother."

For the first time after meeting Keegan, Sept laughed out of pure humor. "Be careful going home and I'll be in touch." She stood until Keegan turned out of the lot, and with her went any suspicion of anything sinister about this crime. It was a robbery gone bad, and that was it.

The little voice in her head was the only thing that put the brakes on that theory.

# CHAPTER FOUR

The pain behind his eyes made him want to rip them out of his head. He'd done what had been asked of him, but nothing had changed. The silence was overwhelming except for the voices that built his thirst for feeling the knife go in. The suddenness of the urge had surprised him more than anything. He had heard no voices of any kind until the night he saw the guy by the Dumpster. His white shirt had been like a blank canvas waiting to be painted.

That's why he'd stripped down despite the temperature. He'd knelt there in the quiet and followed the red blossom across the guy's chest until it spilt to the walkway and around his naked knees. It was the sacrifice his demons had demanded, but the satisfaction was fleeting.

When the blood had first touched his skin, like an electric shock, it had numbed the pain briefly. That pain—his excuse to stop everything—was the one constant in his life now.

At first the agony was so intense it made him pray to die, but then that misery had transmuted into hope. The necessary pain had given birth to the voice in his head, and no woman in his past had been so seductive.

It started the night he'd heard the guy cursing by the Dumpster. The screaming in his head promised him what he craved, if he would make the right sacrifice. He craved a second chance.

But something went wrong. He'd done what was asked of him, and the door he most wanted opened had stayed firmly shut. That's why he'd picked the woman next. The man had been wrong, but the woman's blood should grease the hinges that appeared welded shut.

The images on her chest were like the ones he'd seen in the book.

He'd knelt next to her too but again—nothing. He'd killed her, but instead of salvation, the emptiness had returned. That betrayal had angered him.

"What?" he screamed, and pulled the hair at the sides of his head. "I didn't do anything wrong."

"The first two were to see if you were worthy of even seeing the door."

The voice made him drop to his knees, his hands still pressed to his head. As much as he wanted to hear its promises, it scared him. He unsheathed the knife and placed it on the bed. The blade had been wiped clean, and in its reflection he could see the tears streaming down his face. Against the rotting sheets the knife did appear to be a shining symbol of hope.

"That's not what you said," he yelled directly at the knife. "You said if I killed them you'd give me what I wanted."

"Shut up and stop your sniveling. That's why you're here with me instead of where you want. You're a coward who doesn't deserve to be rewarded."

"I'm sorry...please." He picked up the knife and kissed the blade.

"Are you ready to begin?"

"I'll do whatever you want." He rocked as he held the knife against his chest, as if cradling a lover.

"Perhaps you'll be worthy yet, but first you have to prepare an altar. You've proved you have the courage to begin the journey, but the gods are thirsty for much more."

"Just tell me what you want me to do and I'll do it." His crying had stopped, and he returned the knife to its sheath with forceful authority. The voice was gone now, but he was calm enough to sleep. "Tomorrow night can't come soon enough," he said as he lay down. The bed smelled of mold and mud, but it brought him comfort, and as his eyes closed he thought of where to build his altar.

That he'd thought of it so quickly made him run his fingers along the handle of his knife. "I knew you weren't mad at me," he said to the voice.

"Sleep now, because you have so much more work to do."

❖

Sept's dashboard clock read 12:30 when she parked in front of her apartment in the Quarter. Her pants were a mess, but she pocketed her keys and walked to Pope's Pub on Royal Street.

When she straddled a bar stool the owner asked, "Aren't you a little old for a food fight?"

"Bite me, then pour me a beer."

"What's the matter, sunshine?"

"I've had people chewing me out all day about a pastry chef, and I don't need you piling on." She sipped her beer and felt the cold liquid go all the way down, then chuckled. She'd been at one of the city's best restaurants almost all day and hadn't eaten.

"I take it the cake maker's dead," the owner said as he wiped glasses and put them away.

"He's dead all right, probably the first of many, since he died for his wallet and watch." She drained her glass and waved off another one. "So much for the calm after the storm. The fuckers that kept me hopping before Katrina must be back."

"Sure you don't want another one?"

"Nah, I'm beat. Thanks, man." Sept threw a five on the bar and waved over her shoulder. The bar had become a regular haunt for her after the storm because the owner had never evacuated and never closed, even when the high winds had brushed the Quarter clean. In the months since, he'd listened to her reminisce about Noel and Sophie, and nodded to prove it.

When Sept was a block away from home, she saw a young prostitute she recognized as Erica Median. When she got closer, Erica asked, "Interested in a date?"

"I give Vice another couple of weeks to start cracking down. Don't be in the first batch they sweep up." Sept slapped Erica on the ass when Erica put her arms around her. "Get to bed. This late, you'll find somebody you don't need a date with."

"My boyfriend threw me out and said not to come back without some cash." Erica shook her head to get the strands of dark brown hair out of her face. "No biggie, but these days it's dead out here after nine."

"You need that idiot in your life like you need cancer. How about you stay with me and start again tomorrow?"

Erica put her hands in Sept's back pockets. "You condoning breaking the law, Detective?" She laughed when Sept slapped her backside again but started walking.

After they made it up the stairs and into her apartment, Sept pointed toward the bedroom. "The bathroom's through there."

"You lost a lot of stuff in the storm?" Erica asked, her eyes slowly scanning the main room.

"The more stuff you own, the more you have to clean, so I just got what I needed." Sept opened the refrigerator, which held only two beers and an empty pizza box.

"Yeah, I can see you're a big fan of cleaning," Erica said, staring at the pile of dirty dishes in the sink.

"Who are you, Merry Maid?" Erica laughed, and Sept unbuckled her pants on the way to the bedroom. When she dropped them in the hamper she noticed the multitude of food stains, including some of Donovan's last effort. Shout probably wouldn't do the trick. She grabbed a fresh T-shirt and slipped it over her underwear.

"Mind if I shower?" Erica asked.

Sept had never seen Erica under a good light. She had started hooking after the storm, when her boyfriend had lost his job, so she still had that young, fresh look. A few more months and that brightness in her face would disappear.

"Sure. Take your time." Once the bathroom door closed, Sept searched the top of the closet for the metal box she seldom used to lock away her gun and badge. Then she lay down, ready for another sleepless night.

The tune Erica was humming in the shower and the running water were the last things she heard until four, when Noel appeared, begging her to help find Sophie. Sept dove under with that now-familiar sense of panic that she was already too late.

When the two turned into the water-bloated images Sept's dream always dredged up, she woke up gasping and covered in sweat. Only this time she wasn't alone. Erica hovered over her with her hand above Sept's chest.

"You're okay, it's just a dream." Erica rubbed her hand in a circle. Sept screaming "No" over and over had woken her. "You're okay now," she repeated, trying to ease the look of fear on Sept's face.

"Thanks," Sept said as she kicked the sheet off and sat up.

"Wait." Erica sat up behind her and put her arms around Sept's neck to keep her from standing. "Tell me what's wrong."

"It's nothing—just a bad dream."

"My mama used to call those the night terrors. Said there's only one way to keep them away." Erica ran her hands along Sept's shoulders, down her arms, and up along her back so she could repeat the motion. "Want to give it a try? We had too little sleep for you to get up now."

"What's the cure?"

Erica edged closer and kissed her neck, then her cheek. When Sept didn't push her away she got up and sat on her lap so she could reach her lips easier. "The cure is to have someone love you," Erica said as she traced Sept's lips with her fingers. She could read the fatigue in the dark circles under Sept's eyes, so what she decided next was partly for that and also because she wasn't ready to go back to her asshole boyfriend. "Lift up," she said, tugging on the elastic band of Sept's underwear.

"You don't have to go that far," Sept told Erica, who was now on her knees between her legs.

"Let me, please." The underwear came off easily and she smiled up at Sept before she put her mouth on her. That's all she used as she licked and sucked Sept's clit until it was hard against her tongue. Sept barely made a sound, but Erica could tell by her breathing and the wetness coating her chin that she was close. The moment Sept put her hand at the back of her head, Erica sucked as hard as she could until Sept bucked her hips a couple of times, then lifted her off the floor.

"If that's what your mother had in mind, you two must've had an interesting relationship," Sept said as she lay back with Erica plastered to her side.

"That's disgusting," Erica said, and kissed her shoulder. "After she kissed away the bad feelings, she would sing to us." Erica started to hum, and the tune she picked made Sept's laughter gradually give way to deep, even breaths, a sign she was asleep.

Erica was still awake at seven, and she carefully extracted herself from Sept's side and picked up her wallet. Sept had left it on the nightstand next to her keys and cell phone the night before. She dressed and left without a sound, cash in hand.

At seven thirty Sept's cell phone woke her and she groped for it, feeling drugged from all the sleep. "Savoie," she barked. The light streaming into the room made her put her other hand over her eyes as she fell back into her pillow.

"Where are you?" Royce asked.

"Getting some sleep, like you told me to." Sept held the phone to her ear, the short silence on the other end giving her the chance to listen for Erica, but the apartment was too quiet for her to still be there. "What's up?" She turned her head and noticed her wallet wasn't in the same spot she'd put it down. A hundred dollars was missing.

"You've got another one."

"Am I the only homicide detective left in the city? I'm already working a case."

"Cut the whining and get going. I already sent Nathan out there and he asked me to call you."

She stepped on her discarded underwear on the way to the bathroom, a reminder of her early morning activities. "He did this from his years of experience in the field?"

"Just call the kid and get the details, then phone me when you know something."

He hung up before she could add anything else, so she threw the phone on the rumpled bed and headed for the shower. When she finished she walked naked to the closet to grab something to wear and found Erica sitting on the bed with her legs crossed.

"Are you mad?" Erica asked.

"Should I be?" Sept said as she kept her course for the closet in consideration of time and not because she was uncomfortable naked.

"You were sleeping when I left and you looked like you could use the rest. I wanted to do something to thank you for last night, but I'm broke."

A dark blue pair of pants was next in the lineup, so Sept chose a cable-knit fisherman's sweater to go with them, since she figured she'd be outside in the damp cold for most of the day again.

"No need to explain, but I'd appreciate if you asked first." The bed bounced when Sept sat next to Erica to put her shoes on. "You want to hang out longer? You can, but I've got to go."

"Can you take five minutes first?" Erica took her hand and walked her into the small kitchen, where a pot of coffee and an omelet in the frying pan were ready to be served. "Your change's on the counter."

"You didn't have to go to the trouble, but I'm glad you did. I'm starving." Sept cut the egg dish in half and found plates and mugs so she could serve Erica.

"You really don't mind if I hang here today?" Erica ate like someone who hadn't in a while.

"Watch TV and relax, and when I get back we can talk about your next move. But try and think today whether you still want this guy you're living with. I can't choose for you, but you stay with somebody like that and it won't end well."

Erica pushed her last bit of omelet around her plate and lowered her head. "It's either him or the street. I got no place else to go."

"If you have friends, that's never true." Sept finished and gathered up the dishes and deposited them in her now-empty sink. "Take another shower if you want, and a nap later. Call if you need anything." She handed Erica her card.

"I bought some other stuff so I'll cook, if you want."

"I'm not sure when I'll be back, so hold off on that." Sept hugged her before she strapped on her gun. "Lock yourself in." Erica smiled and waved as Sept closed the door. "What the hell am I thinking?" she asked herself as she descended the stairs. "You don't have time for strays." But Erica was only nineteen, so it wasn't too late to make a positive difference in her life. If Sept's life was built on anything it was that—trying to make a difference.

## CHAPTER FIVE

The park in the uptown section of St. Charles Avenue had made *Gambit Weekly*'s list of bests for "Best Park to Take Your Kids" for ten years straight. The yearly list compiled locals' opinions on best restaurants, happy hours, movie houses, clubs—five hundred things that made New Orleans unique. Sept was sure the scene she drove up to wasn't what the *Gambit* voters had in mind.

"I stopped for coffee," Nathan said, and held up a cup. He took a sip out of the one in his other hand, only to miss the sip hole and spill some down his coat.

"Only your second day and you're already sucking up? What'd you do wrong so early? Hell, I got down here in less than an hour after talking to you." Behind Nathan the left corner of the park was taped off, and the uniformed officers were keeping the press across the street on the grassy center of the avenue.

"I was just being nice because you won't like what's behind door number two. If you want to guess, think of something you've seen recently and go from there."

The traffic slowed as it came even with them, and almost everyone was rubbernecking. She called over one of the uniforms to control the flow.

"Let's see what we got, Detective," she told Nathan, and flicked him behind the ear.

An older woman was on her back, her eyes and mouth open, her arms spread out like she'd been posed. The stab wound in the center of her chest was noticeable because the killer had ripped open her coat and sweatshirt this time. The blood pool was more compact because it had seeped into the dirt surrounding the merry-go-round where she'd fallen. Along the top of her chest were two lines of smears that the bleeding hadn't caused.

"Tell me what you know," Sept said to Nathan as she put on a pair of gloves and booties.

"No ID on her, so I have some guys canvassing and asking if they know her. A couple of joggers found her at six thirty this morning on their way to Audubon Park. The older of them checked for a pulse, so those are his shoeprints next to her head. Other than that, she was stabbed and robbed like Donovan Bisland from Blanchard's." His rundown was numbered in his notebook, and Sept smiled when he checked off each item as he said it.

"Here's a tip that'll keep the brass from ripping your throat out." She stepped closer to the body but kept to the grass for now. "Don't let the media vultures hear you say one crime scene is like another one, that there's a pattern."

"You don't think there is?"

"There are definitely similarities, but they don't need to know that yet." She pointed to the mob across the way. "They catch a whiff of that and the headlines will scare the shit out of even you."

"Thanks," Nathan said from right behind her. "Tell me what I missed."

To Sept the scene was too open for a robbery, even if the usually busy avenue had light traffic after dark. This section of St. Charles had sustained more wind and fire damage than flooding, so it was more populated. A thief with a taste for murder who chose this spot was begging to get caught.

"Did they find any other footprints?"

"You beat the forensics team here, but those were the only ones I saw," Nathan answered. "The only cover he had was the merry-go-round, yet I didn't see much in the dirt around it as far as evidence goes."

Four feet of dirt surrounded the playground equipment, and as Sept made the complete circle, she didn't discover another footprint. This children's play area should've been covered in a variety of prints.

"The killer evidently wiped the entire area clean." Sept knelt in the grass right where it gave way to the play area. "Does someone who does that strike you as a person who's only after small change?"

Nathan crouched down next to her. "What do you mean?"

"Donovan was a victim of convenience. He was in the right place at the right time."

When she stopped talking he stared at her. "Yeah, so?"

"His wallet and watch were gone, but what about that scene, and this one, makes you think someone didn't take that stuff for the usual reasons?" Sept was thinking out loud when George and Alex arrived.

George said, when he was close enough, "Could you tell this creep he can take a day off between this shit?"

"I'll see what I can do." Sept answered like she always did when he complained. "I doubt you'll find anything, but work the whole circle. And get some of the uniforms to walk the area and find what was used to sweep that dirt clean. That might be the only thing you'll find evidence on."

"You heading out?" George asked.

"Nathan and I have a stop to make, so do me another favor and turn the body over to the coroner's office. I need Gavin to look at that wound." Sept was talking about Gavin Domangue, the coroner.

"You got it, darlin'."

As they walked toward the cars, Nathan said, "You don't strike me as the type."

Sept stopped and grabbed him by the back of the collar. "What are you talking about?"

"You know." He laughed, but stopped when she didn't join in. "You're not the type to let some old guy flirt with you."

"Again, what did you promise my father for this job? Because you're an idiot." She smacked him in the back of the head as George cracked up behind her. "The old guy's my uncle, so you're not only an idiot but a sicko."

"Sept, I'm sorry. How was I supposed to know he's related to you?"

"First off, the old shield they fished out of the candy jar should make you more observant. Second, I didn't rip his balls off and hang them from his ears. Keep that in mind should you have an overwhelming desire to call me some pet name."

"Sure thing."

Only after Nathan swallowed visibly did Sept laugh and start walking again. "Leave your car. We'll come back for it later."

"You sure you want me riding with you?"

Sept stared at him over the roof of the car. "You're an idiot, Nathan, but you're mine, so get in."

❖

"Have you heard if Norman and his boys are back in business?" Della Blanchard sat on a stool in the middle of the kitchen at Blanchard's as the staff prepared for the lunch rush.

"Their fields were ruined, so we're using Monty and his brother as our oyster suppliers," Keegan said.

"It'll take forever to recover from this damn storm. Our family's been buying oysters from Norman for years."

"Gran, remember your blood pressure," Keegan said gently, and stirred in the ingredients for the cream sauce they used on their crab cakes while Della ranted. "About half our suppliers were set back, but we assured them we'll take them back when they're ready."

"Because of you, I don't worry about our future, sweetheart. It takes more than good food for this business to be successful. You've learned not only that, but how to treat people." Donovan's assistant handed Della a piece of pecan pie. As her fork went up the hum of the kitchen quieted, since the employees knew this was a test. "Almost, but still very good. Try more butter in your crust next time."

"Thank you, ma'am."

"Please, you're part of our family, call me Della. Let's try the bread pudding next."

"You got it."

Della took another bite of pie before she handed the plate back. "Any repercussions in our numbers from Donovan's death?"

"The detective in charge kept the madness out back so I doubt anyone noticed, and the paper did a decent job with the coverage."

"Is that the idiot who considered you a suspect?"

Keegan laughed more easily now that she knew she wasn't, but she still hadn't figured out why. "She was just doing her job, Gran, and she promised she'd keep me informed." Keegan took a small spoon and tried her sauce, then took it off the fire. "Promise me you won't start making calls."

"Friend of yours?" Della asked. She accepted the tureen of bread-pudding soufflé with warm whiskey cream sauce and took a bite. This one was sacrosanct—no matter who made it, they followed the recipe. "Perfect, thank you."

"Actually, Detective Sept Savoie is more like finding a roach on your plate, but she's determined to hunt down whoever did this."

"Sept? Who names their child 'Seven'?"

"The next time I see her I'll ask." The clock in the kitchen chimed eleven times and everyone took a moment to meticulously clean their station.

"You do that, and I'll see you in a couple of days at brunch. Good luck, everyone." Della kissed Keegan good-bye and gave everyone a short wave before she pushed through the swinging doors.

Keegan still had a little time before the lunch crowd started, so she closed the door of the chef's office and scanned the résumés she'd received. They needed someone to replace their last chef, who'd relocated to Arizona after the storm. So Keegan was trying to find the next Emeril Lagasse. Until then, she was in charge here, with Della's blessing.

From the door, Jacquelyn Blanchard said, "I hardly recognize you since you're not chopping the crap out of something."

"At least one of us learned to cook, princess," Keegan shot back at her older sister.

"Be nice. I came to tell you how sorry I am about Donovan. I would've come sooner, but I've been stuck in city hall with the economic development committee, and you were sleeping by the time I got home."

"It was one of those 'long baths with a large glass of pinot, then off to bed' nights. Sorry. Yesterday was hard enough when the staff found Donovan and called me, but add all the commotion that followed and I was numb. I don't mind news coverage of the restaurant, but not because of this."

Jacquelyn shared the red hair color and blue eyes, but was six inches taller than Keegan. She was as talented at marketing their business as Keegan was in the kitchen, so she was in charge of sales.

"Don't worry. I lit a fire under this downtown yesterday, and the mayor and police chief both promised to make it a priority. This is the last message we need to send out to the world as we try to rebuild." Outside, the waiters put in their first orders of the day, setting the clatter of pans in motion. "You doing okay?"

"Fine. I just miss his laughter in there." Keegan waved toward the kitchen. "Wait, there is something. Could you not light any more fires on this? I know you get results with the guys down there, but the detective working this case doesn't need the headache."

"Do tell." Jacquelyn sat on the desk and crossed her legs, making her skirt hitch up to mid-thigh. "The only time you notice someone is if they have some innovative cooking idea."

"Not true. And all I noticed was that she seems capable of doing her job."

"I'll let you slide on the details because of what you're going though, so consider yourself lucky."

Keegan laughed and nodded. "I appreciate that, but speaking of details, how's it going with Adam?"

"Certain things have come to my attention that make me believe Adam is lower than pond scum, so it isn't going anywhere."

Jacquelyn's tone made Keegan think that Adam was in a dark room somewhere with an ice pack on his groin. "What happened?"

"His secretary, his neighbor, his tennis instructor, and his mother happened. And should I mention the neighbor and tennis instructor are married?"

"He was sleeping with his mother?"

"Sweetie, he's a cheating asshole, but he's not a complete pervert. No, his mother thought I was being unfair," Jacquelyn made air quotes on the word, "when I got upset with her little boy's need not to feel hemmed in."

"He defines monogamy as being hemmed in, I take it."

"Considering I never slept with him, I wouldn't know what all the fuss was about, but I never did think of myself as a good harem girl, so he can define the word however he pleases." She hit Keegan when she laughed. "All right. Enough about me. Tell me what's new with you, or should I say who."

"The lead detective on Donovan's case thinks I was seeing him."

"Ha," Jacquelyn said, and clapped her hands. "If she's that

unobservant she'll never find the idiot who did this. What's her name?"

"Sept Savoie. Mom came by earlier and told me she's assigned to the French Quarter precinct, but she's brought in on major cases since she's one of NOPD's best. Seems we rate as major."

"Who names their child Seven?" Jacquelyn asked, acting as if she hadn't heard the rest of what Keegan had said.

"You sound more like Della Junior every day. I don't know what was on her mother's mind when it came to names, but I trust her."

From her perch on the desk, Jacquelyn tapped her stiletto on the arm of Keegan's chair. "Della Senior told me this trustworthy person accused you at first."

"You haven't lived until you're considered a murder suspect, but as long as the cop's motivated I'd do it again. This isn't a witch hunt to bring down one of the Blanchards." Keegan pinched the tip of her sister's shoe. "Anything else new? I have to get back out there."

"The National Association of Ophthalmologists agreed to have their convention in the city next month, and we're hosting two different nights, so we'll have to work up a menu for them." Jacqueline stood and smoothed down her skirt. "Let's make a date tonight for dinner, but only if you agree not to talk shop."

"Just tell me when and where."

"You pick, Keegan. If not, I'll never hear the end of it if they use the wrong kind of cheese or something."

"Let's try cousin Mackie's place on Bourbon."

Jacqueline hugged her. "I'll meet you there at eight."

## CHAPTER SIX

"It seems impossible, but your victim was stabbed between nine and midnight." Gavin, the coroner, pulled the sheet back just far enough for the wound to be visible. "She sustained only one stab wound, but it was enough. I waited until you got here to open her up, but the blade probably nicked her heart."

"Any similarities to yesterday's case?" Sept asked as she studied the lines that had been drawn on her upper chest.

"Looks like the same weapon in almost the same place."

"How hard is it to do that?" Sept thought about how Keegan's knife sliced through that duck breast.

"It's not easy. If you want my opinion, you're looking for a man with some upper body strength."

"What kind of knife?"

Gavin placed a small ruler next to the wound. "I imagine he sunk it to the hilt, so I'd say a blade of two inches at its widest point. Probably a hunting knife."

"Makes sense. Those are big enough and sharp enough to field-dress a deer. The breastbone on a buck is about the same as this."

After Sept stepped back, Gavin cut down the chest. The retching began and he smiled along with Sept, who pointed to Nathan in the corner. When he started the saw to cut through the chest cavity, Nathan stepped out, clutching the garbage can.

"This is what killed her." Gavin pointed out the small cut in her heart, which he had lifted out to weigh. "This guy is not only determined but has impeccable aim. A mortal wound like this isn't easy in one shot."

"Is it the same guy?"

"All I've got is two dead people who got that way because someone stabbed them."

Sept took a few more notes and did her best to sketch the lines drawn on the chest from the photos in Gavin's file. "Is it the same guy?" she asked again.

"Between me and you and the fly on the wall, it is, and he's gotten a good taste. That means, get ready to spend some time in here with me."

"Thanks, Doc. We'll get back with you as soon as we ID her."

"Tell your partner I've got toothbrushes and mints in my office if he needs them." Gavin kept doing his job as he talked. "Take care and tell your parents hello for me."

"Will do."

Sept shook her head when she found Nathan sitting on the hallway floor. She helped him up and gave him Gavin's offerings.

"You aren't going to make fun of me?" Nathan asked as he rolled his mint around his mouth.

"Watching someone cut a body up isn't easy to do, so no. You need to grab some lunch, even if that sounds disgusting."

Nathan put his hand over his stomach as if that was the last thing he wanted. "I'll trust you on that. Want to join me?"

"Maybe next time. After that, head back to the office and go through old files to see if you find any comparable cases."

"Did the old files survive?"

"Most of the older ones were computer-archived, but you'll have to call around for the others."

"Why am I doing that?"

"Patterns. That's another important lesson. We've had two similar crimes in two days, but before we sound the alarm about a knife-crazed killer on the loose, we have to establish a pattern." The weather had turned colder as the afternoon progressed, and gray storm clouds were gathering over the west side of the city. The damp, cold air made Sept's shoulders ache. "The only way to establish a pattern is through research, so get cracking on that once you get to the office."

"If you're going to do more investigating, don't you want me with you?"

"Nathan, what you're doing *is* investigating. I just plan to walk the scene one more time and check if the guys have identified our victim."

He walked with her to the car and rested his hands on the roof. "My car's over there anyway, so would you mind if I stay with you?" The more distance they put between them and the morgue, the more the color returned to his face. "Your father emphasized how much I could learn from you. I'll stay late and work on the files, but I want to see how you go about this."

"Let's go, then."

When they arrived at the park, the crime unit, as well as the tape and any other evidence of what had happened the night before, was gone. Only a squad car with two officers inside remained.

"You released the scene?" Nathan asked, and sounded surprised.

"When it comes to what I may or may not want, this one's different from yesterday's." Sept waved to the officers as she walked to the merry-go-round. "The brass don't like to publicize a murder for too long, but Blanchard's was out of the way, so I had more latitude."

"What are we looking for?"

"Anything that doesn't belong." Sept stopped at the playground equipment in the spot she figured the woman had been lured to. The blood was gone, hidden under a new pack of dirt the city must've spread out. "Can't do shit about the levees, but they're all over this," she mumbled.

Their victim had been facing the street, but why stop right here and not move when her killer confronted her? It didn't make sense in either case. And where was the killer standing that he didn't alarm the victim? No matter what the woman did, most people were street-smart enough to at least try to avoid criminals.

"Got anything new for me?" Sept asked the cops who'd joined her.

"We just found somebody that might know the lady."

"Where?"

"Small apartment complex three blocks from here. The manager has a tenant that fits the description, and she hasn't seen or spoken to her today."

"Does she usually?"

The officer answering the questions nodded. "The complex caters to the handicapped, and the manager usually checks daily to see if this lady needs groceries or anything. Aside from three walks a day with her dog, this woman was a homebody, even worked from home."

Sept closed her eyes, trying to think of any clues on the victim's body. When she couldn't come up with anything, she asked, "What was her disability?"

"If it's her, then Robin Burns is blind. She lives with her seeing-eye dog and works as a computer programmer."

That explained Robin Burns, if the Jane Doe at the morgue turned out to be her, but didn't explain Donovan. "Any sign of the dog?"

"Not yet. We thought it was more important to find out who was killed."

"And you discovered who she was when?"

"Two hours ago," the other officer answered.

"Funny, I was at the morgue and I didn't see you down there with the landlady for an ID."

"We were told to stay put here."

After Sept took a deep breath, she grabbed them both by the collar and turned them toward the car. "I'm sure your commander would understand if you leave to help with the investigation. Or would you rather sit on your ass looking pretty for the passersby?"

"You want me to pick up the landlord and take her down?" Nathan asked.

"Follow the two workhorses, then get on those files. Call me if you have anything." When the guys started walking away, Sept thought of one more thing. "Did she mention the dog's name?"

"Mike," the first officer said. "Whatever help that is."

"You'd be surprised." It was late afternoon when Sept was left alone, and, as usual, she started at the murder spot and turned her attention outward.

The park was small but popular. St. Charles Avenue ran along the front and another street along the side and back. Only one side was lined by a thick stand of trees, to insulate it from the mansion next door.

Sept started at the sidewalk on the St. Charles side and walked the tree line. She found Mike ten feet from the end. He'd been stabbed and cut badly close to this ribs, but as she bent to check his tags to make sure it was him, he whimpered.

"This is going to hurt, but hang on." Sept cradled him in her arms and carried him to her car. After a few calls to find the police vet, she made it in less than fifteen minutes with lights and siren blaring. She forgot whatever she'd planned for the rest of the day and sat in the waiting room instead.

The doctor came out a few hours later and said it would take time, but Mike would recover. Whoever had stabbed him had missed his heart, but collapsed and damaged his lung.

"We'll keep him a couple of days. I'll call you in the morning with a progress report," the vet said.

Sept shook her head. "He's not mine." As she was about to make some more excuses, her cell phone rang.

"The landlord identified our Jane Doe," Nathan said. "It's Robin Burns, and the last time her friend saw her was at nine. Ms. Burns regularly walked Mike right before going to bed at ten, and she always took that same route."

"Good work, Nathan. We'll start again in the morning." She suddenly felt bad for Mike, as well as the two victims. Mike had probably spent most of his life with his master, who'd depended on him as well. That relationship was over for him now. "Call me when he's able to leave," Sept told the vet.

"I thought he wasn't yours."

"He isn't, but I'll take him until I can figure something else out."

"You want to see him before you go?"

The sarcastic response in the back of her throat died because the vet looked so earnest. Sept nodded instead. The golden retriever had been cleaned, stitched, bandaged, and sedated, so he appeared to be sleeping peacefully. Sept stroked his neck gently.

"It's a shame you can't talk, boy. You could make my job so much easier." When his front paws twitched, she stopped. "Just relax and heal. I'll find out if your mama was somehow connected to a pastry chef named Donovan."

## CHAPTER SEVEN

C an you tell me where she is?" Sept asked whoever had answered the phone at Blanchard's. "This is Detective Savoie and I've got a few more questions."

"She's having dinner with her sister, but I'll give her a message if you want."

"What I want is either a phone number or the name of the restaurant."

"She'll be at Mackie Blanchard's in the Quarter at eight."

At a light, Sept noticed the blood smeared all over the front of her sweater—a reminder of what had happened to Mike. No matter how noble her rescue had been, Mackie Blanchard's would never admit her like this.

Sept grabbed a parking spot a few doors down from her place, then stopped to talk to Madeline Seymour, who lived in the apartment under hers. Madeline had tended bar at Chris Owens's place since she'd been old enough to get through the door.

That had been thirty years ago, and Madeline was still pouring and Chris Owens was still kicking her leg over her head, even though her advanced age was as top secret as what happened to Hoffa. Sept loved talking to Madeline because a five-minute conversation was better than an hour spent reading the paper.

"You look in a mirror recently, Savoie?"

"Why? I didn't think it was that bad yet."

Madeline took a drag from her cigarette and twirled her black bow tie on her finger. "Hell, girl, you're more than easy on the eye, that's not what I'm talking about. I'm just saying that you don't need to be hiring a hooker. And if you feel like you have to, don't go leaving them in your place."

"Wise words from a wise woman. Have I ever asked you why you didn't consider a career in law enforcement?" Sept shook her head.

"If I did that, people wouldn't tell me shit." Madeline laughed. Then she pointed her fingers at Sept like a gun and laughed harder when Sept acted as if she'd been wounded. "Besides, if I became a cop, who'd fill you in on all the gossip?"

"True. Be careful, and come by for coffee sometime." Sept took the stairs two at a time and knocked before unlocking the door. "Erica," she said as she took her jacket off and threw it on the sofa.

"Oh, God," Erica said, staring at her chest. "Did you get hurt?"

"It's not mine, don't worry." Sept stripped the sweater off next and headed for the bedroom and hamper. "I ended up taking a dog to the vet."

"That sounds like you. You're always rescuing the pathetic, aren't you?"

"The dog probably tried to help his master, and you're anything but pathetic." The shirt had traces of Mike's blood on it so she grabbed a fresh one from the rack. "Did you get a chance to think about what I asked you?"

"I know you want to help, and I know I can't stay here forever, but I got no skills, Sept."

"It's 'I don't have any skills,' and that's not true. You just need a break, but it's a lot like kicking dope. If you don't really want to change, you won't." Sept buttoned her shirt and sat with Erica on the bed. "How about we try a step program? But unlike AA, mine only has three."

"What are you talking about?"

"First, you keep doing what you know, only more on your own terms. That way you get ahead faster. Second, you do it until you realize you don't have to, and if you stay in the life it's your decision. And last, if you make another choice, I'll be there to help you through."

"What's the catch?" Erica lifted her feet and sat Indian style. "There's always a catch."

"None, and if you turn me down and go back to the butthead, I'll still be here for you if that doesn't work out."

"I want…I want to feel like I did last night. All I'm asking is a place to sleep where I feel safe."

"Then get dressed and I'll introduce you to a friend of mine." Sept held Erica's hand. "If you don't think it'll work out, you can come back here until we think of something else. Deal?"

Once Erica was ready she stayed quiet as they walked down Bourbon Street arm in arm, mostly people-watching. The sun started to set when they were in the gay-bars section, and Sept kept going until they reached a house on the next block. It appeared to take up half the block, but there was no business name on the bright, shiny red door. The color was the owner's idea of a joke regarding what some parts of the Quarter had historically been called.

As Sept pressed the bell, Erica asked, "What's this place?"

"The friend I was telling you about lives here."

The door opened and an elderly African American gentleman stood erectly in the opening. His hair was as white as Sept's, but while her eyes were almost black, his were a deep, vivid green. He wore a suit that fit the way only custom-tailored clothes do, and when he saw Sept his face relaxed into a smile.

"I'll be, girlie, I feel safer already," Wilson Delacour said, and his voice sounded as if he'd spent his life singing the blues. "Get in here before folks think we're being raided."

"Mr. Wilson, when's Brandi going to let you retire?"

"That girl can't live without me, so I'm here until they carry me out in a pine box." Wilson took their coats and pointed to the room to the left. "You here to see her majesty?"

"If she'll grant me five minutes," Sept said. The front parlor was furnished with French antiques, but Brandi had re-covered most of them in a leopard-skin material.

"Pour a drink if you want, and I'll call her down." Wilson closed the double doors.

"This is Brandi Parrish's Red Door," Sept said, to finally answer Erica's question.

Erica grabbed Sept by the bicep and laughed. "Brandi Parrish the madam? No way. She's a myth that old guys like the one that just left have created because they like to spin a good story."

"I'm a cop, Erica, but you learn certain things fast if you want to stay a cop. When it comes to law enforcement, some addresses don't exist." She took Erica's hand off her arm and placed it in her lap. "I don't care how much evidence you have—the rules are firm. The Red Door falls into that category, and it's not myth."

"And you're all right with that?"

"I do my best to uphold the law, but I've never considered Brandi a threat to anyone."

"Unless I've got a whip in my hand, honey, then I'm plenty threat," Brandi said from a door that, before she opened it, appeared to be a full-length mirror in a gilded frame. Her black hair was pulled back into a cascade of curls, and the negligee she wore accentuated her large breasts and small waist.

Brandi had told Sept she'd been the youngest of five children, and she'd always promised herself that she wouldn't end up cleaning fish or peeling shrimp like most of the women in her family. That drive had paved her way to Bourbon Street as the madam and owner of the Red Door.

"The stories I could tell about my whip would put some color in that head of hair of yours," Brandi told Sept.

"Listening to those stories is what drained the color right out of it." Sept rose and kissed Brandi on the lips. "I'd ask how you've been, but it's that 'whole good enough to eat' thing," Sept said with a smile.

"And all those boys in blue wonder why you're my favorite." Brandi took Sept's arm and led her to one of the settees. "Gonna introduce me to your friend?"

"Erica Median, this is Brandi Parrish."

"Your answer to my problem is to bring me to a brothel?" Erica asked, as if the idea sounded ridiculous to her.

"That's the biggest favor Sept could've done you, so show me some respect or get the hell out of my house. Your sitting in this room doesn't mean anything yet," Brandi said.

"This isn't a brothel, Erica, it's a home. That's what you said you wanted, but you also said this is what you wanted to do. With Brandi you can work, have a place to stay, and have someone to take care of you." Sept spoke, but she was hyperaware of Brandi's perfume.

"What's this going to cost me?"

"I have an empty suite available for three thousand a month," Brandi said.

"Three thousand? Are you nuts?"

"That'll take you six dates. The rest of the month I'll line up as much work as you want, and you can start saving or spending it on whatever you want."

"Or," Sept said, "you can try something novel, like going back to school." She sat next to Erica. "It's up to you, so stay and talk it over. If you decide against it I'll see you back at the apartment later."

"Go on, Sept. We'll come to terms," Brandi said. She accepted another kiss from Sept and waited for Wilson to show her out.

"This is a weird thing for a cop to do," Erica said.

"Sept knows that you can try to change things for the better, but if you're schlepping all by yourself you can't change anything at all."

Erica stared at her for a long minute before she said what was on her mind. "What's that supposed to mean? I'm a whore, so I should be a good one?"

"Actually, *you* think you're just a whore, but she put you somewhere that'll give you the opportunity for something else. Trust me, there's a difference." Brandi stood and opened the double doors. "Would you like to see your new place?"

"Yes, ma'am."

Brandi slightly curled her lips up in a smile before she nodded. "You're off to a good start."

❖

"There's a forty-minute wait," the hostess at Mackie Blanchard's told Sept. "You can sit in the bar if you like."

The place was full, and Sept figured people were anxious to get away from their forced rebuilding. She gave the woman her name and headed for the bar behind her.

"Vodka on the rocks." Sept pointed to the brand she wanted. She wasn't interested in eating, but she didn't feel like going home yet, so she used the excuse of seeing Keegan to stay out. She twirled her glass on the oak bar and let the bits of information from the last two days swirl around her mind. Lost in that process, she relaxed, knowing that sometimes something would pop out.

After Keegan saw Sept in the bar with her head down, she stopped halfway in taking her coat off.

"What's wrong?" Jacqueline asked as she helped her and followed the direction of Keegan's eyes. "Friend of yours?"

"No, I'm just surprised to see her here." Keegan watched Sept's idle movements.

"You've got that look," Jacqueline said, her voice singsongy.

"I do not, that's Detective Savoie."

Jacqueline handed off their coats and put her arm around Keegan's shoulders. The way she hummed made Keegan glance up at her. "You know, sis, if anyone who looks like that accuses you of something and you could end up in handcuffs—I say go for it."

"Are you totally insane?"

"Hardly, and don't play Miss Innocent with me and tell me you didn't notice how good-looking she is. If that's your story, then try telling it somewhere else, because I'm not buying. She could almost make me forget Adam."

"Ha," Keegan said louder than she meant, and it carried across to the bar. "You're not gay, and you'd shave your head before you'd let anyone handcuff you."

"Keep telling yourself that, sweet pea." Jacqueline pressed Keegan closer and winked at her. "Look, your date has spotted us."

"She's not my date," Keegan said in an exasperated whisper. "And if you say anything like that in front of her... Detective, it's nice to see you again." Keegan's voice cracked at the end. "Do you eat here often?"

"Ms. Blanchard." Sept held out her hand. "It's nice seeing you too, and no, I don't. The closest I've come to a Blanchard establishment was the Dumpsters at your place."

"You have something against good food?" Keegan asked.

"My mother's an excellent cook, so no, but I work for the city. Your family's out of my league. Are you going to introduce me?"

Keegan hesitated when she saw the size of Jacqueline's smile. "This is my sister Jacqueline."

"How about we treat you to dinner for all your loyal service?" Jacqueline suggested as she waggled her fingers at the hostess.

"That's okay. I just need to ask Ms. Blanchard a few more questions."

The hostess waited with three menus in her hands.

"You can ask whatever you like, but is there a rule that says you can't do it over barbequed shrimp?"

"Resistance is futile, as they say, so you should surrender while you still can," Keegan said. Sept nodded and followed the two down the steps to the main dining room. "You can order off the menu or leave it up to Jacqueline," Keegan said to her when they sat down.

"How does Jacqueline know what I like?"

"A challenge, I love it." Jacqueline took her menu and left the table for the kitchen.

"It's her way of making up for being the only Blanchard who can't cook." Keegan shrugged. "What'd you want to ask me?"

"I know we had some problems when I asked if you socialized with Donovan."

"You didn't ask me that, you accused me of sleeping with him. Not quite the same thing."

Sept accepted her new drink. "I did apologize for that, Ms. Blanchard."

"So you did." Keegan lifted her glass of pinot. "How about you call me Keegan and I'll call you Sept."

"That sounds good, but I'll give you the right to change your mind once I start asking questions." The answer bordered on flirting, but Sept just wanted to keep up with Keegan. She held her glass up and waited.

"Sounds like you might be seeing the error of your ways, but I'll only drink to that if you answer one question for me."

"I'll give it my best shot." They touched glasses, and the atrocities of the day slipped into the box Sept kept in the back of her mind. "What would you like to know?"

"Actually, two people asked me today who names their child Seven? That's what your name means, right?"

The question wasn't original. Sept had spent a lifetime answering it, but the way Keegan phrased it made her sit back and laugh. "A woman who had six children and was surprised with a seventh. Since my mother definitely didn't want any more surprises, she considered me her lucky seventh. We're French, so she thought Sept was more acceptable than the English version, and she put it on my birth certificate."

"Your mother sounds like an interesting woman." Keegan sat back as well and held her glass with both hands. "She didn't per chance name the other six Un, Deux, Trois, Quatre, Cinq, and Six, did she?"

"Camille Savoie showed more imagination than that with Gustave, François, Alain, Jacques, Joel, and Noel." The door of the kitchen opened, and Jacqueline walked out a few steps and stopped. She stared at Keegan, then turned back again. "Is it just you and Jacqueline?"

"Yes, just the two of us." When Keegan took a sip of her wine, Sept noticed how good her lips looked moistened. "Now, what did you want to ask me?"

"If you ever did socialize with Donovan, did he ever mention a woman named Robin Burns?"

Keegan closed her eyes as if to give the question her full attention. "We'd go out for drinks every so often, and we worked together so I knew a lot about his life, but that name doesn't sound familiar."

"She was blind. Does that help?"

"That I'd remember. He might've known her, but he never mentioned her in our time together. Who is she?"

A waiter came out and set two plates of shrimp down. The appetizers made Keegan turn and glance toward the kitchen. "Jacqueline must still be coordinating the rest of dinner," she said. "Sorry, I'm being rude. Who's Robin Burns?"

"Another case I'm working that has some similarities. I thought you could help me make a connection, if there's one to make."

The forkful of shrimp stopped midway to Keegan's mouth and she put it down. "Someone else got stabbed like that?"

For the first time since they met, Keegan showed the normal emotional reaction Sept was used to as her eyes watered and fat tears rolled down her cheeks. Without thinking, Sept wiped them away with her thumb. Her mother always said that people became good at something like cooking because they had a passion for life in general. To Camille you couldn't be truly passionate unless you took things to heart. Keegan wasn't just a good chef, but obviously a good friend.

"Donovan might've died early, but he was a lucky man," Sept said, and moved closer. "He lived his dream and he had one good friend that I know of, and I'm sure you'll never forget him. I might not have known him, but I won't forget him either. Whoever did this will answer for it."

"They killed someone else, though, didn't they?"

"Ms. Burns was found this morning, and while the crimes were similar, they were different too, so I can't really give you a definitive answer yet." To try to cajole Keegan back into a good mood, she lifted Keegan's fork and offered it to her. "I know it's hard, but try and forget about it right now. If some irate guy comes out of the kitchen complaining about wasted seafood, I'm not running interference for you."

"You think you'll find who did this?"

"There have been some perfect crimes, but usually something of the killer is left behind. My father always says there aren't any ghosts, because only a ghost leaves no tracks to follow. My job is to find that little bit of the killer he leaves behind, and no one's better at it than me."

Keegan took a bite of her food and nodded as if approving of the flavor. A taste of wine followed before she returned the favor and pushed Sept's plate closer. "To anyone else, what you said would sound boastful."

"A lot of people do think I'm an egomaniac." Sept started on her appetizer.

"If they think that, they obviously haven't taken the time to talk to you. To me you're more than passionate about your job, as I am about mine. You come off as a bitch—"

"But a really caring one?"

"Sorry. That came out wrong."

"I'd agree with you, but considering our first meeting I don't blame you at all." Sept had Keegan smiling again, so she was about to say good night when Jacqueline showed up holding two plates. "I hope you brought some of these out for yourself," Sept said, and pointed to the last bite of appetizer in front of her.

"I take it I guessed right on your first course?" Jacqueline held the plates high enough so Sept couldn't see what they were.

"You'd have to be an idiot or have a severe food allergy to shellfish not to," Sept said.

Keegan hid her smile behind her glass, but Sept saw it and joined in.

"Care to make it three for three?" Jacqueline asked.

"If you guessed any kind of liver, you're going to have to admit defeat."

Jacqueline put the medium ribeye down first and followed it with garlic-butter mashed potatoes. The waiters followed with the rest of the food as Jacqueline sat down. "Well, is it to your liking?"

"If you'd brought out a bottle of ketchup you'd have hit the bull's eye," Sept said as she picked up her knife and fork. She laughed when she glanced up at two startled faces. "Don't worry. I only douse my fries in the stuff. I wouldn't dream of putting it on steak."

"Good thing," Jacqueline said as she cut into the same order as Sept's. "I'd hate to ruin a good meal when Keegan cracked you over the head with the bottle."

"You find ketchup unacceptable, Ms. Blanchard?" Sept asked.

"It's Keegan, remember?" She nodded to the waiter when he placed her steak before her. "And there's nothing wrong with ketchup."

"Except?" Sept took a bite, amazed at the tenderness of the meat.

"Except if you put it on perfectly aged meat that Mackie uses his special blend of spices on, then cooks it the way they serve it here. You can do it if that's how you like steak, but it'd be like adding *Dogs Playing Poker* in the background of the *Mona Lisa*."

"She's loads of fun when you take her to Burger King," Jacqueline said in a deadpan voice.

They spent the rest of the meal in easy conversation, mostly about Sept's family and stories of growing up the granddaughters of Della Blanchard. After traditional bread pudding and coffee, Sept felt like taking her pants off, but she had enjoyed the dinner.

"Whenever you'd like to play again, give me a call," Jacqueline said as they left.

"Play?" Sept asked, confused.

"The 'guess what you like' game," Jacqueline clarified. "Only next time we'll play for money."

"You shouldn't have given away your dislike of liver," Keegan said. "Slips like that make you lose your advantage."

"Noted." Sept helped them on with their coats and opened the door. "Thank you both for dinner and for the company."

"It was our pleasure," Jacqueline said, her voice an octave lower, but her jaw clicked shut when Keegan shoved her elbow into her side.

"Keep in touch," Keegan said.

"Will do, and be careful." Sept shook hands with both of them and headed to the car.

"She's not what I imagined after I talked to you this morning," Jacqueline said.

Keegan watched the taillights of Sept's car as it took a right at the corner. She was headed uptown, perhaps for home. "What were you hoping for?"

"I wasn't hoping for anything." Jacqueline handed her parking stub to the valet. "I was more curious than anything. That look you had made me believe you'd found another plaything."

The comment was typical of Jacqueline's forthrightness. "Gosh, you make me sound like a slut."

"Please," Jacqueline said, her hands shoved deep into the pockets of her coat. "Not even close, but you have to admit you like them either self-centered or flighty, though I can relate to that."

"Go on," Keegan said, waving her hands at Jacqueline. "This is so fascinating I can't wait to hear more."

"It's the same inclination Mom and I have, and it's the best way to keep them all at arm's length."

"Enough psychobabble for one night." Keegan kissed Jacqueline's cheek and headed for her own car. "See you at home."

Alone with only Alicia Keys on the radio, Keegan thought about what Jacqueline had said. She'd had numerous relationships, and none of them had gotten past the three-month mark because that's how long it took for her to admit defeat. When that happened, only Jacqueline said anything. Their mother Melinda stayed quiet—not because she didn't care, but because after the death of her lover she'd been as unlucky at love as her daughters.

Sept was out of her range of experience, and that was how she intended to keep it. Especially now that she felt raw after Donovan's death. The last thing she needed was someone who could break through every barricade she'd built around her heart.

# CHAPTER EIGHT

Before Sept went home to an empty apartment, she drove to the park once more. She parked there but headed to the complex where Robin Burns lived, then backtracked to the park.

Most of the streetlights down the path Robin Burns would've taken were working, but that hadn't mattered to her. Robin merely followed Mike's lead on a route she'd probably memorized and could've walked herself, but the outings hadn't been for her. Sept was sure that Robin loved her dog, and the outings had been for Mike.

As she walked, Sept studied the houses along the way and the spots where a predator could hide to pick his prey. The burned-out shell of a house stood a block up from the park, its roof missing, windows blown out, and the front of the second floor black from flames. Only one spot appeared sturdy enough to stand on.

The porch stretched the length of the house, and though the very end of one side had partially caved in, the other side had survived. Something about the abandoned building made Sept stop and pull out her cell phone.

"Nathan." She said his name as soon as he answered. "The burnt house in Robin Burns's neighborhood, did the crime units look inside?"

"Just the porch, but they didn't see anything but the mess the fire department left. Need any help?"

"Where are you?" Sept pulled out her flashlight and stepped up on the porch. "You still at work?"

"I've been reviewing files, but most of the stabbings in the last couple of years happened when some idiot drank too much or tried to solve a bad marriage."

"Get someone to sit on this place tonight. I found something." She flashed the light on the banister. "See you in the morning."

In the corner of the porch she noticed a grouping of small nicks on the banister rail. They were so small that whoever had checked the area had probably missed them, but unlike the rest of the wreckage, they were fresh. Someone must have stood there and waited but, impatient, had picked at the wood with a knife.

Each stroke had cut through the burned wood, but left no noticeable jagged edges. Looking down the street, Sept could see the back side of the park, since the trees had shed their leaves, and also the corner in the opposite direction.

"If I was standing here waiting, I could easily spot someone being literally led by a dog. When they pass I just follow, stab the dog, and then get what I really want."

She called George to make sure he and Alex would be there in the morning. The house was already burned, so it would be easy for someone to destroy evidence they thought they'd left behind.

"You aren't a ghost, are you?" Sept walked to the spot where she'd found Mike but didn't locate any other clues. "But you come damn close. It won't matter in the end, though. No one's so good that I won't eventually catch him."

❖

When his eyes opened, the sun had set and the sheets around him had ripped and bunched under his back. He felt no discomfort, though, as he lay quietly and waited for his only friend.

"You're right. I'm the only one who understands why you hurt." The voice was so real he sat up and scanned the room, sure that this time someone would be standing there. "If you do your job well you might see me, but before we continue, it's not too late to turn back."

"No." He stood up so abruptly his cherished knife fell and embedded itself in the wood floor at his feet. "I'll do whatever it takes, but you promised me."

"Calm down. You have to control yourself or you *will* get caught before you reach the door." The voice was so loud he put his hands to his ears. "From now on I'll call you Novice, because you have a long road before the gods will be fit to send you any favor but me."

"Thank you."

"Get ready, because tonight we hunt again. Only this time you won't find what you're looking for in blood."

"What does that mean?" Novice asked as he yanked his knife from the floor and wiped the blade with his shirt.

"You have to learn what to do so the sacrifices will have meaning, so clear your head of everything else. If you don't, I'll only get weaker."

"Tell me what you want and I'll do it."

"You might turn out to be the perfect student, Novice."

❖

"What's next?" Nathan asked.

It was a good question, but unfortunately Sept had no ready answer. The marred wooden banister was the only clue in the abandoned house. Soot had covered where the killer stood, but he'd dragged his feet on his way to the sidewalk, so she didn't even know his shoe size.

"We wait and we keep talking to everyone who lives within a two-mile radius of our crime scenes. Right now we don't have a choice."

"Wait for what?" Nathan sat in the passenger seat of Sept's car and clicked his pen until Sept grabbed it and threw it over her shoulder. "Wait…you mean we have to sit around until he does it again and hope he screws up?"

Nathan was obviously horrified and Sept figured that if he stuck with this job that reaction would eventually lessen. As a detective you became almost numb to atrocities, and that insensitivity brought its own outrage. But it was the only way to survive the job without going insane.

"Hopefully something will break before that happens, but we have to face reality. Since his timetable seems to have slowed somewhat, maybe we'll get lucky and someone will remember something small."

"Have you at least figured out why?" Nathan asked.

They had been at the burned-out house most of the day, and

Nathan had been quiet as he combed the section she'd assigned him. She assumed he was questioning her now because he didn't want to sound foolish in front of the others.

When Sept remained silent, he said, "Sorry, that's a stupid question."

"If you'd asked me what kind of underwear I use, that'd be a stupid question." She stopped in front of their precinct and cut the engine. "But if it has to do with the case, don't ever think that."

"So why'd he do it?"

"Could be for the thrill, or just to see if he could—who really knows? Why do you think he did it?"

"Because he's sick and sadistic? What guts does it take to kill someone who can't see it coming?"

Sept recognized the signs of frustration. "Don't let your anger get in the way of the work, because if you do, you'll miss everything but the guy holding a big knife. Enjoy your day off and I'll see you on Monday."

❖

For the next week Sept held her breath every time she walked into the precinct, but every morning Royce Belanger shook his head. Their killer had taken two lives, and just when he seemed to have developed a taste for killing, he'd gone underground.

When she dropped into her chair, Royce asked, "You've still got nothing?"

"I've got what I had yesterday, so yeah, basically we got nothing." She rubbed her eyes, trying to wake up. "Maybe we'll luck out and the asshole will come in and confess."

"If you're waiting for that, you need to put in for some time off," Sebastian Savoie said. He'd been in the precinct chief's office for an update. "You have time for coffee with your father?"

"Yes, sir." Sept grabbed her jacket and shrugged when her father shook his head, obviously disappointed in her casual outfit. But jeans were the only clean pair of pants she had left.

There were places closer than Café Du Monde, but Sept knew how much her father loved the beignets and how much her mother controlled his diet. Hopefully the location would improve his mood.

After Sept placed their order, Sebastian said, "Tell me what you've got on this." The wind was really gusting outside so they'd opted for the close-to-empty inside room. "Because if I believe the chief, all you have is two dead people."

"Then you shouldn't think he's pulling your leg every time he tells you something." Sept picked up her water glass and drained it as a way to postpone the fallout. Usually when things weren't going well in your job, you just had to worry about an ass-chewing from your boss, but your father's disappointment was an extra treat.

"Sept, I put you on this even though it wasn't in your area, but the media is starting to smell a bigger story than rebuilding after the hurricane, so I don't want to hear the word 'nothing.'"

"I had Uncle George examine both crime scenes, and all the perp left behind is two dead people."

Their coffee arrived with a plate heaped with beignets. Sebastian picked up one of the fried treats and knocked off half the powdered sugar, probably as a compromise to his wife. "Tell me what you won't tell anyone else."

"It's the same guy, and it *is* a guy." Sept put her elbows on the small round table and lowered her voice. Only four other people were in the room, but she didn't want to be overheard. "If I'd responded to the park scene first, I still would've connected it to the Blanchard's scene, but I wouldn't have guessed how much he enjoyed it."

"You think he's on a schedule?"

"I'm just grateful he didn't start out with a nightly thing."

Sebastian tapped another beignet free of powered sugar and dunked it in his coffee before taking a bite. "So he likes it and isn't predictable. What else?"

"He's good because he's left no trace of himself except the clean stab wounds." A group of rescue workers sat down close to them and Sept stopped talking.

They'd first come to town during the flooding to pluck people from it, but now they lived in a tent city by the river and were helping search for bodies in the miles of ruined neighborhoods. Also, police officers from numerous cities were there helping the NOPD's depleted numbers.

"You're still holding back. What's in your gut?"

"The first two weren't planned. The victims were convenient

targets at a time he was asking himself if he was capable of the deed. If he's been wondering about it for a while, he's sure now. He'll do it until we stop him."

The cups were empty and the beignets gone, so Sebastian put his coat back on and led her into Jackson Square. They stopped in the spot where the president had promised to rebuild New Orleans.

"Standing here, you'd never guess the shit storm we're in," Sebastian said as he stared at the statue of Andrew Jackson. "Something happen this weekend? Your mama's never happy when you don't show up on Sunday."

"I wanted to have something to say when we had this conversation, and I knew we'd have it soon, so I was working."

"That'd be a good excuse for anyone but your mama. Don't let it happen again." They walked through the park to the area in front of St. Louis Cathedral. "What were the designs on Robin Burns's chest about?"

"I don't know." No matter how long Sept stared at those pictures and researched them, she still didn't have an answer. "You have a guess?"

"From your report he knelt in Donovan's blood, then took up finger-painting with Burns. You don't have any idea?" Sebastian asked as if he didn't believe her answer.

"He knows he can kill, knows he likes it, but he still hasn't discovered why. The designs on Robin's chest show he's evolving."

Before Sebastian got into his waiting car, he said, "Sounds like you've got more than nothing."

"What I need, though, is a way to get into this bastard's game."

❖

Sept's phone rang as she walked back to the precinct, and she laughed when she saw her mother's name. "Either you're showing a lot of restraint or you're mad at me."

"You know, Sept Savoie, one of these days you won't have a mother worried out of her mind over you."

"It's lucky that I do," Sept said as she started toward home. "I guess Dad didn't make any excuses for me."

"He took up for you like he does for all of you when you're

working on something, but that's not going to fly this Sunday, in case you're thinking of making it two no-shows."

"I wouldn't consider it. I bet I lost five pounds this week alone." Sept knew how to get her mother to fret about something else.

"I'll make extra this weekend, then." Her mom paused, and Sept knew she was trying not to upset her with what came next. "Your father told me you saw Damien."

"He came by the precinct last week." Sept didn't want to elaborate.

"How'd he look? He rarely returns my calls, and that's not like him."

But elaboration was exactly what Camille wanted, Sept thought. "It'll take time, Mama. He needs to talk to someone about what happened, and until he does, all that stuff he's bottled up is just going to fester."

"You need to talk to him."

"I did. I talked to him, Ralph talked to him, and Gustave stops by his place once a week to talk to him," Sept said of her boss and her older brother. "Damien doesn't want help, but maybe with some more time he'll realize he can't get over this alone."

Camille's sigh came through clearly over the line. "I keep thinking of Noel and how she suffered. Maybe that's what he can't accept."

"Mama, you can't dwell on that." It was easy to say but impossible to believe. Sept drove herself constantly so she wouldn't have time to replay her sister and niece's last moments. "Aren't you the one who told me this happened for a reason?"

"I'm not questioning God, but nothing makes this easier on any of us. Your sister loved Damien with the same devotion I have for your father, so we can't abandon him because it'd help the rest of us forget faster."

"I'll go talk to him again," Sept said, to appease Camille before she started crying.

"And you'll be here on Sunday early."

"And I'll be there Sunday early," Sept dutifully replied.

"Now do your mother a favor and go eat something. Every single one of you took after your father when it comes to getting wrapped up in work and forgetting about everything else."

"Stop worrying, and I'll see you Sunday."

Camille's suggestion would have to wait until she stopped by for a drink. Her phone rang again as she turned onto Royal Street, and she figured her mother knew her better than she thought. "I'll eat something later, I promise."

"Just because I cook doesn't mean you have to eat it," Keegan said.

"Sorry, I thought you were my mother."

"She calls you to remind you to eat?"

Sept laughed. "If that's the only thing she called to remind me of, I'd have it made. What can I do for you?"

"I know it's not your job to provide me with updates on Donovan's case, but I haven't heard from you in a week. Is there anything new?"

From the noise in the background Sept could tell Keegan was at work, because someone was saying her name and something about veal. "If you want I'll tell you how badly it's going."

"How about you give me a couple of hours, then come by? That way you won't have to lie to your mother about eating. I'll trade you a veal chop for some answers."

"You don't have to give me anything."

"Two hours, Detective, and come hungry."

Keegan hung up and Sept thought about the dinner she'd shared with the Blanchard girls the week before. If she'd had to write a review of the evening, she would've focused more on how good Keegan's lips looked after each sip of wine than on the food. "This time concentrate on your plate, Savoie, or you could be in serious shit."

# CHAPTER NINE

When Sept reached Blanchard's she saw only a few diners left in the downstairs main dining room having coffee. She'd had to shower and change, but having spent the day in a burned-out house had left her no choice. She hoped Keegan didn't think she wasn't eager to be there.

The hostess told her, "Ms. Blanchard is waiting for you in the kitchen, Detective."

The cooking staff was gone, and the cleaning crew had started, but Keegan stood in front of the grill with a blue bandana tied around her neck. She flipped two pieces of meat, then stirred whatever was in the frying pan with a flick of her wrist. If Sept tried that move, she'd be cleaning the floor.

"I might have to make something up so you think you're getting your money's worth," Sept said as she peeked over Keegan's shoulder at the pan. "You shouldn't have gone to all this trouble."

"Eating is more than just survival to my family, Detective, so yes, I did, since I haven't eaten either. If it eases your conscience, you can tell yourself this is more for me than you." Keegan put the veal chops on plates, then placed the sautéed-garlic-encrusted green beans she'd saved from the dinner rush next to them. The plates then went into the dumbwaiter in the opposite wall for their trip to the second floor.

"Are you officially off duty?" she asked Sept as they climbed the steps.

"As of two hours ago, so if you need some parking tickets fixed you'll have to catch me in the morning," Sept said as they reached the garden room. The plates and an open bottle of wine and two glasses were on the table by the windows that overlooked the yard.

"Do you drink wine, or do you stick with vodka for all occasions?" Keegan splashed some into her glass and tasted it before pouring a glass for Sept. She was surprised when Sept took the bottle after she finished, then pulled out her chair. When Keegan sat, Sept poured her a glass of the pinot.

"I do drink wine, but I compliment you on your observation skills. I thought I was the detective."

"It's the first mark of a good restaurateur to know what her customers like."

Sept cut a piece of the veal chop and put it in her mouth, and Keegan rested her chin on her laced fingers when Sept closed her eyes and chewed. "How'd you know I like veal?" Sept asked when she swallowed.

"You mean you don't?" Keegan bypassed her plate for the wineglass, content to watch Sept eat. "You can try to lie, but that wasn't the face of someone who doesn't like veal."

"Actually, I don't get to eat it often, but this is the best I've ever had. As for my reaction, usually only my mama brings that out in me on Sunday afternoons when I go over for lunch."

"Thank you for the compliment, Detective, and now that I've proved that I can cook, what have you done to catch Donovan's killer?"

It didn't take long for Sept to tell Keegan what she could. She even asked if Donovan ever walked near the park where they'd found Robin Burns. That conversation was so short that Keegan had gotten through only a fourth of her dinner, so Sept engaged her with other questions.

"So was the infamous Della Blanchard I've heard so much about the founder of the Blanchard empire?"

"I dare you to call her infamous to her face, and no, she wasn't. Her father opened Le Coquille D'Huîte in the French Quarter. Gran started working for him when she turned twenty-two, and from the stories I've heard it didn't take her long to persuade him to buy this place." Someone came and cleared their dishes and brought out coffee with two servings of the restaurant's famous bread pudding.

"If Blanchard was your grandmother's father, how'd you all end up with the name?"

"Della married into another Blanchard family. You know the name is as common here as Smith is in other places."

The old house around them creaked every so often when the wind outside picked up, but the remaining staff quietly prepared the place for the next day's diners. Sept closed her eyes again when she tasted the first spoonful of bread pudding.

"Your mother lucked out and did the same thing, or was your daddy the Blanchard?" Sept asked as she poured the rest of the rum cream sauce on her dessert.

"Nope, my mom was born the Blanchard, and I'll save the story of how Jacqueline and I ended up with the name for our next meal. The only other Blanchard cook in town is our cousin Mackie."

"Sounds like a fattening family to be a part of," Sept said, then finished her dessert. "Are you done for tonight?"

"I just have to call Jacqueline and I'm done."

"You need a ride?"

"My car wouldn't start this morning so I walked, but I promised Jacqueline I'd call tonight so I wouldn't be out after dark alone."

"Tell her I'll take you. I can't cook, but I'm a great driver and escort."

Having Sept take her home wasn't what Keegan had in mind for the end of her day, but despite their first rocky meeting she'd found their evening enjoyable. Sept had an easy manner that made Keegan want to relax and enjoy the moment. Their meal wasn't a date, but she couldn't remember a night when someone wasn't trying to impress her with their culinary expertise or their incessant chatter about why they'd be a perfect companion for her and her family's money.

The silence they shared as Sept drove toward St. Charles in her beat-up Mercury sedan made Keegan think that her escort, as Sept had referred to herself, was a person comfortable with who she was.

"It's the one on the corner," Keegan said, and pointed to the white house. "Can you go around back? I'm sure Jacqueline locked the front gate."

"You live with Jacqueline?"

"She seldom picks up after herself, can't boil water, and loves to dish out advice, but she's a good roommate." Keegan peered out the front window of the car and could imagine what Sept was thinking. "It's not ours, you know," she said in an effort to diffuse what message the colossal structure sent.

"That's a shame."

Keegan stared at Sept. "What do you mean?"

"It's a beautiful house," Sept said, her thumbs drumming the steering wheel. "You look like you belong there, so it's a shame it's not yours. People don't put that kind of details into new construction"— she pointed to the ornate woodwork on the façade of the house—"and you're the kind of person who seems to care about the details that make something special. Why, did I say something wrong?"

"The house belongs to Della. She grew up there, and most people only see the bank account it must take to own it." Keegan tried to sound as apologetic as possible.

"When I first came out of the academy I used to patrol this area. You want to know what I always thought when I saw these places, especially this one?"

Keegan shook her head. "You remember this one?"

"It was the best-looking one on the avenue, but I wondered how much it would cost to heat and cool it." Sept smiled. "People don't understand that the folks inside places like this may have more money, but they share some of the same problems as everyone else. As a beat cop I still knocked on the doors around here because some of these guys beat their wives, their kids are on drugs or in some other kind of trouble, and sometimes they're just nice folks that something bad happens to.

"Keegan, you might have more money than me, but it doesn't define who are you, unless you're the kind of person who lets it."

When Keegan was growing up, her mother Melinda had told her that repeatedly. "What kind of person do you think I am?"

Sept smiled again but didn't answer. Instead she got out and walked around to open Keegan's door. "The way you outwork everyone in the kitchen means you're no snob who uses her name to make her way in life." She held out her hand to help Keegan but let go as soon as she was on her feet. "Considering how you treated me the day we met, you're no pushover, and the way you mourn Donovan's loss means you're a good friend."

"Did they teach you how to be so complimentary in detective school?"

"Camille Savoie taught me my manners, and the academy taught me to put you in a headlock you can't get out of."

When they reached the back door that led into the large kitchen,

Jacqueline was drinking something out of a mug. "Thanks for tonight. It's not often I get a police escort to my back door."

"Not an even trade for the meal you made and for the company. Thanks for both." Sept took her hand again and squeezed her fingers. "Have a great night."

"You too." Keegan wracked her brain for something else to say to extend the conversation, but not in time to keep Sept from walking away.

"Hot date?" Jacqueline asked as Keegan locked up.

"No, and before you give me a hard time, for once I'll admit that I wished it had been. Sept Savoie is as comfortable as a favorite old sweater, but as exciting as cayenne pepper, I imagine." She took a sip of Jacqueline's steaming chocolate and kissed her cheek. "I'd love to be out on a hot date with her, but I don't think she sees me as hot-date material."

"Then the next time you find some reason to see her, try not to look like Chef Boyardee. That outfit is great for the kitchen, but it's as flattering a muumuu."

"Shouldn't we be sure she's gay before we plan my grand seduction?"

"If Sept is straight, I'll be happy to give her some fashion tips to soften her appearance, and she didn't ravish you at the door because she thinks you're too girlie to be gay, despite the unflattering outfit."

"Thanks for the critique, but you should know that spandex chef outfits aren't an option, and silk invites stains."

Jacqueline stuck her tongue out at her and took her mug back. "Forget about the clothes for now, sunshine, and let's work on your snaring techniques. Because if I'm right, you'll have to make the first move."

"How about we wait and see if she's as good at picking up on signals as she is at finding clues?"

"Why the change in your opinion, or have you just realized how hot she is?"

"There's more to life than hot," Keegan said, then yawned. She was ready for a shower and bed.

"Yes, there is, but you're the one who keeps telling me dishes with heat and stirred with excitement are the ones that get you noticed. All this time you've settled for the sorbet served in between courses to cleanse the palate, so why not for once try the course that makes you close you eyes and savor the unique flavor that'll not only taste good, but has presentation?"

Keegan had to laugh. "No wonder you're so good at marketing. You can't cook, but you sure can talk someone into trying anything."

"Does that mean you'll try?"

"It means I'll think about it, but I'll at least call her again. With everything going on right now, Sept has enough pursuits on her hands without me throwing myself at her."

"There's the Keegan we all know and love," Jacqueline said in a way Keegan didn't take as a compliment.

"I know you think I'm boring and unadventurous, but ripping someone's clothes off and sticking my hand in her underwear isn't the way to build a meaningful relationship."

"True, but at least you're thinking about it." Jacqueline slapped Keegan on the butt on the way to her room.

The thought of doing that to Sept made Keegan shiver. What she wanted was what her mother had, but it couldn't hurt to want the happiness to come wrapped in such an enticing package. Could it?

## CHAPTER TEN

O n Sunday Sept walked down to the Le Madeline Bakery close to the cathedral to have breakfast and read the paper. An article in the Metro section focused on the two recent deaths, with a list of questions the police hadn't answered yet. Her name appeared more than she liked, probably because she hadn't taken any of the reporter's calls.

"Did they screw up the croissants this morning?"

It wasn't the voice Sept expected to hear so soon, but then maybe her luck in some things was changing for the better. "It could be that, or maybe that meal Friday night ruined me for anything else." Keegan was attractive, but the blush added "adorable" to Sept's list of her attributes. "Good morning." Sept pushed the chair opposite her out with her foot. "Checking out the competition?"

"More like I was restless, and since City Park is still closed, I opted for a walk in the Quarter."

"Save my seat," Sept said as she stood. She waited in line again to get Keegan some coffee and something from the display case. She added two packs of raw sugar to the French roast and headed back to her unexpected treat.

"Wow, I thought I was the only one who remembered what people like to drink."

"If I hadn't, you would've thought I was unobservant," Sept said, and smiled. She folded her paper and moved it out of the way. "You look beautiful." The words slipped out before her brain could engage, and she wanted to slap herself in the back of the head. "I'm sorry about that."

"For what? You don't think I look beautiful?" Keegan leaned back as if to show off her form-fitting cashmere sweater.

"No, you do. The comment was inappropriate."

Keegan laughed and twirled a piece of her hair. "Telling a woman she looks like shit is inappropriate, Detective, but telling her she looks beautiful usually gets favorable results."

"I'll have to write that down in my notebook."

"Now tell me why, when I walked in, you looked like your coffee tasted sour."

Sept tapped the paper. "This article about the cases I'm working and what an incompetent idiot I am."

"You look incredible yourself this morning."

Sept put her elbow on the table and rested her chin on her fist. It wasn't the first time Keegan had surprised her. "Thank you."

"I'm trying to take your mind off your bad press."

"So you don't think I look incredible?"

Keegan brushed the crumbs from her cheese croissant from her fingers and laughed again. "Don't waste your breath asking questions you already know the answer to." She watched as Sept picked up her own croissant. "And don't eat anything else."

"What, it's going straight to my hips?" Sept asked, but dropped it anyway.

"I don't want you to spoil your appetite. When are you expected at your mother's table?"

"At four, and how do you know that?"

"You mentioned it last night. You have time to take me to brunch." Keegan stood and smoothed her suede skirt. It fell at mid-calf and hid the top of her brown stiletto boots. "Shall we?"

"Sure." Sept stood and put her jacket back on. She'd planned a casual morning of exploration to see what businesses had reopened, then she'd go home to change before she headed to her mother's. Those plans, though, didn't sound better than spending time with Keegan. "Where to?"

"We can walk. The Le Coquille D'Huîte isn't that far."

"If you can make it seven blocks in those heels, I'm game," Sept said as she helped Keegan with her coat.

Their walk was slow and enjoyable, but when they arrived at the landmark, Sept wasn't expecting the entire Blanchard family. She squared her shoulders and stepped forward so Keegan could introduce her to the two women she hadn't met.

Melinda Blanchard, Keegan's mother, took her hand in both of hers and gave her a welcoming smile, as did Jacqueline. Melinda and her daughters had obviously gotten their hair color from Della, since Sept noticed a little red mixed in with the predominant white. "Sept, this is my grandmother, Della Blanchard," Keegan said.

"Mrs. Blanchard, it's a pleasure, ma'am." Sept held her hand out and waited what seemed like a good five minutes before Della accepted it. "Thank you for having me."

"Tell me, Detective Savoie," Della said, and the three other Blanchards physically cringed. "What the hell were you thinking when you treated my granddaughter so badly? Keegan is many things, but she's no killer."

"Gran, Sept was doing her job," Keegan said.

Sept winked at Keegan. "Thank you, but I'm sure Mrs. Blanchard would rather hear what I've got to say about this. I was eliminating her as a suspect, ma'am, and I did apologize after I concluded she was innocent...of that at least." Sept met Keegan's eyes with a smile she hoped conveyed what kind of trouble she was in later.

"She mentioned you did, but I want your word it won't happen again."

"Unless more people are killed in Blanchard's backyard, you don't need to worry." Under the table Sept squeezed Keegan's knee gently and hoped Keegan didn't pour her mimosa over her head. "She's in good hands."

Keegan had her glass pressed to her lips and choked the moment Sept touched her. "Sorry." She held her napkin against her mouth. "I swallowed wrong."

"I'm sure that's all it was," Jacqueline purred.

The meal lasted until two, with Sept answering questions from everyone but Keegan. The more the Blanchard women asked, the more Keegan blushed, but Sept didn't falter. Della was tough, but Sept enjoyed her cutting wit.

At two Della stood and extended her hand to Sept. "You and Keegan were ten minutes late today."

"I apologize, Mrs. Blanchard. I insisted on walking and it took longer than I thought."

"Next Sunday remember to get here no later than eleven."

"I appreciate today, ma'am, but I don't want to intrude again," Sept said, now that she knew this was the Blanchards' equivalent of her mother's Sunday tradition.

"Eleven, or there will be hell to pay," Della said before she kissed Keegan and led Melinda and Jacqueline out.

"I'm sorry about all this," Keegan said.

"Great food, four beautiful women to enjoy it with, and the opportunity to share my life story," Sept said, her eyes on the white tablecloth. "What's there to be sorry for?"

"At least you're a good sport."

"You think you're getting off that easily, Ms. Blanchard? Think again." Sept pulled out Keegan's chair for her and, once they were outside, put her hand on the small of her back to point her toward Royal Street.

Sept opened the passenger-side door of her car and helped Keegan in, and she didn't talk until she got behind the wheel. "Are you up for some retaliation, or do I take you home?"

"Should I be afraid?"

"That depends on how easily you scare," Sept said, and started the car.

❖

Novice stood in the yard of the abandoned house with his eyes closed, his head cocked to the side, and his breath held, checking if he could hear any signs of life in the area. Two finches were moving in the branches of the dead oak tree that was lying on its side, the larger branches not visible since they had crashed through the neighbor's roof. When he was sure he was alone, he moved forward and pressed his gloved hands to the window, but the panes were so dirty he couldn't tell if this place would do. For the first time in the past week he felt like smiling, since it wouldn't be long before he could put all his planning into action, and he wanted his location to be perfect.

He tried to find a spot in the window so he could see how badly damaged the interior was. "Break the glass, but don't touch it," the voice said, and Novice thought it sounded almost giddy.

"I know," he said out loud. "I won't do anything stupid and get caught. This is too important."

Novice turned the corner, and at the side of the house he found the entry he was searching for. The owners had probably enjoyed meals in front of the bay window off the kitchen that at one time likely had a dining-room set in front of it, but now a sofa perched on the ledge covered in broken glass. The storm had been like filling all the homes with water, then turning on a blender. The furniture had floated from room to room looking for a place to land, or get out, so when the owners returned, even the refrigerator that had taken two large delivery men to wrestle into place was now a lawn ornament.

The rest of the glass was easy to kick in, and Novice was careful not to cut himself as he crawled through. From the chaos inside he guessed no one had come back to survey the damage yet, or if they had, they'd stopped at the front door and left.

"They didn't have the guts to face it," he said. The light he had strapped to his head to free his hands illuminated the frames still on the wall. Inside them, the family photos, if that's what they'd been, had rotted into a blob of faded pastels.

"Not everyone has your courage," the voice said. "They don't know what I'm about to teach you."

"What?" Novice moved to the front of the house, where the ceramic tiles gave way to wood floors. The planks had warped, and the mud that covered them made it hard to tell if they were oak or pine. Not that it mattered. It was what he needed.

"That pain and loss make you strong. How can you know what was valuable to you until you lose it? It's the only way you can express how you feel when you get it back."

The front room had a bay window as well, and it was still intact. Some of the living-room furniture was piled against it, but that wouldn't take long to clear away.

"I'll be the best student you've ever had," Novice said. He pulled on his work gloves and started. When he was done, a space in the middle of the room was as clean as possible without bringing in new material. He finished the perfect altar, then said, "I'm ready."

"You are, and so we begin," Teacher said, because in Novice's mind that's what the voice had become.

## CHAPTER ELEVEN

Sept and Keegan left the beauty of the French Quarter for the gray bleakness of the Lakeview subdivision. The old neighborhood had been the site of one of the three levee breaks, and in less than thirty minutes the houses with the manicured lawns had been submerged in fifteen feet of water. Here for miles no one place had been spared, and as Sept drove around the debris still on the street, the situation's bizarreness was apparent in the escape holes in the roofs and the spray-painted information next to the front doors.

The painted Xs on the front of the houses told a story of what the rescuers had found inside and when. Rescuers had put a zero in one quadrant of the X if they had located no bodies, or a number if they had. Most homes had a zero, but Sept pointed to one with a four. That was one of Katrina's stories of woe. In the other quadrant was painted the date they checked, and the last was reserved for pets. In some cases people had returned to find the rescuers had removed an animal when the inhabitants had owned none. The unfortunate animal had floated to their home when it could no longer fight the brown waters.

Every house here told a story, even if the teams searching them had painted their Xs or not, and the silence and gray film the water had left behind told that story. Driving through the areas affected was like entering a black-and-white movie when you were used to high-definition color. Every time Sept returned to the place she'd grown up, she took away an overwhelming sense of sadness. The flood had not only stolen Noel and Sophie, but had washed away the sounds and color that had painted the streets with life, hope, and children's laughter. Those things would eventually return, but it would be a slow, hard process.

"This makes me feel guilty," Keegan said, her head turned away from Sept as she looked out the window.

"Why? Most people would feel fortunate their house was anywhere but here." Sept stopped to give Keegan the option of turning back.

"That's just it. Jacqueline and I had only minor roof damage. It doesn't seem fair."

"This is where I grew up, and where my parents are planning to rebuild. I thought you might like to join me for dinner, but after what we had this morning—"

Keegan shook her head and raised her hand to make Sept stop talking. "I'm not a snob, remember? And I'd love to join you and meet your family."

"They're living in a small trailer parked in front of a gutted house. I don't want you to mess up that great outfit."

"This old thing." Keegan plucked at her sweater.

"Liar," Sept said, and put the car in gear.

The Savoie house was the only one on the block that had a neat yard with Christmas decorations up. When they walked up to the front door, Keegan could see nothing but studs throughout the first floor, but the house was full of noise from people having a good time.

"We gutted the whole thing, but Mama insisted on us rebuilding the kitchen first," Sept said.

"I was about to ask how she fed one through seven if she's living in a trailer," Keegan said. "How'd they find a contractor so fast?"

"That's easy, she gave birth to her work crew."

The conversation stopped when they reached the backyard, and the sudden scrutiny of so many people made Keegan step closer to Sept and wrap her hand around her arm. Compared to her family, the Savoies were a mob.

"Snap out of it, people. It's just Sept," Gustave Savoie, the oldest sibling, said. "Line it up and act civilized."

Keegan walked down the impromptu greeting line and shook hands with each sibling and his family until she reached Camille and Sebastian. "Thank you for letting me come."

"It's about time Sept proves she has a friend, sweetheart," Camille said.

"That won't get her out of working today, though," Sebastian said. "Get changed, Sept."

"You can sit back here and talk to my mom," Sept told Keegan. "I won't be long."

Once Sept had disappeared to the front of the house with her father and her brothers, Keegan asked Camille, "Do you have another apron?"

"Do you cook?" Camille asked, and most of the Savoie wives laughed.

"I dabble a little."

Unlike her family, Sept's didn't ask Keegan one question about herself. Gustave's and François's wives stayed to help Camille, and they were more interested in asking about food. Keegan answered as she cut up everything Camille handed her, and helped put the ingredients together for the jambalaya they were making. She'd never had three hours pass so quickly.

"I thought you said four?" Keegan asked a dust-covered Sept.

"If you're not here by four to put in an hour of work, Camille won't feed you." Sept looped her finger through the neck strap of her apron and tugged. "What's this?"

"I don't sing, so I had to do something to earn my supper." Keegan reached up for Sept's hand. "Don't pout. I didn't mind, and I learned a few things."

Everyone grabbed a plate and went to the large cast-iron pot Camille had placed over the butane burner outside and waited for her to ladle out the rice dish that was full of chicken, pork, and sausage. The family sat at four picnic tables in the yard, and Sept and Keegan shared their meal with Sebastian and Camille. Only Sebastian mentioned the article in the morning's paper.

"I don't control the media, Pop."

"I know," he said, and grimaced when Camille moved his untouched salad closer. "But you know something needs to break on this case before they get cranked up."

"I'll try my best," Sept said, and kept her smile.

Under the table, Keegan had returned the favor from lunch and placed her hand on Sept's knee. The contact was brief, though, since she didn't have the cover of a tablecloth like Sept had earlier. "I wouldn't worry, sir. I'm sure Sept is doing her best."

A couple of hours later everything was cleaned and put away, and Camille walked them to the car with two containers of leftovers. "Get going before you get a flat from all this stuff everywhere and, Keegan, don't be a stranger."

Sept drove, not needing any directions this time, and Keegan closed her eyes and enjoyed the silence. She didn't open them until Sept turned the engine off, but she didn't lift her head from the headrest.

"I didn't think that through real well, did I?" Sept asked.

"Why do you say that?"

"I left you alone most of the time, which wasn't very hospitable."

"Would you feel better if I told you that Camille and the others talked more about you and didn't give me a hard time?"

Sept laughed as she put her keys in her pocket. "Actually, that's way scarier."

"Everyone should have a fan club as dedicated as yours, and you have no reason to apologize. I had a great time today, and I hope you feel the same."

"I do," Sept said before she got out. Keegan watched Sept walk around the front of the car and wipe her hands on her paint-covered pants. "The best idea I had all day was to go out for coffee." She offered Keegan her hand, but this time she didn't let go.

"I'm glad you think so, considering the grilling you got at brunch."

They stopped at the back door, only this time the room was dark. "Everyone should have a fan club as dedicated as *yours*, Chef Blanchard. Some show their devotion differently. They were just looking out for you." Sept took the key Keegan had retrieved out of her purse and opened the door. "Thanks again for the great day."

"You had a lot to do with that," Keegan said, and accepted her key back. She could understand Sept's need to wipe her hands. She was nervous for some reason too. "Maybe if you're not busy this week we could do it again…dinner, I mean."

"I'll call you." Sept touched her fingers again before she stepped back and turned to go.

"Sept," Keegan said, Jacqueline's words about first moves and taking chances in her head.

"Something wrong?"

"Have a good night." She could muster up only so much courage for this kind of thing.

Sept nodded and paused before she moved closer. She placed her hand against Keegan's neck where it curved up toward her jaw and kissed her briefly on the lips. "You too, and tell Jacqueline I happen to like girlie girls."

"What?"

"Just something she asked while you were in the bathroom." Sept kissed her again on the cheek. "See you soon."

Keegan stood there until she heard Sept start her engine. Without turning, she said, "Did you feel sorry for me or something?"

"As if," Jacqueline said, and popped open a soda can. "I wanted to give this a chance, so don't be mad. Your happiness means a lot to me."

Keegan locked the door and hugged Jacqueline. "Mad...as if. Thanks for giving her a clue."

"Yeah, yeah—don't waste it."

"You know me better than that," Keegan said as she started up the stairs. "I've never been wasteful about anything."

"She's not a flan," Jacqueline called after her.

"I realize that, and she's interested. What else matters?"

# CHAPTER TWELVE

Erica stood in front of her closet and flipped through the new clothes Brandi had bought her. It had been less than two weeks, and while she was still a prostitute, she was starting to feel like she was worth something, if only to herself. She had almost turned down the gifts because she didn't want to owe Brandi something she didn't want to pay, but the other girls had reassured her they were only presents. By accepting, she'd also skipped having to face her boyfriend again.

Her dates had also changed dramatically in a short time. She worked as much as she wanted, but the guys weren't anything like anyone she'd picked up in the Quarter.

"I've been out with this john, girl," Tameka Bishop said from Erica's bed. Her suite was across the hall, and she had gotten into the habit of helping Erica get dressed and coming over for late-night talks. "Find something in there that's blue and silky, and you'll be fine."

"What's he do again?"

"He owns a couple of car dealerships, loves the color blue, and he's going to like you." Tameka continued to buff her nails as she talked. "If you want a hint, take a blue condom and put it on for him. You do it right and he'll give you a big enough tip to pay for this place for the month."

"You want me to tell Brandi you want to go?" Erica sat and gladly let Tameka take her hand to buff her nails.

"I've got a date, but thanks. Brandi's getting more calls than ever, so it's a good thing you showed up."

"That must be true, because I've never made so much money in my life."

Tameka leaned closer as if she was ready to share secret information with her. "All these big shots, and that's who they are, from athletes to politicians, just want to pretend for a little while they can still get the girl."

Her laugh made Erica assume that Tameka thought that was impossible. "You're saying their only chance is by paying?"

"Sometimes that might be true, but I'm telling you to pay attention, and try to get something out of this that'll help you in the future."

"You sound like my friend Sept."

"My date tonight is a bank president. When he's bringing me home I always ask him how I can invest my money. Your guy can help you establish credit, but the most important thing you've got to learn is to use these guys as much as they're using you." Tameka stood up and stretched, which made Erica notice how beautiful her legs were. "I've got about a year to go before I have enough to open the dress shop I want. Then I'm only sleeping with whoever *I* want to."

"You think you can help me out?" All the talking Sept had done finally made sense to her.

"What are your plans?"

"Right now…making it through the day," Erica said, and laughed out of disgust. "Being away from my asshole boyfriend is progress, I guess."

"Was he a beater?"

"He thought a good slap was a great way to motivate me to work harder."

Tameka snapped her fingers, then pointed at Erica. "Those days are over, girl. You concentrate on work for now, and I'll share my plans with you until you come up with your own." Erica hugged her and held Tameka, trying not to cry. "Finish getting ready, and don't forget to ask your date for some advice. They love that."

The blue silk dress clung to Erica in a way that made her feel beautiful as she studied herself in the full-length mirror on her closet door. When Brandi came up to get her, she waved and nodded when Tameka invited her over later for another talk. At the stairs she turned around and lifted her hand to Tameka again and smiled. She suddenly wished she could just stay home and spend time with her new friend.

❖

Tameka and her date had ended their evening at a local club not far from the Red Door. Before that they'd enjoyed room service and each other at the Wyndham Riverfront Hotel, but her date had wanted to hold her a few times on the dance floor and have a few drinks.

At two that morning he'd opened the car door to take her home, but she'd kissed him good night because she wanted to walk. Pre-Katrina, the Quarter was seldom quiet at this time of the morning and she'd wanted to enjoy it while it lasted.

That decision was playing through her mind now like an old scratched vinyl record. Just a few years shy of thirty, she had a plan, the one she'd shared with Erica, and one that each date brought her closer to, but she needed to forget about it for the moment so she could concentrate on how to get out of her current mess with as few scars as possible.

She tugged slightly on the ropes tied around her wrists to see if she could free herself. The man who'd grabbed her had also bound her legs apart, which made her believe his sick sexual games hadn't begun, but strangely he hadn't covered her mouth. Not that she was about to scream and provoke him, because after he bound her spread-eagle to the nails that were already driven into the floor, if all he did was rape her she'd consider herself lucky.

After he'd grabbed her, he'd thrown her in the trunk of his car and driven for what seemed like an hour before he stopped. She had heard his car door slam, but nothing else. Left alone, Tameka had tried to work the latch to free herself but couldn't find any kind of release in the total darkness. He'd come back and let her out, his knife pressed to her throat the entire time. As he led her into the house, her street smarts had forced her to look around so she could describe it later, but she couldn't make out much in the quiet blackness of the place.

The only light came from the lantern he'd placed next to her after he'd asked her to undress before he started on the restraints. From her limited view she was lying on the one clean spot in the house, which drove her fear up but not into a panic. He'd obviously planned to bring her here, since the clutter of debris and rotting furniture had been pushed aside, and usually crazies who planned were the kind written about in books after the cops finished dissecting their brains to find out what had fucked them up so badly. Also, he'd folded her clothes in sight of her and taken his time with each piece until he'd stacked them neatly close to her feet.

"I don't know what you want, but I won't tell anyone if you let me go," she said in an effort to start a dialogue with him. After getting her naked, he'd turned away and knelt down to mutter to himself.

"Is this your house?" Tameka tried again, but he acted as if he couldn't hear her. "If it is, don't you have enough problems already? If you stop now I'll never tell anyone."

Tameka kept at it, talking about anything to get through to him, but he wouldn't turn around. She stopped mid-word when he did. Even in the dim lighting she could see the void in his eyes that she wasn't going to breach no matter how long she talked. Instead she concentrated on his face and thought of the best way to describe it. If he raped or hurt her, she would do everything she could to catch him when it was over.

❖

Teacher was happy. Novice could tell by the laughter he heard in his head every time he thought about the sacrifice behind him. He'd been anxious to hunt again after the park, but Teacher had talked him through what needed to be done to get ready.

The red candle he'd brought had nothing to do with lighting, and as he struck the match, the smell of sulfur heightened his senses so much the voice warned him to calm down. This wasn't the time to lose it after all he'd learned and planned in the time he'd taken between killings.

He placed the candle right above the woman's head, and the muscles in her neck stretched as she followed his movements with her eyes. Even in the low lighting he could see her pulse beating rapidly.

"You don't need to do this," she said.

He ignored her as he prepared the ritual he'd have to perform as many times as he was commanded until he was no longer the novice but the master. Once that happened, he'd regain the control he'd lost or, more accurately, the control that had been stolen from him.

With the candle in place he took his knife from the bag that held his supplies, and that was when the woman started screaming.

"You should feel blessed that you were chosen," Novice said, his voice raspy from lack of use.

"You aren't going to get away with this," she said. When Novice cut her left wrist, "Help" roared from her lips, but he tuned her out.

To Novice it wasn't blood spilling to the floor but the paint he needed to fill the empty canvas in the house he'd picked for his first offering to the gods. He put on the surgical gloves he'd purchased and dipped his fingers in the growing pool. On her forehead he drew the number three, and on the tops of her feet he painted a two and a one.

None of the books he'd read told him the sequence of the rituals, but he had Teacher for that, and this was the way to open the path. As the woman cried, he went back to the bag again and took out the potato-sized rock he'd found by the railroad yard. One half was painted black and the other red, and he placed it between her legs.

"Please, if you want you can touch me. Just don't hurt me anymore," she said. Her tears ran from her eyes into her hairline, and the steady stream smeared her makeup. "I can show you a good time."

"What you'll show me is the way," Novice said as he took up his knife. He cleared his mind of her cries for help and concentrated on what he wanted. The book he'd read was adamant about being specific. He moved his lips as he asked, but he kept the wish in his head, not wanting to share it with his sacrifice.

When he was certain that he couldn't be misunderstood, he stabbed her in the abdomen close to her left side. She screamed as her hands and feet rose as high as the bindings would allow, and her head shook as if trying to block out the pain.

"God...please" were her last words as Novice moved the knife toward the right, effectively gutting her. He then cut from her neck to her groin so he could move the skin aside to reach his goal. Her body was still spasming as he reached into her chest and ripped out her heart.

It was warm in his hand, and he closed his eyes from the horror of what he'd done. He opened his fingers to let it go and get away before he threw up, but when Teacher spoke soothingly to him, he squeezed the heart instead and felt the blood trickle down his arm.

"If there was another way I'd tell you, but this is the only thing that will open the door. So take a deep breath and finish. It's your job. If I could I'd do it for you, but it's you who has to prove himself."

Novice did as commanded, but the deep breath filled his nose with the scent of blood, which made him more nauseous. He placed the heart by the burning candle so he could pour the small bottles of cheap rum and water he'd brought with him.

That completed the ritual, and now he felt hopeful for what would come of it. He whistled as he cut the woman free and knocked out the nails he'd driven to tie the ropes to. He would have to make more sacrifices, and he'd need the supplies. But more importantly, he wanted to keep his freedom to finish his work. Teacher had said over and over not to leave anything behind.

"You've earned your rest, Novice," Teacher said.

He was tired, but he was careful on the way home. A traffic stop now would require an explanation for all of the blood on his clothing. "Thank you," he whispered in the car before he started the engine. "When do we make the next step?"

"You have another week to prepare. Then we'll call to the one who understands misery and suffering like no other. You have until Sunday a week from now to build another altar and find the next sacrifice."

Novice rubbed his thumb and index finger together and worked the now-sticky blood like a talisman. He'd sleep because Teacher wanted him to, but knowing when he'd be called on again filled him with the kind of energy that rivaled the anticipation of being with a lover. And that was exactly his goal.

## CHAPTER THIRTEEN

The units you sent out in Robin Burns's neighborhood came back with nothing," Royce said to Sept and Nathan. The station house was full of officers displaced by the storm, but Royce had given them one of the interrogation rooms to lay out what little information they had.

Sept and Nathan had tacked up pictures from both the crime scenes on the walls, and every morning Sept would drink her coffee as she moved from one picture to the next. So far, she had more questions than the photos held answers.

"Not one person who was home saw anything," Royce went on. "What do you have planned next?" he asked Sept.

"I'm considering school crossing guard," Sept said, and winked at Nathan when Royce raised his middle finger in her direction. "What, you don't think I'll look good in the uniform?"

"Stop fucking around and remember to stay away from the press."

"What are we going to do next?" Nathan asked when Royce left the room.

"Since no one is coming forward, it's time to ask these two some questions." She tapped Robin's and Donovan's pictures. "We've got a second victim, and this is what makes it different." She moved her finger to the lines drawn on Robin's chest. "What are you trying to say?" she asked, more to herself. "Find a blowup of just this."

Nathan flipped through the file and handed her what she wanted. "You figured it out?"

"Not yet, but like I keep telling you, I'm an eternal optimist."

"That doesn't jump out about you," Nathan said, then ducked.

"When you start acting like a sarcastic asshole, you show potential, so come on, Wonder Boy. Let's go find some answers."

The weather had warmed enough that two weeks before Christmas they saw people in the Quarter in shorts. When Mother Nature was this schizophrenic, the natives got restless—like when the moon was full—and the police had to deal with more problems, but that was part of New Orleans's uniqueness.

Sept headed back uptown, and as she turned onto St. Charles Avenue, Keegan hijacked her thoughts. She missed her. Their Sunday together had been the best time Sept had spent in forever, and on the way home she had realized that she hadn't mourned Noel and Sophie all day. That alone made her sorry that she hadn't called Keegan yesterday, but trying to find something to move them ahead on this case was taking all her time.

As Sept headed toward the river, joggers crowded the grassy center of the avenue. During the storm, falling tree limbs had shredded the wiring that powered the city's famous streetcars, so runners had a clear path. The oaks that had shaded this street for over a hundred and fifty years hadn't fared well in the hurricane-force winds. Residents also had to wait for the streetcars to be rebuilt.

In the uptown section, Tulane and Loyola University's fall semesters had been interrupted. Most of the schools in the city were damaged and flooded, and the students were in limbo in whatever makeshift classrooms educators could put together. Tulane had been hard at work from the day after the storm, so the repairs would be complete when they reopened in January.

Sept had called before they left the precinct and found the professor she needed to talk to in his office. The lines the killer had drawn had to mean something—or at least she hoped so, because they might open a new area to investigate. The fact that the perp had taken the chance to make them in such an open area made Sept think they held some significance.

"What's this guy do again?" Nathan asked.

"Dr. Munez teaches a sociology class that centers around religious studies."

The horseshoe-shaped parking lot in front of the main building was partially blocked off as a yard crew cut dead branches from the oaks that lined the front of the school. Sept entered from the other side and showed her badge to the overzealous security guard who ran over.

"You want to pray with him or something?" Nathan asked.

"One more question like that and I'll take back my 'potential' comment."

The old stone building had an unused, musty smell as they climbed the stairs to the second floor, but Sept knew it had to do with age instead of Katrina this time. Her full scholarship here had helped her learn as much about the campus as it had the criminal-justice system.

"Detective Savoie?" Dr. Julio Munez waited near the door wearing jeans and a T-shirt showing the school's mascot. The green wave with a snarly face was carrying a football. As a student Sept had never understood how anyone could fear a wave, but August's storm surge had changed her mind.

"Dr. Munez, thanks for seeing us so quickly."

"I have more than enough time on my hands lately, so no need to thank me." He led them to his office a few doors down and cleared another chair for Nathan. "What can I do for you?"

The space was large, since Munez had lucked out and scored an office in one of the oldest buildings on campus, but it appeared cramped because of the numerous idols and other religious artifacts on the walls. Sept recognized some, but others looked more like they belonged in a sex shop than alongside the crucifixes and stars of David.

"Does this mean anything to you?" She handed Munez the photo and started studying the decorations again.

Like Sept had done countless times, Munez studied the photo from every angle. "Is this someone's chest?" he finally asked.

"The designs were found on a murder victim's chest, yes."

"They were drawn in her blood?"

"Yes, sir."

Munez handed the picture back and tilted back in his chair. "Right off, nothing comes to mind. But if you want, I could copy it and research it for you."

"You can't think of anything?" Sept asked.

"Over the centuries, different tribes have used body paint for a multitude of reasons, but that will take time to decipher. Whoever did this might've seen it in a *National Geographic* magazine, or could've simply wanted to see how the blood looked on skin." He shrugged, and his chair creaked. "The lines are so simplistic it could be nothing or part of a ritual I'm not familiar with. I really want to help but I don't know."

Sept gave him the picture again and nodded. "Keep this one, but please don't share it with anyone. If you find anything give me a call." She handed him her card as well.

Once they were outside again, Nathan asked, "Did you see the size of that statue's penis?"

"I think it's the Inca god of fertility, or a little guy with an overinflated opinion of himself. You weren't envious, were you?"

"Yeah, right."

Sept laughed at his blush. "I'm fairly sure knocking a fertility god brings about instant impotence, so tread lightly."

"You're full of shit."

Sept laughed harder at the insult as her phone started to ring. "Savoie," she answered.

"Are you playing hard to get, or are you a jerk?"

"I thought I should wait the requisite two days that it takes to make me not appear to be desperate or a stalker of any kind," Sept said to Keegan.

"You don't strike me as someone who's conventional any time."

"I thought you got to talk to my mother this weekend?" Sept drove back to the precinct in record time. "Hold on," she told Keegan. "Why don't you grab lunch, Nathan, and we'll get back to it this afternoon?"

"Hot date you need to run off to?" he asked.

"You're supposedly a detective, figure it out." Sept pulled away before Nathan closed the door. "Where are you?" she asked Keegan.

"What, now you're in a rush to see me? Is your life usually that blessed?"

"Not always, but I can hope, can't I?" Sept headed back uptown at a slower pace. "How would you like to have lunch with me?"

"Let's not get ahead of ourselves. Explain that question about talking to your mother, and I might tell you where I am."

"You mentioned that I'm unconventional, but after you met my mother you should realize she encouraged that in us, so I hope it isn't a problem."

"You ate with my family and you're asking me that?"

"I have to admit that your family probably rates higher than mine on the unconventional scale. So how about lunch?"

Keegan laughed. "You do realize I cook for a living?"

"I'm offering you a rest." Sept parked in front of Keegan's house. "Or do you break out in hives if the food isn't prepared in a Blanchard kitchen?"

"Funny, Detective…it's your turn to hold on. Someone's at the door."

"Take your time." As Sept waited for Keegan to reach the front of the house, she rested her phone against her chin and regretted not calling sooner.

"You guessed right," Keegan said.

"I'm a trained detective, guessing had nothing to do with it," Sept shot back. Keegan was in her black-and-white checkered pants, but they were topped with a white T-shirt instead of the thick linen shirt she'd seen her in. "Though I thought you'd be whipping up soufflés by now." Sept tapped the glass of her watch.

"I've got a rare morning off since I trust the staff to get things started. All that free time made me realize I hadn't heard from you." Keegan rested her head on the side of the door and tried to sound annoyed. "Is this something I should expect from you?"

"That depends."

"On how much I bitch? Is that the answer you're looking for?" Keegan laughed and stepped back to let Sept in, then started walking.

"More like what job I'm applying for here," Sept said seriously.

Keegan was leading her to the kitchen at the back of the house and stopped so abruptly at Sept's answer that Sept slammed into her back. Sept's hands around her hips kept her from losing her balance and falling. She turned slowly so Sept would hopefully keep her hands where they were.

"Aren't you a little old to play coy? If you're just clueless, let me explain. A girl doesn't introduce you to her family if she's not interested."

"If that was our first date, I've never experienced anything like it." Sept didn't move, seemingly content to have Keegan pressed against her. "Is that your idea of a vetting system?"

"I've tried the usual dating game, with mixed results, so I thought I'd make radical changes this time around."

"What changes are you looking to make?"

"Come with me." Keegan moved to Sept's side and put her arm around her waist and kept it there until they were in the kitchen. Then she put Sept on one of the stools that surrounded the cooking area. Off her feet they were closer to the same height. "I've decided not to take any more shit, which means if you're planning to blow me off at every opportunity for something you think is more important," Keegan made air quotes on that comment, "hit on my sister, or cheat on me—you're free to leave."

"You put up with all that stuff before?" Sept asked in a way that sounded like she didn't believe it.

"Not all at the same time. I'm not a complete moron."

Sept brought Keegan's ponytail forward and pulled on it gently. "Anything else?"

"I'll let you know as we go on, but right now I want to take you up on your lunch offer."

"Where do you want to go?"

When Sept moved to stand up, Keegan held her in place. "We're here, and it's not because I'll break out in a rash if we go somewhere without a relative in the kitchen. I took the morning off so I could make you lunch. Aren't you glad you didn't blow me off and break the rules right away?"

"Are you interested in what I might want?" Sept asked.

"I'm sorry. My little tirade did come off as bossy."

"I knew that about you from the day we met, but I won't hold it against you." Sept laughed when Keegan narrowed her eyes. "I want one thing, and it's been on my mind since Sunday."

Keegan opened her mouth to ask what, but turned all her attention to Sept's lips when they covered hers. Their first brief kiss at the back door had left her wanting more, and now she knew she'd been right about what Sept could wake in her. Sept was vastly different than what she was used to, but in a way they came from the same foundation. Their families were important, and perhaps Sept had been searching, like she had, for the kind of relationship they had grown up witnessing.

"I'm good to go," Sept said when she ended the kiss. "If you've got any other rules, make sure you deliver on one of those before you tell me."

When Keegan heard Sept's voice, she opened her eyes and didn't remember closing them or putting her fingers in Sept's hair. "You've been thinking about kissing me?"

"I'd tell you everything else you made me think about, but you haven't started lunch yet. Since I'm hungry, I don't want to chance that you'll toss me out for, as my mother says, being fresh."

Keegan gave her a brief kiss and pulled her hair just hard enough to get Sept's attention. "I might not be ready for you," she said, teasing before she started lunch.

They talked as Keegan took out the ingredients for a veggie pizza. Unexpectedly, she didn't experience the usual awkward first moves of getting to know someone. Sept sat and joked with her and asked the kinds of questions that put her at ease.

When the pizza went into the oven, Keegan set the timer and accepted Sept's hand as she sat next to her. As the timer went off so did Sept's phone, and Keegan took the dish out and started slicing to give Sept the chance to answer.

"Savoie." Sept pulled her notebook out to write something down as she listened. "Who found it?"

Keegan reached for plates but waited before she put anything on them. "You're blowing me off already?" she asked when Sept finished.

"If you think I'd trade you and that for something else," Sept pointed to the pizza, "then we need to spend more time together so you'll learn differently. I do need to go, though."

"It won't take two days to hear from you again, right?" Keegan got out a disposable container and filled it with pizza.

"If this doesn't take all night, I'll call you as soon as I'm done. Maybe I can give you a ride home."

"I'm kidding. Go to work. Usually the worst thing I worry about is bad eggs, but with you, I don't want to think about it." Keegan held the container as she walked Sept to the door. "Be careful, and don't forget to eat this."

"I'd say my mother's really going to like you, but you've got a leg up on that end already." Sept kissed her again, and Keegan felt like she was being cheated out of the day. "Take care yourself, and I'm sorry we have to cut this short."

Whatever the call had been, Sept must've thought it was an emergency since she slapped a blue light on the roof of the car and sped away. Keegan stood at the door even after Sept was no longer in sight and thought about what had just happened. No one in her family or circle of friends had ever dated a cop, so she didn't know what to expect. But she figured it was a lot like being with a doctor.

The phone tied such people to a world she wasn't familiar with, but if you wanted the chance to be with them you had to learn to share your time with what defined them. And Sept was one of those people who poured her heart into what she did. Someone could probably try to change that, but such a relationship wouldn't last, and it shouldn't.

"Only surgeons and such aren't ducking killers and bullets while they're at work," she said as she closed the door.

"Was it the pants that finally scared her off?" Jacqueline asked, her mouth full of pizza, when Keegan made it back to the kitchen.

"Why are you here?"

"I live here, and I don't have anything until two. But don't worry. I didn't plan to interrupt the kissing." Jacqueline picked off a mushroom and ate it separately.

"How do you know we were kissing?"

"I just finished saying I wouldn't interrupt, but I mentioned nothing about spying on you." When Keegan laughed, Jacqueline bumped hips with her. "You sure about this one?"

"I'm never sure about anything except how much salt to put in a dish, but she seems like a good bet."

Jacqueline took another slice and headed for the stairs. "I'm sorry to hear you say that."

"Why?" Jacqueline began to talk over her shoulder, clearly trying to get a head start.

"I still think she could help me get over Adam." She was running by the time she said his name.

## CHAPTER FOURTEEN

Sept took another bite of the still-warm pizza as she entered the Lakeview neighborhood in search of the address Nathan had given her over the phone. No one had started rebuilding on this block, and there wasn't one FEMA trailer around. Even though the storm had been almost four months earlier, this wasn't uncommon. Sept attributed it to a widespread form of lethargy caused by the enormity of the cleanup.

As she reached the edge of police units parked in front of the house she'd been called to, she took one last bite and closed the box to save the rest. The two cops throwing up across the street provided her first clue that it would be a long day.

"I tried to keep everyone out," Nathan said as she walked up.

"But?"

"But some of them outranked me and told me to jerk off."

Sept glanced across the street. "Would that be the two geniuses who told you that?"

"Yeah, but I can't blame them for their reaction. It's rough in there. I'm not sure who can do something like this and live with himself, but he has no soul."

"Who found her?" Sept saw the news trucks coming up from the opposite side and cursed under her breath. "Hold up," she told Nathan.

"Who's in charge?" she asked the uniformed police who stood in the yard. An overweight man with curly blond hair stepped forward and stuck his thumbs in his utility belt. From his expression Sept knew he was about to lay down some attitude.

"What can I do for you, little lady?"

Since she was at least four inches taller than him Sept wanted to crack up, but behind him the cameras were rolling. "If anyone's in my crime scene, hustle them out before they destroy any more evidence," she growled. "Once that's done, then back them up," she nodded toward the media, "about a block. And in case you weren't briefed, keep your mouth shut, big boy. Now move."

The guy had to pull his pants up as he hustled toward the house, and Nathan pressed his fingers to his mouth to keep from laughing. A minute later five other officers came out of the house and headed toward the growing number of unofficial onlookers.

"Jesus Christ," Sept said in disgust. "By the time we finish going through there, we'll be able to prove they all did it. Weren't they trained better?"

"I doubt even you've seen a crime scene like this, so you can't blame them," Nathan said.

"Let's go see what's so unique about it."

The uniform in charge left one officer inside the door, and unlike the curious group who'd just left, this guy kept his eyes on the street. "You okay?" Sept asked when she saw how he was breathing.

"The smell's kind of overwhelming, but my partner and I'll take it in shifts, so I'll be fine."

Sept nodded and took a deep breath herself when she glanced over his shoulder into the front room. She accepted a set of booties and gloves from Nathan, but she couldn't take her eyes off the floor.

"Let's get started. Give me the whole story of who found her."

"The search teams were making their way down the street when one of them saw the candle through the window. He kept banging on the door, since he thought they were using candles and was afraid they'd burn the house down. As you know, unless you rewire, the power company won't juice the place, and the guy went out back to check but didn't see any sign of work at the box outside."

The warmer weather had sped up the decomposition, and the entrails appeared so inflated and bloated they would never again fit in her abdominal cavity. The body still appeared to be tethered to the floor because the killer hadn't untied her, Sept concluded, until after she died. The woman was spread out like a bug in a display, and her complexion had become blotchy.

"Was the door locked?" Sept asked.

"He said no. After he knocked some more, he tried the knob and went in about three feet before he ran out screaming."

The candle had a thick layer of melted wax, so it had been burning for hours, but it was still flickering. It reminded her of the candles at the front of the statue of the Virgin Mary when she went to church as a child. This candle came in the same red container that they provided parishioners at St. Genevieve about a mile away, and it put out just enough light for Sept to discern the heart lying next to it.

"Did you take a look?" Sept asked Nathan.

"More like a brief glimpse. When I saw what was waiting, I didn't want to fuck up the scene, so I waited for you."

"What the hell is this?" Sept asked when she moved closer, but she figured no one would answer.

She walked slowly around the body, trying to find a place to start. Wherever she picked, it would be a long day.

"Nathan, get on the radio and call the crime scene guys and tell them to bring a generator and some lights. This'll take some time, and we'll be here well after the sun sets."

Alone except for the guy at the door, Sept swept her flashlight to the pile of clothes neatly folded near the woman's feet. At the top was a purse still shut, as if the dead woman had put it down to keep it from getting dirty. Sept opened it and found a small wallet with seven crisp one hundred dollar bills and a driver's license. The name Tameka Bishop didn't sound familiar, but her address did.

"Fuck," Sept said. The money made sense now, and she wasn't looking forward to telling Brandi Parish the news.

She took her flashlight back out and clicked it on. By Tameka's feet were holes in the floor, and with a quick flick upward, Sept saw the same thing by her hands. The holes piqued her interest, but not as much as the numbers on her feet. They tickled something in her brain, and when she put Tameka's purse down she almost threw up, but her reaction had nothing to do with the gore.

On the soles of her feet the bastard had drawn the same lines they'd found on Robin Burns. "No fucking way."

"Do you need something, ma'am?" the young police officer asked.

"Just talking to myself, don't worry about it."

"I wasn't gone long enough for you to go crazy," Nathan said.

Sept waved him over and pointed to what she was staring at. "This look familiar?"

"Shit," Nathan said as he squatted next to her. "It can't be the same guy, can it?"

"It's the same guy, but he's added some tricks to his game. He's evolving, and this time he needed privacy to get all this done. He's nuts, but not enough to attempt this somewhere like the park or Blanchard's."

Sept moved the beam of her flashlight to Tameka's ankles. "He must have tied her to something in the floor, and from the looks of it she struggled." She moved closer to look for any details in the thin bruise circling her ankle.

The wound pattern came next, and she glanced at Nathan to make sure he was okay. If an autopsy had made him ill, this was much worse, and she didn't need him throwing up on the body. He nodded as if reading her thoughts. "I think he started here." She pointed to the lower left side of her abdomen.

"Why? Up to now, if this is the same guy, he's done it with a stab through the heart."

"Her heart is lying over there like some kind of offering, so he didn't follow his usual routine." She took her pen and carefully lifted the open flap of skin in the spot she was talking about. There was too much blood to see if there were any nicks on the floor. "The way this cut tapers to nothing here," she pointed to the underside of Tameka's right breast, "means he cut in an upward angle, but we can't be sure until Gavin checks it out."

"It's not like he'll have a lot to do once we get her out of here. This asshole more than gutted her."

Sept noted the rest of the injuries as she went along, but she held little hope of finding any other clues. With the quick, seemingly unplanned crimes this guy had left nothing behind, so with as much time as he wanted to get the blood thirst out of his system, there would be less than before.

George arrived as Sept reached Tameka's head, the candle still flickering right above it. Their silent guard at the door finally showed some life and stopped him from entering. "Nathan, make a note to find out how many religious-supply stores are still in business. If it's anything like the grocery stores, it should be a short list."

"You got it, as soon as we get back to the office. What do you want to get from that?"

"I want to find one of these." She indicated the candle.

"Sept, come on. The mosquitoes are starting to get bad out here," George yelled from the door.

"Let them in," Sept said to the officer.

"Fuck me." George stopped at the edge of the clean part of the floor. "What the hell?"

"Some sick fuck had a good time with her," Sept said. The part of the floor that was still dirty did hold some marks this time, and she shone her light to the trail that led back to what used to be the kitchen. "You guys start in here, and if it takes another memory card for the camera, get every inch from every angle you can think of."

"What's with the numbers on her feet?" George asked as he set up the spotlights.

"If you find a note with an explanation, let me know."

Sept followed the smudges to the window, and she could visualize him climbing through, stepping on the broken glass. The light was fading so she went outside to check for footprints. In the yard she spotted a trail from the window to where the dead grass was still thick.

She found a few good prints in the accumulated mud carried in by the flood, but something was odd about them. She crouched down to explain the ridge detail that would let them narrow down what kind of shoe it was, but saw only the general shape of the shoe. Whoever had walked through the yard seemed to have had wood slats tied to the bottom of his feet.

"Anything?" Alex held up the camera with one hand and swatted away bugs with the other.

"Call in another team for out here and tell them to bring plenty of plaster to make casts of these."

"Sure thing. It'll give me a break from being in there."

Sept went back inside but this time carefully entered through the window. She used her flashlight in a sweeping motion, trying to find something out of the ordinary, which was almost funny when she thought about what the house looked like on the whole. "Maybe I should try to find something that's actually in place," she said to herself.

"No prints so far," George said. He was using a blue light to try to map the blood splatter and any other body fluid in the room. "Gavin's office called, and I told him to hold off until you were ready."

"Besides Robin Burns, have you ever seen this?" Sept showed him the line drawn on the bottom of Tameka's feet.

"I've never seen it done before, but the crazies who sit up nights thinking about what to do next to fuck someone over are always coming up with new shit to freak us out." George took a handheld spotlight and shone it on the pile of stuff up against the front window. "Doesn't look like he touched any of that, but we'll go over it just in case."

"You do realize that we'll see this again until we catch this guy, right?"

"Been around long enough to know that."

"I'm not questioning you, but I'm telling Dad to send the word down that as we find these to assign you. We'll have better luck finding the differences if we're working together."

George held the light as Sept walked the room. "You should call him now and show him what we're up against."

"I'm planning to, but I want to contact someone else first." Sept stared at the body as a whole and thought she was on the right track. The candle was the proof. "Are you done?"

"No. I'll go hit the bedrooms first, then head to the kitchen and go through that section you said he came through. Sometimes even the most careful person screws up where he thinks you won't look."

Sept nodded as she flipped through her notebook searching for the number she needed. The sun was starting to set, but the sweat was dripping down her back. Nathan came back in when Sept started to dial, and he walked around the body again.

"Dr. Munez," Sept said, and the name made Nathan stop and face her.

"Detective Savoie?"

"I don't mean to bother you so soon."

"I'm working on finding what you want, but I'll need more than a day."

Sept laughed and shook her head. "I'm not calling about this morning. First, I want to know how squeamish you are."

"Depends. If it has anything to do with rotten seafood, count me out."

"I'm at a crime scene, and I want you to come out here and tell me if this one explains the symbol I showed you earlier. Before you agree, you need to know that this is rough."

"If you think I can help I'll be happy to try. What's the address?"

Sept put her hand over the mouthpiece. "Nathan, go pick the doc up, and I'll deal with my father until you get back." Just then Julio called her name. "Sorry, you won't need the address. My partner should be there in about twenty minutes, and he'll get you through the police line."

"Your dad's coming?" Nathan asked.

"I'm sure he'll still be here when you get back so you can get in some ass kissing, if that's what you're worried about."

"I only wanted to thank him for the chance to work with you—no need to be an asshole about it."

"I'm yanking your chain—no need to act so whiny. Go get Munez and fill him in on the generalities. I want him to keep his stomach contents in place, but I want him to tell us the first thing that comes to mind." Sept aimed the spotlights toward the ceiling. Tameka had already been violated enough. "He might not know anything, but I still want that initial reaction."

"Be back as soon as I can. Call if you want anything else."

Sept could hear George talking to Alex and the other team that had arrived, but she didn't move from her spot close to Tameka's head. After Sept became a detective, she'd found that when she spent time alone with the bodies of the victims and the places they'd died, the answers came easier. Only Tameka stayed as silent as she was still, and Sept attributed it to the crime's senselessness.

When Sept's father answered, she said, "Dad, I know you're getting ready for dinner, but you need to get over here." She gave him the address and closed her phone. She wanted to wait and tell Brandi in person. Sept knew how she felt about her girls and how hard she tried to keep them safe.

"Was that what happened to you?" she asked, but it wasn't that simple. Brandi chose her clients too carefully for the freak who did this to get past her.

"Ma'am, Chief Savoie's here," the officer at the door said.

"Jesus," Sebastian said as soon as he laid eyes on Tameka. "How'd you catch this?"

"I put the word out that no matter where a knife job went down, it was mine. We lucked out this time because it's our guy."

"Nothing about this resembles your guy."

When Sebastian saw the strange but simple symbol and learned that the blood was drawn by a knife, he cursed softly.

"You were right, kid. This guy's got a good taste and he's found his gig. I know you'll bitch, but you need some help, and tomorrow you're going to get it."

Sept put her fists on her hips, matching Sebastian's stance. "I'll take whatever you want, but whoever you bring in understands Nathan and I are the primaries."

"Don't worry about that, but unless you plan to work twenty-four-seven you need some help running everything down. Get back to it, and I'll be at your office first thing in the morning."

If she nodded, Sebastian would be out the door and out of her way. Because he was her father, Sept knew he never wanted to appear to show favor, but he also didn't want to give the impression that he doubted her ability.

"Nathan wouldn't forgive me if you left before he had the chance to tell you how wonderful you are."

"Where is he?"

"Picking up a Tulane professor I need to talk to."

Her father laughed. "He's not that bad, is he?"

"A little eager, but that never hurt anyone."

"Did he tell you where I found him? Why he got what he asked for?" Sebastian asked. He had followed Sept to the other side of the room to look at the numbers and symbols on Tameka's feet.

"Where'd you find him?" Sept checked her notes as she moved around.

"He was one of those elite cops who eventually brought the Dome under control when all hell broke loose in there."

The world had witnessed the city fall into chaos in the New Orleans Superdome and the convention center. Both had turned, during the moments before the storm came ashore, into the shelters of last resort. Thousands of people with little or no supplies and water huddled inside as downtown filled with water. As the winds peeled sections of the Dome's roof off, some of those inside began to abuse the weak.

Once the worst of the storm was over, it had taken the National

Guard and the police inside to seize control of the building and the situation. Sept had fired her weapon in the line of duty, which was unusual.

"I guess I was too busy to notice him."

"He noticed you, and while he didn't rack up any heroics, he didn't run from his post. I wish I could say that about every cop on duty that day. So when he found out who you were, he made an appointment with me and asked."

"And here I thought he promised to wash your car for the next year."

Sebastian laughed again and held his hand out to George. "Hey, brother, it's like a family reunion in here," he said to his brother-in-law.

"If you suggest that to Camille, call me ahead of time so I can watch her kick your ass."

"Sept," Nathan called from the door.

"Excuse me," Sept said to Sebastian and George. She walked out to the small cement portico at the entry of the house. Julio had his back to her and was staring at the media, who showed some life at their arrival. "Dr. Munez," Sept said to get his attention. "I wanted to give you another chance to skip this. We could always cover the scene through pictures."

"If you trust me, I'd like to help in person."

"Go ahead, and we'll cover it however you want." *Let's just hope we don't have to clean off the victim when you throw up on her.*

# CHAPTER FIFTEEN

Whatever reaction Sept had expected, Julio Munez falling to his knees wasn't it. She and Nathan looked at each other, and Nathan moved closer to Julio and put his hand on his shoulder. "You okay, Doc? Do you need to step out for some air?"

"When was she found?" Julio asked.

"This morning, and we think it happened sometime last night."

Julio didn't get up, but he did turn around to look at her. "Why do you think that? Are you sure?"

"I haven't brought the coroner's office in yet, but I'm fairly sure," Sept said. "Drawing from my Catholic background, candles like that don't last more than three days in warm weather, but bodies don't either. From the level of decomposition, I'm sure she hasn't been here that long." She waited for him to stand, but he turned to Tameka instead. "Like my partner asked, are you all right?"

"Are the marks you showed me somewhere on her?"

"The soles of her feet. Does it make sense to you now?"

"I recognize it, but none of this makes sense."

Sept nodded, even through Julio hadn't turned around again. "Take your time, Dr. Munez, but when you're ready I'd like for you to tell us what you think."

"May I get closer?" Julio asked from his position ten feet from the heart and candle.

"George, you finished on this spot?"

"There's nothing there, but make sure he puts some gloves on."

Properly attired, Julio walked on his knees until he could lean down and almost lie on the floor to smell around where the heart was placed. "I thought so," he said.

"Anytime you're ready," Sept reminded him again.

Julio got to his feet and took the gloves off, then reached inside his shirt and took out a strand of something he wore around his neck. "Are you familiar with the Santeria religion, Detective?"

"Santeria, like voodoo?"

"Only those who don't understand Santeria call it voodoo."

"Explain it to me," Sept said, then focused on the scene, trying to see it in a new way. "I've always thought they're the same thing, but I didn't know human sacrifices had anything to do with either."

"They don't. In Santeria some rituals call for animal sacrifice, but no true practitioner would take a human life."

"But this looks like a ritual killing to you?" Sept asked. "If it does, I want everything you know."

"The killer knew the basics of the rituals." Julio stared at the candle, head, and rock. "Santeria is a religion the slaves brought here to keep their own beliefs even if they'd lost their freedom. So they wouldn't get caught, though, they adopted a Catholic saint to represent each of their gods."

"Smart," Sept said as she took notes. "If they were caught worshipping, then it was a saint instead of something that would've gotten them a beating."

"Perceptive, Detective. That's exactly why they did it. The rituals have been handed down from one priest to another."

"Somebody went off the deep end of the crazy pool, then," Sept said. "What does all this stuff mean? I appreciate the history lesson, but we need a place to start to find this freak."

"The symbol on the picture you showed me is the shepherd's hook of Elegua, symbolized by the Holy Child of Atocha." He pointed at the rock painted red and black. "Each god has his favorite colors, numbers, sacrificial animals, foods, herbs, and ornaments."

"This Elegua's favorite colors are red and black?"

"That's right, as you can see not only by the rock, but also by the choice of candle container. If you smell the floor it's aguardiente, or strong rum," Julio said. George stepped forward and took more swabs than he had already. "Elegua loves that as well as standing water. The priest usually takes sips and spits it on the sacrifices he's left."

When Sept opened her mouth, George said, "I got it. I'll take plenty of samples for DNA testing."

"His numbers are three and twenty-one." Julio pointed to Tameka's forehead and feet. "His days are Monday or the third day of each month, so yesterday is correct on your part."

"So we can expect six more of these?"

"There are more gods than days of the week, Detective. This person has committed blasphemy against the gods he wants to honor, but he obviously doesn't care about that. He'll do it until he gets what he wants."

A light rain started to fall, and when Sept heard it she hoped the crime unit had finished gathering evidence outside. The only good thing about rain now was that it brought with it cool winds that made the inside of the house bearable.

"What else can you tell us?"

"Why he chose Elegua," Julio said. He had turned away from the body and was seemingly happy to stand close to the door.

Sept could tell he'd had to force himself to look away, but the calmer he got, the more he ran his fingers along his necklace. "Can we get you some water or something?"

"I don't think I could swallow anything right now, but thanks."

"These things aren't easy, but you're doing great." Sept put herself between him and the body to block his view. "You'd started to tell us why you think he did this."

"Elegua guards the path and the door," Julio said, then took a deep breath.

"The door to what?" Sept thought she'd have to rip Julio's fingernails out to get him to speed up his answers.

"For those who believe, Elegua and the others are called Orishas, and Elegua is the intermediary between us and the other Orishas. The ritual performed here was more elaborate than the picture you showed me earlier."

"If you had to guess, why'd someone do this?"

"Find his offering and it might give you a clue."

Sept turned around and scanned the room. The guy took the time to clean where he'd be working, and kidnapped someone whom he then disemboweled. Granted, she was no voodoo expert, but the whole of what she saw was obvious to her.

"The body wasn't the offering?" she asked, and hoped she didn't sound sarcastic.

"Think of it this way, Detective. When you make a call, you need to put a dime in the phone." Julio took a deep breath as if to find the courage to turn around. "She's the dime," he pointed to Tameka, "and the things you see are the area code and number he dialed. What you need now is the conversation he had. Elegua was summoned so he'd open the door. That I know for sure."

"But not why?" Sept nodded and took a few more notes. "Nathan, get the coroner in here and tell him from head to foot, and to take his time."

Nathan stepped around to where Gavin had been waiting right outside in front of the bay window.

"If you don't mind, Dr. Munez, I'll have one of the officers give you a ride back to your office or home. Just tell him where you'd like to go."

"Will you call me if you find any more like this?"

"Of course, you've been a big help." Sept smiled, then realized how tight her face had become. "I do have one more question. Granted, you teach all this at Tulane, but you seem more versed in it than I would've thought. Why is that?"

"I'm a professor by profession, but I'm a Bablawo by faith."

"Could you repeat that, only in English this time?"

"A Bablawo is a high priest in the Santeria faith. That's why I know a true believer didn't do this."

"Uh-huh," Sept said, and fought the urge to take him in for questioning. "Thank you for waiting until now to share that with all of us. Where you were last night? I'll have to wait for time of death to pinpoint what part of the day I need an alibi for."

"I was in Baton Rouge from noon until early this morning. I'm teaching a class at LSU until Tulane starts up again. But like I said—"

"I know, a true believer wouldn't have done this. But you have to admit, for a nonbeliever, he had more than just the basics down. The only thing he got wrong was using a girl instead of a chicken."

"Elegua prefers goats and roosters. He finds chickens an insult."

"I'm Catholic, and the only sacrifice you make during mass is five bucks when they pass around the collection plate. The priests find chickens insulting too."

"You can joke, Detective, but whoever killed her was serious in what he wants from the Orishas."

"When the guys finish going through the room, what are we looking for as his offering?"

"It can be wrapped in a shepherd's hook, which could be a small stick that resembles the design under her feet, or it could be something as simple as a top or marble. Elegua is considered playful, so don't discount any children's toy. The offerings are usually left at an entryway, and for the Orisha to have accepted the offering, one has to have been left. Otherwise the asking for something was all for nothing."

"Sorry to interrupt, Sept, but the guys are finished outside and we'd like to start in here," Alex said. He and three other crime scene investigators with him were all in their socks. They knew better than to track mud into a crime scene, and their shoes were caked.

"Let Gavin remove the body first," Sept said, then explained what else to look for.

"And this offering, you sure it's here?" George asked. He had walked over when Alex showed up.

"He followed the rest of the ritual, so it should be," Julio said. "But then, he wasn't supposed to kill someone, so who knows?"

"I appreciate all the information, Dr. Munez, and please remember what I said about not speaking to anyone about this. Have a good night and we'll talk soon," Sept said and walked him to the street to the waiting patrolman.

"Sept, if we find something I'll call you, but we'll stay until we're done," George said when she got back to the front door.

"Thanks. I'll be up if you need anything. She was one of Brandi's girls, so I'm going by to talk to her." Sept moved aside as Gavin's assistants came in with a body bag. "See you in the morning, Dad."

"Good call on the professor," he told her. "Go home after Brandi's. You two aren't going to solve this tonight, so get some sleep."

Nathan followed her to the car and sat in the passenger side. "You want me to come with you for the death notification?"

"You heard the boss, get some sleep. I'll handle the visit and get a lead on who Tameka was out with last night. After our meeting with my father in the morning, we'll start there." Sept waved to him as he ran for his car, then put her hand down on the container Keegan had given her earlier. Two pieces were left, but she had to agree with Julio. No way could she swallow anything right now.

"Just my luck to meet a woman who actually knows how to cook, and I get some religious wing nut who kills my appetite." Sept started the car and headed for the Quarter. It was late, but for Brandi and her girls, the day was just beginning.

❖

Wilson still had his tie on, but he'd answered the door without his suit coat. "Aren't you up past your bedtime?" he asked Sept.

"Crime never sleeps in this town, you know that."

"But neither does the fun." He let her in and walked her to the kitchen where his dinner plate was waiting. "If you're here for Brandi, she's gonna be busy for a while. You want a drink or something?"

"Maybe later, and you know I wouldn't ask you to bother her unless it was really important." Wilson nodded and let out a long sigh. "It's important, Wilson."

He picked up the phone on the wall by the door and spoke softly. "She said to wait in the office, and she'll be right down. You want me to walk you?"

"Finish up," Sept pointed to his plate, "and thanks. Again, if I could've waited, I would've."

"Don't apologize, Sept. You treat Brandi and me with respect, so you always gonna get the same in return. Tell her to call me if it's something bad." He shook his head. "Brandi's tough as they come, but bad news puts her out."

"Will do." Sept walked to the room at the other end of the house and sat in one of the leather wingback chairs across from Brandi's desk. The mahogany walls were lined with books, and the matted frames held an array of pictures of Brandi with political and business leaders. To them her money was just as green as everyone else's, no matter how she earned it.

"The only reason a detective shows up at my house at this hour is if they want a freebie or they've got bad news." Brandi took a seat next to her and crossed her legs. She had on a long silk nightgown and her feet were bare, but her hair wasn't as perfect as Sept was used to seeing it. "Considering I've been offering you a taste since you got out of the academy, only to be turned down, you're here to tell me something's wrong."

"Tameka Bishop" was all Sept said. Brandi squeezed the arms of her chair. "She still one of yours?"

"I rent her a room upstairs."

"Come on, Brandi, I'm not here to fuck with you. Is she one of your girls?"

"She left for a date last night, and since she's reliable I figured the gentleman wanted more than one night. He's a regular and she's never had any problem."

"I need to talk to him."

"No," Brandi said, her voice close to a shout. "You know better than that, no matter how much I like you."

"I just left a hellhole where some asshole did things to her that were beyond cruel, and Tameka's probably only the first of many. What's his name?" When Brandi's lips started to tremble, Sept slid off her chair to her knees in front of her. "He can come here, and he only has to talk to me, but I do need to see him."

"She's dead?" Brandi asked.

Sept held her hands and nodded. "I'm sorry."

"She was one of the ones who would make it out of this life. She was so close."

"That's why we have to work together. This is a seriously twisted guy, Brandi, and I've got to find him before he kills someone else." The tears ran down Brandi's face but she smiled at what Sept had said. "I promise whoever her date was won't be mentioned in any report, and I won't embarrass him, but I need a name."

"When you see him you won't need one," Brandi said as she wiped her face. "Tomorrow night at ten I'll invite him over for a drink. Why don't you join us then?"

"Thanks, and if you could do me another favor. Tell Wilson to call the girls who are out tonight. Give them the message to be extra careful and have their dates walk them to the door. If they can't, or someone's not back in time, call me."

Brandi put her arms around Sept's neck and kissed her cheek. "I'll do it myself, don't worry, and when you're done with Tameka, call me. She's my responsibility and I want to do right by her."

"I'll let Gavin know. Sorry I bothered you so late. I'll let myself out."

"So you know, Tameka and Erica became good friends in the short while she's been here. She's out tonight, but if I call you after I tell her, I expect you to do right by her."

Sept kissed her cheek in return before she stood up. "You've got my number, but if she's around tomorrow I'll talk to her then, no matter what."

"It's that heart that makes you one of the good ones," Brandi said, and this time kissed her on the lips.

# CHAPTER SIXTEEN

Sept closed the red door gently behind her and leaned against it. She was tired and damp from the rain, yet she doubted she'd sleep if she went home. Pope's Pub was still open, though, and if she couldn't fall asleep the old-fashioned way, she'd chase it down in a glass full of vodka.

Her phone rang as she closed her car door, and the melancholy disappeared when she saw Keegan's name on the display. "I thought you offered me a ride home?" Keegan asked, without preamble.

"I thought you'd be asleep by now." Sept knew if Keegan was still at the restaurant, she was purposely waiting for her.

"I'm at home and I'm in my pajamas, but I'm too aggravated to sleep."

"Why, did you burn something tonight?" Sept sat in front of Brandi's and watched the few stragglers on Bourbon Street.

"I haven't burned anything since the fourth grade."

"Does this aggravation have something to do with me, then?"

"I was expecting a call from you, at least, and since you answered right away it means you weren't busy, so maybe it has a little to do with you."

Sept laughed and tried to remember when a woman who wasn't her mother had actually scolded her on the phone. "Would you believe I just finished for the night?"

"Where are you?"

The answer of the Red Door, Sept guessed, would get her a quick disconnect, but her father had told her the only way to make any relationship work was to be honest. No matter how incriminating the answer, it proved you weren't doing anything wrong. The ending to that lecture was that Savoies had patrolled the streets of New Orleans too long for one of his kids to screw up that legacy by actually doing anything wrong, so honesty won out.

"I'm right outside the Red Door." Keegan didn't hang up on her, but there was a long stretch of her breathing on the other end. When Sept's mother did that, she was usually trying to find less harsh words than "You're an idiot."

"Keegan?"

"Is there somewhere else in town called the Red Door that isn't the Red Door I'm thinking about?"

"Maybe, but I'm sitting outside the one you're probably thinking about. If you're interested, I do have a good reason for being here."

"It's your birthday and they sent you a coupon?"

Sept laughed again, even though it wasn't a great idea. "I left today to investigate a homicide. The girl who was killed lived here, so I came by to tell the owner what happened. Now if the *Times Picayune* calls you tomorrow to ask what you know, I'd appreciate if you didn't repeat what I just said."

"Sorry, but I didn't expect your day to end in Brandi Parrish's parlor."

"It surprises me that you actually know Brandi Parrish, but we'll get to that later. Would it make you feel better if I told you that my day almost never ends like that?"

The question made Keegan laugh. "It's that *almost* that makes me worry."

"True, but I could've just omitted the address and told you it was the end of a long day." Sept started the engine and headed toward Pope's. "My job and yours are the same in that we can't pick who we serve. If they show up, we can't take a pass when we don't like what they do for a living."

"Is this my trip to the woodshed?"

"It depends on if you think you need a good spanking," Sept said. "I was planning to call you, but most people are asleep by now, so I thought I'd be civilized and wait until morning."

"If my family heard you right now, they'd bring you up on harassment charges for threatening a spanking."

"Your family, huh?" Sept reached the intersection that would lead her to Pope's, but she hesitated. "I'm not interested in what they'd do, but your opinion is important. And I didn't threaten you with anything."

"I finally found someone who isn't in awe or terrified of Della? This is as good as a perfect soufflé."

Sept laughed and made her decision. "So you forgive me for walking out on you today?"

"It was work, Seven, and work I understand. If you leave me to run over and hang out with Brandi Parrish when it isn't job-related, we'll have problems. That seem fair to you?"

"More than fair, and Seven—that's cute." The city felt unnaturally quiet as Sept drove with the window open. Her clothes were still damp from the heat of the crime scene and the rain afterward, so she'd rolled the window down instead of opting for the air conditioner. "How was your night?"

"Busy but good, or at least better than yours, from what you've said so far. What did you eat besides a veggie pizza?"

"Not a whole lot," Sept said, and got another long pause. "Keegan, you still there?"

"I'm still here."

Sept found a parking spot with no problem and let her head fall back when she turned the engine off. "Something the matter?"

"I'm sorting out my plan of attack."

"Sounds interesting. Who's on your hit list?"

"You. Strangely enough, you tell me the truth about the Red Door, but taking care of yourself, not so much. Define for me 'not a whole lot,' because to me it means not a lot, but something even if it was just a peanut. Is that the case?"

"Let me rephrase, then. I ate pizza and nothing else. Happy?"

"No. That pizza was hours ago, and it was purposely light so you wouldn't get sleepy."

"You could've arrived with dinner at the right time, and I still would've passed. Not that you're not a great cook, but the scene didn't stimulate the appetite." The stretch Sept did when she got out of the car popped her back in a way that made her feel better. "Not that any of them do, but this one was tough."

"Still, you should eat something. I have stuff in the fridge."

"Then come open the door and let me in," Sept said as she rested her free hand on the back door of Keegan's house. They hadn't known each other long, but she figured the sight of Keegan and her company would be better than the drinks at Pope's Pub.

The kitchen light went on, and Sept smiled at Keegan's pajamas. Blue silk pants with a ratty T-shirt weren't what she would've pictured. "Not too close," she warned when Keegan opened the door. "I'm sweaty, and the place I spent the day hasn't been touched since the day before Katrina. I could be a walking mold specimen."

Keegan ignored her and hugged her. "You look awful."

"Then I look as great as I feel," Sept said, and laughed. It didn't matter that she'd left the crime scene. The images of Tameka's body would be tough to dispel without a severe blow to the head.

"Come in here," Keegan said, and walked backward so she wouldn't have to let go of her. "Sit," she said, when they reached the stools where Sept had sat earlier.

"Do you entertain here a lot?" Sept put her hand on the U-shaped counter, her eyes taking in everything about the space.

"My great-grandfather built this house, and once you walk through every room you can tell where his heart was." Keegan's back was to Sept as she took things out of the Subzero. "This is the largest room in the house and a lot of people have been through here since then, but he wanted a space where he could visit while he did what he loved. He would cook as his friends talked and watched."

"Family tradition, then," Sept said, her eyes on Keegan's butt when she bent down to retrieve something from one of the bottom drawers.

"It is." Keegan turned around with a few containers in her arms. "Though I doubt anyone leered at him while he did it."

"How do you know? If his butt was as cute as yours I'm sure he must've had some admirers." Sept rested her head on her fist and winked at Keegan.

"I thought you said you were tired." Keegan reached for a bowl and cracked three eggs into it with one hand faster than anyone Sept had ever seen.

"I am, why?"

"Because you're incredibly feisty for someone who's tired." Keegan moved on to some peeled vegetables.

"Maybe your butt is like a shot of adrenaline." Sept smiled lazily as a blush colored Keegan's neck. "I'm sorry. I shouldn't give you a hard time, considering how nice you're being."

"No need to apologize, as long as you find my ass more enticing than Ms. Parrish's. But if you don't, then consider this one of those times when I'll find it acceptable for you to lie."

"I don't need to lie about that." Sept stood up and stretched again, making the leather of her holster creak. "You win that contest hands down."

"Aha," Keegan said as she slid the pile of vegetables into a hot frying pan. "That means you have enough data to make a comparison. Are you an ass woman, Detective?"

"I'm a whole-package kind of person." She wanted to put her arms around Keegan, but the grime of that house bothered her. "And I like the package I'm looking at right now."

"Are you going to beat your chest to impress me?"

"That did sound rather chauvinistic." She watched as Keegan added pieces of roasted chicken to the pan to heat before pouring in the eggs she'd beaten with cream. "And that smells really good."

"I've always thought an omelet satisfies your appetite, but it's not rich enough to keep you up all night."

Sept leaned against the counter as Keegan flipped it. And when she seemed satisfied with the other side, she flipped it again onto a plate.

"What do you want to drink?"

"Whatever goes with egg," Sept said when Keegan handed her the plate. "It doesn't matter, I'm not picky."

Keegan took out two beers and joined her. "What happened today?"

"You don't want to know," Sept said before she took her first bite. "Or at least you'd be better off not knowing."

"It was that bad?"

"I consider myself a veteran because of all the homicides I've worked, and tonight was the worst thing I've come across."

Keegan put her hand on Sept's back and rubbed a small area, not seeming to mind the damp shirt. "You want to talk about it? It might help."

"A cook and a shrink?"

Keegan took her hand back. "I'm a chef, and I just wanted to help."

"I'm sorry again. It wasn't my best attempt at humor, but I *was* kidding. I should've gone home and let you alone, because after today, I'm not the best company."

"Why'd you decide to come?"

Sept put her fork down and faced her. "Because I missed you today, and the thought of not seeing you would've made what I saw that much worse. You remind me that for all the ugliness, I still have something beautiful in my life to look forward to, and that helps."

It was too much to say to someone she'd recently met, but again Sept had decided to be honest. Keegan was beautiful, and watching her chest move as she took a breath didn't dispel the image of Tameka's mutilated body, but it made it more manageable.

Keegan put her hand back and smiled. "That was sweet."

"I'm sure it raises some alarms on your stalker radar, but I'm too exhausted to find another way to put it."

"I'm glad you didn't."

Sept went back to her plate, shocked at how hungry she suddenly was, but she couldn't possibly eat the whole thing. "Does this reheat well?"

"If you want another one tomorrow I'll be happy to make you one, but sadly this one's going in the trash." Keegan emptied the plate. "You want to lie down for a while?"

"Not unless I spend the night. If I fall asleep here I don't think you'll be able to wake me up." Sept raised an eyebrow when she noticed it was almost two in the morning.

"Nothing wrong with that."

"I'd love to accept the offer, but my father's expecting me at nine." Sept drank the rest of her beer and handed the bottle to Keegan. "I should be done earlier tomorrow, so how about dinner? Only you have to let me take you out."

"You don't have to do that, but I do want to see you." Keegan placed her hands on Sept's stomach and slid them to her back. When she was done they were close enough to kiss. "Wouldn't you rather a quiet night in?"

"Sure, I'd love that," Sept said, but tilted her head back and kept her lips out of reach when Keegan tried to kiss her.

"What's wrong?"

"You're okay with seeing me, right?"

Keegan couldn't get Sept to lower her head either. "Of course I am, so tell me what's wrong."

"Then why don't you want to be seen with me in public?"

Keegan laughed at first, then let Sept go when she didn't join in. "I'll let that slide since you're tired and you're not thinking straight. I realize it's been a while since I've dated, but I didn't know inviting someone over for a romantic dinner is an insult."

"If I apologize again I'm going to sound like a broken record, but I'm sorry. How about if I call tomorrow and we'll do whatever you want, with the exception of one thing."

"I can't wait to hear this," Keegan said, still sounding miffed.

"Don't ask me to cook anything."

Keegan laughed and dropped her head so her chin hit her chest. "You're like a refreshing cliché."

"That's an interesting thing to say. What's it mean?" Sept took the chance and moved forward, glad when Keegan opened her arms to her.

"You're a sweet, stylishly challenged idiot who grew up with a mother who's a genius in the kitchen, yet her daughter can't cook."

The weight of grief combined with her day cracked Sept's veneer, and she opened her mouth to take in a lungful of air. But the tears fell anyway and turned into sobs. She'd never learned to cook because she hadn't wanted to, so Camille had spent hours sharing her secrets with the one person who wanted to be the one to pass them to the next generation. But Noel had taken all that knowledge with her, as well as the little girl she would've taught it to.

When Sept became aware of her surroundings again, she was lying on the kitchen floor with Keegan holding her. This had never happened to her, and she was upset that when it finally had, it was with Keegan. She stared at the small black and white tile on the floor and tried to think of a way to make it out the back door without any more embarrassment.

"Are you okay?" Keegan asked.

Keegan might've been smaller than Sept, but she was strong. Sept could tell in the way she held her. "I will be, if we make a deal that this never happened." She had to clear her throat because it felt so raw.

"How about we make another deal instead?" Keegan tightened her arms but didn't try to move Sept's head. "I'm not sure what happened, but it's nice that you trusted me enough to show me that you aren't strong all the time. You can trust me."

"I…thanks for that," she wanted to tell Keegan, but the words wouldn't come. "I should go home so you can get some sleep."

"Not on your life." Keegan kissed her temple and helped her up. "You're going to take a shower and lie down."

"I can't. I've got that meeting in the morning."

"You'll be there on time, I promise." Keegan led her up the stairs and handed her a clean towel when they were in her bathroom. Sept accepted it like she was now running on autopilot. "Take your time and leave your clothes on the floor."

The hot water felt good as Sept stood motionless in the shower. "Time to snap out of it before you freak this girl out," Sept said to the rack of shampoo and conditioner. But when Keegan had mentioned her mother and the kitchen, Sept had compared Noel and Tameka.

Both of their final moments had been horrific, and while she would never consider putting Noel in Tameka's place, at least the people who cared for Tameka had closure. Since Noel and Sophie had never been found, Sept felt cheated.

The water started to cool and Sept washed off before it got cold. When she pulled the shower curtain back, she saw that a pair of boxers and a T-shirt hung next to the towel. The boxers appeared big enough to fit her, which left the question of who they belonged to. She didn't have any other option than to put them on, though, since her clothes were gone.

When she stepped out Keegan was sitting on her bed, and she appeared tense. "I'm sorry for coming unhinged like that. It wasn't anything you said."

"Are you sure? Either you're really sensitive about not knowing how to cook"—Keegan stood, put her arms around her waist, and smiled—"or there's something else to that story."

"There is, but you had no way of knowing, so don't worry about it."

"Do you want to lie down and talk?"

The invitation to lie down sounded great; Sept was so tired it hurt to keep herself upright. "I'm not trying to blow you off or hide anything from you, but can the talk wait?"

"You don't have to say anything to me if you don't want to. As I said, sometimes it helps if you're willing to say it out loud. If you share it with someone, then maybe it won't be so hard to carry the load."

"Sounds like it might be a good idea to stay in tomorrow night, if you're still willing. I'll share all my problems, and that way you can feed me and send me on my way if it's too much for you." Sept lay down and smiled up at Keegan when she joined her.

"Close your eyes and don't worry about me sending you anywhere." Keegan kissed her forehead and put her arm over Sept's chest. "Even if I tried, Jacqueline would claim you before you reached the door."

# CHAPTER SEVENTEEN

K eegan admired how long Sept's lashes were in the sunlight. They were still as dark as her eyes, compared to the completely white hair. Keegan was glad Sept hadn't dyed it, because the color suited her.

She glanced back at the clock once more before she trailed her finger down Sept's forehead to the end of her nose and to her lips. The relaxed features tensed enough for Keegan to know that Sept was waking up.

"Good morning," Sept said without opening her eyes.

"Good morning." Keegan stretched out on top of the covers next to Sept and ran her fingers through her hair like she had the night before. "Is this enough sleep for you to be okay at work?"

"What time is it?"

"Fifteen past seven. I would've let you sleep longer, but I didn't want you to have to rush." Sept had gone to sleep immediately, and Keegan had stayed up an hour afterward to watch her. Sept didn't appear innocent and young when she slept, contrary to the old saying. She didn't look haggard or old, but her rapid eyelid movements indicated that she was trapped in a bad dream.

When a door slammed down the hall, Sept lifted her head. "Thanks for last night."

"That's Jacqueline coming back from her run, and you don't have to thank me because you'd do the same for me." Keegan kissed Sept's forehead and folded the blankets back. "Take another shower, then meet me downstairs."

She waved to Sept from the door before closing it. The night had been way too short in that she needed more sleep, and she'd enjoyed the way Sept felt beside her. She hadn't had anyone stay overnight in this house in a couple of years, but the nights had never been lonely. That only happened when you allowed someone in so deep that they left a void when they decided to leave.

"You've been mighty domestic this morning," Jacqueline said as they descended the stairs together. "Laundry, French toast, and ironing all before eight—I'm impressed."

"It was a rough night and I didn't want her driving. We went over all this already."

"Sweetie," Jacqueline put her arm around Keegan's shoulders and pressed her cheek to the top of her head, "you can wake me up demanding boxers whenever you want. But remember that no matter what, you can talk to me about anything."

Keegan handed her a bowl of oranges and a knife. "Thanks for saying that, and for the boxers."

"Adam's loss, so tell Wyatt Earp she can keep them," Jacqueline said as she started the juicer. "Did you read the paper this morning?"

Keegan shook her head.

"According to the headline, some poor woman was killed in a satanic ritual."

"Leave it to them to get it wrong," Sept said. She dropped her shoes by the table and crossed the room to kiss Keegan. "Thanks for taking care of my clothes and me."

"Sit and get your shoes on and tell us why the paper's wrong."

"I can't comment on an ongoing investigation, but I *can* say it was no satanic killing."

Jacqueline finished her juicing duties and poured three glasses. "If you can't comment on what happened, what are the benefits of having you around?"

"I come in handy if you have outstanding parking tickets, and if you get arrested."

Keegan laughed and held her spatula out like a pointer toward Jacqueline. "Keep Sept in your good graces, then, because if anyone's likely to get locked up, it's you."

"True, but my money's on Gran to be the first."

They spent the meal Keegan had prepared laughing, which was what Keegan had wanted. She couldn't protect Sept from what she saw or the crazy people who wanted to hurt her, but while they were together she could try to give her peace. Even if they were never more than friends, she'd try to give her that.

"I'll see you back here tonight, then?" Sept asked before she left.

"Why don't you pick me up at the restaurant? I'll have Jacqueline drop me off." The hip holster Sept was wearing creaked even now that it was dry. Keegan didn't touch it, but she did run her fingers on the shield Sept had clipped to her belt as well. "Call me if you need anything before that."

"The same goes for you. You know that, right?" Keegan nodded and opened her mouth when Sept kissed her. It was the kind of kiss you shared after spending a passionate night with someone and you wanted to make them feel loved.

Their night hadn't had any of the usual passion, but Sept had clearly put as much compassion into her touch as she could. Keegan felt like she was immersed in a warm lake with a strong undertow like the ocean's. She felt safe in Sept's arms, but she could be swept away by passion just as easily.

"The French toast was great, but it doesn't compare to this," Sept said, and kissed her again. "I'll see you tonight."

"It's a date."

❖

When Sept arrived at the precinct, the pictures from the new scene were already up. There were so many that her father had moved them to a larger space on the second floor. She sat and drank the coffee Keegan had handed her before she left, watching as Alex methodically pinned up the new ones. He clustered them by body part, just as he had done with Donovan and Robin Burns.

"Good morning," she said as he finished the last of the stack, the images of Tameka's heart completing the weird collage. "What time did y'all finish up?"

"A crew's still working. George is there because he wanted to make sure they were doing okay. He said he'll be back in time, though, so don't worry." Alex sat next to her and stared at the wall of pictures.

"Did you guys find the sacrifice Dr. Munez talked about?"

"We took that front room apart and didn't find a thing."

"Then whatever was going through this sick fuck's pea brain didn't count for anything." In the light of the upstairs bullpen, Sept could see how attractive Tameka had been.

"What a waste, then," Alex said. "But why does this Munez guy think the killer would've left this thing?"

"Because these gods he's trying to please are obviously big fans of a well-written note." Sept drained her cup and set it aside to wash later. "How the hell should I know? When I was growing up, you used a strand of rosary beads to communicate with God—or as a weapon, depending on which nun you happened to be sitting next to when the sisters made you go to church. The way those women could wield those things would make a dominatrix proud."

Alex laughed and nodded, and his long, jet-black hair fell into his face. "I remember those days, and I don't miss them."

Nathan came in and sat on Sept's other side. He plucked at the ironed crease in her shirtsleeve and wiggled his eyebrows.

"Fuck off, wonder boy," Sept told him.

"And good morning to you, sunshine. How'd last night go with Ms. Parrish?"

"Not great, but Brandi's a survivor." When Nathan plucked the crease on her pants again, Sept pinched his earlobe between her fingers.

Sebastian entered and said, "Do I need to separate you two?" He was followed by Royce and someone Sept wasn't expecting. Everyone in the room stood.

"Detective." Fritz Jernigan stood in front of Sept and held out his hand. The tall, fit African American man had a great smile. He and Sebastian had gone through the academy together, and since then Fritz had made it all the way to the top and recently become chief of police. "Your dad tells me we're in for a wild ride with this one."

"If you look at the crime scene photos, you'll see he's right, sir. This guy puts a new spin on murder, and it seems like he's gearing up, but we'll do our best before his kill count gets any higher."

"I told Sebastian and Royce to make sure you get whoever and whatever you need to make that happen. If you run into any snags, let me know, and I expect regular updates."

"Yes, sir, of course." The others remained on their feet until Fritz left, followed by Royce.

"You heard him, tell me what you need," Sebastian said.

"If another one of these scenes is found, no one goes inside to sightsee until Nathan and I finish." Sept dropped back into her seat. Her clothes might've looked great after Keegan got through with them, but she was still exhausted. "And I want George and Alex on this. They've worked all three scenes so far and it'll be easier to compare evidence."

"You need more that that," Sebastian said as he moved from picture to picture.

"If you want to add detectives to this just pick another team, but Nathan and I are primary."

"We're strapped, so your choices are some beat cops or the feds." Sebastian glanced back at her as he said it.

"I'll take care of it, then," Sept said. "Guys, give me a minute here." Sebastian didn't take his eyes from the picture of the candle and the heart until they were alone. "Strapped? What kind of shit is that?"

"Fritz doesn't want to turn this into a feeding frenzy when it comes to the media, so low-key is how he wants to play it."

"How do you want to play it?"

"I taught you, so I trust you, but we need more people. Not a knock to you, but we both know what this is going to become if we ignore it. Pick your team of uniforms, but choose wisely." Sebastian put his hands on her shoulders and whispered the next part. "I love Fritz like a brother, but if this goes south it'll be about politics, not family, and he and the mayor will be looking for someone to blame. Don't let it be you, kid."

"Thanks, Dad. I'll keep you in the loop."

Sebastian kissed her cheek and hugged her. "Go to work. You can tell me about it Sunday."

"Sounds good."

"Is Keegan coming with you? Your mama and sisters-in-law really liked her."

"Get out of here, and tell Mama if she wants the scoop to call me."

## CHAPTER EIGHTEEN

The morning went by quickly as Nathan checked a few things out for Sept and added the first two people to their team. Lourdes Garcia and her partner Bruce Payton had actually called her first. They'd been the first two to report to Blanchard's when Donovan had been discovered.

Sept had accepted them even though she'd realized that they were using the opportunity as a springboard on their detective's exam. Right now Sept needed ambitious people.

"Where do you want us first?" Lourdes asked.

They'd ordered lunch in so Sept and Nathan could catch them up to speed, and so Sept could plan their investigation. "This last place had more evidence than the first two, but still nothing of the killer."

"Are we sure this guy did the others?" Bruce asked.

"I'm sure about Robin Burns, and ninety-five percent about Donovan Bisland," Sept said. "He found his signature with Tameka, though, so that's where we'll start. You two track that candle down for me. Try every location in the city still selling them right now, and call me if any of them have to do with Santeria or voodoo."

"We'll start now," Bruce said.

"Sept, can I talk to you first?" Lourdes looked concerned.

When they were on the back patio that some of the secretaries used for lunch, Sept asked, "What's wrong?"

"Before I get too involved in this case I want to make sure you're cool with the fact that my mom, Maria, believes in Santeria."

For a moment Sept felt like she'd been asleep half her life and had woken up in a place she didn't recognize. Since when did so many people practice something she personally found bizarre? "If you can vouch for her that she didn't do this, we're good."

"I can even give her an alibi."

Sept laughed. "Then we're cool. Hell, if she's willing, she might even be able to help us."

Lourdes appeared relieved as she headed back inside, and Sept took the opportunity to call Blanchard's. "Keegan Blanchard, please." The warm temperatures were gone and Sept was feeling the chill through the cotton of her shirt. "Detective Savoie," she said when the suspicious-sounding person on the other end asked.

"Are you calling to try and impress me, or to cancel our date?" Keegan asked. "If it's to cancel, should I remind you that I washed your underwear this morning?"

"My ass is too grateful for me to consider canceling." Sept held her hand up to Nathan when he came outside.

"Stop by your place and pick up a jacket."

"Not a change of clothes, huh?"

"I think we've established what a great job I do with the laundry, so don't worry about it, but it's too cold to be running around in shirtsleeves. If you won't do it for yourself, think about me. I can't have the sniffles and cook."

"With incentive like that, consider it done." Sept pointed at Nathan and glared at him as he inched closer. "I'll see you tonight."

"Stay safe, Seven, or I might have to get rough with you."

Sept laughed, then stopped as she faced Nathan, who was less than two feet away. "What's so important that you're willing to lose a few teeth?"

"Brandi Parrish called."

She waited for him to say something else, but he delivered the news like he was announcing he'd won the lottery. "And?"

"She wants to know if we can come over."

"We?" Sept narrowed her eyes.

"All right, you. She wants to know if *you* can come over now, instead of tonight."

"And you thought you'd tag along? Is that what you're so peppy about?"

He lowered his head a little and shrugged, making him seem like a six-year-old whose mother had told him there'd be no Christmas that year. "You don't have to take me and I'm sure you won't, so forget it."

"Have you ever been?" Sept walked around the building to where she'd parked her car, happy that she wouldn't have to reschedule Brandi and her mystery man.

"No." Nathan followed like an obedient puppy.

"You do realize they don't walk around naked and fuck in the living room, right?" She laughed at his blush. "Come on, eager beaver. Let me introduce you to one of the places in New Orleans that doesn't exist."

Tameka's last date was definitely innocent because life was never that easy, but they still had to talk to him on the off chance he'd noticed someone hanging around.

Sept stopped at her apartment for a jacket on the way to Brandi's. When they arrived Wilson made it to the door in only a few seconds, as if he was expecting them, and Sept shook hands with him and introduced him to Nathan. The house was quiet, with only a radio playing forties music filtering in from one of the rooms.

"I thought you were coming alone?" Brandi asked, and Sept almost laughed at the way Nathan's mouth made a perfect "O," probably because of her negligee.

"This is my new and inexperienced partner, Nathan. Go easy on him."

"They gave you a rookie?"

"Yes, so tell me what I want to know, since I'll probably be dead by next week."

Brandi smiled, but only one side of her mouth lifted. "At least he's cute." When Nathan blushed again she added, "And bashful too. How sweet."

"I hadn't noticed." Sept took her notebook out as a hint that they were there for a reason. "But he's as trustworthy as an eagle scout."

"In the office, then," Brandi said as she took Wilson's arm and stepped away.

Nathan followed Sept down the hall and said nothing.

"Whoever is behind that door, no reaction, okay?" Sept turned her head when he didn't say anything, but he nodded.

When they reached the study Sept took a breath before she turned the knob. From the back, the silver-haired guy in the pinstriped jacket could've been anyone, but when Sept sat next to him, she had to fight hard to follow the advice she'd given Nathan.

He was the president of one of the larger banks in town and a frequent dinner guest of Sept's parents because he'd grown up with her father. And he was a married father of four with thirteen grandchildren. She should've paid closer attention when Brandi had said that she wouldn't need a name, but Brandi couldn't possibly know just how well Sept knew him.

"I came because I realize you won't make this any worse than it has to be," he said, his eyes glued to the wall the entire time.

"Embarrassing you isn't my aim, sir, but you were the last person to see Tameka alive."

"The second-to-last person to see her alive. There's no way I had anything to do with her death. We've had a standing appointment for two years."

"Sitting with you at my parents' house with your wife, I would've never guessed this." Sept placed her hand on his forearm with her father's advice in mind. Every story always had two sides, even if one side was lame and inexcusable. "I'm sure you have your reasons for befriending Brandi and her girls, and that you did won't leave this room."

"Sept, you have to believe me. I had nothing to do with this."

All the people Sept interviewed said they had nothing to do with anything ever. Every crime was committed by some guy who never slept and had an insatiable appetite for mayhem.

"Just give me a breakdown of the time you spent with her, and try to put times in when you can."

He described their time in the hotel room, when they left, and the drinks and dancing afterward. "I opened the car door to take her back and she turned me down. Said she wanted to walk, and I knew better than to argue. When Tameka made her mind up, no amount of money could persuade her."

"No one on the street stood out?"

He closed his eyes like someone had photographed the scene and painted it on the back of his eyelids. "It was late and I didn't see anyone at all. Despite what you must think of me, I'm a gentleman, Sept. It was less than a block."

"I'm not here to judge you, only to do my job." Sept stood and Nathan popped up as well. "If I need to talk to you again, I'll call."

"Did she have family?"

"She had Brandi and the girls here, from what I understand. We'll find out if she did during the investigation."

"Thanks."

Sept guessed he had more to say, starting with the desire to help those left behind. As she shook his hand, the memory of him offering the same thing at Noel and Sophie's memorial services was vivid.

"I'll be in touch," Sept said.

"About your father…" He left it hanging for Sept to finish.

"Don't worry, sir. He won't find out unless you tell him, but if you lied to me today, my obligation stops there."

"I understand."

Sept and Nathan left him in the study and headed for the front door, where Brandi was waiting. She'd changed into a business suit and swept her hair up and pinned it. "One thing before you run off. She's in the parlor," Brandi said to Sept.

She then took Nathan's arm. "While your partner deals with a chore, would you like to try one of Wilson's peanut-butter cookies? They're heavenly, Detective."

Erica sat on one of the antique sofas with her hands covering her face. When Sept sat down, she raised her head, and the redness of her eyes showed she'd been crying for a while. Sept opened her arms and Erica fell against her.

"Listen to me," Sept said as her crying slowed down. "No matter what, you call me if you have a problem with anyone. I brought you here to be safer, but I don't want you to think of it as a long-term fix."

"Where am I supposed to go, back to the idiot who turned me out in the first place?"

"Think of something and work hard to get it. If you need any motivation, remember what happened to Tameka. I don't want that for you, and you've got too much potential to do this for the rest of your life."

"I can really call you?"

"Anytime you want and for anything you want to talk about, and no walking around here at night alone." Sept dabbed a tissue under Erica's eyes.

"Brandi already warned us."

"Have your dates drop you at the door, and when they can't, you really need to call me." When Erica nodded, Sept squeezed her.

"You're gonna catch him, right? Tameka was my friend."

"I'll do my best."

❖

When they reached the car, Nathan said, "Lourdes called. They found something they thought we should check out. It's not far."

"Where to?"

"Mendoza's House of Spirits." Nathan read the name from his notes. "On Chartres."

The name sounded familiar, but Sept drew a blank. She drove a few streets over and peered up at the old brick building that was probably one of the first built in the city. The person standing on the other side of the street, not the building itself, jogged her memory.

"What's to check out?" Sept asked.

"There was a break-in, and the only things taken were candles and a couple of books. Here's the missing inventory the owner's come up with so far."

"Red candles?"

Nathan nodded. "Along with a few other colors."

"Uh-huh." Sept put her hand on the door latch but hesitated.

"You okay?"

"I'm fine, but could you wait up a second?" Sept opened the door and crossed the street to where Damien stood rocking from foot to foot. "Out walking again?"

"Until they let me come back to work I don't have much else to do." Damien stopped rocking but started fidgeting. "Remember this place?"

"It was one of our first calls together, and now I'm back for the same thing." The last time Sept had seen Damien, he had only looked unkempt. Now he smelled like that was exactly what he was.

"What's a homicide detective doing investigating a robbery?"

"Part of my case led me here. Why don't you wait, then I'll take you to lunch."

"Sure, I'll be here." Damien's smile didn't erase the sadness etched in his features.

She crossed the street again and glanced back to make sure Damien wasn't leaving. Inside, a woman was standing with Nathan at the counter with examples of the different candles stolen.

"Detective Savoie," she said, and held out her hand. "I'm Estella Mendoza."

Sept guessed she was Hispanic, and she stopped when the woman pinned her with eyes so light gray they appeared white.

"Are you the new owner?" The bits of the first time she'd been here were coming back, but she didn't recognize Estella. "It's been about five years, but I remember another woman, who resembled you."

"Good memory, Detective. I inherited the store from my mother. She told me about you, and when your partner mentioned you, I knew my mother's watching out for me. You caught the others who violated this place."

"I was in a uniform then, and the punks hanging on the corner weren't that hard to figure out." Sept bent down and examined the saints embossed on the front of the lined-up candles. "This is all that's missing?"

"I took out one of each, and if it had just been this, I wouldn't have bothered to call it in. The stolen books were the only copies in existence." Like Dr. Munez, Estella ran a bead necklace through her fingers.

"What were they?"

"Works that have been in my family for years. They're the handwritten instructions of all the rituals to call the Orishas. My great-great-great-grandmother started them, with the help of those who worked the old magic back then."

"All the steps were in there?" Sept didn't straighten up, but she turned her head in Estella's direction.

"The rituals can never be completely written down, because they won't work without advanced knowledge. The masters don't want the novices to try things they shouldn't."

"Did the books have anything about a sacrifice?" Sept was mentally cursing. The investigating officers probably hadn't fingerprinted the place over candles and two books. It was a missed opportunity, though she doubted that the thief had left any fingerprints.

"Nothing about a sacrifice, but there wouldn't be any reason to record that. Those who know would make that before they began the ritual." Estella put her hand on Sept's forearm. "Why do you need to know that to find whoever robbed me? Or better yet, how do you know to ask that at all?"

"I'm not here to investigate your robbery, Ms. Mendoza, but I'll do whatever I can to find your books." Those were the most important because they'd already found part of what was stolen. The red candle burning near Tameka's body came from these store shelves, but the books were well hidden somewhere. She'd find them only when she found her killer.

"God bless you," Estella said, then shivered. "You'll need it. Whoever stole my books is opening doors he's got no business with, and it'll burn him in the end."

Julio Munez said he had no idea why the guy had killed Tameka, but Sept believed everyone had a theory, if given a chance to share it. Selling charms and hex dolls to tourists might have paid the rent, but this business thrived by selling to those who believed in the power of the Orishas.

"Why would someone kill in the name of Elegua?"

"Kill a person, you mean?"

Sept nodded.

"Killing's never acceptable, no matter how important what you seek is. It's a sin."

"I realize that, no matter who or what you pray to, but what if they did?" Sept persisted.

"They want Elegua to open the door so they can talk to the other Orishas, since Elegua is the gatekeeper." Estella shut her eyes tight. "That's what's usually done, but if someone was killed, I can only guess that's why. What the killer wants will come only with the next sacrifice."

"Thanks anyway, ma'am," Sept said, and handed Estella a card. "And if you could keep this conversation between us for now, I'd appreciate it."

"Of course, and good luck, Detective. Hopefully you're wrong about the killing. Like I said, no novice with a book should be attempting to wield that kind of power."

## CHAPTER NINETEEN

The smudged mirror was cracked in the upper left-hand corner, but Novice didn't care. He stared at his sweat-covered naked body and repeated his wish. He wanted his vision to come true here in front of the mirror so he could relive some of his favorite memories, but so far there was only silence. The silence and his reflection, and that wasn't what he expected.

"I did everything asked of me, and nothing," he said as he tapped the glass with the tip of his knife. More than anything, he wanted to smash the mirror into tiny pieces, but he couldn't. It was the door he'd asked to be opened.

"If you don't have the guts to see this through, tell me now so I can stop wasting my time," Teacher said in a low, menacing voice. "Who are you to question me or make demands? Like I found you, I can find someone else who's more worthy."

"Wait," Novice said, dropping his hand with the knife to his side. The blade was sharp enough to open a small cut on his outer thigh. "I only thought that I would be given a small glimpse."

"You'll get that after you do as you're told. You act like a spoiled and selfish bastard, and you wonder why you lost so much?"

Novice clenched his free hand into a fist. "I don't care what you promised me." He was so angry that spit landed on the mirror. "Don't say that again. My family was stolen from me. I loved them and did everything I could to keep them safe."

"If you want to be left alone…again, all you have to do is say 'Go,' and I'll disappear."

The anger that had pulsed through Novice so strongly just moments earlier shattered like a plate falling on marble. "Wait, please, you're all I've got, and now they're hunting me."

"Question me again and I won't give you the choice. I'll be gone and you can shout your wishes to the wind. I can guarantee, if that happens you'll never get the answers you're so desperate for and the wolf on your trail will devour you, because we both know she's more than capable." Teacher stopped long enough for the silence to close in, and Novice started crying. "Stop it, and get ready. We don't have much time and we have an altar to prepare."

"What about my wolf?"

"As long as you have me, nothing and no one can touch you. If the wolf gets too close, we'll set a trap she won't walk away from."

"Thank you, Teacher," Novice said with his head lowered.

❖

"Son of a bitch," Sept muttered when she stepped out and Damien was gone. The interview hadn't taken that long, but she saw no sign of him in either direction. He'd been on foot, but something had spooked him, and Sept made a mental note to drive by his place and check on him.

Starting their careers, then working in a patrol car together had forged their friendship to the point that Sept had a hard time imagining Damien not being a part of her life. When he'd married Noel, Sept had stood up for him, and they had truly become family that day. She'd driven him to the hospital the day Noel went into labor and held Sophie the day she was baptized. All that history meant nothing, because when she saw him now she had no clue what was going through his mind. It was like staring at a stranger.

"What's wrong?" Nathan asked.

"My brother-in-law disappeared on me."

"Want to track him down?"

"We don't have time." Sept scanned the area again, trying to find some sign of Damien. "Let's go visit our favorite coroner and see if he found anything."

"How's Ms. Blanchard?"

After Sept keyed the ignition, she turned toward Nathan before she put the car in gear to try and figure out if he was being sarcastic. "She was great the last time I saw her. Why?"

"It's an innocent question people ask when they're trying to get to know each other." He laughed, and to Sept he sounded nervous. "After you ruled her out as a crazed killer, she seemed nice."

"She's better than nice, and I can't believe you're a gossip hound."

"Is that bad?"

"That depends on if I hear from anyone else at work how nice Keegan Blanchard is. Get me?"

"Can I tell you something and not have you think I'm a geek?"

Sept laughed as she turned into the parking lot across from the coroner's office. "Sure, but you're working on the assumption that I don't already think you're a geek."

"Funny," Nathan said. "I know this is a temporary assignment, but I want to work with you. So if I'm slacking in any area, let me know. I want to prove that I'll be a good partner, and that means I'd never betray your confidence."

"Relax, Nathan, you're doing fine." Sept reached into her pocket and took out a roll of mints and handed them to him. "Here, this should make this visit easier. It did for me at first."

When they arrived, Gavin was putting Tameka's body back in a drawer. He explained the wounds on the body and how he figured Tameka had sustained them, from the cuts on her wrists to the gash that had gutted her.

"I've been doing this for a long time, Sept, and if I never see anything like this…" It took Gavin a few seconds to flip through the pictures to find what he wanted. "The cut, if you remember, was done in what seems to be one swipe, but her heart"—he pointed to a spot on the picture of Tameka's heart as it sat in a pan—"was ripped out of her chest. That takes a degree of cruelty I'm not familiar with, and I don't want to be."

"Did you call Brandi Parrish?"

"I still have to gather some evidence, but I'll release Tameka to her as soon as I'm done. She's at peace now, but that was a hell of a mountain to climb to get it."

"You're a good man, Gavin." Sept handed him the photo back and nodded. "You're the side of the scales that keeps the world balanced."

"I don't know. These days it seems like there's more of them than good guys. Best of luck to you, because I don't want another one like this one on my table."

Nathan popped another mint in his mouth and offered one to Sept. "What are we missing?" he asked on the way back to the precinct.

"It's something, because as meticulous as this guy is, he'll do something that'll trip him up." Sept glanced at her watch and noticed it was after five. Another long day where she felt like she'd walked in small circles that got her nowhere but frustrated. "For all his careful planning, he's crazy. And crazy people have a tendency to do crazy shit."

"What if he's not?"

"God help us," Sept said, and meant it.

❖

"Make sure you order extra veal." Jacqueline sat in Keegan's office with papers spread out everywhere. "The private party next week offered it as a choice of entrée, and no one went with the chicken."

"Smart group, and I've got it covered. Just remember that after that, we need to shut down for at least a week. The lights in the center room upstairs keep flickering, and I'm sure it's the wiring."

It was their weekly meeting, and Keegan always really looked forward to it since, aside from business, she got to enjoy Jacqueline's company for hours without interruption. Today, though, she couldn't help but glance at the clock every few minutes, and because she was anxious for the day to end, the hands of the damn thing seemed to be nailed down.

"Earth to Keegan." Jacqueline snapped her fingers in front of Keegan's face. "What's wrong?"

"Nothing, sorry."

"Tell me or I'll pin you until you squeal."

"You're wearing a skirt and you haven't done that to me since I was five," Keegan said, and scooted back when Jacqueline made a halfhearted lunge toward her. "And I'm worried about Sept."

"I know you are, but you're going to have to learn to live with what she does or move on to someone safer."

Keegan stared at Jacqueline's mouth as she said it and still couldn't believe she had. "That somehow makes me sound shallow."

"No, it doesn't. This is new to you, which makes me worry." Jacqueline stood and put her arms around Keegan from behind. "I already know you care, or else you wouldn't have been ironing so early this morning. You don't even do that for me."

"Maybe you don't bring out the mother hen in me," Keegan said, and lifted one of Jacqueline's hands and kissed the back. "Like I said earlier, she had a rough night and I was trying to help out."

"I'm sure you'll be fine, but don't forget that I'm right down the hall from you most nights. I'm your favorite sister, I love you, and I'm available for conversation at all hours."

"Thanks." Keegan sighed and picked up one of the menus in an effort to change the subject, but dropped it quickly. "Why couldn't she have been a chef?"

"That's an easy one," Jacqueline bent over and whispered in her ear. "It'd be like dating yourself, and no one in the kitchen would be able to concentrate. They'd all be looking at her ass all night, including you."

From the window they saw Sept standing in the middle of the kitchen with her back to them and her fists on her hips. She'd changed clothes, wearing her leather jacket, and three of the wait staff were talking to her.

Her stance telegraphed her confidence, but Keegan knew she had a vulnerable side as well. "You know I'm not into looks," Keegan said, but her eyes followed the path from Sept's shoulders down her back to the long legs covered by black slacks.

"I know, you like her for her mind"—Jacqueline moved so she was behind Keegan again, "her sense of humor"—she raised her index and middle fingers—"but that's not what makes your pulse race, is it?" She placed her fingers on Keegan's neck. "There's a little hedonist in all of us, and thank all that's holy that's true when the right opportunity comes along."

Jacqueline sounded so logical that Keegan nodded, then smiled when Sept turned around. "I appreciate the pep talk."

"What else are big sisters for?"

"Have you cooked your share for today?" Sept asked from the open door.

"It's not like we have a quota, Detective," Keegan said.

"Then how about an earlier night than we planned?" Sept stood with her hands still on her hips, making her jacket flap open enough for the butt of her gun to show now that it was in a shoulder holster.

Keegan glanced at the nine millimeter before she settled on Sept's eyes. Today they appeared like black pools that hid nothing of who Sept was and what was in her heart. "Did you have a better day?"

"No one died, and that's always a good day." Sept relaxed her stance and moved closer. "I'm here with you, and while I don't have as much experience with what that's like, I'm predicting that's always going to be good as well." At the end of her words Sept stood in front of Keegan and kissed her.

"A cop who sounds like a poet." Jacqueline rubbed Keegan's back briefly when the kiss ended. "That's a keeper, sis."

"Can we finish tomorrow?" Keegan asked Jacqueline.

"Sure—go have fun."

Keegan looked up at Sept's mouth and tried to suppress the need to enjoy it for the rest of the night. They had made their date to talk, to learn about each other so they could move forward, but right now all Keegan wanted to do was be romanced.

"What's going on in here?" Sept tapped her finger gently against Keegan's temple. "Change your mind?"

"Absolutely not, I'm just glad to see you. What are you in the mood for?"

Sept kissed her again and rested her forehead against Keegan's when their lips parted. "I know you love to cook, but how about a drink first?"

"You're not hungry?" Keegan asked, enjoying the way Sept's hands felt on her hips.

"One drink and then I'll do my best to help you in the kitchen."

"Do I have time to change out of the unflattering outfit Jacqueline loves to tease me about?" Keegan plucked at her top.

"You're fine, so tell the children good night." Sept cocked her head toward the kitchen.

"I don't know, Seven. You looked like you were doing great in there with my staff."

"They were asking me about Donovan's case."

Keegan accepted Sept's help with her coat before she took her arm. "What's funny about that?"

"They weren't laughing about that." Sept held the car door for her. "They were shocked you let me back in the building after how things went that morning."

"And that was funny?"

"The part about me threatening you with handcuffs is what got them going." Sept parked on the street close to the Café Du Monde. It was usually a tow zone even for official vehicles, but most of the businesses in the area were closed for the day, and the visiting police officers from other states and emergency workers had headed back to their camp site two blocks away.

Sept grabbed a small bag from the backseat before she opened Keegan's door and took her hand. The walk to the levee wasn't long and the benches at the top were empty, so they picked the first one they came to.

From her bag Sept took out a bottle of wine and two glasses and went through the process of opening it. "When I started college I lived in a small apartment uptown that made me feel like someone had placed me in a soundproof room," Sept said as she poured.

"Why'd you think that?"

"When you grow up with six other siblings and all of a sudden you're alone, you go into shock. As much as I complained about the constant commotion in our house, I missed it when I left."

Keegan accepted her glass and sat slightly sideways so she could look at Sept as she spoke. "That sounds normal. Jacqueline and I were the only ones, but when we lived apart while I was in culinary school and she was starting her job, I felt a void. Having Gran offer us the house brought us even closer." The sun was starting to set and Keegan didn't remember ever watching it from here. "To a beautiful night." She lifted her glass to Sept in a toast.

"And many more like it."

They took a sip and Keegan felt it go down smoothly. "I didn't mean to interrupt you."

"You didn't, but let me finish so we can get to the enjoyment part of our evening." Sept stared at the brown water of the Mississippi River and let the strong current swirl her back to the times she was dredging up. "At least one night a week I'd meet one of my siblings here to watch the sunset."

"That sounds sweet," Keegan said, and put her hand on Sept's shoulder close to her neck. She twirled a lock of hair around her finger and smiled when Sept leaned toward her.

"It was a good way to catch up since my brothers were either already on the force, in the academy, or ahead of me in college. The one I missed the most, though, was my sister Noel. She decided on the University of New Orleans, where she was working on a teaching degree."

"I didn't get to meet her last Sunday." Keegan prided herself on her ability to remember names and people. "Did she relocate after the storm?"

"Not exactly." Sept took a deep breath, then a sip of her wine. "Right here was where we met and continued the talks we'd had most nights sharing a room at home. I could tell you every one of Noel's wishes for the future, and every one of her secrets."

"I don't think she'd appreciate you doing that," Keegan said, in an effort to make Sept smile.

"Noel's dreams weren't anything you had to keep secret. She lived them after she found her happiness." Sept looked at her briefly before she turned back to the water. It was cloudy, but the descending sun would peek through every few minutes.

"What happened?"

Before Sept began, she warned Keegan that she'd never told the story from beginning to end. She'd only examined every aspect of it when she woke from her nightmares. The middle haunted her because she could only guess at that part.

"Every day, we took turns going to the makeshift morgues," Sept said softly. Throughout the story she paused and breathed deeply, in what seemed to be an effort to keep her emotions from spiraling away from her. "So many faces, but none of them were the ones we were looking for. We went until there were no more nameless faces to search through."

"They were never found?" Keegan closed her eyes at how horrific that fact must have been to live with.

"They're gone, and I never understood it."

Keegan took Sept's glass from her and placed it and hers on the ground so she could get nearer. "What do you mean?"

"They lived close to one of the breach sites, but even if they'd been washed away in the current they should've been found eventually."

"There's still hope. From what I read in the paper, the search teams are still finding the missing." Keegan lifted her other hand and pressed her palm to Sept's cheek. "I'm so sorry for your loss, and for saying something to remind you of it."

"You didn't do anything wrong, so don't apologize. I just don't expect it to still hurt so much."

"Of course it still hurts, it hasn't been that long." The sun made its final descent and the darkness closed in around them. "Don't beat yourself up over this, and don't feel bad about last night. If something happened to Jacqueline I'd be a wreck, and after spending time with your family I know you're as close to them as I am to mine."

"Thanks, and I'll take you up on that if you don't blame yourself for yesterday as well. When you mentioned cooking with my mother, I thought about how much Noel loved to do that." Sept put her arm around Keegan and brushed away her tears with her thumb. "Yesterday started really great. Then I was thrown into the hell of someone's making, and you unfortunately got the end of that."

"I'm tough enough to handle some bad nights. After a while you'll see I have a few myself, if enough goes wrong in a day. I feel for you, though. Losing your sister was bad enough, but add your niece—it's a wonder you and your family are doing so well."

The guys a few blocks away had started a volleyball game, and Keegan figured it was to blow off steam. Their shouts and laughter were easy to hear since there was no other activity to compete.

"My mom has this strong faith that made us all believe everything would eventually be all right. That helped, and then we started working on the house, which was even better." Sept smiled as Keegan ran her fingers methodically through her hair. "That my parents lost everything was a blessing in a way, because it brought us together to rebuild it, which helped us recapture the happy memories of Noel."

"I hope you know I'm here for you as well. Even if we only become good friends, I want you to be able to let some of your emotions out like you did last night." Keegan kissed her chin and stopped her head massage to trace Sept's eyebrows. "Didn't that make you feel better?"

"As embarrassing as that was, I do feel better." Sept took her hand. "And I'm interested in becoming more than friends."

"I'm glad you said that." Keegan's ears got hot when Sept kissed her palm. The sensation made her nipples tighten, and she was glad for the thick cotton top. "Because I want much more than friendship too."

"What's making you blush?" Sept asked, her fingers skimming Keegan's cheeks. "You okay?"

"I'm fine, and I'm not blushing." She laughed at Sept's expression. "You're raising my blood pressure, Seven, live with it."

The tease made Sept lower her head and kiss her as if she had all night. Keegan opened her mouth and accepted Sept's tongue, and her ears got hotter. Not that she wanted to compare Sept to anyone else she'd been with, but it was difficult not to. The way Sept kissed made her look forward to the next level of their relationship because if she put so much into a kiss, she had to be the kind of attentive lover who would make you crave to be touched.

"You ready to go home?"

The urge to give in to whatever Sept wanted was on the verge of coming out of her mouth, but that's not what Sept needed right now. "Come on, I promised you dinner."

"You did, and I said I'd help." They walked back to the car, and on the train tracks between the levee and the street, two young punks stopped and stared.

Keegan moved closer to Sept and put her hand on her back under her jacket. Between the story Sept had told her and the time afterward, Keegan had forgotten they were in one of the most unpopulated spots in the city, despite the team of police about a quarter of a mile away.

"How you lovebirds doing?" the taller guy said with a smile that only made him appear more cruel.

That he talked to them at all made Keegan grab the back of Sept's pants, and she tried to calm her breathing. "Unless you want to start your night someplace you aren't going to like, I'd move on, slick," Sept said.

"What, you give advice for a living?" The same guy kept talking while his friend tried to get behind them.

Sept slowly handed the bag with the wine and glasses to Keegan and smiled at her. The move, Keegan realized, was to free her hands, but she didn't want to move away from her. Keegan said her name, ready to follow any instructions Sept had.

"Stay with me, okay?" Sept smiled in a way that Keegan thought was meant to reassure her. Her relaxed facial features didn't give their would-be muggers the incentive to pull any weapons other than the knife held by the guy slowly circling them. In a flash, Sept had her gun in her hand and pointed at his head.

"Actually, I don't get paid to give advice. I get paid to drop scum like you in a dark hole with big horny guys named Bubba, so get your ass on the ground before you get there from the bullet I'm going to put in your head." The taller guy started to move and Sept pointed it briefly at him. "Don't make me say it again. On the ground facedown—now," she yelled. Their inexperience and age gave them away when they dropped like they'd fainted.

A call to the dispatcher brought a couple of units down, and they took the pair along with their two knives into custody. "We were only talking here," the guy who'd first approached them said. "You can't get arrested for that."

"Process them and put them in with the baddest ass you have," Sept told the officer. "Even if they get cut loose tomorrow, they might learn a lesson."

When they were back in the car, she said to Keegan, "You okay? I'm so sorry about that. I should've thought this out better."

"That doesn't happen to you often, does it?"

"That's the first time it's ever happened to me, and I hate that it did when you were with me."

"It's not like it was your fault, but you're sure exciting in more ways than one." Keegan put her hand on Sept's heart. "That was scary, but thanks for keeping me safe. It's crazy, but you made me feel like nothing bad could happen to me."

"Still, I should've handled it better."

"We're both here and we're headed to my kitchen instead of the hospital. You couldn't have handled it better, in my opinion." Keegan moved closer and kissed Sept's cheek. "Want to learn to cook the perfect piece of salmon? I can almost guarantee there are no knife-wielding crazy people in my house."

"I'd love to." Sept wrapped a lock of red hair around her index finger. "You are so beautiful," she said softly and as reverently as a prayer.

"I've never felt that way until now," Keegan whispered back. "And unless you want your coworkers to know how much I like you, put this thing in gear."

# CHAPTER TWENTY

Novice sat as still as possible, even though rats were crawling along the rocks next to him. He had known where his prey might go, and when she had left Blanchard's and pointed her car toward the French Quarter, he had sped ahead and got ready.

From his perch close to the water he had heard only the murmur of Sept and Keegan's voices, but that was enough. Sept liked this girl. He could tell from the way Sept held her when she kissed her, and how she'd proven herself in battle.

"See," Teacher had said when Sept drew her weapon fearlessly. "That's how you protect your own and why her woman will remain true. The gods reward that by giving her a woman who won't be taken away."

Novice wanted to yell back, but he knew the taunt was a test, because any sound meant surrender. So he waited until the area grew quiet, as when he and Teacher had arrived. He chose the bench Sept and Keegan had and pressed the heels of his palms to his eyes.

"Tell me what you've learned," Teacher said.

"What do you want to know?"

"Who is the warrior god?"

Novice pressed his hands harder against his face until his eyes hurt and rocked in place. These tests were hard without the crutch of the books he'd taken. "Chango," he said suddenly.

"Very good." Teacher's voice sounded as if it were coming from the water. "Your worst enemy will not stop until your heart is in her hand. She will succeed."

"No, she won't. You said the gods would bless me if I believed.

Sept would treat the gods with nothing but contempt. She believes in nothing."

"She believes in the battle—it's what defines her. That's true, and you know why it is as well."

Novice moved his hands from his eyes to his ears. "No, you're lying."

"Your fear holds you back, so no one claims you. But she, without trying, is a child of Chango."

"I want that," Novice said, spittle spraying the front of his shirt. "I want that," he repeated, and beat his chest with his fist.

"Then prove yourself by showing what you know," Teacher said before he fled from Novice's head.

"You all right, man?" The guy who asked looked like he'd been with the two robbers the police had taken away.

"I'm not okay," Novice said as he stood.

"You want me to call someone for you?" The guy moved closer, as if trying to get a better look at his face.

Novice could narrow his vision to just one spot. That gift from the gods made it impossible for him to miss, and in his mind, as quickly as Sept had drawn her weapon, he pulled his knife from the sheath on his leg and felt the warm blood on his palm.

The man who gurgled his last breath facedown and slumped on the bench was to Novice no sacrifice or gift, but proof that he was as much a warrior as anyone else. He left a message, so in a way his victim was a gift, only to Sept. It was also a present to himself, because the body would draw Sept's attention away from what he had to do.

"Let me show you what I know," he told Teacher as he pulled his jacket tighter around him and his hat lower. It was going to be a busy night.

❖

"Simple is always best, remember that."

Sept nodded, even though Keegan couldn't see that her eyes had wandered from Keegan's sure hands to her backside. When they'd arrived, Keegan had changed into her pajamas and come back downstairs with the boxers Sept had worn the night before.

"At this rate the only thing you'll learn is how to pick my ass out of a lineup." Keegan turned her head away from the filet of salmon she'd been cutting into serving portions and tapped the tip of her knife on the cutting board.

"Simple is best," Sept repeated dutifully. "See, I'm paying attention." She stood next to Keegan with the ingredients she'd been sent to find.

"Uh-huh." Keegan didn't sound convinced, but she didn't push Sept away when she kissed her. "I'm glad you're here." Keegan wiped her hands on a kitchen towel, then patted Sept on the butt.

"Are you sure? Our night didn't start off too well."

"However our night started is a memory now, and yes, I'm sure. Right now there isn't any other place I'd rather be or any other person I'd like to be sharing time with."

"Me too," Sept said, then lowered her head again. They'd started dinner after they'd changed clothes, but it'd been a slow process in between kisses and caresses. As Sept allowed herself to enjoy Keegan's company, she felt like someone who'd been sick for months and she'd discovered her cure to rejoin the living on Keegan's lips. "You're the best thing that's happened to me in a long time."

"My sister's right. You're a cop who sounds like a poet." Keegan molded herself to Sept's body and moaned when Sept put her hand flat against the small of her back.

"Where's Jacqueline tonight?"

"Working late, then grabbing dinner, probably at the restaurant."

"She's doing that because of me?"

"She volunteered to give us some privacy." Keegan's fingers scratched at the elastic of Sept's shorts. "It's not something she's had to do in a long time, so she didn't mind."

When Noel had gotten married and pregnant soon after, she'd quit school. She'd explained to Sept she'd made her decision because family was the most important thing to her, not to please Damien. In Noel's mind, family was the one constant that filled the void caused by the pain life threw at you, and it made the celebrations of your happiness that much more special.

Keegan obviously felt that way about Jacqueline, and Sept didn't want to make her choose between them. "We have a lot of fish here. Why don't you call her?"

"She's fine," Keegan said.

"I'm sure she is, but tonight isn't a one-shot deal. And if it's okay, I plan to spend a lot of time with you, so it'd be unfair to make her eat out that much." Sept pressed Keegan closer. "When we move to the naked cooking lessons I'll make her reservations myself."

"You're too much, Seven."

Jacqueline arrived thirty minutes later and laughed at Sept's total concentration when Keegan had her put kosher salt and cracked pepper on the fish so they could throw it on the indoor grill. "You should be ready for chef status at Blanchard's by next week," she told Sept.

"I'll leave that to the experts, since I doubt I could charge fifty a plate for this." As Sept spoke she measured four minutes on her watch and flipped the pieces over.

"I'm sure you could get away with it if it's coming out of Keegan's kitchen." Jacqueline sipped her wine and winked at Keegan, who was making a salad. "Should we set a day aside every week to have pajama cooking night?"

"Just as long as you actually wear some, you're invited," Keegan said, and threw a broccoli floret at her.

Sept scooped their main course onto the platter Keegan had handed her and placed it in front of her teacher. "Does it look edible?"

"You did great." When Sept put her arms around her, Keegan dropped her salad tongs.

"You're a generous grader." The next kiss was softer, but Sept squeezed Keegan's butt, since it was well out of Jacqueline's line of vision. "Let's eat."

Before Sept could protest, Keegan served three plates, placing the food on them so they looked like they'd come from Blanchard's. She squeezed a good amount of lemon on each piece of fish before she handed it over, and nodded as if approving when Sept carried them to the table.

"I should've listened to my mother when she said cooking was fun."

"You can tell her that Sunday, and that I can teach you plenty more."

"I can't wait to start," Sept said, and Jacqueline rolled her eyes like she didn't believe they were talking about food. "You'll see what a quick study I am."

## CHAPTER TWENTY-ONE

Surely he could find something in the damn place to use, Novice cursed in his head. He'd cruised the street for less than an hour before he found what he needed to prove himself both to Teacher and his hunter. Only one of them could win this battle, and it wouldn't be Sept Savoie.

Finally, in the stockroom, he found a roll of twine next to a roll of brown wrapping paper. It wasn't as good as the cord in his kit, but it would work.

When he returned to the front of the store he'd broken into, Frieda Hearn sat whimpering where he'd left her. Unlike with Tameka, he couldn't afford to have someone interrupt him, so he'd gagged her, then checked her ID. It wouldn't please the gods as much to not hear as her life left her body and to not know her name. When Tameka succumbed to the pain, certainly Teacher had heard, but the blood would have to do this time.

Frieda kicked Novice's cutting hand when he tried to straighten her out to tie her legs, and he panicked as his fingers momentarily went numb. He wanted to hit her but didn't have time for pettiness, so he flicked his knife against her chin. She sounded like she was choking against the gag at the sudden pain of the deep cut, but she did stop struggling.

"Like I told the others, you should be grateful I picked you. I'm offering you forgiveness for your life. Now you're worthless, but when I'm done you'll go to my gods wearing a cloak of redeeming blood," he said as he tied her ankles to the counter legs.

The knife cut easily through her clothes next, and he folded the remnants neatly and stacked them close to her feet. He made the necessary markings with the blood from her face, and only when he admired his artwork did he realize he was humming.

"Before we start…" He put his hand on Frieda's chest and closed his eyes. It had been a lifetime since he'd touched a woman, or at least that's how it seemed. With his eyes shut he could almost pretend she was his wife, but the moaning behind the gag ruined it for him. "Tell them I'm trying my best to get to them. What happened," he looked into Frieda's panic-filled hazel eyes, "it was my fault, but I'm doing my best to do as I'm told so I'll see them again."

He cupped her cheek with his hand and leaned closer to her face. "Remember what I said—it's important." The muffled crying ceased in one loud moan.

Then only Teacher was in his brain. The way Teacher chuckled as he started his true work meant he'd made a good choice. That laugh combined with his humming made this one easy. Novice's lack of nausea assured him that he was evolving and growing into his new life.

Novice held Frieda's heart in his hand and said his wishes aloud as he lit the white candle. "Remember what I told you," he said to the bloody organ. "You hold my heart just like I do yours." He laughed because the words struck him as funny. In his mind Teacher's laughter mingled with his until it was almost the same voice.

"Remember, because I've forgotten nothing, and I want it all back. I'm tired of paying for my own sins."

❖

"You have to get some sleep," Keegan said, and pointed at Sept to drag her attention to her face. "I mean it. If tonight proved anything to me, it's that you have to be sharp." When Sept sucked her finger in to the knuckle, any other reprimand was impossible to deliver.

"Then I guess I should get going," Sept said when she let go, right after biting the tip of Keegan's finger gently.

Keegan nodded but didn't move from her spot, and didn't protest when Sept lifted her shirt off. The way Sept stared at her chest made her nipples pucker until she felt like they were truly connected to her groin. She was like a pot of water under a low flame. Instead of getting up to let Sept go, she tipped her hips forward to make more contact with Sept's middle.

After dinner Sept had helped her clean up the kitchen. Jacqueline had wished them good night and taken her dessert upstairs, and she wouldn't bother them again unless they had to evacuate for a fire. Then Keegan had led Sept to the den, sat her down, and offered to feed her the coconut cream pie she'd brought home. And the easiest way to do that was to straddle her hips.

"You want me to go?" Sept asked, and Keegan nodded. She ran her finger through the meringue of the pie and painted Keegan's right nipple with it. The slight touch made Keegan hold her breath and stop nodding when her head fell back. "You don't really want that, do you?" Sept painted the other nipple.

"At this point I don't see me ever winning an argument or saying no to anything you want," Keegan said as she straightened up. The way Sept was looking at her made her feel desirable.

"I'm only trying to thank you for making me a coconut cream pie. Did you guess it was my favorite? Or do you have special powers of divining what I like to eat?"

Keegan brought her hips down harder, trying to make the contact bring some relief to the pulsing between her legs. "Desserts really aren't my thing, so I'll pass along your compliments to our new pastry chef." She anchored her fingers in Sept's hair while Sept thoroughly cleaned off a nipple.

"Do that, but I'm sure they must have taught you in culinary school that presentation is ninety percent of any dish. At least it is in my opinion." Sept cleaned the other nipple with the same slow dedication. "If coconut cream wasn't my favorite, it would be now."

"Your mother told me."

There was still half of the large piece Keegan had cut for them to share, but Sept pushed it away. "Why would my mother tell you that?"

"I asked," Keegan said as she unbuttoned Sept's shirt. She had it completely undone when Sept lifted her hand and placed her fingers in the hollow under her throat. "I want to feel you."

"I want that too, but we have time," Sept said, and Keegan followed the trail of Sept's fingers as they traced an invisible line down her chest and between her breasts to the slight swell of her belly. The path ended when Keegan grabbed her wrist and leaned forward to hide her body. "What's wrong?"

"I'm not the skinniest woman you've ever been with, am I?" The shape of her body never bothered her until times like these, when she secretly wished for Jacqueline's tall, slender figure.

"What does that have to do with anything?"

Keegan could tell Sept was confused, so she sat up again and retraced what Sept had done, only this time on Sept's body. When she stopped right above the elastic band of the boxers, she couldn't find any extra skin to pinch. Sept was in extraordinarily great shape.

"Nothing, but I can try to lose weight if you find that more attractive." The offer would be a sure mood killer, but Sept had penetrated some of her defenses built by experience, and the accumulation of those experiences made her ask before she got hurt.

"You would lose weight for me?"

And there it was in one simple, hopeful question. "Sure, I could try. If that's important to you, though, I should warn you that I'm not great at it." *I will not cry*, Keegan chanted in her head.

"You're a great chef," Sept said, and sat up so she could hold her. "You run a successful business," she kissed her forehead. "But you're a certifiable but adorable idiot."

"Gee, thanks."

"Well, you are if you can sit on top of me and ask me that. Only an insane person would tell you they want you to lose weight."

"Are you only saying that so you won't hurt my feelings?"

"No. I happen to think you don't need to change a thing about yourself."

Keegan rested her forearms on Sept's shoulders and tried to laugh. "It's a small hang-up of mine, so forget I said anything."

"I have a better idea," Sept said, and helped Keegan stand up.

Any worry on Keegan's part that their night was over ended when Sept picked up the pie plate, put it on the coffee table, knocked some of the cushions to the floor to make room, and took her shirt off and lay down. She then opened her arms for Keegan to join her, and when she did Sept promptly rolled her over to her back.

"My mother can tell you what my favorite pie is, as well as what she cooks every year for my birthday, since we all get to request something.

But if you want the answer to what I find attractive in a woman, only I know that." She placed her hand on Keegan's hip as she spoke and left it there. "If you want to know, you have to ask me."

Keegan's brain had kept a perfect score of the wounds she'd received in her life, but her heart spoke as she looked into Sept's eyes and easily asked, "What do you like in a woman?"

"I like a smart, funny, compassionate woman with rosy pink nipples and curves." Sept started to move her hand, and her touch made her words believable. But the truth was in her eyes, not her fingers. "Believe what you want, but I found all that in you the moment I saw you."

"Now I know you're lying." Keegan covered Sept's hand with hers when she reached her breast. "When we met, you thought I'd killed someone."

"You can't hold that against me forever, and I worked to prove I was wrong." Sept lifted her hand with Keegan's and kissed Keegan's palm. "Right now I don't want to know that anyone has ever touched you before me. Not because I'm the crazed, jealous type, but because this time belongs to us." She kissed Keegan's lips next but didn't let go of her hand. "But the day will come when I'll ask you that, and I'll be very interested in the answer."

"Why?" Keegan asked, and ran her fingers over the familiar territory of Sept's brows. It still surprised her how dark they were compared to the hair on her head. "*Are* you the crazed, jealous type?"

"I want to know so when the opportunity arises I can kick their ass for making you doubt yourself." Sept kissed her on the chest right above her heart. "You're beautiful on the inside," she kissed lower, "and I realize that's what you say when you want to make someone feel better."

"Don't forget 'you have a beautiful mind.'"

"You've got your feel-good lines and I've got mine, so don't interrupt me." Sept licked Keegan's nipple that was now so hard it was dark red. "You're beautiful, Keegan, and I wouldn't change anything about you."

"Another feel-good line?"

"It's a more dignified way to let you know I think you're hot, and you turn me on." Sept placed Keegan's hand flat on her chest and covered it with her own. "I could tell you something to be nice, and fake it if I really tried, but you'd see through that." She dragged their hands down until they went under the elastic of her shorts and didn't stop until Keegan knew the truth of what she was trying to say. "Some things can't be faked, and this is my usual reaction to hot women who turn me on."

"I'm not interested in hearing about any one woman who turned you on before me either, but I do want you to touch me," Keegan said, and she shivered at how wet Sept was.

"Like I said, we have all night," Sept said, but to Keegan she sounded winded.

"But I can tell you want to go faster." Keegan teased her by applying more pressure to what felt like stone under her fingers.

"You're trying to rush me?"

"Come on, baby, there's slow and there's excruciating." Keegan almost came when Sept sucked her nipple in and impatiently tugged down her pants. Before Sept could get her hand anywhere near where Keegan wanted it, her cell phone started ringing. "Please tell me you don't have to answer that."

"Think nasty thoughts and I'll be right back." Sept kissed the nipple she was headed to next before she got up.

The phone was sitting next to the gun holster Sept had taken off when she arrived and Keegan had asked her to change, and she'd actually forgotten about it. Sept stood in only a pair of underwear and kept her eyes on Keegan as she spoke. It was like lying under a scorching sun. This tall, somewhat unpolished cop made Keegan want to sit with her legs spread apart and beg to be touched.

"Gran would be so proud," Keegan said quietly.

"Rope it off, call Nathan, and give me twenty minutes," Sept said, then listened. "Just keep the area clear and call me if you have any problems with anyone telling you otherwise."

"Do I have to put my nasty thoughts on hold?" Keegan asked as she sat up and tried to put her hair in order.

"When I catch this asshole I'm going to kick his butt in repayment for tonight, and yes, put all those on hold." Sept grabbed her shirt but her pants were upstairs. "Keep in mind I'm the crazed, jealous type."

"You don't have to be—I'm enthralled with you now." She slipped her T-shirt back on and led Sept upstairs. "That's what I remember Della telling my grandfather all the time."

"If I had a choice, I wouldn't pick work, since I'm more than enthralled with you."

Keegan kept going until they were in the bathroom. "A shower would be a good choice before you go."

"Great idea," Sept said, and took Keegan's shirt back off. "Join me."

"I do that and you'll need more than twenty minutes."

It was the shortest but most erotic ten minutes of Keegan's life and left her knowing she'd need another longer shower, only with cold water, when Sept left. She watched Sept dress, adding the last piece of her wardrobe downstairs when she strapped on her gun.

"I'm sorry about this," Sept said at the back door.

"Don't be, Seven, but I expect you to make it up to me. And I'd eventually like to hear about what drags you away in the middle of the night."

"It's not that I don't trust you, but because we both don't need to know every vivid detail of some sick person's fantasies."

Keegan held on to her jacket opening. "Ugly things are like big pieces of furniture, don't you think?"

"How so?"

"They're easier to carry if two people share the load," Keegan said and kissed her. "Get to work, and be careful."

"Get some sleep and I'll call you in the morning." Sept put her arms around her and held her. "We'll reschedule tonight, and I promise I'll make sure I can turn my phone off." Sept kissed her, stepped out, and motioned for Keegan to lock the door.

"When you catch this guy I may kick his ass myself," Keegan said as she watched Sept walk away. "And I won't reconsider unless this guy left a note with a map to his house pinned to the body Sept's going to investigate."

## CHAPTER TWENTY-TWO

Sept sighed as she turned into the parking lot that ran behind the Café Du Monde and the shops beside it. With each block she passed she got angrier that they'd called her back to this place. Her skin crawled at the possibility the guy she was chasing had been here.

Lourdes stopped her at the steps that led up to the bench on the levee where Sept had taken Keegan earlier. "You need to know that it's definitely our guy, and this one seems personal." A flash of Tameka's body made Sept peer up toward the line of benches. If he had the audacity to do that to someone here, they'd have to deal with a stack of bodies before she caught up with him. "Why do you think he'd pick this place?"

"I was here tonight with a date."

"Here, as in the general vicinity?" Lourdes asked.

"What bench is the victim on?" Sept started the walk up, curious now as to what awaited her.

"The guy's slumped over the first one on the right."

"Then let me rephrase. I was here with a date on that particular bench." The area around the bench was roped off, and Bruce was doing a good job of keeping everyone on the other side of it. The two officers who'd called it in were on the other end, talking to the group of visiting police that had wandered over from the camp.

The guy was slumped over the bench, one of his arms dangling over the top swaying in the slight breeze. When Sept shone her light she noticed a small pool of blood on the wood slats. However, the most interesting thing about the scene wasn't the familiar shepherd's hook finger-painted in blood, but the number seven with a line drawn through it on the man's forehead.

"You think it's the number of kills?" Bruce asked Sept as she carefully scanned the body from head to toe.

"Only if we missed some bodies, and considering where we found the last one that's possible, but this one is probably a warning to me."

"How do you figure?"

"Sept…it's the number seven in French," Lourdes told Bruce.

"Shit, you probably think I'm an idiot, but it's been a long day."

"Don't worry about it." Sept shone her light on the man's feet, which were soles up with just the toes hitting the ground. "Who found him?"

"We lucked out," the primary officer who'd responded said. "A group of highway patrolmen from Illinois found him, since this is their usual jogging route."

"When George and Alex get here, make sure they take a picture of this guy so one of you can drive it over to central lockup. I was out here earlier and had to call in two punks looking for an easy score."

"What's that got to do with this guy?" Nathan asked. He'd jogged up and was still breathing hard.

"They're all wearing the same jacket. If it's gang-related I don't recognize the colors, but I'm not working the streets searching these guys out. Some new blood's come to town after the storm, trying to carve out their piece of the action. Maybe that's all this is, but like I told Lourdes, I doubt it." Sept continued to look for any other markings on the body.

"You didn't see this guy earlier?" Nathan asked.

"The two guys I had taken downtown were only armed with knives, so maybe this guy was their backup. But when he saw me draw my weapon he hung back, not wanting to get one of his friends shot."

Nathan put on a pair of gloves he dug out of his pocket and felt along the guy's waistband. "If this one had a gun or knife, it's gone now."

"That means he probably didn't have either one."

"The killer might have taken it as a souvenir," Nathan said.

"Our guy's not a tourist, and this was quick and unplanned."

Nathan moved to the back pocket of the loose jeans and pulled out a wallet. "Take me through it, then."

"Our guy was sitting here and this poor bastard walked up for some reason and got stabbed," Sept said, and accepted the wallet and opened it in search of ID.

"Did he speak and tell you what happened when you first got here or something?"

"Put your detective hat on, Nathan, and take in the scene." Sept spoke softly so as to not embarrass him. "When you walk up to something like this, you immediately ask yourself how this guy got dead. What happened, where was he standing, how far away was the killer, and what was he killed with? You try to answer as many of the questions on your mental list as you can here so you spend less time chasing down the answers."

"He got stabbed."

They picked the body up gently, with help from Sept, to check if that was the right answer to the first question.

"If he landed like this, he had to have been standing close to the bench to fall forward at that awkward angle." Nathan answered the second question Sept had posed, and she nodded. "Like in Donovan's scene, our perp had to have been standing close to get a kill in one shot, and he took the time to write a number seven on his forehead. What's that about?"

"I brought Keegan here earlier to watch the sunset and have a glass of wine. We talked for an hour before we left to go to her house for dinner."

"Here as in this park?" Nathan pointed to the ground.

"Here as on this bench." The body had no more answers than Nathan had, but they needed to find something much more important. "Either this guy is one hell of a guesser when it comes to my dating patterns, or it's one hell of a coincidence, or—"

"Oh, my God, he followed you here?" Nathan said. "You didn't see anyone?"

"It was a date, Nathan, not a surveillance job."

"Do you think he's targeting you?"

"I need a little time before I can answer that." She turned and looked out over the water. No one treaded water here and survived because of the current, but there was one way to hide.

The Corps of Engineers had long ago covered the levee along the river in this area with stones, since they were less susceptible to erosion.

The incline was steep enough that, if you sat quietly, you could escape detection unless someone on the benches looked straight down.

When she'd been here with Keegan, Sept had glanced out over the water, but she had been more interested in their talk than in spotting someone playing a serious game of hide-and-seek. If he'd sat there and watched them, because Sept didn't believe in so fortuitous a coincidence, he'd seen her with Keegan. Considering how Keegan was dressed and the fact that this freak who had a morbid fascination with people's hearts had clearly followed them, he knew exactly who Keegan was and where to find her.

As soon as Keegan answered her phone, she asked, "You miss me already?"

"You know it." Sept tried her best to keep her voice upbeat. "As soon as I'm done here I'm coming back, no matter how late it is, but until then I want you to do me a favor."

"If it has to do with stilettos and fishnet stockings, I'm too short to pull it off."

Sept laughed so quickly that she snorted, which in turn made Nathan, who was standing next to her, laugh even louder. "I'll be the judge of that, but that's not the favor. Is Jacqueline still there?"

"She should be. I didn't hear her go out, and she's too old to sneak out the window anymore."

"Go wake her up and ask her to help you lock all the windows and doors, and don't answer the door for anyone until I get there."

"It would've been better if you'd asked for the shoes and hose, Seven. What you're asking is scaring me."

"Hold on." Sept put her hand over the bottom half of the phone and faced Nathan. "Get a car over to her house uptown and tell them to sit outside until I get there. I can't prove he was watching us earlier, but I don't want to take the chance and have something happen to her."

"You got it." Nathan headed to the group of officers talking to their visiting brothers.

"When I get there I'll explain the whole thing. I'm probably being paranoid, but if I'm wrong, I want to err on the side of caution, as they say. Keep the phone with you, and if you hear anything out of the ordinary, call me."

"You're coming back tonight, right?"

"I have a few more things to do and I'll be there."

"Stay safe until then, okay?"

Sept scanned the inquisitive crowd and tried to single out the one who was watching but wasn't curious. "You too, and I'll call you when I'm close so I won't scare you."

"It's too late for that."

"Sorry, sweetheart, I'll try and make it up to you later." Sept hung up and waved to George as he walked over. "Tante Fern will think you're having an affair," Sept said, using the French word for "aunt."

"When I get these calls she gets the bed all to herself, so I think she secretly likes them," he said, then put his hand on her shoulder and squeezed. "What we got now, *cher*?" George asked, as he put his bag down. Since they were mostly alone in a sea of people, he called Sept what his parents often did, which loosely translated to "loved one."

She pointed to the guy's forehead. "I think it's a personal note to me, but this time I won't need any professor to tell me this means, 'Sept, I'm going to get you.' As much as I like getting mail, I would've preferred Hallmark."

"Bastard should know it's not a good idea to poke the bear with a stick."

"The bastard is off his rocker, so I'm guessing he doesn't know any better." When Nathan stepped back and held his thumb up with the other hand, meaning a car was headed to Keegan's, Sept knocked her fist against his. "Before you start anything, Uncle George, take some shots of the crowd, and try to get everyone. Nathan and I'll watch, and if anyone tries to walk away we'll chase them down."

"You think he's here?" George asked.

"I think he was here earlier, and if he has that kind of superiority complex, he has the balls to come back and check on his handiwork and laugh at what bumbling idiots we are." Sept told him about how she'd started her evening, which made George take double the shots.

"Want us to do anything else?" Lourdes asked, with Bruce standing next to her.

"I hate to make you wait until all this dies down"—Sept waved to Alex as he joined George—"but could you two hang around and assign someone to sit on this spot until I get back in the morning?"

"Anything in particular they should watch for?"

"Just the general area, but no one, and I don't care who they are, gets down on those rocks until I get back here. I'd do it now but I don't want to miss anything." Sept stared down into the darkness of the levee slope, trying to imagine where the killer sat and listened to the story she'd told Keegan. "This guy knows who I am, and it's time we balanced that out by trying to get closer to him."

"Don't worry. We'll take care of it," Bruce said.

"Don't make a big announcement about it, and tell whoever stays to park their unit down the street. If he took the chance of coming out here once tonight, maybe we'll luck out and he'll be back."

As everyone did their job, Sept and Nathan walked toward the wharves of the Port of New Orleans. They'd been closed since the storm and had only recently started receiving small shipments to gear them up for full operation after the first of the year.

"How ordinary must you appear that you can stab someone through the heart and simply walk away?"

"Did you say something?" Nathan asked.

Their footsteps sounded loud against the wood of the pier, and Sept felt like an idiot for not asking herself that question before. "Think about it, Nathan," she said as she slowly swept the shadows with her flashlight. "What does this guy look like that no one notices him?"

"What do you mean?"

"So far we have four victims that we know of. It was easy to find Donovan, as well as Robin Burns and this guy. The fact that we stumbled over Tameka accidentally could mean we have more like her and we just haven't found them yet. Of the four, one of them was blind, so we'll have to take her out of the equation, but the other three, what was their excuse?"

Nathan held his hands up as if he didn't know how to answer the question. "Excuse for what? I'm sorry. I don't know what you're talking about."

"When you work scenes like Tameka's in your mind, you want to believe this was some bloodthirsty monster, but in the end the truth is what makes you shiver. Because when the media talks to the neighbors they can't believe that the killer was Joe Blow, who lived a quiet life with his two poodles. Killers like this one never turn out to look like the monsters our head wants them to be. They're successful for so long precisely because they blend in."

"Like Ted Bundy?"

"It makes sense, doesn't it, and explains why Donovan, Tameka, and that poor bastard back there let this guy so close."

"They thought he was harmless."

Sept nodded and felt like she was finally making some headway. "You heading back to Keegan's?"

"I owe her a big explanation, along with an apology. The fact that some homicidal maniac might have seen us together, then killed some guy so he could finger-paint some more, should make a huge impression on her mom, sister, and grandmother."

"Hey, I'm new to this, but I haven't heard very often of these types of people targeting the police that are after them. That's right, isn't it?"

Sept nodded and rolled her shoulders, trying to loosen the tightness. "Most of the time, but it's not unheard of."

When she got back to the levee, the techs were gathering evidence and Lourdes and Bruce were watching the crowd. "You heading out?" Lourdes asked.

"Yeah, but I'll be back first thing in the morning. If they find something, call me tonight. He's close, I can feel it, and he's made this personal. The other murders were for something else, but this one tells me that he thinks I can't find him. I don't scare that easy, asshole."

## CHAPTER TWENTY-THREE

The drive back to Keegan's was fast and quiet, and Sept had time to arrange her thoughts. She was missing something simple, but for the life of her she couldn't figure it out. It was unlikely for the killer to get away with three of the four murders without detection, considering what public places he'd picked, but he had. And after Tameka she thought he'd found his "thing," but now he was back to the quick kill.

When she turned off St. Charles she stopped and talked to the patrol guys sitting in the car in the front of the house. They reported that the street and the house were quiet, except for Keegan and Jacqueline looking out the front windows every so often.

"Thanks, guys. You can take off." On the way back to her car she punched redial. Keegan picked up on the first ring. "You want me to come in the front or the back?"

"Park your car, because you're not going anywhere else tonight. I don't care who gets killed."

After Sept entered through the back door and enjoyed a hug and a kiss from Keegan, she spotted the pie they'd had after dinner sitting out on the table, with a carafe of coffee. "I'm going to gain a hundred pounds at this rate," she said.

"I'll think of some way for you to work it off, but right now I want you to have a piece of pie and tell me why a police car's been parked in front of our house all night long." Keegan stripped Sept's jacket off.

"We'll have pie later." Sept took her hand and held out her other one to Jacqueline, then walked them to the den and the large sofa. "I was called out for a murder in the French Quarter. The victim was found lying across the bench where we had our drink earlier today, Keegan, and whoever killed him used his blood to paint a seven on his forehead with a line drawn through it." Sept kicked her shoes off and put her feet on the coffee table.

"You think the number had anything to do with you?" Jacqueline asked.

"That's the only clue the perp left, but yes."

Keegan didn't say anything, but she held her hand to her stomach.

"Donovan's was the first in a spree of homicides that have left me with four open cases, if you count the one tonight."

"And they're related how?" Keegan finally asked

After Sept described the series of murders, she said, "The game's changed, and if he's targeted me and he's crazy, I don't want him coming after you."

"What does that mean exactly?"

"That I'll be here every night sleeping on this great couch, and that you need to stay in contact with one of us at all times. If I could, I'd put a unit with you, but the department will never approve that." She kissed Keegan's temple. "No matter what, you have to promise that you'll never be alone and you'll be hyperaware of your surroundings."

"Is there some reason you have to sleep on the sofa?"

"I haven't been asked to sleep anywhere else."

"While you two work out the details, I'm going to bed," Jacqueline said. "But don't even think about trying to sneak out of here before I get to talk to you some more, Sept." She kissed both of them good night and waved as she disappeared up the front staircase.

"You okay?" Sept asked when Keegan got even closer and almost straddled her legs.

"I feel more weird than anything. I don't normally have some psycho killer watch me while I'm out on a date, but considering who my date was, I don't have anything to worry about."

Sept put her fingers under Keegan's chin and brought her head up. "I'm serious about you being careful. Trust me when I tell you that you *do not* want to put yourself in any situation where this guy gets a crack at you." The kiss that followed was full of enough passion that Keegan lay back and dragged Sept with her. "I don't want anything to happen to you."

"I'll be careful, but I'm not sorry to have a bodyguard sleeping with me every night, and she won't be on the sofa. Let's go upstairs."

The bed covers were thrown back in a heap, clearly because of Keegan's quick exit from the bed after Sept's first call from the scene. If that had frightened her, Sept couldn't tell as Keegan began to undress her. She removed each item, then folded it and hung it on the back of the chair close to the bed. When Keegan was done, Sept stood naked before her with only the light from outside shining on her body.

"I believe you promised to make something up to me," Keegan said as she peeled her T-shirt off and wiggled her butt to work her bottoms off.

Sept gazed at Keegan's naked body, and her groin tightened. She'd never thought she could be turned on solely by looks. But Keegan changed that because of the way her breasts appeared slightly heavy but would seemingly fit perfectly in her hands, and the way that overall she embodied Sept's concept of femininity.

"What?" Keegan said in a tone that hinted at self-consciousness.

"You need to get used to me staring at you." Sept finally stood behind her and rested her hands on Keegan's hips. "When I do, it's not because something's wrong, but because you're incredibly beautiful and sexy."

"You must get lucky a lot."

"I thought it was taboo to talk about past experiences when you have someone naked standing in front of you." Sept tried to take it slow, but the feel of Keegan's skin made her want to move closer and memorize every curve. "And even if it wasn't, I'm not in the mood to talk about anything or anyone right now."

When Sept cupped her breasts, Keegan took a deep breath and Sept smiled. They were definitely the perfect fit. But she just had to move her right hand in the opposite direction until it nestled between Keegan's legs.

"What are you interested in talking about, then?" Keegan said as she put her hand behind Sept's neck and laughed.

"I'm interested in a long conversation about plenty of things, but first I want to show you how much I want to be here with you." When she spread Keegan's sex, Sept took a breath at how wet she was. "Is this all for me?"

"One of my secret recipes," Keegan said, and Sept laughed.

Sept turned her around and kissed her until Keegan brought her hands up and combed her fingers into Sept's hair. The house was quiet and the floodlights outside produced just enough brightness for Sept to see that Keegan's nipples were as hard as hers, and in that moment she wanted to touch Keegan until she lost herself in the experience.

When their lips came apart, Keegan said, "Touch me."

Sept came close to orgasm when Keegan encouraged her to lie on top of her and she spread her legs. In the brief minute Sept stopped to enjoy the position they were in, her phone started ringing. "Fuck me," she said, knowing she couldn't ignore it.

"I'm trying my best, but if you keep running out the door it makes it more difficult."

"With any luck, Nathan has a quick question." Sept moved to get her pants. "Savoie."

"Sept, this is Bruce. I hate to call so late, but do you remember Estella Mendoza?"

"I talked to her the other day about a robbery at her store. Why?"

"You need to get over here." Sept could hear a woman crying in the background.

"What happened?"

"We have another one, and our guy took a little more time."

"Shit." Sept gave quiet acknowledgment of what her night had turned into. "Did you call Nathan?"

"He said he'd be right here."

"I'll be there in a few, but call the unit and get them back out here."

As Keegan held herself off the bed by her elbows, she said, "Please tell me you don't have to go."

"Trust me, I'm in as much pain as you are. I don't want to, but I have to."

"Do we have enough time to do something about that pain?"

Sept threw her pants back on the chair and lay next to Keegan. "When I finally get to touch you, I don't want to have to run out the door right afterward."

"You're right, but I don't have to like it," Keegan said, and kissed Sept's chin when Sept put her arms around her.

"Try and get some sleep, and don't forget to go with Jacqueline in the morning."

"You're a riot." Keegan bit her on the neck. "I couldn't sleep now even if I wanted to."

"I don't want to be blamed if you oversalt something, so try your best." Sept kissed her again.

"Before you go, remember that you have to make this up to me, but you have to be in one piece to do it. Be careful, and I expect you back here tomorrow night, ready to close the deal."

"It's refreshing to finally meet a girl who knows what she wants." Sept held her until she could almost hear her watch ticking. "I'm so sorry about this."

"Pull out your magnifying glass and big pipe, Seven, and find this guy."

## CHAPTER TWENTY-FOUR

Estella Mendoza was slumped against the front of her building with her hands covering her mouth when Sept drove up. Whatever was inside appeared to have molded her face into the definition of horror.

Lourdes came out the front door and waved Sept over. "I had Gavin's staff come in to give us a time of death so we could figure out the sequence of events tonight."

"What's his opinion?"

"The guy in the park came first, and then he came here with this girl. I only saw pictures of the first crime scene with Tameka, but this one looks a lot like it."

The first time their perp had brought his own supplies, but this time, with the help of the stolen books, he'd had everything he needed on the shelves of the store. From Sept's first impression, he'd had to improvise only on what he'd bound her with, and he'd left her tied spread-eagle in the middle of the floor.

"Same wound patterns as before, but with subtle differences," Sept said to no one in particular.

"Hey," Nathan said as he bounded through the door and put on a pair of booties. "This guy is putting a serious hurt on my sleeping patterns."

"Among other things," Sept said softly as she squatted close to the woman's head. A white candle was burning and a number nine was on her forehead. "We need Dr. Julio to pay us another visit."

"I'll try him."

"While you do that, I'll see if we can get a head start on this." Sept looked at the heart on the floor and bent down far enough to sniff the large wet spot around it.

"What is that?" Nathan asked, then swallowed hard.

"Smells like nothing, so I have to guess it's water." Sept stood and pointed him toward the door. "Should we ask Estella her opinion—if she can handle it?"

"Can't hurt, unless she filleted that woman like a trout."

Estella was sitting on the curb with her eyes closed and her lips moving like she was chanting something. As Sept walked up she glanced at Estella's clothes and concluded that she had indeed walked in to find the carnage the killer had left behind. She couldn't possibly have done that and walked away without a drop of blood on her unless she'd showered and changed, but Lourdes's interview stated that she had an alibi for the window of time when the killing took place.

"Ms. Mendoza." Sept said her name to get her attention. "I'd like to ask you a few questions."

"Why did this happen here? The women in my family and I have helped so many communicate with the gods we worship here. All that blood… We'll never wash away the taint, no matter how hard we scrub."

"If you remember, I talked to you about another killing that was a lot like this one." Sept leaned against the light pole close to Estella and flipped through her notes. "For that one I spoke with Julio Munez from Tulane, who helped me navigate what the killer left behind."

"I know Julio, and if he shared anything with you I'd believe it. He's a true disciple who knows the rituals as well as I do."

"I learned that all the rituals have meaning to one god, so I want to ask you about what was done to that girl in there."

"If I can help, I will. No one deserves that, especially in the name of any religion," Estella said forcefully.

Sept nodded and flipped to the new page in her book where she'd written just a few lines. "What god does the number nine represent?"

"It depends. What else did you find?"

"A white candle and an organ cut out that was doused in what appears to be water."

Estella pulled her necklace out and ran her fingers along the beads. "The warrior king Chango is a powerful Orisha with a huge following. He's a ladies' man and has more than one wife. One of them, Oya, is known to be compassionate and has power over the dead. The very few santeros who dare to use body parts in their ceremonies in Oya's house wish to summon her."

"Oya's house?"

"Any cemetery is her domain." Estella appeared to be gathering strength as she spoke.

"I thought you and Munez said no one killed in the name of any of these gods."

"It's a sin to take life, Detective, and I don't know of a religion where it would be considered acceptable. But once God has taken the person's spirit, some consider the shell left behind an offering. It does happen occasionally, especially if you need to create powerful magic."

"Thank you, and we'll try and get this place cleaned up as soon as possible."

Back inside, Sept walked the scene with Nathan, and they located the shepherd's hook on the bottom of the woman's foot and the pile of clothes neatly piled nearby. On top was a small purse with an ID and fifty-two dollars inside.

"Frieda Hearn. Run that name and see if anything pops," Sept told Nathan.

"Anything else?"

"We have the hook at the bottom of the foot, but a completely different set of clues around the body, which Estella said are for a different god. What does that tell us about this guy besides he's crazier than a flock of loons in heat?"

"That his mother neglected him as a child?"

"What's his mother got to do with this?"

"I don't know, but all those guys they catch after they've killed enough people to fill the Superdome always say it was their mother."

"How about we try and focus, Dr. Freud?"

"He's trying different ones until he gets the results he wants?"

"That's what I think, so that answer is as close to genius as you're going to get tonight." They walked the rest of the scene together, including the storeroom in the back.

Julio Munez showed up thirty minutes later and hugged Estella before he turned to Sept for another teaching session inside. He didn't add anything new to Estella's information except that Friday was also one of Oya's favorite days to receive sacrifices made in her name.

"If we're looking for the sacrifice you talked about," Sept said as George and Alex took samples around the room to see if the killer left any other clues this time, "what's it going to be?"

"Assuming he stole Estella's family's books, he wouldn't know that part of the ceremony, which he proved by not leaving one at the first murder. So you might not find anything."

"Hypothetically speaking, if he did somehow miraculously start channeling the gods he wants to impress, what are we looking for?"

"Oya's representative is St. Theresa, but her symbols are a crown with nine points and a hoe, pick, gourd, lightning bolt, scythe, shovel, rake, ax, and a mattock hanging from those points. Or possibly a spear, a lightning-bolt symbol, or a dried seed pod." Julio counted them off on his fingers as if he didn't want to forget any of them. "The sacrifice can be tied to any one of those, or to a statue of St. Theresa herself, but I'm betting you don't find anything because this is just a pretender of the faith."

"Who sat around and thought of all this stuff?" Sept said, almost without realizing the words were coming from her mouth.

"The Catholic religion is as full of ritual as any other, so don't ridicule something you know nothing about, Detective."

"I'm not making fun of anyone and I put all religions in the same category, Dr. Munez, so don't take offense."

He tore his eyes away from the body to look at Sept. "Call me Julio, since we'll probably be spending a lot of time together. And because religion is something I've devoted a lifetime to, I'd like to hear your thoughts."

"Surely you have people more versed on the subject than I am to talk to. My opinion shouldn't matter." Sept stared at the flickering candle and imagined what kind of detachment from reality you had to be suffering from to kneel next to this woman and gut her like that.

"It does matter, because until you understand how someone can be deeply moved by what he believes, you will never get close to this person. Faith is a two-way street, and how you practice it depends on what you hope to gain by it."

Sept recalled the nuns of St. Genevieve and had to laugh. They might have devoted their lives to their faith, but they could sure nail you with a rosary or a yardstick when the mood struck them. "Religion to some, especially the most pious among us, is a crutch that they use to fill some void that no one else can. When I was forced all those years ago to attend church, the people who acted the holiest were the ones who couldn't fit in anywhere else."

"That's true, but some practice to find salvation or favor with the gods, and others practice to find the excuse to do things like this. People who blow themselves up in crowded marketplaces or fly planes into buildings act in the name of their god, and they expect a divine reward." Julio pointed to Frieda's body and the area in general. "We look at this and see the workings of a sick mind, but the person who did it sees nothing different than the little old lady who attends church every day and drops a quarter into the collection box to light a candle. This is how he interprets his faith, and what we need to find—and fast—is what he's praying for."

"No clues at all from what you see here." Sept walked around and squatted down next to where the killer had tied one of Frieda's ankles to the leg of the counter. "Excuse me, Julio," she said when she ran a gloved finger over the intricate knot. "George, make sure you save these knots when the coroner's office cuts her loose."

"Sure thing," George said.

"I'll take care of it," Alex followed up.

"Thanks, guys. I'll see you in the morning at the station." Sept cocked her head in the direction of the door. "Would you like to finish our talk, Julio?"

Outside, Julio walked Sept to his car and put one hand on the hood. "I wish I could tell you something else, but I'll have to do some research before I can add anything."

"I appreciate you taking the time, but nothing jumps out at you from what he left in there?" Sept felt like she hadn't slept in a week, and the day was already starting to wear on her.

As Julio rubbed his chin she heard the rasp of his five o'clock shadow. "This is only a guess, but from what I know of the Orishas he's tried to leave sacrifices for, he's trying to open the door that leads to the dead."

"Excuse me?"

"He sacrificed the first girl to Elegua, the guardian of entrances and paths and the first to be called in any ceremony. This one is a gift to Oya, who has power over the dead. Like I explained before, the ceremonies and what Orisha someone picks is like using a pay phone.

Tonight he killed to speak to someone who lords over those who've passed."

"He's calling the dead?" Sept asked seriously.

"I don't know that for sure, but perhaps. If that's the case, we haven't really narrowed it down, because there are a million reasons people want to talk to the dead."

"Call me if you find anything, but don't worry. I'll be in touch this week." Sept shook hands with Julio and waited until he was behind the wheel before she headed back to her own car and aimed it toward her apartment. The sun was starting to rise when she parked and trudged up the stairs, wanting nothing but to fall into bed and sleep for a few hours.

The bed was unmade, which saved her the trouble of having to pull back the covers, and after she'd stripped down to her underwear, she sat on the edge hard enough to bounce and dialed. "Hey, I wanted to let you know I came home for a few hours to get some sleep, and I figured you'd be getting ready for work. I'll call as soon as I'm up and maybe we can have lunch. Remember to be careful and try not to be alone." Keegan's cell had gone straight to voicemail, but that didn't concern her since she knew the unit she'd sent over would be there until shift change, which wasn't until after seven that morning.

When Sept plowed into her pillow, the tension drained from her body and the last thought that flashed through her mind before she fell asleep had nothing to do with new relationships or fear of nightmares. Why would someone want to call the dead?

## CHAPTER TWENTY-FIVE

I really appreciate this," Keegan said to Madeline Seymour, Sept's neighbor, as she unlocked the door to Sept's apartment.

"Whatever you do, don't make any sudden noises to jar her awake. If you get shot I never saw you and I have no idea how you got in here. Do we understand each other?" The cigarette bobbed in Madeline's mouth as she spoke.

"I'm not planning on any noise, and jarring her awake is the last thing I have in mind." Keegan smiled, waved, and closed the door on Madeline in an effort to get away from the smoke. She scanned the apartment in search of the kitchen and laughed when it took a blink to find it. "This tiny space and so little furniture, if there was a fire and I was an insurance adjuster, I'd turn her in for arson," Keegan said to the bags she carried.

The refrigerator was so white and empty it almost blinded her, aside from the two containers she was sure held the cure for cancer in the cultures growing on whatever they once were. "Seven, what the hell are you doing to yourself living like this?"

The constricted space and lack of furniture didn't bother her because they reminded her of Sept's personality—simple and straightforward. What you saw and heard was who Sept Savoie was, and if you didn't like it, you had a problem with the truth. What bothered Keegan was Sept's poor eating habits as she ran from one crime scene to the next.

"Woman cannot live out of Styrofoam containers alone," she said as she threw the spoiled food into the trash before she moved to the bedroom.

Sept was lying on her back with the sheets pooled around her hips; her breathing was slow and deep. In the light of day Sept looked solid, since even in sleep her muscles were distinctly defined. "It's like winning the lesbian lottery," Keegan whispered, and started to strip.

After her sleepless night, she'd taken the morning off, but any plan to cook Sept breakfast would have to wait. She wanted only to join Sept for a long nap to shake off the fatigue. When she was naked she put her hands on the mattress to see if a wild punch was coming her way, but all she got was a glimpse of Sept's dark eyes as they opened briefly and she laid her arm across the bed as if in welcome. Keegan closed her eyes as soon as she was pressed against Sept, and the last thing she was aware of was the steady beat of Sept's heart under her ear.

❖

The clock was flashing on 9:00 when Sept woke up, which meant the electricity had gone off again as the crews tried to repair lines downed during the storm.

She had to move Keegan off her so she could reach her watch. Surprisingly, her cell phone was mercifully quiet, but more surprising was waking up to find Keegan naked in her bed. With the heater on, Keegan had kicked the sheets off them completely, which gave Sept a clear view of her backside. The desire to touch her was as strong as it had been the night before.

"Are you still trying to commit my ass to memory?" Keegan asked.

"I'm actually trying to figure out if I need to cuff you." Sept moved her hand from Keegan's shoulder to her butt. "Are you a cat burglar disguised as a chef?"

"I can debone a chicken in less than five minutes, but don't worry. Locks aren't another of my specialties." Keegan kissed the side of Sept's neck. "You should be thanking God I'm not the killer you first suspected, because your neighbor let me in awfully quick when I asked. That makes me wonder." Keegan bit the spot she'd just kissed.

"What?"

"How many other women she's let wander in here?"

"If you really want to know, it isn't a revolving door." Sept rolled over and put Keegan on her back so she could touch her. "Before you, I was dating my job more than anyone else."

"We have to do something about that, Seven." Sept was stretched out next to her, but that must have not been good enough for Keegan, so she pulled her on top. "You need a little more of this and that in your life."

"I'm willing to take suggestions." Sept licked one of Keegan's nipples. "You're right." She licked it again and enjoyed the way Keegan's hips pressed toward her. "A little of this..." She sucked on it this time until she heard Keegan moan. Then she moved to the other nipple and gave it the same treatment, followed by a gentle bite before she let go. "And a little of that, and I feel better already."

"If you tell me you have to go anytime soon, I'll punish you in a way you won't forget anytime soon." Keegan put her fingers on Sept's nipple as she spoke and squeezed just enough to get her attention. "Do you have to go anywhere?"

"I worked most of the night and I did promise to keep you safe, so I think I deserve some downtime." She raised herself far enough to move down and ran her tongue down Keegan's body as she went. "And if it's okay with you, I plan to spend it making up for having to leave you last night."

"I'd love that." Keegan reached down to bring Sept back up. "You said last night that we had all the time we wanted to enjoy this."

"I'll go as slow as you want, or we can wait until you're ready."

"After you drove me insane last night I'm more than ready, but I want slow." The weight of Sept on her made Keegan feel like she'd finally found the anchor to keep her rooted in her dreams. That was different from being dragged down in the mundane dreariness her life had become while they tried to get their businesses back to their pre-storm level. "I want to enjoy every bit of you, and I'm glad we got interrupted last night."

Sept began to roll off her but Keegan kept her hands on Sept's face. "If you're not ready to do this, I'll totally understand. Don't do it because you think it's what I expect," Sept said.

"I didn't mean that I'm glad we had to stop because I was having second thoughts," Keegan said, and brought Sept's head down so she could reach her lips and kiss her. She slowly sucked Sept's tongue and came close to breaking the contact when Sept pumped her hips into the mattress. "Last night was last night, but today I get you here all to myself, and I get to touch you in the light. It's like a gift."

"Last night I wanted to show you how much I've come to care about you. I wanted you to see what was in my heart," Sept said as she gazed down at Keegan. "And in my life, except for my family, I don't remember ever wanting to do that for another person."

"Then I consider myself fortunate."

Sept rolled off only partially so she could run her hand down Keegan's body. With her head on the pillow, Keegan watched the path Sept's hand took between her breasts, down her belly, and over her groin, down her thigh until she reached the inside of her knee.

"You are so beautiful," Sept said as she lifted Keegan's leg to rest it over her body, leaving her open.

Keegan was about to beg Sept to touch her, since she was dripping. "Like I've told you before, I've never felt like that until you looked at me. You were right. You can't fake that, because now that I know you, I'd be able to tell."

Sept's fingers felt like silk as they made their way through her red hair. She moaned as Sept went to her opening and came up until her fingers rested right under her clitoris. The way she pushed down made Keegan feel like screaming. Her groin was pounding, and she craved the contact that would bring the relief she'd been waiting for not for days, but for what seemed like her entire life.

She liked sex, but had never been with someone who took this kind of time. She'd never been with someone who clearly savored the sight of her as well as the touch. Sept might've not known how to boil water, but she knew the exact recipe for making her crazy.

Sept swirled her index and middle finger until they were wet. Each tight circle brought her around Keegan's clit, but she hadn't touched it yet, and each time she didn't, Keegan lifted her hips, trying to entice her to put pressure where she most needed it.

"I really want to put my mouth on you," Sept said.

"And I really want you right here next to me, so think of something else," Keegan said, and was amazed she was able to form words, much less coherent sentences.

Sept smiled and glanced down as if thinking about the challenge.

She lifted her fingers, which were visibly wet. "I bet this is like your cooking," she said.

The loss of Sept's hand made Keegan feel cold. "What do you mean?"

"I read some of your reviews, Chef Blanchard, and the word used most often to describe your style is 'unique,' especially regarding the flavors you create in the kitchen." Sept brought her fingers up but didn't put them in her mouth. Instead, she slowly painted Keegan's lips until they were coated in her essence. "I bet this is unique as well, and I can't wait to taste."

As soon as Sept finished speaking, she brought her mouth down and claimed Keegan's lips so they could both enjoy what she was talking about. And at the same time she brought her hand down again and squeezed Keegan's clit and tugged it up and down before sliding her fingers in and burying them inside her.

Keegan dropped her head to the pillow and shut her eyes tight. The sudden onslaught of sensation erased any inhibitions she might have had with Sept, and when Sept started to pull out, she clenched the walls of her sex, wanting to keep her in place. "Don't get distracted now, Seven," she said when she opened her eyes and saw Sept looking at her breasts.

"It's hard not to." Sept kissed the closer one right under the nipple. "When I touched you, your nipples got hard."

"Think what'll happen to them if you make me come," Keegan said, and hissed out a long breath when Sept covered her clit with her thumb.

Keegan opened her mouth to say something as Sept pulled her fingers out, but when she buried her fingers again, her thumb rubbed against Keegan and made the orgasm Sept had so carefully built start down a fast slide of no return. As Sept moved her fingers in and out she kept her eyes on Keegan's, and Keegan couldn't look away as the sensations built so much she thought she'd damage something if they couldn't finish.

Sept's movements were slow, and she smiled as Keegan felt her lungs shrink like they couldn't inhale enough air. She was wet, her skin felt like someone had given her a shot of adrenaline, and she wanted Sept to go faster and harder, but she couldn't say anything for fear that

Sept would stop. Her movements became jerkier as she lost control of her hips, and then Sept lowered her head, kissed her, and sped up her hand.

This was the permission Keegan needed to close her eyes and clutch onto Sept and ride out the explosion that washed through her like a New Orleans rainstorm in July. The kind of storm that came on so fast that the best thing to do was to stand and enjoy it as it soaked you through and cooled you from the summer heat. Sept had begun more slowly than such a storm, but in the end Keegan could feel her in every pore of her body, and the yell she let out when she reached orgasm made her want to laugh, since it was as out of character for her as running through the French Quarter naked.

"No." She grabbed Sept by the wrist to keep her hand in place. "Stay inside me."

"Are you okay?" Sept raised up on her other elbow.

"I will be, but right now I'm trying to figure out what you did to me," Keegan said, and turned her head on the pillow so she could look at Sept.

"Do you mean that in a good way or bad?"

"Honey, I'm sure even if you don't date much, when a woman screams in your ear and draws blood by raking her nails up your back, it's a good thing." Keegan licked her lips right before Sept kissed her again, and as soon as their lips touched, she was shocked at how quickly her passion stirred back to life. She couldn't help the groan that escaped when Sept took her hand back.

"Don't worry," Sept said as she rolled over and covered Keegan's body with hers. "That was just the appetizer."

Keegan bent her head back so Sept could put a row of kisses down her neck. "If that was the appetizer, I'll be unconscious by dessert." With Sept on top, Keegan found how easy it was to reach all the interesting parts. If Sept planned to touch her again, she would have to wait. She reached between Sept's legs and found her ready.

It didn't take much to make Sept collapse, trapping her hand between them. "I'm no chicken, but I think you just deboned me," Sept said.

"And it could become habit forming," Keegan said as she ordered Sept's hair. When she'd decided to take the morning off, she hadn't necessarily planned to spend it like this, but she wasn't sorry. "Are you ready for something to eat?"

"Now there's an offer I can't pass up." Sept lifted her head so quickly that she startled Keegan.

Before Keegan could move to get up, Sept slid down her body and lowered her head between her legs. The twinge that had started almost immediately after Sept had made love to her blossomed into another orgasm before she really had a chance to enjoy it. She wasn't disappointed, though, as Sept sucked her in and brought her to orgasm again.

"Thank you." Sept moved back up and put her arms around her when Keegan rolled on top of her. "That was delicious."

"If you want anything else you'll have to wait until I can move any part of my body again," Keegan said, and kissed Sept's chest. "We'll be doing this a lot, won't we?"

"When you're not in the kitchen and I'm not out chasing bad guys, I'll meet you right here," Sept said, and cursed under her breath when her phone suddenly came to life. "Wait, don't move," she told Keegan when she started to roll away.

"I'm not upset," Keegan said, and kissed her forehead. "As a matter of fact, give whoever is on the other end my thanks for not interrupting us until now. A few minutes ago there would've been trouble." She waved as she headed toward the bathroom.

"Nathan, you do realize you have the job, right? You don't have anything to gain from kissing up now." Sept watched Keegan's butt as she walked away. At the door Keegan turned around and shook her head.

"Sorry, I got up an hour ago and couldn't go back to sleep," Nathan said. "I checked in and found a message from Gavin. As he went through the autopsy, he discovered something, and he wants us there before he finishes."

"Did he give you a time?" The conversation was getting more difficult as Keegan came back out of the bathroom, still naked.

"He said he's not busy, so whenever we want to stop by would be good."

"Good. Give me a couple of hours and I'll pick you up." Sept snapped the phone shut and threw it on the empty side of the bed. "I did say I was looking forward to the naked cooking lessons," she told Keegan when she stepped in and found her pouring ingredients into a bowl.

"Before I do all this, I guess I should ask if your oven works." Keegan took a few more things out of the bags she'd brought in.

"The last time I heated a frozen pizza, it worked fine."

"Sometimes, sweetheart, it's best to answer with simple answers like yes or no," Keegan said as she mixed the contents with her hands.

"That's good advice when you're testifying in court, but I don't get what it has to do with my oven."

"It doesn't have anything to do with the oven, but everything to do with the words 'frozen pizza.' Should I start listing all the reasons why that's totally horrible for you?"

"You and my mother will get along great," Sept said as she put her arms around Keegan and peeked over her shoulder to see what she was doing.

"I'm sure we will, but your eating habits are about to change drastically." Keegan pulled the dough she'd made and dropped it in small dollops onto a baking sheet.

"If you expect me to start complaining, it's not happening."

"I give you credit for not running for the door and forgetting my phone number. Most people would be worried about the U-Haul by now." The biscuits went into the spotless oven, and Keegan glanced at the wall clock as she closed the door. "And I won't fuss because I want to be right, but because I don't want to visit you in the hospital when you have a heart attack from a buildup of frozen pizza."

"Like I said, I'm not complaining, no matter why you fuss. I like the fact that you care about me at all." Sept moved closer and put her arms around her. "Like you said, no matter how we met or started our relationship, I'm glad we did."

"And you wonder why I feel so lucky," Keegan said, then kissed Sept's chest. "You could turn a girl's head with talk like that," she said in her best Southern belle accent.

"Want to take a shower with me, Scarlett?"

"I will in fifteen minutes." Keegan pointed to the oven.

They took their time enjoying the simple breakfast of biscuits with homemade strawberry preserves and café au lait that Keegan had made.

Keegan sat on Sept's lap, content to split her time between watching Sept eat and savoring her fingers as they roamed over her body. Sept kept it up when they stepped into the shower, and Keegan teetered between arousal and comfort. Her worry didn't begin until Sept strapped on the shoulder holster and clipped her badge to her belt.

"I know this sounds juvenile, but have you ever considered doing something else?"

"Not really, and it has a lot to do with my family. I'm sure my dad would've understood if I'd wanted to, and my mother would've been thrilled if I'd gone into banking or something equally mundane." Sept finished buttoning the heavy linen top that Jacqueline loved to tease Keegan about and kissed the top of her head.

"What made you want to do this?"

"My family has lived the history of this city by protecting its streets for as long as I can count. When I was a little kid, I knew early on that when it was my turn, I'd want to do the same thing. It takes all different types of people to make a community, and it's the Savoie family tradition to keep order in the one we've called home for generations. That's what my dad has always told us, and he's right." Sept kissed her cheek this time. "That's the best answer I've got."

"Thanks for sharing it with me."

"Did you ask for some particular reason?"

Keegan put her hands around Sept's neck and felt the top edge of the leather holster. "I'd tell you, but the question's too premature."

"If I guess right, will you tell me?" Sept sat her back down on the sofa and held her hand. Keegan nodded and kept her eyes down. "Most of my brothers are married and have kids, and when they first met their wives their question about the job had to do with worry and how they would learn to live with the reality of it. Am I in the right ballpark?"

"I'm not in the same category as your sisters-in-law, but when I see you put on all that stuff I think about what you're going out to do, which does drive me a little insane."

Sept put her arm around her and lifted Keegan's head with her other hand. "It gets easier, but only with time. It's that day-after-day experience that'll show you that I leave and come back, and while it'll never be a nine-to-five job, it's a job. I just hope you give it that much time."

"I'm not going anywhere, Seven, and if you ever get hurt, can I remind you about this conversation?"

"As many times as you'd like." They shared another long kiss before Sept helped her to her feet. "Right now, though, we have to begin that experience gathering of yours, because I have to go to work."

They walked downstairs together, and when they reached the street the beat cop about twenty feet away with his partner stopped and opened his arms to Keegan. Sept propped herself against the front of her building and watched what seemed to be a touching reunion. As Keegan hugged the guy she kept her eyes on Sept the entire time and smiled.

"Sept, this is my friend Tom from high school." Keegan walked him over and put her arm around Sept's waist.

"How's it going?" Sept asked as she shook his hand. "And you?" She shook his partner's hand next.

"Pretty good these days, Sept. This area's so quiet now, I keep wishing for a bar fight or two," Keegan's friend said.

After a few more minutes of small talk with the two, Sept apologized for having to leave.

"We have to get going too, but it was good seeing you again, Keegan." He tipped his hat and they started their patrol again.

"I'll see you tonight at the house, right?" Keegan asked Sept.

Sept opened the door to Keegan's coupe and helped her inside. "With any luck, I'll be done way before that and can pick you up at the restaurant."

"Are we towing my car home, then?"

"If you can walk from your house, I'm sure I can too." Sept reached through the window and kissed her. "Drive safe, and keep your phone handy in case you have to call me."

"You do the same, Seven, and I'll see you tonight."

## CHAPTER TWENTY-SIX

Nathan was waiting in front of the precinct when she drove up, and he appeared as wiped as she felt. But Sept wouldn't have traded her morning for a month of sleep. "Anything new since the last time we talked?" The traffic had picked up and more shoppers were out carrying bags with Christmas-related things printed on the outside of them.

"You did get a call that didn't make sense, but I took a message anyway." He handed over the slip of paper when they stopped at a red light.

The name Dr. Glass didn't sound familiar. "Did they say what they wanted?"

"He's a vet and said your dog is ready to go home. Actually, he said he's been trying you for days but you haven't gotten back to him. You didn't tell me you had a dog."

"I don't have one. Remember the night I walked Robin Burns's crime scene and found her dog Mike? He was stabbed and left for dead, but I took him to the police vet." When they arrived at the coroner's office, Gavin was standing outside smoking a cigarette.

"What are you going to do with him?"

Sept drummed her thumbs on the steering wheel as she tried to find the right answer. "I checked with the service that places the animals, and she said he'd probably be retired, but that would be up to the vet. Besides, I don't have room for a dog."

"You're not taking him to the pound, are you?"

"Even if I wanted to, I don't think they're operational yet after the building flooded. Let's finish here and go pick Mike up. I'll think of something."

Gavin took the last drag off his smoke as they walked up and leisurely stubbed it out in the ashtray that looked like it had been there since the 1940s. "You two need more sleep," he said.

"I'd love nothing better, and I'm sure Nathan isn't used to staying up past nine," Sept joked back. "What you got for us, Doc?"

"I found something but left it in place until you got here. If all this shit is eventually going to give me nightmares, I want to know I'm not alone as I sit up watching old reruns of *Seinfeld.*"

Frieda Hearn's body was lying on the exam table when they entered, and Sept could see that even in death she displayed the terror she must have faced right before the killer made the savage gash up her middle. She handed Nathan another canister of mints but took one for herself before she let go of the can. Gavin had only slightly enlarged the cut they'd seen the night before, but after he clicked on the spotlight Sept could see why.

The killer might have ripped her heart out like he had Tameka's, but in this case he'd inserted something. "What is that?" Nathan asked as he peered over Sept's shoulder where Gavin was pointing.

"I might be wrong, but from my old churchgoing days, this looks like the bottom of one of those small plastic saint statues they sell in the religious gift shops around town," Sept said as she studied the chest cavity to see if the killer had left anything else. "I'll bet you lunch that it's St. Theresa."

"How in the hell can you talk about food right now?" Nathan asked, sounding queasy. "If you're hungry, you're not human."

"I ate breakfast, don't worry, but by noon I promise you won't be thinking about this." Sept scanned the room for a box of gloves and put some on. "Do you mind, Doc?"

"Be my guest. That's why I waited."

The small plastic statue had been shoved in and embedded in the soft tissue of Frieda's chest, and it made a sucking noise when Sept pulled it loose. Nathan was working his mint in his mouth like it would stave off any embarrassing reaction he might have.

"Is that St. Theresa?" Gavin asked.

"You're talking to a fallen Catholic, Doc, but our killer is nothing but considerate." Sept turned the piece around so they could see the name engraved on the bottom, even though it was coated in blood. A piece of paper was wrapped around the statue and tied with a piece of the same twine that Frieda's legs and arms had been bound with. "You think it's a confession and a picture of him in the act?"

"I'd swear you were crazy, but this is the definition of crazy," Gavin said, and laid out a section of sterile paper so Sept could put it down and preserve all the evidence.

Carefully, Sept lifted the twine off the top of the statue and unrolled the paper. The plastic image of the Carmelite nun was relatively clean, considering where it had been, with traces of blood only on the top and bottom. She had to hold the paper with her fingertips to keep it flat, and in large typed letters the note said,

*I want a second chance.*
*I will serve until you see how worthy I am.*
*I want back what was stolen from me.*

"If that doesn't clear it up, then I don't know what will," Sept said. "Being cryptic must be something all these guys learn in serial-killer school."

"You have no clue what it means?" Nathan asked.

"'I want a second chance' has to go with the last line of 'I want back what was stolen from me.' We need to figure that out, and I have a feeling we'll be getting the chance real soon, because he needs to get a little more detailed." She couldn't see anything on the paper or about the print that could lead to their guy, but it would go to the lab anyway so they could check it for traces of prints or DNA.

"You're right, I guess, if you take the second line to heart," Nathan said.

"It means he'll keep killing until he gets back what was stolen and gets his second chance," Sept said. She bagged the note and the statue and initialed the outside before she handed it over to the lab technician Gavin had called. "Thanks, Doc, and if you find anything else, call us."

"What's next on our list?" Nathan asked.

"We find out who Frieda Hearn was and why this guy would've targeted her. After that, I have a dog to pick up and find a new home for."

❖

Novice stood naked in front of his mirror again and kept his eyes closed as he mentally intoned a chant he'd made up. In each hand he held something he'd kept from his sacrificial victims. They were significant to him, but he doubted his hunter had noticed anything missing from either scene. After each one was dead, Novice had tied a small lock of hair together and snipped it off. It would stay soft and remind him of the two women who had brought him closer to his goal.

His lips moved as he chanted Tameka and Frieda's names, along with the name of the gods he'd gifted them to. When he opened his eyes he still didn't see what he wanted reflected in the mirror, but he had come to accept one fact. Gods, no matter which you prayed to, needed the respect they were due, which meant numerous sacrifices.

"I know what you want now, but you have to realize I'm willing to give it to you, and I don't give a damn who's after me. Sept Savoie is a good hunter, but up to now her prey has been weak and easy to catch." He ran the strands of Tameka's hair along his jaw. "I'll be anything but weak and easy. That means I'll not only get what I want, but I'll be free to enjoy it for as long as I want, while she runs around chasing the crumbs I've left her."

"Before you start boasting like that, you should remember the lessons your Sunday school teacher taught you," Teacher said.

"The truth isn't bragging," Novice said defensively.

"Only a man who humbles himself before God will know salvation. Sept has everything she wants, and she keeps it because she doesn't run around yelling about how wonderful she is."

"Sept will always be considered sick and perverted, so don't preach to me about anything, especially about God. If He gave a fuck about me, my wife would be in that bed with her legs spread and waiting for me, and my child would be running through the yard playing and laughing. But they aren't"—his voice had risen so much that his face and chest had gotten red and blotchy—"so don't fucking talk to me about God and what the fuck He wants." He punched the wall next to the mirror hard enough that the pain shot through his arm and he dropped the lock of hair.

"Calm down, you idiot. I look at you like this and wonder why I waste my time," Teacher said, his voice stern enough in Novice's head that he dropped to his knees to pick up the hair and stayed there. "You're a maggot and will always be one until you please the gods who are willing to listen to you at all."

"You're right, Teacher, I'm sorry."

"At least you figured out that what you have believed in all your life is wrong. God has abandoned you, and if you even think to show Him any kind of favor, such as acting disgusted at what I ask you to do, He can have you back."

Novice held both locks of hair in one hand and rubbed them on his face for a little comfort, since Teacher offered none. "I promise I'll listen only to you."

"You have to start carrying me with you no matter what you're doing. You're strong enough to do what you have to as the man everyone expects you to be, but keep your eyes open to what I need from you." Teacher's voice had become so soft and seductive that Novice's penis stirred to life. "Can you manage that?"

"I'll do whatever you need me to," Novice said. Beads of sweat were forming along his hairline, and his erection in the mirror appeared foreign to him, like it belonged to someone else. His grief had killed his sexual drive entirely.

"See what I can do for you." Teacher's voice became softer and morphed into something new but familiar. The stern voice of his instructor sounded feminine, but not like just any woman's. "I know you miss me, my darling."

"Oh, God," Novice said, and choked on a sob that deflated him quicker than if someone had kneed him in the groin. "Please don't go."

"Close your eyes and listen to me," Teacher said, sounding exactly like Novice's wife. "Show me how much you missed me. Let me see that."

When he looked at his reflection, his erection was back and he happily wrapped his hand around it. He wasn't giving in to the pleasure for himself, but for his wife. "I've missed you so much," he said as he stroked himself.

"I know, love, but I'm here now and you're not alone." The laugh Novice thought he'd never hear again filled his head as his hand sped up. "Let go for me."

He wanted so much to please her that he leaned back on his feet and pumped his hips along with his hand. It was easy to imagine her straddling him as he gave her what she'd begged him for. From the time they'd met he'd taught her how to please him, and it didn't matter if some lessons had been hard for her. She'd learned to beg even if she really didn't want it.

The roar he let out as he climaxed was liberating, and he stilled his hand but didn't let go of himself as he sat back on his feet. He'd forgotten about the calm that came after releasing all his tension, but now the release brought not only calmness but resolve. He needed to prepare another altar and leave another gift for not only the gods, but for Sept as well.

"We're together again, my love, and with more sacrifices I'll get to feel you as well as hear you," Novice said out loud.

"I have every faith in you."

Novice laughed in a way he hadn't in the months since his wife and child had died. He was back in control, and no way would Teacher leave him now, no matter what he did, because as he had before her death, he owned her. His wife was his to do with as he pleased, no matter what name she went by, and now that she'd revealed herself, he'd continue to call her Teacher until the time came to show her who really was in charge. When that happened, he'd put her back in her place for all the misery he'd suffered since she'd left.

"If you want another sacrifice, you'll have it." He stood up, walked to the misshapen dresser, and opened the top drawer. The flood had swollen and warped the wood, so it had taken him a few hours to get the damn thing to work. The drawer pulled easily now, but the piece of furniture still appeared like a heap of trash.

"Even if someone stumbles in here, they'll never find these," Novice said as he took out the books Estella had been kind enough to leave in the store for him. He turned to the page with a sketch of St. Barbara at the top. "If we face a warrior and hunter, it's time to honor the chase," he said. St. Barbara stood almost arrogantly as she held her sword, but even though she was a woman, she embodied the most powerful of the Orishas. It was time to pay homage to Chango.

"This one will have to be something special, so I hope you're ready, Sept, and you aren't so caught up in chasing that girl's ass you're not worth the importance Teacher has placed on you."

## CHAPTER TWENTY-SEVEN

You've been over here so much, people will begin to talk," Brandi said as she stepped into her home office to meet with Sept and Nathan. "And I can't have anyone maligning the character of two of New Orleans's best." She laughed as she took her seat behind the traditional oak desk. "What can I do for you, Sept?"

"Are you familiar with a Frieda Hearn?" Sept had made Brandi her first stop in this part of the investigation to hopefully save some time walking the streets in search of the answers she needed.

"If it's the Frieda I'm thinking of, she's a decent person engaged in one of the world's oldest professions. She just wasn't in the league with my girls and our clientele. Why do you ask?"

"She was killed last night." Sept watched Brandi's face, which showed a fleeting stab of pain. "I wanted to confirm my speculation, so thank you."

"Wait," Brandi said when Sept put her hands on the arms of her chair to stand up. "Should the girls and I be worried about some maniac out there targeting us?"

"No matter what, you and yours should always be vigilant, you know that, but I haven't figured this one out yet. We have a pattern, but three of my victims don't make sense."

"I know you won't share the details, but you're saying three of them weren't prostitutes, but two of them are?" Brandi lifted one of her legs and folded it under her, making her jeans pull tight. "If that's true, how do you know it's the same guy?"

"I know, and I want you to be careful. He doesn't seem to be targeting anyone per se, only someone who's out and convenient.

Tameka was one too many for you. Talk to everyone living here and tell them to keep their eyes open."

"Thanks, Sept, and if anyone on the force will spend time figuring out who did this, you will."

Brandi walked them to the door and Sept let Nathan go out first. "I can't stress this enough, Brandi. If you hear of anything or anyone you think is hinky, let me know. I'm tired of this guy being so far ahead of me."

"You'll be my first call." Brandi put her hand on Sept's face and smiled. "You always are, but since you haven't made a move to kiss me good-bye, I think I might be out of luck when it comes to wearing you down."

"I make a better friend than a lover, but she thinks otherwise, so I'm willing to try and prove her right." Sept took Brandi's hand and kissed the back of it. "You'd like her."

"If you're willing to take the chance, I'm sure I would. Tell her for me that she's a lucky girl."

"Will do, and I'll be in touch."

Sept walked to the car without looking back and didn't hear the red door close until she was about to open the car door. Her friendship with Brandi could've easily become something else, but knowing that Brandi still worked on occasion would've driven her crazy.

"Want to knock off a little early today and pick this up first thing in the morning?" she asked Nathan.

"Sure." He rubbed his eyes and yawned. "Where do you want to start tomorrow?"

"Let's review everything we have so far. Sometimes when you put all the information in front of you, something small pops out that makes you feel like an idiot for missing it in the first place." Sept drove back to the precinct slowly, finding that she missed talking things out with a partner. What had started as a reluctant relationship had started to gel, and she was beginning to enjoy being around Nathan.

"I'll call the team together."

"Wait up on that. We'll go through it first. All that chatter when we're crammed in there makes it hard to think. And check if the lab has results from the note we found."

"Will do, and don't forget to call me if you hear anything before that."

Sept nodded as she parked next to his car. "Have a good afternoon off and try to get some rest."

She headed to the vet's office next and took the opportunity to call Keegan. "How was lunch?"

"Mine was great, but I bet I can list exactly everything you've put in your mouth today."

"There are so many ways I could respond to that, but I'll be good and tell you I had to skip lunch because I was working." At a traffic light Sept stopped next to a police cruiser and waved to the guy driving it. "I mentioned lunch to Nathan, but we were at an autopsy and the poor boy was gagging enough."

"Anything new and fascinating happen today?"

"I'll tell you later, as far as the autopsy is concerned, but I had to go see Brandi Parrish again to ask about the new victim. Now I'm on my way to pick up my only witness at any of the crime scenes."

"We'll get to Brandi Parrish when I see you and can pinch you if I think any funny business is going on there, but as for the witness, that's great. I thought you didn't have any leads."

A couple of canine units were parked in front of the office when Sept arrived, and she came close to laughing at Keegan's little jealous streak. "I don't have many leads, and when I introduce you to my witness later, you'll see what I mean."

"Are you off for the rest of the day?"

"I am, but I have to run by my house first and pick up a change of clothes before I come over. Do you have to work tonight?"

"Unfortunately, yes, but if you want, you can come keep me company."

The offer should have made her cringe, considering how she felt about cooking, but she was looking forward to watching Keegan do what she loved. "What if I sit in your office and work on some things, and then I'll go home with you from there?"

"And maybe after you've finished studying all that gore, you'll be interested in learning to cook something new."

"Maybe," Sept said, and laughed. "I'll see you in about an hour, so be careful."

The lobby of the office smelled like dog food, and some clients were sitting with their pets, waiting to be seen. "Sept Savoie. I'm here to pick up a dog I left," she told the receptionist. The woman buzzed her in and had her wait by her desk. A few minutes later the doctor came out leading Mike on a leash.

"It's a good thing you were able to leave him so long. I've taken the stitches out so you won't be due back here for a couple of weeks, and as you can see, he's doing great."

Mike sat at the doctor's feet with his tongue hanging out as he seemed to study Sept with an open, friendly face. The spot where he'd been stabbed had been shaved, so the long, thin pink scar was visible. Sept stared back at him and felt bad for the animal that had obviously been talented and dedicated enough to serve a blind person. Those days were probably over.

"He's still not a hundred percent, since the bastard who did this cut him fairly deep, but we were lucky that the blade went between his ribs and didn't break anything," the vet went on.

"If he was a working dog, can I call someone so they can place him again?"

"Only time can prove me wrong, but I think we can consider Mike retired. He probably had a couple good years of service left because of his age, so he's lucky enough to enjoy his retirement." The doctor petted Mike under his neck with genuine affection. "He's a great dog. You should consider keeping him, Detective."

"My hours would make him miserable, but I'll find him a good place." Sept took the leash from him and shook the vet's hand. "Thanks for patching him up."

As Sept walked him out, Mike stopped at the door and looked back. She could swear it was his way of saying good-bye. In the car he sat in the backseat and gazed out the window, and all she could hear was his breathing. Hopefully Keegan wasn't allergic to dogs.

"If only you could sit with a sketch artist and tell him what this asshole looks like, Mike," she told him as she walked him upstairs to her apartment. "That'd save me a lot of trouble and most probably someone's life."

❖

After Sept packed a bag, she put Mike back in the car and drove to Keegan's. She left her stuff in the backseat and shouldered only her bag filled with her case files and held Mike's leash. The afternoon had turned cloudy and chilly, but she figured she could make it to Blanchard's on foot before any rain fell.

As they walked, Mike's training and instincts kicked in as he stopped her from crossing the street until he could check to see if it was safe. How many times had he done that for his late master on their nightly walks before some idiot cut Robin Burns's life short? When they reached the restaurant, Sept stood at the windows by the kitchen and waited until Keegan noticed them. The first patrons wouldn't arrive for dinner for a few hours, so she could introduce Keegan to Mike and walk him home after she sat in the garden and reviewed her files.

If Keegan was allergic to dogs, it wasn't apparent as she knelt next to Mike and gave him a good rubdown, which seemed to make Mike happier. "I take it you like dogs," Sept said.

"Where'd you get him? He's beautiful."

"Mike Burns is my one and only live witness. He was Robin Burns's guide dog, and I had the vet patch him up. Now I have to find him a new owner."

Keegan gave Mike a little more attention before she stood and kissed Sept hello. "You don't have to do that right this second, do you?"

"I thought we could sit out here and work for a while before I walk him back and put him in your yard, if you don't mind."

"Honey, you can't leave him in the yard. He's used to being inside," Keegan said as she put her arms around Sept's waist.

"I wasn't going to leave him out there alone. I was going to sit with him, since some people don't like dogs inside."

"I let you inside, didn't I? And I didn't even know if you were housebroken." Keegan spoke in a teasing voice as she neared Sept. "I'm sure this guy is housebroken, so it's not a problem."

"Good to know," Sept answered drolly, but kissed Keegan again when she tilted her head up.

Since only the kitchen staff was in the restaurant, Keegan led them into her office and closed the door. Sept used the small desk as Mike lay nearby and stared at her. The staff talked and joked as they started the dishes for that night, but Sept tuned them all out as she went through the notes and pictures of every crime scene. She lined up small prints of all five victims and how they were found laid out, and she took her time going down the line.

Sept was no profiler, but something was odd about how different each scene was from the other. The first and the third held the most similarities. The killer had murdered the two men quickly, almost like he was trying to quit smoking and only needed a quick hit to get over the craving. He'd taken his time with Tameka and Frieda, but with Tameka he'd found a deserted spot and completed the process leisurely. Only, according to the religious expert, he'd forgotten the most important aspect of it. With Frieda he'd gone through the ritual completely, but he'd picked a place where he'd been forced to rush the kill before Estella returned to her apartment over the store.

"Either you're a planning fool who considers every aspect of what needs to be done, or you're a lucky bastard who's flying by the seat of his pants and timing has been on your side." Sept spoke to the pictures and smiled down at Mike when he moved over and put his head on her foot. "Which is it, buddy? Is this guy smart or lucky?"

For a dog he was quiet, but Sept enjoyed his expressive face. She petted him as she continued to go through her papers. At a few minutes before seven everyone in the kitchen stopped and said hello to someone who'd arrived through the kitchen entrance. Sept gazed at the guy standing in the kitchen and her pictures, and something clicked.

The new arrival was a New Orleans police officer who, like so many other businesses in the city, the restaurant had hired as a guard. It was a good opportunity for the guys who did it to earn extra money, and the business benefited because they were trained police and not some idiot pawning himself off as a night watchman.

Donovan, Tameka, Frieda, and the guy in the park had allowed the guy close, so they had to trust that person, even if they didn't know him.

"He's dressed like a cop," Sept said quietly, making Mike sit up. Robin couldn't see, but that's why Mike hadn't reacted when the guy was close. She didn't know the details of guide-dog training, but she guessed they were taught not to react to the uniform. "You thought he was there to help, didn't you?" she asked Mike.

The proof was right in front of her. No one in the kitchen had blinked when the guy walked in. Even Keegan had proved it that morning when she hugged her friend hello. Granted, she knew the guy, but most people approached by a uniformed policeman welcomed him into their personal space, or at least let him close enough to end up with a knife through the heart.

"Fuck," she said in disgust. "If that's true, he'll be that much harder to find." The city was full of cops and national guardsmen from all over the United States. "Whatever kind of uniform it was, that's what got this guy close enough," she said to Mike and the top of the desk.

"Ready to take a break?" Keegan asked.

Sept scooped the pictures up and put them back in the folder. She didn't want to give Keegan nightmares. "I was getting ready to come talk to you."

Keegan put down a bowl with rice, vegetables, and barely cooked veal for Mike. "I thought I'd feed you two before I get crazy in there." She put the night's fish special down for Sept next.

"Good to see the dog rates before me."

"I'm sure in the end he'll follow directions better than you do," Keegan told her before she bent down and kissed her.

"Can I ask you a few questions?"

"As long as I can walk out of here not blushing, you sure can," Keegan said as she sat on the edge of the desk close to Sept.

"Those will come later, don't worry about that," Sept told her, and put her hand on Keegan's knee. "My questions actually have to do with work."

"Anything I can do to help catch Donovan's killer is important to me. What do you want to know?"

"The night that happened, did you have a policeman on duty?" The policeman who had sparked Sept's idea was standing close to one of the stations with a plate in his hand, talking to some of the staff.

"Al was Jacqueline's idea when we reopened after the storm. He works from opening until closing and mostly stands out front to give people a sense of security. Do you think he had something to do with this?" Keegan put her hand over Sept's.

"No. I know Al from some of my cases, but seeing him out there gave me an idea."

"Do you want to share it?"

"We'll discuss it tonight when we're alone. Right now I want to talk to Al before he goes on the clock for you."

"You can do that after you eat. I'm sure having two of you out there won't throw people into a panic." Keegan moved her plate closer and cut off a piece of the fish and fed it to her.

"Don't tell my mom, but that's better than hers," Sept said when she swallowed, which earned her another kiss.

"Your secrets are safe with me, and you're sweet."

"This is delicious, and I'm not the only one who thinks so." Sept ate another piece and pointed to Mike, who was walking his bowl across the room to make sure he got every bit. "I'll pick up some dog food tomorrow."

"I'll take care of that. You concentrate on work, which is more important than shopping." Keegan laughed when Mike jumped up and put his paws on her thighs as if wanting to be petted. "What are you going to do with him?"

"See if someone at the precinct's in the market for a new dog. If not, maybe one of my brothers will take him."

"Before I say this, let me preface it by saying that you don't have to worry about the U-Haul. What if I keep him, and since you'll be around a lot more, you can spend time with him when you're at my place?"

"Does this mean you want to wear my high-school ring?" Sept asked as she put the last piece of fish in her mouth.

"Do you even know where your high-school ring is?"

"You'll have to wait and find out. Right now I want to talk to your rent-a-cop." When the dog dropped down close to Keegan's feet, Sept stood up and kissed her. "You want to stay here or come with me?" Sept asked Mike. The sound of her voice prompted him to lie down and stare up at her, his head on Keegan's feet.

"Does this mean we can keep him?" Keegan asked.

"If he wants to be kept, then I don't see why not. Though he acts like if I tried to ship him off somewhere he might bite me in the ass."

"You staying out with Al all night?"

Sept shook her head and put her files back in her bag before she left the room. She trusted Keegan, but didn't want someone else to get an unforgettable shock.

The restaurant patrolman was keeping visible in front of the restaurant, tipping his hat at the patrons as they arrived. Sept recognized Al since he had done a brief stint in the French Quarter. A few years from retirement, he was one of those guys who obviously loved putting on the uniform every day; he was always immaculate.

"Hey, Al, they feeding you good in there?" Sept asked, and knocked her knuckles on the side of the building.

"Best gig in town for an old bachelor like me. How you doing, Sept? Your mom and dad making out okay?" Al held his hand out and shook hers with a strong grip.

"Living in a small trailer together, they're learning all kinds of stuff about each other. I don't mean to bother you while you're working, but can I ask you a few questions?"

"You still investigating Donovan's murder?" Al shook his head and propped himself against one of the columns that lined the front of the building. "Hell of a nice guy, that one."

"Were you here that night working?"

"I was here until ten. My commander had scheduled me for five the next morning, and I wanted to get a few hours' sleep before I went out on patrol. I didn't find out about Donovan until the next morning, when I heard about it on the radio."

Sept watched him as he answered, and from her experience he was telling the truth. "You were here that morning? I don't remember seeing you."

"They had me driving around the east. People were looting some of the houses where folks have tried to come back and rebuild, so there was a push to put more people on the streets. I volunteered to help, so I couldn't get out of it. You know how shitty things have been on the street."

"And getting shittier by the day, my friend. Did you see anyone hanging out around here or doing some drive-bys lately?"

Al smiled and gave a short wave to a group handing their car keys over to the valet. "It's amazing how many regulars the girls have here. I've learned the faces of lot of these people, but none jump out as strange." He pulled out a pack of cigarettes and offered one to Sept, then lit his and took a deep drag before he continued. "I've stayed on some nights when Donovan was in there doing his experiments, as he called them. He was an interesting fella who had a fucked-up life before he started working for the Blanchards."

"Fucked up how?"

"Not every parent is accepting of their children's choices as yours and Mrs. B., Sept. Donovan told me his folks threw him out when he was sixteen and never came looking for him with a case of remorse. I wonder if they even know he's dead." Al flicked his ashes into a glass ashtray. "On nights I didn't have to be anywhere early the next day, I'd stay and talk to him. Maybe if I'd been here that wouldn't have happened."

"You know better than to dwell on *what ifs*, Al." Sept looked down the street in both directions to see how many of the windows were lit. Maybe they'd missed a witness, but she saw only the same places she and Nathan had canvassed. "Can I ask you one last thing, and it stays with us?"

"Ask away. You don't have to worry about me shooting it up the flagpole."

"Standing out here, have you ever seen another patrolman or a regular unit who does some drive-bys? That might strike you as strange, but I really need to know."

"Just the regular guys assigned to the neighborhood. They cruise by, but I wouldn't say it's a nightly thing. You looking for more witnesses or something?"

"Nah, I had an idea, but you make me think I'm on the wrong road. Thanks for your help, man." She handed him one of her cards and shook his hand again. "My cell's on there if you think of anything else."

"Will do, and if you need to talk to me here's my number." Al took a pad from his front pocket and wrote his number on a blank sheet and tore it out.

Sept headed back inside but didn't want to go through the restaurant, so she walked to the side to make her way around to the kitchen door out back. Unless Al was some master killer as well as an accomplished liar, he wasn't the missing piece to her theory.

Inside, she watched as Keegan worked, running her kitchen like a machine with every part functioning perfectly. Mike hadn't moved from his spot on the floor, and Sept spent some time petting him, being careful to stay away from the tender spot where he'd been stabbed. For a wounded dog, Mike was the most docile animal Sept had ever been around.

"Five dead people, and a city full of cops and military personnel. If I'm right, this shouldn't be hard at all," she said, and laughed.

## CHAPTER TWENTY-EIGHT

At a little after ten, the kitchen slowed down and Keegan walked back into the office with the night's numbers. She dropped everything into the top drawer of her desk and held her hand out to Sept. "Take me home. If you're still hungry I'll make you something when we get there, but right now I want to go."

"Why? You looked like you were having fun in there."

"It only takes one person who thinks food needs to be the consistency of shoe leather to be safe enough to eat to sap the fun out of the night. Every once in a while we get someone who sends stuff back so often you want to ask them to go home and cook it themselves, since we obviously don't know what we're doing."

"Don't worry. You're done cooking for tonight. And for future reference, I won't ever send anything back unless you feed me liver." Sept put Mike's leash back on and opened the door for them.

"Why? How do you like liver prepared?"

"I wouldn't send it back because you cooked it wrong. I'd send it back with a note asking what the hell you were thinking, because I hate liver, in case you've forgotten." She shivered for better effect and Keegan laughed. "You can make me sleep on the couch if you want, but don't ask me to eat liver."

"Noted, Seven, and we have a problem." Keegan held Sept's hand and walked close to her. "Good night, everyone, and thank you for a great night," Keegan told the staff as they made it to the back door.

"What's the problem?" Mike was pulling on the leash like he wanted to lead, and Sept let him, to see where he'd take her. The trip ended in the garden, where he stopped to mark a tree.

"I'm in the coupe, and you'll have a hard enough time squeezing in there, even without Mike." When Keegan said Mike's name, he came to her and sat so his head was under her hand. "You up for another walk?"

"Sure. That might be good for him, since he's used to it."

The night was cool but Keegan unbuttoned her top. "Think about how many years Robin must have done that. She couldn't know some crazy person was waiting for her. That's the thing that hits me the most when I read about stuff like that or watch it on the news."

"What's that? We can compare notes." The neighborhood was quiet as they strolled to St. Charles Avenue, and Sept was happy to see that a lot of the houses not only had life inside, but some Christmas decorations.

"When someone decides to cross the line and start killing people, we're the ones who have to change our lives." Keegan sounded disgusted as she leaned into Sept. "We're the prisoners even though we're following the law."

"That's why I love doing what I do. What you're saying is true, but it's up to me to make you forget about things like that."

"You said you'd tell me what's going on with this guy you're chasing."

Sept gave enough details so that Keegan could visualize what they were up against, but not enough to make her sick. She finally told her about the autopsy she'd been to that day and what they'd found. The note still didn't make any sense, but now something on the edges of her brain was starting to take shape. Nothing solid yet, but it would eventually come to her and she'd feel like an idiot for not thinking of it before.

"He put a religious symbol inside her chest?" Keegan asked as she grasped Sept's waist tighter. "Isn't that taking your faith to an extreme?"

"I'm sure God is used to people doing things in His name, but this guy isn't interested in the run-of-the-mill religion. He's into something called Santeria, and from what my Tulane professor tells me, he's calling the dead."

"I don't mean to change the subject, but what does Brandi Parrish have to do with all this, and why do you keep going to see her?"

A few joggers were on the wide median of St. Charles, and most of them waved at Sept and Keegan.

"Tameka was the first girl he carved up as what he assumed was a sacrifice, and she was one of Brandi's employees."

"You're such a diplomat, honey."

"Well, technically Tameka was her employee," Sept said, and kissed the side of Keegan's forehead. "When we found her she still had her ID on her, and I recognized the address. I didn't know the second girl we found, but from her clothes I could guess what she did for a living. I went to see Brandi today because of the old saying."

"Go ahead and tell me, because I have no idea what you're talking about."

"The whole 'it takes one to know one' concept. Frieda didn't work for her, but Brandi knew who she was."

When they were in front of Keegan's house, Mike stopped walking and sat next to Sept. He barked once and shook his head. "I think he's asking you for a coffee break," Keegan said as she took his leash off. "So he's targeting prostitutes."

"If it were that simple I could probably give Vice a good description of what to look for and be done with it, but it's not. I don't think he's targeting any one person or profession. He's not a sexual sadist or a calculating killer. I think opportunity motivates him." After visiting three shrubs Mike came back and barked again, so Sept put his lead back on.

"But he took so much time with some of his victims, including Donovan, that it doesn't make sense to me that he's an opportunist."

Sept took them the back way so she could grab her bag. "His victims are what I meant. He doesn't strike me as the classic hunter most serial killers are, but he obviously watched us that night at the levee. That's why I'm serious about you being careful."

"I will. I don't want to be a sacrifice for anything." The house was quiet and Jacqueline's car wasn't there, so Keegan didn't shout for her. "Did you find out what tragic thing happened in his life that would make him call the dead in such a unique way?"

"What do you mean?" Once the door was closed, Sept let Mike off his lead and watched him as he went on a quick smelling tour around the kitchen.

"You don't think he's trying to reach George Washington, do you? If he's come up with this elaborate calling plan, he must want to talk to someone he lost that didn't sit well with him."

"Why do you think something tragic happened to him? The guy could just be nuts."

"I'm not saying he isn't, but if something happened to someone like Jacqueline, I might want to talk to her again, even if she was dead. Trust me, I'd draw the line at cutting people up to do it, but it would be tempting." Keegan put her arms around her. "If you had the chance, wouldn't you want to talk to Noel and Sophie again?"

Sept's phone rang, and even though she didn't recognize the number on the screen she answered. "Savoie."

"Sept, I hate to bother you, but I thought of something and didn't catch you and Keegan before you left," Al said.

"What's that, Al?" Sept asked so Keegan would know who she was talking to.

"No one stood out walking or driving by the restaurant, but someone did walk by twice in the last couple of months. He didn't make much conversation, but he was friendly enough."

"Anyone I know?"

"You know him well enough to be related to him. It was your brother-in-law, Damien. When I first saw him, it took me a minute to place him, but it was him. Poor guy looked lost, but you said to call if I thought of anything, and that's all I've come up with."

"Thanks, Al, that helps. One other thing, were you working the next night?"

"I was tired as hell from being on the early shift, but I was there. I didn't want to disappoint Keegan and the others."

"You didn't happen to see Damien that night, did you?" Sept tried her best to keep her voice calm.

"No."

"Thanks again, then, and remember to call me no matter how trivial anything you think of might seem."

The word "fuck" exploded in her head at what Al had said. When she'd seen Damien in front of Estella's, she'd thought he was simply restless and wandering around, but placing him near Blanchard's showed more of a pattern. Perhaps Damien wasn't just trying to work out his grief on his own. The implications made her want to throw up.

"What's wrong?" Keegan asked when Sept let her phone drop on the counter. "You're white as rice. What's the matter?" she asked again when Sept didn't answer.

All of sudden the note they'd found in Frieda's chest made perfect sense. *I want a second chance.* Of course Damien wanted a second chance, so he could evacuate Noel and Sophie before the storm surge killed them. *I will serve until you see how worthy I am.* He would keep killing until he got that chance. *I want back what was stolen from me.* After months of thinking about it, that's what he'd come to believe. His wife and child had been stolen from him, and no matter how many more people had to die, he was determined to get them back.

"Sept, honey, you're scaring me. What's wrong?" Keegan put her hands on Sept's face as if to get her to focus.

"Sometimes what you seek is right in front of you, but you want more than anything to be as blind as Robin Burns so you don't have to see it."

"What are you talking about?"

"About nothing I want to prove, but I think I know who did this."

# CHAPTER TWENTY-NINE

You can't be serious," Keegan said, followed by a laugh that was more nerves than humor. "Sept, your sister was married to this guy. I might not know him, but if Noel was anything like the rest of you, she'd never share her life with someone who's capable of the things you told me."

"If this was July of this year, I'd say you were right. He couldn't possibly have dreamed this up, but this isn't July. Damien talked Noel into staying put and it killed her. That fact changed him into someone I don't recognize and don't really want to get to know." Sept took the chance that Keegan and Jacqueline kept their vodka in the freezer and opened it in search of a bottle. She poured herself a small glass, but Keegan took it out of her hand and shook her head.

"That was the answer when you didn't want to let anyone in, sweetheart, but those days are over. If you need a crutch I might fit better." Keegan pressed herself to Sept's side and lifted Sept's arm over her shoulder.

"I already have a mother," Sept said, and closed her eyes at how harsh that sounded.

"Trust me, I'm not applying for that job. But, like Damien, you didn't talk to her or anyone else, did you?"

"What was I supposed to say? That I missed my sister, that when she died I lost something of myself that I'll never get back? I could sit with some shrink every week and cough up all my feelings, but for what?"

Keegan let her go and stepped slightly away. "If you want to drown yourself and any feelings that might actually help you get past what happened, go ahead. I can't force you to talk, and I sure as hell can't force you not to kill off another slew of brain cells with Grey Goose. But you can do it somewhere else, because I refuse to watch."

The urge to leave gripped Sept around the throat so tight that she came close to walking out the door. "I don't need to drink. It just helps sometimes to numb the stuff I'm tired of thinking about and can't do anything about."

"That's not numbing anything, and you'll never truly get over missing someone who was that important to you."

"Gee, thanks," Sept said with a laugh. "I feel so much better now."

"I didn't tell you that to make you feel worse, Seven. What happened to Noel and Sophie unfortunately can't ever be undone, but you can honor what they meant to you by learning to be happy again." Keegan came back when Sept opened her arms. "Do you think if things had been different and you had been lost in the storm, Noel would've made Sophie stop finding things to be happy about because you were gone?"

Sept kissed her forehead. "Does this mean you're applying to be my shrink?"

"I'm applying for the 'something to be happy about' job. Please don't think I'm trivializing what happened to your family, but I want you to trust me by letting some of that anger and sadness out." Keegan lifted her arm and made a muscle. "I'm tougher than I look, believe me. I can handle it."

"I'm sure you can, since we got through our first fight in less than ten minutes."

"You showing up at my restaurant and accusing me of murder was our first fight, sunshine."

Sept put the glass in the sink without drinking any of the vodka and took Keegan's hand to lead her to the sofa. "That wasn't a fight. It was more like you ranting at me and me not kissing you to get you to pipe down."

"For a cop, you sure have a faulty memory."

They laughed, but as soon as they sat down, Sept sighed about what had upset her in the first place.

"Unfortunately, my memory is too good sometimes, and some of the things that didn't make sense before now fit perfectly in a scenario I don't want to contemplate."

"You don't really think Damien could've done this, right?" Keegan took her top off and leaned back against Sept's chest in only her undershirt. "How about in exchange for cooking lessons you give me detective lessons?"

"I don't have any proof, but think about this." She explained what Julio had said about calling the dead, the fact that no evidence was left at any crime scene except the bodies and decorations, and that when they worked together, she and Damien had answered a call to the store where Estella's books were stolen. "It's not a slam dunk, but the first thing my father taught me was that there was no such thing as ghosts."

"What does that mean?" Keegan asked as she massaged the back of Sept's neck.

"That's what hasn't clicked for me until now. When we're called out on a case, the killer usually leaves something behind. Not necessarily fingerprints or DNA, but something like a footprint or other clue." Sept thought through all the crime scenes, and the closest to a tip-off was the impressions in the blood next to Donovan's body.

"You haven't found that at any of these murder scenes?"

"I have a plain footprint at Tameka's scene, and knee prints in blood at Donovan's. That's it, and who better to cover up a murder than a cop?" Mike joined them on the couch and, when Keegan started petting him, plopped against Sept's other side. "I've never thought of committing anything close to murder, but if I did, I'd know exactly how to get by with it."

"What kind of cop is Damien?"

"He never wanted off the streets, but he would've made a good detective. Some guys love the streets so much they have a hard time sitting and waiting for the next job to come along, so they stay in the patrol car."

Keegan stopped Mike's rub-down and sat up. "What kind of father and husband was he?"

"Noel wasn't a complainer, but if he'd been anything other than what he portrayed she would've said something. She never did, so to me he was excellent at both jobs. Why?"

"I just don't think a good father stabs people through the heart because his wife and child died in a flood. It doesn't make sense, but I'm sure you have a job to do."

"I do, but right now I'm interested in going to bed." Sept stood up and pulled Keegan to her feet. "Go on up. I'll be right behind you."

"Do you want anything?"

"I'm just going to let Mike out one last time. I'll be in time to tuck you in." Once Keegan was up the stairs Sept did let the dog out, but she also called her older brother Gustave. After briefly summarizing what she'd been talking about with Keegan, she asked, "Can you and Jacques take turns tonight keeping an eye on him?"

"I don't have a problem doing that, Sept, but there's no way this is true."

"No one wants that to be true more than me, but I can't let family blind me. If I wake up tomorrow to another girl with her guts spilled out on the floor, I don't deserve to wear this badge."

"Okay, but tomorrow morning I want a meeting with you and Dad so you can tell me everything that brought you to this conclusion. Pinning someone, no matter if we know them or not, isn't like you."

"I'm not accusing him of anything, and I'm sure as hell not going to take the easy out on this, Gustave. I just want to be sure."

"That's good enough for me. We'll keep him under surveillance tonight, then I'll call François and Joel to pick it up in the morning. Get some sleep. Dad told us how hard you're working this."

Mike followed her up the stairs and to Keegan's room. He started sniffing all the furniture in the room again as she undressed and headed for the bathroom. When she came out he was lying on the blanket Keegan had put down for him, his eyes already closed.

"Everything okay?" Keegan asked.

"Not yet, but I'm working on it," Sept said as she pressed up to Keegan's back and kissed her neck. "Good night and thank you for not kicking me out for being such a butthead."

"And have you go running off to Brandi Parrish? Not on your life, Seven." Keegan laughed. "I might not kick you out, but making you change places with Mike might be a possibility."

"I'll try to remember that."

# CHAPTER THIRTY

The next morning when Sept opened her eyes, Keegan was already awake and practically lying on top of her, so Sept caressed the soft skin of her back. "This'll give me something to think about later today when I have to meet with my father and tell him my theory."

"Meeting with your dad is a great idea, no matter what you're thinking about." Keegan laid her head on Sept's chest and fanned her hand over her breast.

"Why do you think so?"

"You're tenacious if nothing else, honey, and until you prove Damien didn't do it, you won't be happy." Keegan propped herself on her elbows, put her hands on the sides of Sept's head, and pulled her hair slightly. "Am I right?"

"I do want to be wrong this one time. Right now I'd rather think about other things." Sept rolled them over so she could better touch Keegan down the length of her body.

"Have I told you how sexy I've come to think white hair is?"

"Lucky for me I happen to have some," Sept said before she took Keegan's nipple into her mouth. "That's how I feel about the color red."

She took her time making her way down Keegan's body. This time Keegan didn't stop her as she came to rest between her legs and spread her sex open. "You okay?" she looked up and asked.

"I will be in a minute, unless you stop. Then there'll be a lot of pinching going on."

Sept moaned when she lowered her mouth, but not as loudly as Keegan. It took only a few passes of her tongue to make Keegan's hips start to move. She kept her mouth in place as Keegan grabbed her hands and interlocked their fingers. When Keegan pressed down, almost breaking her fingers, Sept sucked her in and didn't let go as Keegan rode out the orgasm.

Keegan smiled lazily as Sept took her in her arms and rolled her over again. They lay there as the sun started to rise outside and Mike yawned next to the bed. "I forgot he was down there," Keegan said.

"If you don't tell him we were fooling around, I won't," Sept said. "Stay put and I'll be right back."

"You're leaving now?"

"I'm going to let him out. If you come home earlier than I do you, can you spend some quality time teaching him to use the toilet so I won't have to get up," Sept said, and patted Keegan on the butt. "I won't be long, I promise."

She put on the T-shirt and boxers Keegan had laid out for her and headed downstairs to the kitchen door. Mike did his usual sniffing tour before he picked an acceptable tree. As they returned, Mike led this time, and in the room Keegan had propped the pillows against the headboard. "Think he wants to watch television?" she asked as Sept stripped again. As soon as Sept sat down Keegan straddled her thighs.

If the question had been serious, Keegan didn't wait for an answer as she put her hand between Sept's legs and stroked her until she grew rigid. Sept opened her mouth to the kiss Keegan initiated, but had to break it off as the orgasm ripped through her much too fast for her liking.

"Tonight I'll take the scenic route, but you looked so good I had to have you now," Keegan said after she placed a series of gentle kisses along Sept's jawline. "I hope you realize how glad I am you're in my life."

"Hopefully you'll feel that way for a long time." Sept opened her eyes and was surprised to find Keegan's swimming in tears. "What's wrong?"

"I'm happy, and this is what happens when it gets a little overwhelming. Sorry. And why wouldn't I feel that way?"

"Relationships are hard, and being in one with a cop makes things a little more difficult. I'm waiting for you to get fed up with the hours and the scars that cases like this leave behind." Sept shrugged, but she believed that honesty either dispelled your fears or brought them to a quicker realization.

"You asked me who in my life made me feel so inadequate about my appearance. It was this woman I dated for a couple of months before I couldn't take the little snide comments anymore and threw her out of my life." Keegan moved her hand up and placed it between them.

"Okay." Sept dragged the word out, not understanding why Keegan had shared that with her now.

"I'm not trying to change the subject, Seven. I'm trying to make a point."

"Which is?"

"I know what I want, and I'm not going to punish you because of what you do for a living. We might not have a lot of history on our side, but in this short amount of time you've made me feel…" Her voice cracked and one tear escaped.

"It's okay, baby, just say it."

"You make me feel beautiful, and wanted."

Sept wiped under her eye with the pad of her thumb. "You should feel that way because you are, on both counts. But if anything is bothering you about the job or you have any questions, promise you'll tell me."

"Only if you'll tell me what you're doing, like you did last night. I won't run to the press and leak what we talk about. Knowing what you're working on helps me worry less. Crazy, huh?"

"Not really, and last night helped me as well. I can go over something a million times, but sometimes saying it out loud makes me think in a new direction."

Keegan rested her forearms on Sept's shoulders and put their heads together. "Then we'll talk a lot, make love, cook together, and before you know it you won't be able to live without me."

Mike barked once and put his paws on the bed. "Considering you're the only woman I've ever introduced to my mother, and who's talked me into keeping a dog, I'd say we're off to a good start."

After they showered together, Keegan sat on the bed and watched Sept dress. Sept winked at her as she strapped on her gun, and Keegan smiled. "I did forget to ask you one thing."

Keegan stood up and handed Sept her badge. "What's that?"

"This idiot who made the snide comments, what was her name?"

"Mercy Alderson, why?"

"The gym owner Alderson?"

"Thus the snide comments about the fact that I don't have a six-pack." Keegan ran her fingers along Sept's abdomen. "You, she'd love. Forget her, though. Believe me, there's nothing to be jealous about."

"I didn't ask because I was jealous. I just want to know who to do the extensive traffic stop on whenever I get the chance," Sept said before she turned and opened the door for Mike to go out first.

"You're kidding, right?" Keegan called after her, but all Sept did was laugh.

❖

Keegan made them all an omelet for breakfast, and she and Jacqueline sat and watched Sept as she listened to someone on the phone. She was pressing her thumb down so hard on her fork it was starting to bend.

"You told me you two could handle it," Sept said. "Great, you can explain that to Dad this morning." She snapped her phone shut and expelled a long breath. "Fuck."

"You don't like my eggs?" Keegan asked, in an effort to break the tension on Sept's face.

"Sorry, I love your cooking. It's my brothers who need a kick in the ass."

"What'd they do?" Keegan asked.

"I called Gustave last night and asked him to keep an eye on Damien until we talked to Dad today," Sept said, then took a bite.

"I'm not sure when you accomplished that, but okay. What happened?"

"The two ace police officers lost him around eleven when he walked to the docks." Sept glanced at her watch and started eating faster. "I'll tell you about it tonight, but I have to go so I won't be late."

"Call me later," Keegan said.

"Be good and remember to be careful," Sept said as she bent down and kissed her. She put her jacket on next and kissed Jacqueline on the cheek before she left. The door closed behind her and Mike sat up as if to see what was going on. A second later the door opened again and Sept stuck her head in. "You want me to find someplace for the dog today?"

"His name is Mike, and I thought we agreed to keep him."

"I didn't mean give him away," Sept said, and shook her head. "More like doggie day camp or something."

"Honey, parts of the city don't have running water yet, and you think there's a doggie day camp open?" Keegan put her hand on Mike's head and scratched him behind the ears. "Go to work, and I'll think of something so he's not here all day by himself."

"See you tonight," Sept said, and winked before she closed the door.

"Let me get this straight," Jacqueline said when Sept didn't come back. "She has brothers?"

Keegan laughed. "Here I thought you were going to ask me about the dog."

"Actually, I'm glad to see a dog in the house. If not, I was going to have to ask you what you did to her earlier to make her bark like that," Jacqueline said with a laugh, and Keegan figured that's why her ears were suddenly hot. "But back to my question, she has brothers?"

"Five, but most are married."

"Which means some aren't." Jacqueline persisted. "Are they anything like Sept?"

"I met them last weekend at dinner, but I mostly talked with Sept's mom and her sisters-in-law. If you want, you can tag along this time, but you either have to cook or paint. Pick painting and you'll see all the eligible Savoies in action."

"You have a deal." Jacqueline tapped the top of Keegan's hand with her fork. "Now tell me about the dog."

Keegan gave her the short version of what Sept had told her the night before, but left out most of the details. She hoped Jacqueline wouldn't ask about Sept's recent phone call and why it had upset her so much.

"So what do you plan to do with him this morning?" Jacqueline asked.

"I thought Mom might take him until you're done later and go pick him up." Keegan smiled sweetly and batted her eyes at Jacqueline, trying to act innocent.

"Stop it before you sprain something on your face. I'm tied up with Gran all day, so you'd better pray Mom is in a babysitting mood."

"Let's hope she is, and isn't in an asking-questions mood."

"Ha, when isn't she?" Jacqueline asked. "Your best bet is to drop Mike off and tell her he's her new grandchild. That should shock her long enough for you to escape."

"I tell her that and she'll handcuff me to a chair until I tell her everything." Keegan got up and Mike followed her to the sink. "Come on, buddy, it's time to introduce you to the rest of the Blanchard clan."

# CHAPTER THIRTY-ONE

Gustave and Jacques were already sitting at a table with coffee and beignets in front of them when Sept arrived. The waiter followed her and took her order for just coffee. "Okay, explain how you lost him," she said.

"We'll give you all the details as soon as you explain why we were tailing Damien in the first place," Jacques said.

"If that's how you want to play it, let's wait for Dad and we'll get screamed at all at once," Sept said. "You know I wouldn't ask you to do something like this if it wasn't important, no matter who the person is."

Sebastian emerged from the backseat of his car and tapped on the window to send his driver away as he nodded in their direction. When he sat down he pointed to the coffee cup and beignets, then folded his hands in front of him. "I'm looking at a lot of gloomy faces. What's up?"

"Sept had a crazy idea that she wants to share with you," Jacques said before he shoved a whole beignet in his mouth.

"You do know that if he wants you to answer something, having your mouth full isn't an excuse to not answer, right?" Sept asked as she shook her head.

"It worked when he was three, so he thinks it still will," Gustave said with a laugh.

"What's the crazy idea?" Sebastian said.

Sept went through her whole rationale, combined with the fact that Damien was in the vicinity of the first crime scene. Her father didn't appear convinced until she explained Julio's supposition of the killer's motives and Keegan's innocent question as to why someone would call the dead. After that, all three Savoie men put their elbows on the table and leaned forward.

"I'm not saying it's him…at least not publicly, until I can prove it. A big part of me wants nothing more than to believe in that guy we all knew when he started dating Noel. There's no way in hell that guy does this, but Damien has changed. After what happened it's like he's touched in the head," Sept said, and felt disgusted. "If by some wild chance Damien *is* doing these killings, I don't want another body on my conscience."

"Where'd he go last night when you followed him?" Sebastian asked his sons. Jacques picked up another beignet and shoved it into his mouth, so Gustave answered.

"Jacques drove until Damien parked and started walking. Then I followed on foot. He left Lakeview and parked on the cusp of the Marigny and started from there," Gustave said, talking about the Foubourg Marigny just below the French Quarter. "Since the streets are so deserted by then, I had to give him a pretty good head start, but I kept up until he got to the Quarter and went up there." He pointed to the steps next to Café Du Monde that led up to a plaza built so you could get over the seawall.

"You lost him after that?" Sebastian took a bite of his own beignet.

"I even called Jacques so we could split up, and we couldn't find him."

"So basically you lost him in the one location where a man was stabbed through the heart simply so the killer could use his blood to finger-paint a seven with a line drawn through it on the poor bastard's forehead?" Sebastian was obviously keeping his voice down only because they'd picked a public place to have this meeting.

"We didn't lose him on purpose, Dad, and Sept didn't explain everything to us. Not that it would've made a difference," Gustave said. "He flew up those stairs and disappeared when he got to the other side."

Jacques finally spoke up. "We're all forgetting Damien might be a little off, and who wouldn't be, considering, but he's a good cop. He disappeared last night because he spotted us and his training kicked in."

"That's what worries me the most about this case," Sept said. "Dad, you always taught us to look for the clues because there's no such thing as ghosts, but this guy is just that. He leaves behind the blood and shit he needs to complete his rituals, but nothing else. No fingerprints or DNA. Nothing that would give us a lead. He's not a ghost, but whoever it is knows damn well how to scrub a crime scene to leave it pristine."

"All right, before we go hanging the boy, find him and bring him in for an unofficial chat. He's been calling about wanting my help to get back to work, so use that angle. I want to see for myself if there's anything to this," Sebastian said. "If he won't do that, then bring him to Sunday dinner and we'll all talk to him there."

"We'll do our best," Sept said as Gustave and Jacques nodded.

From there, Sept left to pick up Nathan and headed for Damien and Noel's house. She hadn't been there since the day she tied a boat to the roof in search of her sister.

She parked in front, next to the nondescript white FEMA trailer Damien was living in, and stared at the ruin of what was once the center of Noel's dreams.

"Nathan, I'm going to trust you with some information, and I don't expect for it to go any further than here for now. Do you understand?"

"You can tell me anything. We're partners, and even if it's temporary, I'm someone you can work with and I'm watching your back." He turned slightly to face her. "What's wrong?"

She told him everything. "There's a chance Damien's doing this." She then described what had happened to Noel and Sophie. "I'm sure you know all this from the gossips in the department, but their deaths probably snapped something in him."

"Let's see if he's here, and we'll play it however you want."

It didn't take much imagination to picture Sophie playing in the front yard, especially the way she used run toward Sept whenever she came over. A lump formed in Sept's throat when she saw the little bicycle she'd given Sophie for her birthday lying in a rusted heap in the yard. Damien apparently hadn't moved anything since the water had gone down, probably to preserve some sense of the family he'd lost.

Nathan knocked on the trailer door, and when no one answered he banged on it with his fist. In between the knocking, the television blared from what looked like a white aluminum box. It was the only noise that broke through the depressing stillness that enveloped the place.

"He's not here," Nathan said as he walked around the trailer, trying to peek in the windows. "Want to search the house?"

"Sure, since he was nice enough to leave the door open." If she found something, they most probably wouldn't be able to use it without a court battle, but she needed to know more than she needed to follow the rules.

No one had touched the inside since the day of the storm. The pictures still hanging on the wall had become blobs of color, and the furniture gave off a rotten odor that made Sept's nose itch. A clean patch on the doorjamb to Sophie's room appeared to have come from Damien standing there and gripping the area to stay upright as he grieved.

From what she could see, the only spot in the house that received regular visits was the master bedroom. The surface of the bed was rumpled as if Damien had just gotten up, but the sheets were rapidly disintegrating. "What the hell are you doing, Damien?" she asked herself as she scanned the room for anything more out of the ordinary. If she'd listened to her mother she'd have realized how off track Damien was becoming.

"You want me to put out an APB on him?" Nathan asked.

The word yes was ready to leave her lips, but she held back, granting Damien one last shred of trust. "Give Gustave and Jacques a day to find him. They know all his haunts, so it shouldn't take long."

"Are they joining our team?"

"I'm sure they bought in after last night. Let's look closer at the place, and then we'll drive around and see if we spot him."

Sept put on gloves and searched the rooms for anything to tie him to the victims that had crowded the morgue since Donovan went down. She couldn't find anything in the bedroom, which would be the most likely place, since the rest was definitely untouched.

That left only the trailer, and again she wanted to take a look inside. She had Nathan wait outside while she picked the simple lock and went in. Every surface in the place had old food wrappers piled up, and dirty clothes lay heaped next to the bathroom. He must have slept on the small couch and stared at the television, because the bedroom was untouched, unlike the one in the house.

She slowly went through everything and had to stop occasionally to wipe her nose, irritated by the stale smell of urine that permeated the rooms. Damien had apparently given up on life, and only his constant wanderings kept him from blowing his brains out. When she found his uniform she wanted to vomit. It hung neatly in a cleaner's clear plastic bag on the back of the bedroom door, as if he was preparing to wear it.

"What the fuck is this, Damien?" she asked as she raised the plastic covering and ran her finger along the badge and ribbons he'd pinned in their rightful place. "Are you going on some patrol no one knows about?" Damien's gun and utility belt were in the top of the closet, and she took them with her and placed them in her trunk. If by some wild chance they missed him, she certainly wasn't giving him the edge of a weapon.

"Come on," she said to Nathan. "Let's drive and see if we spot him." She forgot all her plans for the day as she drove toward the French Quarter and the last place her brothers had seen Damien. "Gustave," she said into her phone.

"Found something?"

"More questions than answers." She turned down the street that would lead them to Café Du Monde and parked closer to the docks than the café. "Listen, I need you to pick up his car and deliver it to Uncle George. Have him go through it, and tell him to call me if he finds anything."

"Already on it. I had it towed an hour ago, and George and Alex are examining it right now. Dad reassigned Jacques and me for now, and we're out looking for Damien."

"What'd you tell George?" Sept shut her door and headed toward the docks.

"I didn't have to, he recognized it. All he said was they'd take care of it and call when he was done. Where are you?"

"At the docks." Sept stopped at the edge and peered toward the benches where she'd brought Keegan. Everyone in her family knew she loved the spot, and Damien was part of her family.

"We covered that already."

"I'm not here expecting to find him. I want to check something out." She walked slowly along the slope of the levee.

"What are you doing down there?" Nathan asked as he followed her from the top.

"Looking for evidence. When we found Frieda's body I didn't have a chance to get back here." She came back up and joined him until they reached the bench, then carefully climbed down over the rocks until she was close to the water. "Sit on the bench and let's try something," she called up to Nathan. She took her time until she found a place with flat rocks.

"Are you sure you don't need help?"

"If you sit you'll be helping enough." She crouched, praying something had been left behind, and in a crack in the rocks found the evidence that proved what she already knew. The gold button resembled the ones on the pockets of the NOPD regulation uniform. "If you're looking over the water, can you see me?" she asked Nathan as she sat down and stretched her legs out.

"Not really, and if it was night, you'd be invisible unless you made noise."

Damien had put on his uniform and lain here as she told the story she was sure he didn't want to hear again to a woman who, unlike his, was alive to hear it. "Is that what made you mad enough to kill two innocent people? No matter what, this has to stop, Damien."

❖

"I thought today would never end," Novice said as he lay back in the abandoned backyard and enjoyed the stars as they started to appear.

"You did well in carrying out my instructions," Teacher said, the voice again authoritative and distinctly male. "You managed to make it through the day in the disguise everyone recognizes while you listened to what I had to say."

"Of course I did, I'm not an idiot." Novice pulled his hair in aggravation. "It was hard not to laugh out loud at Sept and the others as they chase their tails. They're no match for me, and I'll prove it tomorrow night."

"Are you sure you're ready?"

"I plan to take another step toward my goal, which means Chango will have to wait, but it'll show Sept how close I can come to her without her finding me." The slight breeze picked up the hair that had fallen on his forehead and Novice combed it back.

"You're playing a dangerous game. If you get caught, who do you think will protect you?"

"You were a stupid bitch when you were alive, which makes me wonder why I'm trying so hard to talk to you." He screamed so loud his head hurt. "Sound like my father all you want, but we both know I own you. So shut the fuck up and stop threatening me."

"If you don't want to hear me, then you won't," Teacher said with finality, and disappeared in a way that Novice knew he was gone.

"I said don't threaten me," Novice yelled, and laughed, but heard only silence. "Come back, you know how I get. I can't help it if I get mad, but it's your fault anyway."

The creaking of the child's swing set, its loose parts blown by the wind, was the only response. Novice closed his mouth and his mind to Teacher's voice, but he didn't have to try hard, because it was gone.

"Shut up if you want, but after tomorrow when the gods finally notice how faithful I am, you'll beg me to come back. I'll give them and the hunter something they won't soon forget."

## CHAPTER THIRTY-TWO

Y ou accused my granddaughter of murder and now put her in danger?" Della asked Sept as they had dinner that night in the kitchen at Blanchard's. "I don't know about your family, but in ours that's not how we define progress."

"Mom, I'm sure Sept didn't want anything to happen to Keegan," Melinda said. She put her hand over Sept's as she spoke. "And that's a lovely dog you both have now, dear," she told Sept.

"Thank you." Sept smiled and continued eating.

"You two got a dog together? What's next, monogrammed towels?" Della asked, but nodded to the waiter when he refilled her wineglass. "We'll discuss the domestic stuff in a bit, but right now I want to discuss how Keegan's in danger from some nut."

As Sept took another bite of steak, she didn't say anything, but she studied the four women. When she'd showed up after Keegan's call, the rest of the family was already waiting at the chef's table in the kitchen, including someone she hadn't previously met, Melinda Blanchard's girlfriend, Carla St. John.

"Sept hasn't done anything wrong, Gran, and I'm not in danger since I'm sure she'll catch whoever this is," Keegan said, her hands on Sept's shoulders.

Since Sept's arrival, Keegan hadn't moved very far away from her and hadn't said much. "Thanks for the confidence," Sept said.

"Keegan, didn't you have something to show Sept in your office? You mentioned it earlier," Jacqueline said, her finger tapping her wineglass in a way that seemed to annoy Della.

Sept pushed away from the table even though she hadn't touched half her plate. After the door shut, she closed all the blinds so the eyes trained on the room couldn't see what was going on. "Your version of 'guess who's coming to dinner' boggles the mind, sweetheart."

"It's not like I planned this," Keegan said, her arms wrapped tight around herself. "It's their version of a job performance review."

"Then you certainly don't need me here," Sept said.

"Why wouldn't I?"

"Obviously Della would rather see you with a dentist or someone with the right name," Sept said, realizing that with each word out of her mouth she sounded increasingly childish.

"Funny, I thought I made my own decisions about who was in my life, and I was even more under the impression it was you." Keegan moved forward, since clearly Sept wasn't going to. "Are you mad I didn't tell you about Carla?"

"I'm curious why you wouldn't."

"Carla's a new addition to my mother's life, and I don't think of her as someone to trot out in the family receiving line." Keegan stopped and leaned into her without dropping her arms.

"You did say that was a story for another time." Sept put her hands on Keegan's hips. "In case you missed it, this is another time."

"My two moms raised us. Melinda was our birth mother and Sybil Calhoun was her partner. They were way ahead of their time. We lost my mom Sybil six years ago to lung cancer, and Melinda has just started dating again." Keegan rested her ear on Sept's chest. "I'm having such a hard time seeing her with someone else that I feel like I'm ten, so I'm sorry I didn't mention her before now."

"Della doesn't have a girlfriend, does she?"

Keegan laughed so quickly she snorted. "She's as heterosexual as Jacqueline, and once you spend more time with Jacqueline you'll see how man-crazy she is. And to clear something up, Della doesn't dislike you because you're not a dentist. She doesn't trust you yet because you're dating her granddaughter—there's a difference."

"She thinks I want to take advantage of you?"

"I certainly hope so." Keegan finally looked up. "I thoroughly enjoy it when you do. That's why I asked you over. I missed you today."

Keegan's gaze made Sept want to make some profound declaration, but it was too soon for that. No one dropped to one knee and said *I love you* so soon without the other person thinking they flew some major freak flag.

"Is there…" She didn't know how to finish the question.

"What are you thinking so hard about? Remember that life is sometimes like cooking fish—simple is best."

"Is there some way to tell you how much I care about you without scaring you off?"

"I think you just did," Keegan said, and stood on her toes and kissed her. "Think you can face the rest of dinner now?"

"Sure. It'll give me good practice for Sunday brunch, since I'm sure I'll be the headliner again. Unless Jacqueline decides to bring one of those tattoo artists from the Quarter as her date."

After waving Keegan off when she offered to bring her a fresh plate, Sept pulled her chair back in and picked up her fork. As it approached her mouth, her phone rang and she came close to laughing at the sour expression on Della's face. "Sorry about this but I'm on duty," Sept said, standing up and moving away from the table before she answered it. "Savoie."

"I'm at the lab and wanted you to know that the note we found in Frieda Hearn's body came back completely clean," Nathan said.

"Nothing on the paper or the printer?" Sept walked to the back door but stayed inside.

"I had them check everything, and they said in both cases it's the most common type used. They can probably tell you what kind of printer it came from, but there's like a gazillion out there."

"I'll give this guy credit. He sure is stingy with evidence. Even if it is Damien, we'll never prove it unless we actually catch him in the act."

"I know you're having dinner, so I checked with Gustave and Jacques. They're taking a few hours off, then they'll get back to it, but they haven't had any luck."

"How about the unit at his house?" Sept laughed when Keegan took her plate and dumped the contents in the trash and threw another steak on the grill.

"They just changed shifts, but nothing so far. Your dad put the word out quietly with a few guys he trusts that he needs to talk to Damien."

"Thanks, Nathan. I'll pick you up in the morning so we can do some of the canvassing ourselves." She hung up and dialed her father's number. After it went to voicemail, she said, "Hey, Dad, if it is Damien and you have him delivered to the house, make me the first call after you receive word. I know how you and Mom feel about him, but you've seen the crime scenes. He's got a problem, and I don't want that to hurt you or Mama."

"You don't have to go, do you?" Keegan asked.

"I'm not that lucky," Sept said before slapping her gently on the butt and giving her a quick kiss. "Sorry again for the interruption," she told Keegan's family when she sat again.

"Actually, it's nice to see someone who takes her job so seriously," Della said in an abrupt about-face. "It makes me feel better about paying my taxes."

"Keegan gave you a hard time while I was on the phone, didn't she?" Sept said with a laugh.

"That should tell you how much she likes you," Della answered with a laugh too. "Even though you look like someone who can take care of herself, she did give us a stern talking-to. You should know that my granddaughter seldom gets so bent out of shape about anything but bad food. Hopefully you'll live up to all her concern."

"Don't worry, Mrs. Blanchard and Ms. Blanchard." Sept turned to Melinda. "Keegan is in good hands."

"Make sure if we're talking about your hands and Keegan that you behave," Della added in a way that made Sept start to think she was making headway with her.

The rest of dinner was more relaxed and Sept excused herself after dessert to see about Mike. She'd left him in the garden with a few toys and a bowl of water. The area was fenced and he was sitting close to the bench under one of the oak trees when she stepped out. He'd evidently lost the ability to play, or forgotten that side of himself when he became a work dog, so she tried to spend a few minutes a day trying to get him to relax by throwing him a ball.

He sat up and trotted over with the rubber cat Keegan had bought him and dropped it at Sept's feet. "Did Keegan feed you, boy?"

"He had dinner before you got here," Keegan said from behind her.

"At this rate he's not going to want to leave your side."

"If I keep feeding you, do you think you'll feel the same way?"

Keegan brought her out another cup of coffee and put her arm around Sept's waist.

"Even if you didn't. How much longer are you going to be?"

"We're busy tonight, so at least another three hours. Think you can be done with whatever you have to do by then?"

"I want to take another drive through Lakeview and see if I spot Damien. I need to find him before this gets out and some trigger-happy idiot takes care of it for us before he gets his fair shake. He deserves that." The need to go was pulling at her, but not as strongly as the need to stay. "I'll be an hour at most, if you promise not to go home without me."

"You've got no worries there. I'll wait however long it takes for you to get back, since I've been looking forward to going home with you tonight. Go ahead, and I'll say your good-byes for you. Take Mike along for company."

Sept drove to the neighborhood, hoping to catch a glimpse of Damien in the shadows. She knew he must be running after Gustave and Jacques had followed him the night before. The thought that desperate men only got more that way when they felt cornered made her expand her search and send a prayer up to Noel that she would find him before anything else happened.

It was past eleven when she got back to the restaurant and Keegan. Diners were still in the downstairs area, and the kitchen was in high gear when she walked in, so she sat at the now-empty chef's table and watched as Keegan walked from station to station making sure everything was up to standard. In the commotion surrounding her, Sept let her mind wander, not letting herself get bogged down on any one thing.

Once Keegan had finished and turned her way, Sept pondered the rest of the evening and how she wanted it to go. If how she felt about Keegan wasn't clear to her before, this was the biggest clue of all. Before now, no matter what was happening in her life, the case never stopped for her. She'd work until she dropped, and after a few hours of sleep she'd start again. The case was still in the fringes of her mind, and she knew every day brought her closer to the answers she sought, but at that moment feeling Keegan pressed against her until the sun rose again was the most important thing to her. It's what made the days worthwhile.

## CHAPTER THIRTY-THREE

S ee you guys tomorrow." Roxie Stevens waved to her partner and the two others they worked with and got into her car. After the storm their assignments had changed somewhat. Electricity might not have returned to large swatches of the city, but prostitution had.

Vice was slowly getting back to what they did best after being reassigned to things like search and rescue and patrolling the more desolate areas when the looting started to increase and make the news. Now they were back on the street trying to nab those who turned to sex to make an extra buck or forget their problems. Saturday night in the French Quarter was beginning to liven up with the holidays, and Roxie was glad she'd started that diet she'd promised she'd stick to after Thanksgiving—spandex was the most unforgiving fabric she'd ever had the pleasure of wearing.

She stopped at the A&P grocery store in the French Quarter and shook her head when the older gentleman who usually checked her out gave her a wolf whistle as she headed for the door. He obviously liked her undercover clothes, and she was glad he didn't ask her for a date. It was almost midnight, but she craved a bowl of Cheerios before bed and her work schedule had left her pantry empty. "Bowl of cereal and getting these damn shoes off sounds better than winning the lottery," she said to herself as she parked as close to her apartment on Royal Street as she could get.

Roxie grabbed her two bags and purse and juggled them to go to the other side to grab the last two bags. If she could avoid making two trips up and down the stairs, her aching feet would appreciate it. Novice seized on that moment of nonattention as he brushed off the sleeve of his uniform. The shoes were the only thing not regulation. He'd spent nights filing down the soles to get rid of any distinctive tread.

"Hey, is it quiet tonight?" Roxie asked when she spotted him under the streetlight. She was coming around to the other side of the car for the rest of her things. "Or is something going on I don't know about?"

"You know how it is," Novice said, and shrugged. "Can I help you with that?"

The bag with the milk and eggs was the only one left. "You don't mind? It's been a hell of a night and I'm ready to sit down."

"No trouble." He took three of the bags from her and waited for her to show him the way. His skin prickled as they passed Sept's apartment building. He'd spotted Roxie the previous night and followed her home. Once he'd seen where she lived, he'd decided where his next altar would be.

Her garish shoes clicked on the pavement in a steady beat as she moved to the next building, but Novice didn't take another step. If she was ready to get off her feet, he was ready to accommodate her. "Can I ask you something?" Novice said, in an attempt to make Roxie turn around.

"What's—" The rest of what she had to say was replaced by her loud moan as her body twisted violently when the leads of Novice's Taser gun connected with her chest. The jar of pickles she'd picked up shattered when she dropped the bag, but all Novice did was cock his head to the side as he waited for her to pass out from the electric current. "No one can tell me I'm not blessed by the gods," he said as he put her grocery bags right inside the door that led to the stairs. He placed his hands under her arms and dragged her up the stairs, then picked the lock.

This would require another gag, but the location was worth the silence as he worked, since what he was getting ready to do would not only frustrate Sept beyond reason. It would also get Teacher to talk to him again. This time he had everything he needed, including one of the books he'd taken from Estella's store. He wanted to get this one right for two reasons. People sacrificed things for love to this god, who was married in the higher realm to Chango the warrior god.

"You're the luckiest one so far," Novice said to Roxie as he put a red rose behind one ear, then stripped off his shirt. "What can be nobler than to give your life for love?"

When Novice used his knife to cut through her clothes, Roxie pulled on her bindings, as if she knew what trap she'd fallen into. He sliced everything until she was naked, then took time to fold the pieces and lay them at her right foot. From his kit he took five copper pennies and lined them up along her forehead, only to have Roxie shake her head and knock them off.

"I can see you're going to be uncooperative," he said, and without warning plunged the knife low enough that he imagined it went through her womb. He paused before he took it out, as the memories of doing this before made him almost forget that he couldn't linger too long. "It doesn't matter, though. There's always more than one way to do something this important."

He dug his fingers into the hole he'd made and wet his fingers with her blood. Carefully, so he wouldn't leave any fingerprints, he smeared a large swath across her forehead and waited for it to start to dry. That's what he used so the pennies would stay put, even though Roxie still had the strength to fight him.

"I call on Elegua to open the door I want." He drew the shepherd's hook under Roxie's left foot. "And I call on Oya to show me the land of the dead." He drew the number nine under her right foot. "The one I love lives there with my child, and I want them back with me."

He took the candles out next and lit a yellow and a red one and put one on each nightstand. "When you get there, order them back," he told Roxie. Her eyes opened wide as he raised the knife again and stabbed her in the lower belly once more, but this time he brought the knife up and toward him.

The act felt so good that he stopped when he reached her rib cage and was surprised he was breathing heavily. A swell of conflicting emotion settled over him like a bucket of warm water poured over his head. He was turned on, humbled, and grateful all at the same time because this woman he barely knew was willing to do this to help him get what he wanted.

"I'm glad you were willing, because I couldn't do it, no matter how much someone needed it."

He spoke to the lifeless body as he put on a pair of gloves for what he had to do next. It wouldn't take long, since he figured Sept was predictable, and when he opened the closet he saw he was right. The box she used to lock up her gun was on the shelf in the closet toward the front. That went next to Roxie's head, and inside he put a small piece of coral and a sprig of rosemary. In the top he sat the statue of Our Lady of Charity with the note he'd written.

*You walk in the land of the dead, but not for long. If the warrior tries to stop me from what I need to do, that's where I'll send her and those she loves. Remember that I fear no man or woman, and there is no place that I can't enter to do what needs to be done. Nowhere.*

He stared at the altar he'd built and tears blurred his vision at the power that came over him. Sept seemed to have locked all of her strength in this box. "Only one thing missing," he said, as if he were checking things off a grocery list.

Roxie's heart came out easily and made a dull sound when he dropped it on the bottom of the box. He then searched Roxie's purse. He hadn't cared to search the others' things, except to find Frieda's name, but they didn't possess an NOPD badge. He took it out of its cheap leather holder and drove the fastener through her chest over where her heart had been. He wanted Sept to have no doubt of what he'd taken.

Laughing, he stepped into the bathroom to wash the blood off his arms. After he put his shirt on and tucked it into his pants, he walked around the apartment to see how Sept lived.

"This is the house of a warrior," Novice said, as he turned in a slow circle in the main room and saw no personal objects. "I weighed my life down with the emotional baggage of a family, but I took care of that."

"You did, but it's still haunting you, isn't it?" Teacher asked.

Teacher was criticizing him again, but Novice knew only that Teacher was back and as thirsty for more as he was. "I told you I'd keep going until I was rewarded, and tonight's special."

"It's actually genius," Teacher said with a small laugh.

Novice puffed up like a peacock and ran his hands along his chest. Then he noticed the button on his breast pocket was missing and panicked. He ran back into the bedroom and dropped to his knees next to the bed, but the damn thing wasn't there. After searching for over twenty minutes he still couldn't find it.

"Sept," Madeline called up the stairs. "You up there?"

From his calculations, the neighbor was early. He'd have to do something about her because the stairs were the only way out.

"You okay? You dropped all your groceries down here." Madeline climbed the steps holding the bags. "Is this some ploy to make me carry your shit up?" She made it inside the door, her usual cigarette hanging from her lips. "Where do you want this?"

Novice swung his baton at her head and watched her crumple to the floor. "Filthy habit," he said when he ground out her cigarette under his shoe.

"What about the button?" Teacher asked.

"It's probably at home or the dry cleaners." He put his cap on low on his forehead. "I'm not worried about it."

"You should worry about everything, especially the small things. The small leaks, not the big cannon shots, can sink you."

"Right now I'm only interested in one thing, so don't ruin it for me." He packed everything he'd used in his bag and flung it over his shoulder. After checking the apartment one last time, he picked up Sept's phone and dialed her cell-phone number. It rang only three times before she answered, but he wasn't worried since she was with Keegan Blanchard again. He'd be long gone by the time she got here.

"Savoie," Sept said.

"Ask yourself why the gods have forsaken you," Novice whispered as he admired his work one last time.

"Who is this?" Sept asked. "And how did you get into my house?"

"Who am I?" He continued to whisper. "Someone who has not."

"Not what?" Sept asked. Novice could hear the siren in her car and laughed. Sept would never make it in time.

"Been forsaken by anyone. Have a good night, warrior. You'll need it." Novice put the phone down and took a deep breath. The smell of blood filled his lungs and intoxicated him. "You'll spend plenty of overtime on this one, warrior, but you don't have enough hours in the day to find me."

The smell from the broken pickle jar permeated the stairwell as he descended, but the siren sounded close. It couldn't be Sept, but he took the rest of the steps in a run, and on the street he forced himself to walk slowly until he reached the corner a hundred feet away. Once he reached it he ran, because the screech of tires meant Sept or someone else had already reached the scene.

"I'm not worried about anything," Teacher chanted repeatedly as Novice's lungs began to burn, until he reached his car and threw everything in the passenger seat. His hands shook so badly as he took out his key he had to try several times to put it in the ignition. He was safe, but the fear was making him crazy, though not enough to speed out of the area like he'd run. After another deep breath he turned on his radio and started for home so he'd be ready to continue the game when the call came.

"I'm not worried. See, no matter how close she is," he said of Sept as he listened to her call for backup from the front of her apartment, "it isn't close enough." He *had* heard her siren. Perhaps Keegan wasn't as enticing as Novice had thought.

"No woman is going to make her lose her focus," Teacher said. "Unlike you, who let a woman drive you to distraction."

"If you think that, you don't know anything about me." He banged his fist into his steering wheel. "I got rid of my distraction, in case you forgot."

"Yes, but you didn't leave it buried, did you?"

## CHAPTER THIRTY-FOUR

Get over here now," Sept yelled into the phone as Nathan and she stepped around the spilled bags of groceries. "And get units on the streets looking for anyone dressed like a cop. I don't care who they are. Detain them until we finish here."

The apartment's front door was open, and she sped up when she heard moaning. Whoever was inside was still alive. "Nathan, you with me?" she asked, even though he was pressed almost against her back.

"Right here, partner."

They went through the small place slowly, with guns drawn, ignoring for now the two women they glanced at. Everything about the scene practically screamed how close they'd been—from the water in the bathroom sink to the off-the-hook phone.

"Madeline, can you hear me?" Sept knelt next to her and put a towel to the back of Madeline's head, but all she did was moan. The cut had bled enough to stain the back of her white uniform shirt. "Nathan, call for a bus and for the team to get over here."

"You do realize that's Roxie Stevens in there, don't you?" Nathan asked as he came from the bedroom.

"Let me call my father and take care of the living first. Maybe we'll get some idea of who this fucker is, then I'll worry about who he left on my bed."

Sebastian finally answered his phone. "Dad." Sept motioned Nathan over to hold the towel to Madeline's head. "I need you to come to my apartment, but drop Mom off at Blanchard's before you go, unless one of the boys can sit with her."

"What's going on?"

"He left another one for us in my place, on my bed," Sept said, and her father simply hung up. Her next call was to Keegan. "Hey, sweetheart."

"Hey, there. Promise me a vacation when all this is over. It's a sin that we're both working on Saturday night. You left so early this morning it feels like days since I've kissed you."

"You got it, and as soon as I see you I'll kiss you a month's worth, but right now I need to know if Al's working tonight." Sept walked into the bedroom, and any memory of the morning she'd spent with Keegan in this room was replaced with what she was staring at.

"He's outside as usual, why?"

"I have another one, and he left her in my apartment." Sept stopped when Keegan gasped from her end. "This one might take a little longer because I know her."

"Another of Brandi's girls?"

"A fellow officer from our precinct who worked Vice. I'll tell you all about it, but right now I need to talk to Al."

"Hold on," Keegan said, and her voice was replaced by soft classical music.

Al came on. "Hey, Sept, you need something?"

"You're on the city clock now, Al. I need you to stick with Keegan until she's done. See if you can get Jacqueline there as well, then escort both of them home and sit in the house until I get there. I'll have my father call your superior and give him the heads-up on this. Don't let anything happen to them." Sept could see that Roxie's eyes were still open.

"Do what you have to do and take your time, I got this end covered."

"Thanks, Al, I owe you." Sept waited for him to put Keegan back on.

"Honey, do you need anything?" Keegan asked.

"Stay with Al, and tell Jacqueline no dates tonight. Be safe, and I'll be there as soon as I can."

"Seven, you're in more danger than I am, so you take that advice too, okay? Gran was over here again tonight asking about you, so I can't have anything happen to you. You've evidently broken through her hard shell."

"All I care about is breaking through your defenses, babe. Having your grandmother like me is an added bonus. Talk to you later."

The ambulance had arrived while Sept was on the phone, and when she stepped back into the front room Madeline was on the gurney with her neck secured. Her eyes were open but her pupils were noticeably different sizes. She motioned Sept closer.

"Sorry if your place is trashed. I came up to make sure you were all right, but this happened," Madeline whispered, as if talking normally was too painful.

"Don't worry about the place. Did you see him?"

"Hit me from behind." Madeline was panting as she closed her eyes. "Sorry, it hurts like a mother."

"Take it easy and let them check you out. I'm the one who's sorry, but thanks for looking out for me. I'll be by the hospital later to check on you."

After the paramedics left, only those designated to Sept's team were allowed access. George and Alex took pictures, then searched for fingerprints. Sept barely paid attention to them as she checked for anything missing. In the closet, a blood trace stained the edge of the shelf where the killer had reached for her safe box.

"Man, I'm glad I'm not the one who has to inform Roxie's family," George told Alex as he swirled his powder brush along the headboard of the bed. "I never worked with her, but she seemed like a sweet girl."

"We never met," Alex said.

"Makes me want to call all my kids and make sure they're all right," George said as he pulled prints from the section he'd been working. "You want them to grow up and be happy, but when they're out of the house and you see shit like this, you go crazy."

"Makes me glad mine's still young," Alex said.

"How old's your little boy now?" George asked him.

"Almost four, and I really miss him."

"Where is he?" Sept asked with curiosity.

"My wife and son are living with her sister in Mississippi until we can do something about our house. She didn't think it was safe to be around while we're rebuilding, and the trailer FEMA gave us is barely big enough for me, so they visit when they can."

"That sucks," Sept said, and put her hand on Alex's shoulder. "I'm sure you miss them."

"It's tough, but a lot of people are in worse shape than we are, so I'm not complaining."

"Anything, guys?" Sept asked.

"Probably a good set of your fingerprints on every surface in here, but we won't be able to tell until we run all these," George said.

"You gonna read the note?" Alex asked.

"I have to wait until we get it back to the lab later tonight, but y'all will be the first to know." Sept gave the box and all its contents to one of George's men, who put the whole thing in a bag and tagged it, then left it where it had been found.

"Sept, Commander Savoie's here," Nathan said.

"Another present for you, kid?" Sebastian put his arm around Sept since they were alone in the small foyer outside her apartment. "Tell me you're a step closer to stopping this shit, because I just came from Fritz's office and he's losing patience with the slow progress."

"We're still looking for Damien, if only to question him, but there's no sign of forced entry." She pointed to the door. "We didn't find any fingerprints except probably mine, and he called my cell right before I got here. If Nathan and I had left ten minutes earlier we'd have him in a holding cell with the blood still drying on his hands."

"Are you absolutely sure this is Damien?"

"Dad, I'm not sure about anything. Aside from everyone else in the family, Damien is the only one who knows where my extra key is, and none of you did it. I'll admit a lot of people have my cell-phone number, but how many of them could've pulled this off?"

Sebastian walked through the place to the bedroom and grimaced when he saw the death mask frozen on Roxie's face. "Have you had your hocus-pocus guy interpret the scene?"

"I'm sure he'd love your description of his profession," Sept said as she glanced at Nathan.

"He's on his way, sir," Nathan said. "I called him twenty minutes ago."

Julio arrived as George and Alex were finishing their field work. "I should know what we're up against now, but each time I join you I'm more appalled."

"With any luck this will be our last one, Julio." Sept shook his hand and tried to refocus him. "Take your time and make notes, if you want. We must be missing something."

Julio stood close to Sept as they studied the now-familiar wound pattern. "Whoever's doing this is probably a novice."

"Why do you say that?"

"Because the gods he's sacrificed for have made sense to me, but not this one." He pointed to the five pennies stuck on Roxie's forehead in blood. "This Orisha is Oshun, the god of lovers, who is married to the most powerful of the Orishas, Chango, the warrior god. Did he remove the heart again?" Julio asked after he glanced at the burning candles with nothing next to them.

"He did, but he placed it in something this time." Sept pointed to the safe box now encased in an evidence bag. "It's where I keep my gun when I'm at home. Why doesn't this one make sense?"

"The first one opened the door to the other gods, and the second god had power over the dead. He's obviously trying to talk to the dead, but no one would ever sacrifice something, much less someone, to a god who watches over lovers. You give Oshun gifts that reflect the living, not the dead." Julio studied the safe box and scratched the top of his head.

"So this one is called Oshun, what else?"

"She is represented by Our Lady of Charity and is married to the warrior god Chango. If this had been done in his name, I could understand. Those whom Chango favors usually get what they want, since none of the other Orishas want to go against him." He turned and faced Sept, appearing to have thought of something. "Whose house is this?"

"Mine, though I haven't been here much lately." Sept peered up from her notes and tapped her pen on the page. "Why?"

"I'm no psychiatrist, but I don't think this was a sacrifice. Well, partially one, but more like a gift to you."

Sept ran a hand along the top of her head, making her hair swirl in crazy directions, but she didn't care. "Now you lost me."

"Think about where this was done and who he killed."

"I knew Roxie, but we were never lovers." Sept's face got hot since her father was standing nearby.

"That's not what this is about. You're chasing him down, and he knows that somehow, and he killed someone you work with where you live. It doesn't get any more personal than that."

Sept told him about the killer's phone call while he was still in the apartment. "He called me 'warrior.'"

"Then the next god he'll try to impress is Chango. By calling you warrior he must think you're already a favorite of the warrior god, but in his mind he's better, since the other Orishas are helping him. I'll put something together for you, but I want you to meet someone." Julio stepped out of the room and took a deep breath once he was well away from the bedroom. "I realize you put no faith in this religion, Sept, but this person can give you more insight than I can."

"Insight how? You've done a great job so far."

"I believe, and I'm a high priest because I know the academic side of things and all the rituals. But you need to meet with the high priestess Matilda Rodriguez. Matilda is the best conduit between the world of the Orishas and this one that I know."

"If you can set it up, I'll be happy to go." Sept held her hand out to him. "Is there anything else?"

"What did the note say? If you can't tell me, I'll understand."

The bag was still in the bedroom, and Sept wasn't opening it here no matter how curious she was. "I'll tell you what. If you want, you and Nathan can drive it to the lab, and once all the tests are done, you two can read it."

"I'm glad you trust me this much. The killer's evolving. The books didn't mention the sacrifice, but he got it right this time, all the way down to the pennies."

"Actually, he's gotten it right twice. In the rush to chase down some leads, I didn't get a chance to show you the first note. We found it in the second victim killed like this."

Julio nodded almost absently and didn't seem to realize he was still holding Sept's hand. "Can I see that one as well?"

"Sure, but remember our deal. You can't share this with anyone, especially the notes, since those won't be released to the press until we know we have the right suspect behind bars."

"You have nothing to fear from me, Sept. I'll see you later," he said, and finally released her.

## CHAPTER THIRTY-FIVE

The night dragged on as Sept took the place in sections, starting at the foyer downstairs close to Madeline's apartment. She only left for a few minutes to talk to the clerk at the A&P about when Roxie had made her purchases. With Nathan at the lab, Sebastian helped her work the scene.

"What's your take so far?" Sebastian asked as Roxie was put in a body bag and carried away.

"She left work and he followed her. This one was specific and targeted at me."

"Why do you think that?"

Sept held her finger up as she called the hazard cleanup guys to arrange for them to take the blood-soaked items to the lab. "I'm following my instincts."

"What's the scene telling you?"

Sept sat on the hood of her car and took out her notebook. "Roxie was on duty tonight on the new crackdown in the Quarter. She got off, went to the grocery, and was planning a night in, from what the clerk said. Our guy must have followed her from the station house and grabbed her in front of my place. I didn't realize she lived so close to me."

"Still, the distance from her place to yours could've made it a spur-of-the-moment thing."

"If it hadn't been for the call to me afterward and how he staged the scene this time, I might agree with you, Dad. The note tied around that little statue might give us what we need to know for sure."

Sebastian sighed and stared up at the window to Sept's bedroom. "I've been to all these, and I just don't see Damien doing that." He folded his arms over his chest. "Does that make me sound crazy or gullible?"

"No one wants to believe someone they love is capable of this kind of violence, and if it's him, I can only blame the stress of what happened." Sept mirrored his actions and followed his eyes up. "If it turns out to be Damien, I'll always be ashamed for not realizing how much trouble he was in, but I'll do my job."

"If it's him, all of us will do our job. Stress is one thing, kid, but your sister would die a thousand more times if she knew this." Sept could tell he was angry. "I think of Noel and Sophie the first thing in the morning and right before I go to sleep. You know I'm not much on praying, but after you mentioned who you suspected, I started praying you were wrong for once. Your sister's memory deserves better than that."

"I'm not sure, Dad, but he's the only one I can put near any of the crime scenes who lost someone recently and has knowledge of these rituals."

Sebastian's back straightened. "What the hell makes you think that?"

Sept told him about the robbery they'd investigated together at Estella's bookstore years earlier. "We didn't talk much about it afterward, but Estella's mother told us what the place was about and offered us a session if we were interested. When you're grasping at straws trying to dig yourself out of a deep depression, anything can pop into your head. Maybe on one of his walks he passed there and he used the little knowledge he had to get to this." Sept shrugged and yawned. "Stranger things, you know."

"You need to get beyond conjecture and on to some solid facts." Sebastian put his hand back on her shoulder and squeezed. "I have faith in you to get us there."

"Thanks, Dad, that still means a lot to me." Her phone rang and she hoped it was Keegan. She wanted to hear her voice after the day she'd had. She checked the called ID before answering. "Hey, Nathan, you have anything?"

"They went through everything in the bag, and like before, there was nothing we could use, but the note confirmed what Julio told you." Nathan read it to her. "I'll drop a copy off to you before I head out."

"Why in the world does this guy think I'm a warrior?" Sept said, and pinched the bridge of her nose. This case had more turns than a roller coaster and none of it made any sense, but she had no patience when people started doing weird shit in the name of religion.

"Julio had a theory about that," Nathan said.

"What? I don't hide my sword and shield well enough?"

"No, you ass, but you do handle yourself in a way that would please this god Julio keeps going on about. He called that lady he told you about, and she's waiting for us at nine tomorrow morning."

"Good work, Nathan. I'll meet you at the office first."

"Anything else you want me to do tonight?"

"No. They're locking up the scene now and I'm heading over to Keegan's for the night. From what that note said, I'm not comfortable leaving her alone at all."

"Take care, and call if you want me to do anything."

"You're a good man, Nathan. Good night."

Sebastian laughed and stood up after glancing at his watch. "You can thank me later for the great partner. He seems like a quick study."

"You're just happy you found someone who puts up with me, or at least has for more than a week. Go home, Dad, and I'll see you and Mom tomorrow." She hugged him and kissed his cheek.

"We're wiring the upstairs back part of the house, and don't forget to bring Keegan. I'm sure there's a bunch of things your mother and the girls haven't told her about you yet."

"Not funny, old man." Sept walked him to his car and closed his door once he was behind the wheel. "Drive safe and kiss Mom for me."

"You too, and don't take your eyes off Keegan if you can help it."

"Don't worry about that," Sept said with a wink.

❖

"You almost got caught, but you rallied well," Teacher said as they drove home. "Even the warrior was impressed by what you were able to accomplish."

"I killed some bitch right under her nose in the one place she's used as a revolving door for women. That life of filth isn't hard to work around," Novice said as he took off his shirt and admired the whiteness of his chest in the mirror. "You might think she's strong, but she's really a weakling with a penchant for picking up whores."

"Still, her record is impressive since you're the one who's bragged on it for so long. Even your wife got tired of hearing about it."

"I wasn't bragging about Sept, you idiot. I've always hated that smugness she wears like that damn leather coat. It makes me want to hurt her."

"Are you sure about that? Like I said, your wife got tired of listening, but she might have been hanging on your every word, wanting to know what it was like to spend some time with a weakling who loved to screw around like she knew what she was actually doing."

"I don't care how hard I have to work, but as soon as I can feel you and touch you, I'll be tempted to stick a knife so far into your chest that you won't be able to bother me again." Novice slammed his fist so hard into his chest that he coughed. "Why the fuck are you even here, if you're just going to make fun of me?"

"I'm not teasing you, Novice. I'm only trying to make you better than anyone who's come before you. You've finally caught the eye of those you worship so well. You give them what others are not willing to, especially Chango."

"Tell me what I need to know," Novice said as he slapped his knife against the side of his pant leg.

"The woman you killed tonight had power because of who she was and what she did for a living. The other two came easy because they carried no real consequence if you were caught." Teacher's voice was still male, but it was as seductive as any lover. "A cop, though, that carries consequences, and it pays off in the power you gain."

"Do you mean another one like that one, and I'll get my wish?"

"Remember, the harder the sacrifice is to make, the louder it shouts to the land of the dead. If you pick the right one, the god you want to attract can't possibly continue to turn a deaf ear."

"Who carries that much power?" Novice asked, feeling like a young boy asking for a treat from his mother.

"Think about what you want and how Chango will finally throw that door open for you to walk through at will. It will take a thousand whores or just one worthy opponent. Who do you think that is?"

"You want me to kill Sept Savoie?" Novice was surprised at the question, but he wasn't opposed to the target.

"Who carries more power? Didn't you feel it tonight when you held her things in your hands? That wasn't your imagination working overtime. It was real, and it can be ours for eternity if only you have the courage to see it through."

"Then we'll leave her a trail of bread crumbs to lure her where we need her?" Novice walked to the window of the bedroom and looked out at the backyard. Sept would die there, where her blood could soak the ground and make his dreams grow into reality.

Novice laughed at how good simply the idea made him feel. For the first time since his wife had left him, he felt alive and full of purpose. His days would no longer drag out like roads through the desert.

"Don't get too comfortable in the land of the dead, my love. Soon you'll return to me, only this time you'll be mine so completely that I won't let you go."

"That can be true, if you do your part. To attract a god, you must bring down his greatest disciple."

## CHAPTER THIRTY-SIX

Please tell me you don't have to go to work," Keegan said with her eyes still closed. "I want to stay here all day."

"I'd love nothing better, but you're not talking me into something that'll make Della come down on me like a ton of bricks, young lady." Sept put her arms around Keegan now that she was fully awake. "And I can't tell you that I'm not working, because I am, but only for a while."

"That sucks. Today's Sunday." Keegan's whine woke up Mike, and he trotted to Sept's side of the bed and put his paws right next to her.

"I see, she's in charge of feeding you, but the other not-so-nice chore belongs to me." Sept kissed the top of Keegan's head and pulled the covers back so she could get her shorts on. It was two minutes past seven when she glanced at the clock, and as she went downstairs she felt slightly tired, but nothing like when she woke up from one of her nightmares. "Go on, boy, and I'll take you for a walk later."

Mike ran around the backyard a few times before he flew past her and up the back steps. When she made it back in, he was lying in her spot with his head down and his tail wagging, almost as if he anticipated that she was about to play with him. Instead of shooing him off right away Sept looked at what she considered a perfect picture. Keegan and Mike defined happiness for her and made love possible.

"I'm sure if you ask nicely he'll move," Keegan said, and smiled as she held her hand up in invitation.

Nicely wasn't what Sept thought Mike wanted, so she wrestled him off the bed and laughed as he licked her face between barks. When they were done he stayed at the foot of the bed and put his head on his paws.

"What were you thinking so hard about over there?" Keegan asked.

"It wasn't anything bad, I promise."

"If it's good you have to share it." Keegan maneuvered herself on top of Sept as she spoke. "That's the law of good relationships."

"That would explain why I've never had one before now. No one told me that." Sept finger-combed Keegan's hair back, taking time to scratch her scalp.

"Will you think I'm nuts if I tell you that I'm in love with you?" Keegan said, and opened her eyes. In the morning light they appeared as blue as the ocean.

"That's what I was thinking about when I came in. Noel always said, 'When it's real, it'll take the blink of an eye to fall into the one thing you never want to escape from.'"

Keegan blinked a few times, then said, "I'm sure I know what you're talking about, but would you explain a little better?"

"It's probably different for everyone, but last night I realized something about you." Sept rolled them over and held herself up and off Keegan. "I love my job, and before I met you, last night and the days I've been having at work would've been hard to take a break from. Nothing was important enough to distract me from what had to be done."

"I don't want to come between you and your job, Seven."

"You're not. I've discovered that I need both things to balance me out, and in the end I'll be better off for it."

Keegan placed her hand against Sept's jaw. "What do you need?"

"To try and build something with you that makes what I do worth it to me. Up to now I've enjoyed the thrill of the chase, but when it's over I have nothing but the anticipation of repeating it when I'm needed." Sept kissed her and wanted to finish dispelling the uncertainty she saw in Keegan's eyes. "I love you, Keegan, and when I walked in here and saw you and Mike, I realized that I might not have been looking for you, but I found you. I haven't been this happy in forever."

"I guess this means you don't think I'm crazy."

"Not at all, but if you are, it's the good kind of crazy."

Keegan kissed her again. "Could you say it one more time?"

"I love you, and I'd love nothing better than to show you how much, but right now you'll have to take my word for it. Nathan's coming by in a bit and we have an appointment to see a high priestess."

"That's something you don't hear every day. Can Jacqueline and I come with you?"

"Sure. With any luck she'll read your tea leaves so you can be sure of what a great deal you're getting in me."

Keegan pushed on Sept's shoulders to move her. "If she's telling me deep secrets about you, let's get going."

Sept pinned her to the bed and smiled down at her. "Tell me something good and I'll be happy to let you up."

"I love you." Keegan said it, and her body relaxed so much that Sept went down with her. "I do, very much, and I can't wait to tell Della."

"She's not going to ask for a blood sample, is she?"

"More like a criminal background check and a good set of fingerprints." Keegan rolled away, got up, and headed to the shower.

Sept couldn't be sure, but she thought Keegan wasn't exactly making a joke.

❖

"What's the bag for?" Sept asked Jacqueline later when they were all in her jeep.

"Keegan said we were going to your parents' after this, and I thought I'd tag along. That is, if you don't mind."

"I don't mind, but I thought you couldn't cook." Sept looked at her via the rearview mirror.

"I wasn't planning to cook," Jacqueline said sweetly, and winked at her. "I thought I'd help you and your brothers with the house."

"What's the catch?" Sept asked.

"I want to meet your family and help. That's all."

"Uh-huh," Sept answered, but then they arrived at the address Nathan had given her.

As she put the vehicle in park, Sept didn't know what shocked her more, the surrounding area or the house they'd stopped in front of. The lower Ninth Ward had received more coverage than any other part of the city from the time Katrina had come ashore because the area had swirled with more rumors than flood water. A barge had broken free in the canal and caused the levee to give way, and it was still sitting in the middle of one of New Orleans's oldest neighborhoods.

The rumors had sprung up when a lot of the citizens still in their homes, since they had no means of evacuating, heard a series of what they described as explosions, and then the water came crashing in. They believed the government was trying to get rid of an area comprising mostly poor African Americans by flooding them out and blaming Katrina. The mayor's office and the Army Corps of Engineers blew it off as the overactive imaginations of a group already stressed by the situation.

In the end, miles of homes were flooded, and in some cases the elevated homes were carried blocks from their original locations. Driving through the streets that had been cleared, it was hard to accept that so much had been lost in so little time, but the house in front of them appeared neat and totally lived in. The lawn was green, and the wrought-iron fence that surrounded it was freshly painted.

"Either she knows the best contractor in the city or she really can control the gods," Keegan said when Sept clicked open her door.

"Or maybe the tea leaf–reading business is more lucrative than running a restaurant," Jacqueline said.

"Let's see which of you is right," Sept said.

The house wasn't very big, but it had a deep, large porch along the front, and before they reached the steps, Matilda Rodriguez came out carrying a tray with a pitcher and glasses on it. She poured a glass of lemonade for Sept first and handed it to her when she was close enough.

"Detective Savoie, I'm glad you came," Matilda said, with the slightest hint of a British accent. She was dressed in a bright yellow dress with matching head wrap, which wasn't really appropriate for December, but it complemented her light brown skin so well that Sept had a hard time imagining her dressed any other way. "Welcome to my home," she said as she continued to fill glasses and hand them out. "Please sit, since it's so nice out today." Matilda was slight, but her voice held an unmistakable strength.

"Julio said you might be able to help us interpret some things," Sept said as she joined Keegan on a two-seater piece of furniture.

"Do you like your drink or does it need more sugar?" Matilda asked Keegan. "You might not be able to create many sweet things, but you like the taste of sugar just as much as all the condiments you use, don't you?"

"It's fine," Keegan said, and looked at Sept with wide eyes.

"Don't worry. I don't have any more card tricks to share with you to prove I know what I'm talking about," Matilda said, and laughed. "Although you should know that you've chosen well. You two are well matched, but you'll only stay that way by walking the path of truth. That won't be hard, though, since you've fallen for what I believe is the noblest of warriors I've seen in a long time," she said, her words for Keegan again.

"Now that we've gotten Keegan's love life cleared up, do you mind answering a few questions for me?" Sept asked, and opened her hand when Keegan reached for her.

Matilda nodded toward Sept. "What would you like to know?"

"I'm sure you're familiar with Estella Mendoza."

"Estella is one of my dearest friends, as was her mother. Estella told me you had the pleasure of meeting her mother before her death."

"I did," Sept said, then finished her lemonade. "I'm sure you know about Estella's missing books."

"I'll help you with whatever you ask of me, Detective, but I would like to ask you a favor in return." Matilda placed her hand over Sept and Keegan's.

"If it's something I can do, sure," Sept said.

"The books are evidence when you find the man who's doing this, but after that, they must be returned to Estella for safekeeping. They are our only evidence of our history and our faith, and I'm sure you'll do everything you can to get them back to her."

"That's reasonable, Mrs. Rodriguez. What has Julio shared with you?"

Matilda pulled her necklace from under the collar of her dress and ran her fingers along the glass beads. "Someone out there is committing murder in the name of our gods and has no business doing so. Julio didn't share the details, but I could feel the disgust of what he'd seen, just like I could feel the unrest in the land of the dead."

"Uh-huh." Sept was willing to give Matilda some leeway in what she believed, but what Sept needed was facts. "He's been able to walk us through some of the crime scenes, and he thinks whoever is doing this is a beginner who's bending the rituals for his own needs."

"We call them novices, and when they decide to use the faith for ill purposes they are sometimes as dangerous with a little information as a seasoned practitioner is when they decide to use the faith for ill purposes." Matilda closed her eyes momentarily and took a deep breath. "This novice might have started with the faith in mind, but now the taste of blood and the power that comes from it drive him."

"I'm a Catholic, ma'am, and I know that when a person confesses, a priest is bound by his faith to not reveal what that person has told him," Sept said in an effort to steer the conversation in a useful direction. "Are you bound by those same rules?"

"I saw you admiring my house when you arrived," Matilda said, and Sept noticed that Keegan and Jacqueline seemed fascinated by this woman. "Do you know why I'm like an oasis in a desert of destruction?"

"We had a few theories."

"From the day I returned here and found that the storm had washed away much of what my late husband and I worked so hard for, my children have strived to get me back to where I feel most comfortable. And I don't mean just my biological children. From the day I started practicing Santeria, I've had a following of children who seek guidance to see them through hard times and help to find love and all the other things that make us human."

"I'm glad they have such faith and obvious love for you, ma'am, but that doesn't answer my question."

"If you came to me, would you like it if I shared your secrets with someone, even if they were in a position of authority?"

Sept laughed. "That answers my question. What if I tell you my theory of this case and you add any insights. Sort of like one of your consultations."

"Like I said, I'll be happy to help in any way possible, but I can't make you listen to me, especially since you've made up your mind."

"I may not understand Santeria, but I do promise to listen," Sept said as earnestly as she could.

Matilda laughed and all of them smiled. "I wasn't talking about the faith, Detective. I was referring to your case. You've made up your mind and you're not willing to bend. But if you don't, you'll never find the truth, even though it's right in front of you. As for what I believe and how I worship, you're going to be like a donkey."

"You have a polite way of calling someone a jackass," Sept said. She decided even if this was a wasted trip when it came to the case, she was glad she had come.

"I would never do that, but donkeys are stubborn creatures you have to lead to water and sometimes knock them in the head to make them drink. You won't believe what I'm telling you until you catch your killer. That is the true difference between the true believer and the skeptic—faith."

"I agree with you about that and about the fact that this guy is using Santeria as an excuse to kill. But I believe he'll keep using the ritual because in his sick mind he wants what the religion can give him. He lost someone dear to him, and he wants that last conversation with her that all of us would like if we realized someone close is going to die."

"If you know all that, what do you need from me?" Matilda asked as she took a cigar from her pocket and prepared it to smoke.

"I want a place to start looking for someone who might be my killer. Please don't think I'm asking for someone's secrets. I want what my parish priest would tell anyone if someone asked him if I was Catholic. There's no sin in that, is there?" Sept relaxed back into the seat and put her arm around Keegan.

"What do you think you'll get from that list, your killer?"

"Actually, I don't believe that at all."

Matilda struck a match and puffed on her cigar to light it. "Then again, why ask me?"

"Like you said, I have my theory of who, but if I'm wrong, something you and Julio said could lead me in the direction I need to take. A novice is someone who might not know much, but someone in his or her life sparked the quest for knowledge. Your list of names probably won't contain the killer, but I do believe it contains the person who touched this person's life and introduced him to your faith."

"Interesting train of thought," Matilda said. From her other pocket she took a necklace similar to the one she wore and had been touching earlier. She took a deep puff from the cigar and blew the smoke on the strand of red and white glass beads. "I'll give you what you ask for, as well as this." Matilda held the necklace in front of Sept's face. After she took another deep drag from the cigar, she blew around Sept and Keegan's heads.

"I've seen Julio with one of these on, but it was a different color. What are they?"

"You wear a badge so people will know you're a police officer, but this shows believers which Orisha guides your life. You are not a believer, but I want you to wear this for protection. After you leave here you can take it off and have a good laugh at the crazy lady who speaks nonsense, but you are a child of Chango whether you choose to accept it or not."

"Why do you think that?" Sept asked, before Matilda had a chance to place it around her neck.

"His colors are red and white, his image so we'll know him is Saint Barbara, and he is the most popular of the Orishas, but his attacks are sudden and devastating. He is the one Orisha everyone wants to follow. But true children of Chango aren't recruited, they are born. They are unbending in their strength and beliefs, and they will not back down from any situation no matter their fear. Those are the qualities of a true Chango child, and that is you." Matilda placed the necklace around Sept's neck, and Sept didn't stop her. "I want you to recognize all the signs of Chango's identity because I believe he is the next god your killer will sacrifice to, and you will need the protection of your Orisha."

"Thanks, and when this is over I'll bring this back to you." Sept didn't move as Matilda tucked it into her shirt and patted the area over her chest.

"It's my gift to you, Detective, because I want you to know what Santeria truly is. What this man is doing in its name is a travesty, but you will deliver us from this heretic." She then took a sheet of paper off the tray she'd used to bring out the drinks. "Here is your list."

"Thank you." Sept accepted the list and handed it to Nathan.

"Only one more thing, then I'll let you get back to your day." Matilda stepped back so she could address both Sept and Nathan. "Who you seek will only be found by family."

"What exactly does that mean?" Sept asked, and came close to shaking her head. This woman wasn't very different from the card readers around Jackson Square. Anything could become the truth they told you if they were vague enough.

"That's simple enough for you to remember."

"Thanks for your time, ma'am," Sept said as Keegan stood after she'd squeezed her shoulder.

"Please call me Matilda, for you will be no stranger here."

## CHAPTER THIRTY-SEVEN

Do you think she knows who it is?" Nathan asked as they drove back uptown.

"She'll tell you once we do all the legwork and finish our investigation. This guy wasn't hatched, so of course he has a family," Sept said with a laugh.

"Don't make fun of her, baby. She did give you a pretty necklace," Keegan said, then brought their linked hands up so she could kiss the back of Sept's. "Do you recognize any names on that list, Nathan?"

"A few, but the only one I've met is Maria Garcia. That's Lourdes's mother."

"We'll need her working with us this week," Sept said. They had reached St. Charles Avenue and weren't far from the Blanchard girls' house. "Just one second and we'll leave for brunch," Sept told Keegan, once they were next to Nathan's car. She turned to her partner. "It's Sunday and I can't ask you to work, Nathan, but if you have some time, drive around and try to spot Damien where I showed you this week. As soon as I'm through with my family obligations, I'll pick up your slack."

"Will do."

"Tomorrow let's meet with Lourdes and review this list. Matilda probably didn't give us everyone, because it took money to transform that place. I bet a month's pay that the people who paid for it aren't on there."

Nathan folded the paper and put it in his jacket pocket. "You think Lourdes and her mom can expand on this?"

"Can't hurt to try. If it's Damien, I know where the idea would've come from, but if it's not him, maybe we'll see another link."

"Go have fun and I'll get started."

"Call me later, and if you're still out I'll meet you."

When Sept got back into the car, Keegan said, "You could've invited Nathan, Seven. He looked hungry enough."

"I'm sure Nathan wants to take a drive, then spend the rest of the day with his family. If he's smart, that's what he'll do. We have a hell week ahead of us, even if there aren't any more murders."

They arrived at Le Coquille D'Huîte ten minutes ahead of time, but Della and Melinda were already waiting. "Where's Carla?" Sept asked under her breath as they approached the table.

"She usually has rounds on Sunday mornings, so she can't make it," Jacqueline answered.

"Either that or she can't stand facing Gran every week, so she gets dressed and pretends to go to the hospital," Keegan added.

"We can lay bets on who's right and I'll let you know next week, if you want to," Sept said. "I can get Nathan to follow her."

"Follow who?" Della asked.

Keegan kissed Della and Melinda hello. "Sept was telling us war stories, Gran, but it's not dinner conversation. Are we late?"

"I see that you're trainable, Detective," Della said, and opened her arms to Sept.

"I woke up extra early, not to repeat my mistakes," Sept said. She kissed Della, then Melinda, when Keegan cocked her head in her mother's direction. "Good morning, Ms. Blanchard."

"Please, Sept, you're a regular. Call me Melinda."

"She's a regular as long as she doesn't screw up," Della added, and the staff came to attention when Della sat down.

"Gran, you promised to behave," Keegan said as Sept pulled out her chair, then Jacqueline's, and ended up behind Melinda's.

"I will, as soon as Sept answers a few questions." Della gave the headwaiter a small wave. "What happened at your apartment last night?"

"The paper should hire you," Sept said, nodding to the waiter when he placed a bowl of soup in front of her. "I thought we did a decent job of keeping it quiet, so how did you know?"

"I have my ways, so please answer my question."

"There was an incident that involved a fellow officer, and that's all I can tell you right now," Sept said, then tried Jacques's method of evasion and shoved a spoonful of soup in her mouth.

"A dead girl in your bed doesn't sound like a small incident, Sept, and I hope you have the common sense to stay with the girls until this is all over," Della said, watching Sept scoop up more soup. "If you haven't already moved in, let me know and I'll have your things delivered immediately."

"That's so open-minded of you, ma'am."

"I need you there protecting my family. No one said anything about any fringe benefits."

Sept opened her mouth to respond and Keegan kicked her under the table. "You don't have to fall for everything she tells you," she told Sept. "And do we need to review Jacqueline and my ages again?" she asked Della.

"Keegan, I love you but you're ruining my fun." Della appeared in a good mood until Sept's cell phone went off. "I thought we had a deal?"

"I'm not usually this rude, but I can't turn off my phone in the middle of an investigation." Sept stood and handed her napkin to the waiter who was waiting behind her. "Hey, Dad."

"Promise me you'll keep your cool when I tell you this, especially since you're coming over this afternoon."

"What did Mom do?"

"Damien came by late last night while I was still at your place."

Sept felt like punching the wall but contented herself by biting her bottom lip. "I thought you said one of the boys agreed to sit with her?"

"Your mother talked Joel into going to the store for her right after the phone rang. Before you start, I explained why we want to talk to him."

"Was this before or after she told you we were crazy and Damien could no more kill someone than she could grow horns and moo?"

Sebastian laughed from his end. "It was before, and that's not important."

"What'd he say?"

"He wants to meet, but on his terms, and he left a number where you can reach him." Sebastian gave her the number and she wrote it on the back of a matchbook. "Let me know what he says," Sebastian said before he hung up.

"You look like you're about to bolt," Keegan said when she joined her in the entrance to the restaurant.

"Could I use the office to make a call? I don't want to bother anyone if I have to yell." Sept was completely serious. "Depending on how that goes, I'll be right back."

Keegan led her to the event coordinator's office and closed the door behind them, then sat in the guest chair while Sept took the desk chair. The number Sept dialed rang twice before Damien answered. "Don't think of hanging up on me or I will seriously kick your ass when I catch up with you," Sept said.

"Tell me why my family is following me and I might be willing to listen to anything you have to say. Because I doubt Gustave and Jacques came up with that one all on their own."

"Dad wants to talk to you about getting you back to work, and you've vanished. What's up with that? I go by your place and you're not there, you don't call any of us, and you run away from Gustave and Jacques. If I didn't know better, I'd say you're trying to hide something or you feel guilty about something."

"You know what I've been fighting, but I'm not stupid, Sept. You don't send out two guys to tail someone unless you've got something else in mind besides offering them their job back. Don't lie. Tell me why they were riding me the other night."

"Did it ever occur to you that you're part of a family? That when you lost, you didn't lose alone? No, you shut yourself away in that house that's falling in on itself and to hell with the rest of us." Sept knew she was taking a chance talking to him like this, but she had very few options, and guilt and anger were her best bets. "I don't give a shit what you think, but Gustave and Jacques were looking for you because Dad asked them to."

Damien didn't respond to Sept's tirade, and Sept could hear only the wind blowing wherever Damien was. She knew most would try to keep him talking, but she needed the time for him to bite on the bait she'd thrown out.

"Did it ever occur to you that I didn't reach out to any of you because I thought you blamed me for what happened? Hell, *I* blame me for what happened."

"That's a lot to carry alone, brother," Sept said, and meant it. "I can't make you believe me but none of us blame you, and I'm glad you called Mama, because she believes that more than anyone. It's time to rejoin the people who love you, and you've got to know that we aren't waiting to condemn you."

"I can really go back to work?"

Sept locked eyes with Keegan and hoped she wouldn't read anything into what she had to do. To be successful as a cop, you had to know when to bend the truth to the point that you heard the creak that warned you it was about to snap, but that's as far as you could take it. In the rest of her life, Sept had no room for lies and the problems that stemmed from them.

"I told Dad I saw you and what you said about being ready to come back. He thought that was a great idea since the force is so shorthanded right now, and we've been looking for you ever since."

"You all having dinner at the house this afternoon?"

Sept took a deep breath. She could start reeling him in now. "Around four, like always. Why don't you come a little earlier, and we'll get business out of the way before Mama puts out the food."

"I'll be there," Damien said, and sounded the happiest Sept had heard him in months.

"It's a clichéd saying," Keegan said when Sept hung up and closed her eyes to try to ease the pain in her heart. "But it'll be okay. If you're right, a lot of things in your life will stay the same."

"What's that?" Sept asked, and her body came to life when Keegan put her arms around her.

"Damien will still be your family, and despite his faults you'll still love him." Keegan ran her hand up Sept's chest. "He'll be all those good things you remember about him, and because you did the right thing, a lot of people won't have to share what you felt when you lost Noel and Sophie." Keegan moved her hands higher and massaged Sept's neck. "Doing the right thing has its rewards and its downsides, my love, and whatever those are, we'll get through them together."

Sept could smell Keegan's perfume and feel the heat of her body, and she couldn't hold back from kissing her any more than she could manipulate time. And when their lips met, Sept pressed Keegan up against the desk. It was crazy, but she wanted her right then.

"Baby, please," Keegan said when Sept pushed her farther up on the desk so she could reach the hem of her skirt.

"I'm sorry." Sept stopped halfway up Keegan's thigh.

"Nothing to apologize for, if it's something we both want," Keegan whispered in her ear as she reached for Sept's hand.

"Are you ready? I feel bad enough that I've taken this much time from your family meal." Sept started to straighten up, but Keegan grabbed her by the wrist to keep her hand in place.

"I'm ready, but not to go downstairs right this second. It's not nice to make someone this wet, then leave her hanging." Keegan guided Sept's hand down and let go when they reached her underwear. "But if you don't want to be rude, I'll make a bet with you."

"What?" Sept said, and cut off half the word when she pushed the silk aside and felt how ready Keegan was.

Keegan reached for the fly of Sept's pants and had it open before Sept could come up with any excuses as to why they shouldn't be doing this in the Blanchards' flagship restaurant. "If I put my hand in here and you're not wet, we'll go back downstairs no matter how turned on I am, and how much I want you," Keegan said.

Sept was already wet, but if by some miracle she hadn't been, she would've been soaked after Keegan finished talking. "I want you so much."

"Part of my job is to give you what you want when I can," Keegan said, and spread her legs open wider, "and right now I can." As she spoke, Sept buried two of her fingers deep inside her, and Keegan ended her declarations with a moan.

They both fell silent after that as Keegan hooked her legs behind Sept's, and Sept leaned into her when her pants fell to her ankles. Sept's mind went blank as she gave herself permission to enjoy the moment. Keegan reached the pinnacle of her orgasm first, but Sept didn't stop moving her hand as she felt her own coming on.

"God," Sept said, her throat dry from all the heavy breathing.

"And you doubted you'd have fun at brunch," Keegan said as she held Sept and rested her head on Sept's shoulder.

"You must not have explained the menu well enough." Sept kissed the top of Keegan's head and straightened up. "Thanks for that."

"It was a mutual pleasure, baby, and you looked as tight as a fricasseed chicken skin. What's coming might be hard on you, but I want you to remember that I'm here and I will be, no matter what."

"I love you," Sept said, and kissed her before bending down to put her pants back on. "How about we finish brunch, then head to my parents' earlier than usual?"

"Damien's coming?"

"That's what he said, and I want to be ready." Sept helped Keegan down and followed her to the bathroom upstairs. "With my dad and brothers all there, we won't need to call for backup."

"Can we tell Jacqueline a little of what's going on, just in case?"

"If you want, I can take you both home," Sept offered. "Actually, I think that's best, since I don't want you caught in the crossfire if there's any."

"Jacqueline and I know how to duck better than anyone you know, so forget about trying to ditch us."

"Everything okay?" Della asked when Sept helped Keegan back to her seat.

"When this case is over, Mrs. Blanchard, I promise I'll hand you my cell phone when we arrive," Sept said as an apology.

As a waiter put down fresh plates, Della said, "Let me tell you something. While you were gone, Jacqueline sang your praises, and I can see how Keegan feels about you by that sappy look on her face. That kind of devotion doesn't come around very often, and I've been privileged to see it only a few times. As long as it's work dragging you away from our table, you do it well, and when you return, you call me Della."

"The level of devotion is mutual, ma'am, and I have every intention of doing right by Keegan and your family."

"While you're being so noble, you might want the waiter to bring you some club soda before that lipstick stain sets on your collar," Della said, and slapped hands with Jacqueline.

"You would pick now to limit my consumption of vodka," Sept said to a scarlet Keegan, which only made the three others laugh harder.

## CHAPTER THIRTY-EIGHT

Their brunch lasted another hour, then they drove to Lakeview and Jacqueline met the rest of the Savoie clan. Work was forgotten as the boys spread out in different blocks surrounding the house to watch for Damien. After hours there was no sign of him, and when Sept dialed the number she'd reached him at before, the phone just rang.

After nightfall even Camille momentarily doubted Damien, but she was the first to remind them that they didn't have any evidence. Sept tried to believe that as she drove to work the next morning and joined Nathan in their command center.

The new crime photos were up, and Sept felt strange as she stared at her apartment in each of the frames. Roxie had been autopsied and nothing foreign had been found, so that report was sitting on top of the conference table.

"Anything new?" Nathan asked.

"Same as what I told you last night, only Fritz and my father have reassigned the rest of my brothers for now, since they know where to look for him if he's following any regular routine."

"Good morning," Alex said from the doorway. He had a tray of coffee cups and a box of donuts. "How was the rest of your weekend?"

"Not great, since some freak killed a girl on my bed and attacked my neighbor," Sept said. "You look chipper, though. Did your wife come home?"

"Still with her family, but I did talk to her briefly." He put his stuff down, opened the box, and slid it closer to Nathan. "I was on my way to meet George at the lab to review the evidence we collected, but I thought I'd stop and see if you needed anything from us."

"Just the report when you're done." Sept shook her head when Nathan held the box up; she was still full from the breakfast Keegan had made her. "Tell George if we're not here to call me, and we'll swing by and pick it up."

"You joining the search for Damien?" Alex asked.

"That's covered, so we're running down a few names in connection with this religion our guy is sacrificing all these girls to. I'll check with you later and see what kind of progress you're making." Sept gave the pictures one last glance before she motioned to Nathan she was ready to go.

"What names?" Alex picked up one of the donuts and split it in half before he took a bite. "That must have been hard, considering this isn't your usual religion."

"To get the right answers you have to ask the right people the right questions, Alex," Nathan answered for Sept. "We found the right woman and she gave us some leads, so we'll see you later."

"Yeah. We met with Matilda Rodriguez yesterday, and she didn't give us anything except some names," Sept said before she followed Nathan out.

"Lourdes called this morning and said her mother got a call from Matilda last night, and she's willing to help us with these people," Nathan said.

"What's that?" Alex asked, pointing to Sept's open shirt collar. "I've never known you to wear jewelry."

"A gift from Matilda to help my mojo," she said, then turned back to Nathan. "Let's stop by Lourdes's mother's first." Sept glanced over the list as they walked to the car.

"Sept," Alex called down the hallway. "One last thing. If you believe the killer isn't really part of this religion, why waste your time talking to people who are?"

"Covering my bases, so when Fritz threatens to fire me I can tell him we chased everything down."

"Thanks for the information. I was wondering how your end works."

"No problem." Sept faced Nathan again and shrugged. "If he puts in that kind of time in the lab, we'll have it made."

"I don't know him that well."

"He's a bit of an odd duck, but my uncle George says he's thorough."

Lourdes was waiting for them outside with her partner Bruce. "Follow us to my mother's."

In the car, Sept drove while Nathan flipped through crime photos again. "Did the guys finish canvassing the area around my place? Since it was the Quarter, someone should have seen something."

"One of your neighbors down the street said he heard the sirens, but they're so commonplace now he didn't bother to look out the window. And a couple of people were walking around, but they were a few blocks up, closer to the Royal Orleans Hotel. I had them ask specifically if they saw anyone wearing a police uniform, and the guys said all they saw were the units who responded to the scene. No one in an unmarked car."

"Great," Sept said, and stopped behind Lourdes at the traffic light that separated the French Quarter from the Garden District. The day was starting to become overcast, and she took a few minutes to stare at the window displays at Canal Place shopping center, trying to think of something to get Keegan for Christmas. When her cell phone rang, she was so zoned out it startled her.

"Savoie."

"I never took you for an idiot, warrior," a voice said, muffled and distant-sounding.

"I never took me for an idiot either, so we agree on something." Sept pulled over and pointed to the pictures Nathan was looking at, then her phone. She put her hand over the mouthpiece and said, "Call Lourdes and tell her to hold up. It's him."

"We have more in common than you think."

Before she answered, she jotted down the number she'd briefly seen. "I doubt that, since I'm crazy about only a few things, and you're plain crazy."

"I know all the things that make you sweat, warrior, starting with that little piece that's heating up your bed at night. But wait, your bed is a bit bloody, isn't it?"

"What do you want? And why don't you stop playing these games and talk to me like a man, instead of hiding behind the handkerchief covering the mouthpiece. Or can you only get a girl if you tie her up and cut her to pieces when she still tells you to go to hell?"

The caller took a deep enough breath that Sept heard it even through the handkerchief. "You'll pay for that."

"Give me a time and place, and I'll be happy to meet you and talk. From what I've seen of your work, you definitely need someone to talk to."

"Shut up. You're only trying to provoke me, and I'm smart enough not to fall for it."

"You're right. How about I shut up and you tell me what you want." Sept closed her eyes and tried to concentrate on the noises coming through the line. If it was Damien, he'd picked a more populated spot this time, since she could hear people and cars this time, instead of only wind.

"I want a lot of things, including your respect."

"Tell me about it, and maybe I can help you before anyone else gets hurt."

"Warrior, I told you in my note that I'll have to keep sacrificing until I get what I deserve."

She could hear his smugness, which stemmed from the perfect crime scenes he'd left, and since anger wouldn't work, Sept decided on another tactic. "No matter what, you can't bring her back. She's gone, and the storm is to blame. You aren't alone in your grief, but no one else is trying to change what they can't."

"Like I said before, I didn't take you for an idiot. But if that's what you think, the gods have placed way too much faith in you."

"If I'm wrong, then explain it to me." Sept finally detected a familiar sound.

"Fine, and I want to work things out with only you."

"That's not a problem, so let's hear it."

"Sit in your office and wait for my call." He fell silent long enough for Sept to think that he was done and simply had left the receiver off the hook. "Wait for me and I might return something that belongs to you. Decide to ignore me and I'll be happy to build another altar and leave you another blood-soaked room with no trail to follow."

"Wait." Sept yelled into the phone, but this time he had left it off the hook, and no amount of screaming would make him come back on the line. "Fuck," she said as she slapped the blue light on the top of the car. "Get someone to my parents' house and make sure my mother's all right," she told Nathan.

"Lourdes, get back to the station and sit on my phone. If it rings and it's some fucker with a muffled voice, tell him I'm checking on my family before I go back to the office, since I don't trust him to take my dog out for a piss. Then tell Royce to cover the block where the steamboat's docked. I could hear them tuning the organ in the background."

The siren cleared a path to Blanchard's and Al stood up when she screeched to a stop in front. "Hey, Sept, what's going on?" Al asked as she ran by him on her way to the kitchen.

"Baby, what's wrong?" Keegan asked when Sept slammed into the kitchen, making the door swing so hard into the wall it knocked off a few pots hanging nearby.

"Where's Jacqueline, your mother, and Della?"

"Jacqueline had to leave for Houston this morning. I told you that. And my mom and Della should be at Gran's home office."

"What's the number?" Sept said, and yanked the phone off her belt.

Keegan took it out of her hand and dialed for her. "I'm sure once you've finished taking a Blanchard inventory, you'll tell me what's going on."

"Della. Hi, it's Sept. Is Melinda with you?" Sept's relief made her so weak she collapsed against the wall. "No, ma'am. I'm sorry to bother you. I will ask you a favor, though. If anyone from the police department except my father Sebastian, my partner Nathan, or me contacts you about anything, do not go anywhere with anyone in a uniform. I don't care what the emergency is or what their reasoning is. You check with me first, okay?"

"I'll be happy to do that, if you tell me why."

"Your family takes nothing on faith, do they?" Sept asked with a laugh.

"I let you come to brunch, that's faith enough for now. Make me a great-grandmother, and I'll stand on my head if you want."

"I'll work on that, but for now, the killer I'm chasing just called me, and he knows more about me and the people close to me than I feel comfortable with. I have an officer here with Keegan, but I want to make sure the rest of you are all right as well."

"Thanks for calling me, then. If some killer's after us, it's good to know that I haven't given you a hard enough time that you'd give him a free shot at me."

"I thought about it, but we might need you to sit the dog when this is over," Sept said, and laughed. "Remember what I said and I'll call you later."

As Keegan waved to Nathan and dragged Sept by the belt to her office, she said, "Do you need to phone anyone else, or do you have time to tell me what's going on? It's not that I'm not happy to see you, but you have a way of scaring the shit out of me."

"He called me again this morning, and in a roundabout way he threatened the people I care about. I don't mean to scare you, but I'm here because I'm scared, and I'm not afraid to admit that to you." Sept hugged Keegan to her and kissed her. "When he said he'd give me back something that's important to me, I had to come make sure you were all right."

"Honey, you have Al so hyped up that I keep bumping into him when I try to season anything. At this point I'm sure he'd rather face a firing squad than tell you that he let something happen to me." Keegan kissed her on the chin. "I'm fine, but I need you, so that means you have to put your head where it belongs and get this guy. If you don't, you won't take me on vacation until this is over, and I want to model swimwear for you."

Sept looked at her and knew Keegan was trying to be brave and cheer her up, but the concern wasn't completely hidden because Keegan's hand slightly shook as she brought it to Sept's face. "If you want me to concentrate, you shouldn't mention you in a bathing suit."

"It'll be fine, Seven," Keegan said, and pressed her lips to the back of Sept's hand.

"Call Jacqueline and check on her. I have to get back to my office and wait for another phone call, so promise you'll stick to Al."

"Any more stuck and people would start to talk," Keegan said. "If you get the chance, call me later and let me know what's going on. And whatever happens, you be careful. You're a good cop because you're a risk taker, but remember that you're a good cop with someone waiting at home."

"What do you want for Christmas?" Sept asked, trying to take Keegan's thoughts in a different direction.

"I want two things this year, Santa."

"Name them."

Keegan wrapped her arms around Sept's waist and put her chin on her chest. "I want a whole day with no phone, no gun, and no work."

"I think I can promise that, little girl. What else?"

"I want you to not think of me as the crazy chick who's packing up the U-Haul and knitting a sweater for our dog."

Sept had to laugh. "I'll be happy to indulge you anything, if you explain that last statement."

"I want you to give up your apartment and move in with me. It might be too soon, but you shouldn't live somewhere that some psycho broke into and killed someone on the bed. You could indulge me by moving in with me and Mike."

"Do you know how to knit?" Sept asked, before kissing her.

"I started on the matching sweaters the day you brought Mike home."

"I'm not saying no, but we'll talk about it when I get home tonight."

Keegan squeezed her one last time around the waist and let her go. "I'm leaving early today, so call before you come back here to pick me up."

"Will do, and don't try to ditch Al."

❖

"I called ahead and had Royce take care of everything," Lourdes said through her car window when Nathan and Sept walked out.

"Thanks, I'm headed back there now." When Sept got back in the car, she called the office and asked Royce if the guy had called back, then asked to be patched through to her desk. Her boss said that any calls for her were being routed upstairs to the room they'd been using so the tech guys could set up a trace.

"Everything's quiet for the moment," Royce said, "but get your ass back here when you can. I want you on the phone with this fucker if he does decide he wants you to be his new best friend."

"I'm almost there, so keep him talking if he does decide that. Did the search around the Jax Brewery shopping center pan out?" Sept asked and, frustrated, felt like punching the steering wheel.

"I have people covering the area, but nothing so far. If it's Damien, no one's spotted him."

"Thanks, Royce, see you in a few." Sept hung up and called Lourdes, who was still behind them. "Can you break away and get your mom and bring her to the office? If we're going to be stuck inside all day, we might as well get something done."

Before they reached the office she'd contacted her brothers, who still hadn't gotten a glimpse of Damien, and her father, who was giving Fritz a progress report.

"Did he have anything new?" Nathan asked.

"We can hold Fritz off for another couple of days, but then we have to send in the feds. We don't often see serial killers in New Orleans, but with everything going on, Fritz wants something else to blame the feds about if we can't turn up anything."

"We should have zip by then. Does that mean we give up?"

Sept parked in front of the building and left the blue light on top of the car. "Somebody's taking this away from us over my dead body."

Before Sept went inside, she scanned the block, looking at every face to make sure Damien wasn't watching them. If he was there, he was well hidden, so she went in and took the steps two at a time to the second floor. While she stared at her office phone, willing it to ring, she called Estella at the voodoo shop on her cell.

"How long ago did you take over for your mother?" Sept asked her.

"My mom died two years ago, but I worked with her three years before that."

Sept asked Estella to close her eyes and gave her a detailed description of Damien. "In that time, has anyone resembling that come in?"

"We have tourists all the time wanting to buy those little souvenir hex dolls, but I'm really good with faces, and I don't remember anyone like that. Some guy who might be who you're talking about has walked past here, but I've never actually talked to him."

"Anyone else come in who asked a lot of questions?" Sept waved to George and Alex as they came in and dropped another report on the seat next to her before leaving again. "If I sent a police artist down there, could you remember enough to make a composite of the guy?" Sept sat up in her chair and put her hand up when Nathan stepped closer. "Great, I'll have my partner there in a bit with someone."

"You got something?" Nathan asked.

"She said a guy who came in a couple of times gave off a vibe, her words," Sept said, relieved, because the man Estella had described didn't sound at all like Damien. She might have held some unresolved feelings against him because of Noel and Sophie, but she wanted more than anything for it not to be him. Estella had said, though, that she was sure the guy had worn sunglasses and a low-pulled baseball cap, which made it harder to guess his true appearance. "With any luck we can get something to work with."

"You sure you want me to go?" Nathan asked.

"Get the artist on the phone and head over there." They were alone in the room now. "Don't worry. I'm not going anywhere without you, but hurry back."

"You ready for us?" Lourdes asked as she guided an elderly woman in front of her.

"Come on in." Sept stood and held her hand out to Maria.

Like Matilda, the woman before her wore a bright dress that reminded Sept of summer. She smiled and sat across from Sept at the table.

"I'm not sure why I'm here, but I talked to Matilda and we want to help any way we can," Maria said in a soft voice. "Lourdes told me you want me to look through a list of names."

"I want a little more than that." Sept took out the list and handed it to her. "I'd be really surprised if our killer's on this list."

"Why do you say that?"

"After meeting you, Matilda, and Estella, I doubt that anyone who believes like you do would kill in this manner."

Maria picked up the list but didn't lower her eyes. "What do you want me to do, then?"

"Tell me everything you can about the people on here. My mother always says that everyone has a story. The ones on this list aren't any different."

Maria took the sheet, put on a pair of glasses, and didn't say anything as she scanned to the bottom of the page. Then she talked for an hour about the families of everyone on the page she knew, if she was that familiar with them, and about any friends they'd brought to the ceremonies.

She was on the third-to-last name when the phone rang. "Savoie," Sept said, as she smiled at Maria.

"You don't listen very well, do you?" the voice asked.

Sept pointed at the tech manning the recorder. "I'm here, aren't I?"

"But you aren't alone, are you? And don't even try to lie. Like I said before, I know all about you." A clicking sound came through the line, and Sept could only guess that he was hitting his teeth together. "All that glory they dump on you is a pile of shit. You need a million people around you, showing you where to look for the answers."

"At least I know when to ask for help," Sept said, hoping to draw out the conversation so the tech could trace the call definitively.

"What's that supposed to mean?"

"That you need counseling before you kill someone else. No matter what good you think you're getting out of this, it's wrong." The tech wrote something down and signaled with his fingers like he was pulling a string between them, which meant to stretch it out a little more. "You said you wanted to work with only me, so tell me where you'd like to meet, and I'll be there."

"I'll call you soon. Before you and your little helpers start planning where to set your trap, remember that I'm watching you. When I say to come alone, that's what I mean. It's the only way you'll get back what belongs to you."

"What, no hints?" Sept asked with a clearer head now that she knew Keegan and her family were safe.

"You're the decorated detective, figure it out."

"Wait," Sept said, but the line had gone dead. "Tell me you got something?" she asked the tech.

"It's a cell number that matches Roxie's," the guy said. "He must have stolen it from her after he killed her. I narrowed it down to within a block in the French Quarter, but that's as good as it gets."

"Which block?"

"One block near Jackson Square, ma'am."

"Lourdes, your mom," Sept said to Nathan as he came in, and she turned him around.

"I'll stay with her," Lourdes said, standing behind her mother.

Nathan ran alongside Sept with a folded sheet of paper in his hand. "Any luck, in case we actually spot this asshole?" she asked him.

"It's something, but you aren't going to like it," he answered as they hit the street with the siren blaring.

She took the drawing and laughed. "Great, it's the Unabomber." The sketch resembled the composite the FBI had put out for years regarding the famous mail bomber.

They stopped in front of the park right across the street from where their fourth victim was found on the levee and circled the square, taking different sides. After a few turns and a walk through the place they didn't spot anyone, but instead of going back to the office, Sept drove back out to Damien's house.

"You think of something else to look for?" Nathan asked.

"I'm missing something, and I want to know what he took with him that he's been able to stay away so long." She walked through the damaged house again, trying to remember the order of the chaos from the last time to see if anything was different. Sophie's room appeared the same, but Sept looked through the closet in the master bedroom more closely. The stuff hanging in there was stiff with mold, with only a few pieces of Noel's showing any color at all.

Damien's side was more interesting. From the cut of the shirts she could tell nine of his uniforms were hanging there rotting away—the department assigned patrolmen ten. The one she'd seen in the trailer outside had to have been the one he was wearing the night of the storm.

"Keep going through here and see if you stumble on anything," she told Nathan.

The uniform in the trailer still hung on the door of the bedroom, but it had a small rip in the top of the plastic, as if Damien had lifted the covering off to get to the clothing. Unlike the ones inside the house, this shirt had both buttons on the front pockets missing. "Son of a bitch," she said, because for every step she took forward in proving Damien innocent, the evidence knocked her back ten.

"My memory must be shot, because when I was here before, I could have sworn this thing was immaculate," she said to herself as she closed her eyes and tried to picture what she'd seen the first time. Time made her admit that she couldn't with conviction say the shirt had its buttons.

As she turned to leave, something on the floor near the bed lit up like a neon light. No way had she missed this when they were there before. She pulled out her cell phone and dialed.

"Nathan," she said when her partner answered, "grab an evidence bag from the car."

"You got something?"

"Get the bag and I'll be happy to show you."

When Nathan arrived, Sept had picked up the small statue by placing her pen in the hollow section underneath. "Which one is it?" he asked.

"St. Barbara, who I believe is the sign of this Chango one." Sept dropped it in the bag and studied the surface from all sides. "It looks clean, but we'll take it back and see if we get anything off the surface." Before she left, she went through the closet in the trailer and picked up the three pairs of shoes Damien had inside, but all of them had a tread, including the polished shoes under the uniform.

"If his fingerprints are on that, shouldn't we put out the word before he picks up someone else?" Nathan asked.

"This is a sticky situation, and the only thing I'm sure of is that we won't have a say in what's reported to the media." Sept closed the door and walked to the car parked down the street.

"Why a sticky situation?" Nathan asked.

"In times like this, you can't report that you should be on the lookout for a killer cop without the overstressed public going over that much-talked-about deep end."

Nathan slipped the bag into his jacket pocket and walked faster to keep up with her. "What happens then?"

"No one will ever admit it publicly or talk about what needs to happen, but Fritz will put out the word to find him, and some cop will solve the problem by either cuffing Damien if he's asleep or putting a fifty-cent bullet into his head, which will save the taxpayers a million-dollar trial."

Sept stopped in the middle of the street and faced him. "Don't look so shocked, rookie," she said, putting her hand on his shoulder. "It's like bringing him home before his home is so tarnished that it'll take longer to fix than this city. The police department took enough body blows after this shit, and Fritz can't afford any more."

"Your father would agree to that?"

"Don't ask anyone in the Savoie family to pull the trigger, but there aren't enough of us to keep someone else from doing it. And Damien isn't helping us by going underground."

"Hey, Sept," the officer behind the wheel of the police car called out to her. "Thought you'd be out searching for this guy."

"No one has come or gone from there since the patrol has been out here?" Sept asked.

"Just the crime scene guy, but he went over the place and left. Haven't seen anyone else, and at night we move closer. Your old man put a car out back too."

"Did you talk to the guy who was here?"

"He waved before he went in there with his kit, but whatever he was there to do didn't take long."

Sept glanced back at the trailer, trying to gauge how far away it was from where the guy was parked. "Did you get a good look at him?"

"Yeah, I guess, but it's not anyone I've seen before. He had on one of our NOPD jackets, so I let him do his job."

"If anyone else shows up, whether they're on police business or not, call me and give me a heads-up." Sept scanned the street in both directions. Not one house was being renovated or rebuilt. The gray gunk that the water had painted every surface seemed to have coated the street and the life it once housed, and everything had died.

"You got it," the officer said, and shook hands with her and Nathan. "Hopefully we'll get some action soon, because this place is some kind of dead at night."

"Count your blessings, then, and hope it stays that way."

# CHAPTER THIRTY-NINE

"Did you hear the disrespect in her voice?" Novice asked his reflection. He was so angry that the veins in his neck stood out in vivid detail.

"Why should the warrior show you any kind of respect?" Teacher asked. "So far you've touched nothing of hers except someone who walked around the same building she works in."

"But I have." Novice walked to the window and tapped on the glass pointing to the playhouse in the back. "I have someone so she won't have to die alone."

"So she'll know right before she dies how brilliant you are?" Teacher laughed so long that Novice put his fist through the glass he'd been staring through. "That will only show her what a coward you are. You're going to hide until you have her tied down and the knife at her gut. There's no sport in that."

"What more do you want?" Novice screamed and pressed on the sides of his head. "You're driving me crazy for nothing because you never give in on anything."

"Do this one thing and I'll show you what you most want to see."

"Ha." Novice shattered the next pane. "You've said that before."

"I always deliver on my promises. Name one instance that I haven't."

He flexed his hand, relieved that he hadn't cut himself. He reviewed all his conversations with Teacher, and the fact that he couldn't remember Teacher ever reneging on an agreement made him want to put his hand through another pane, but he breathed deep instead.

"What do you want me to do?" he asked.

"Today is Monday, isn't it?" Teacher's tone had returned to that seductive tenor that made Novice crave the feel of hot blood on his hands. "One day ought to be enough, if you are the warrior you say you are. If you plan to continue to use the blade for your sacrifices, there is one you need to pay your respect to before you call on Chango. Tomorrow you'll be ready to do what needs to be done."

"With pleasure."

❖

"I know you miss Tameka, but it's time to get back to work," Shawana Dempscy said as she stood in front of Erica's bed with her hands on her hips. She was the latest addition to Brandi's house. "It's what she would've wanted."

"How do you know what I need or what Tameka would've wanted?" Erica turned her head only slightly to look at Shawana before she stared at the wall again.

"Girl, I've known Tameka from the first day of kindergarten. I could tell her what she wanted before it even occurred to her." Shawana sat on the bed and put her hand on Erica's head. "She told me all about you and how much she liked you. Said she was even sharing that dress-shop dream with you."

"I can forget about that now, and go back to hookin'."

"Not while I'm around. You're going back to work, but under Brandi's protection, and when we put enough money aside we'll open a shop and name it Bishop's, like Tameka wanted." She moved her hand to Erica's shoulder and shook her. "Come on, I know you got some money saved, and since Tameka left me her money, we don't have much more to go. We both lost our best friend, so we're going to have to get used to each other, but that's what we got."

"Why are you being so nice to me?" Erica finally turned around to lie on her back and accepted the tissue Shawana held out to her.

"We're both suffering, so why do it alone? I don't know about you, but I'm ready to find something to be a little happy about and honor my friend all at the same time."

"You're right...I guess." As the words left Erica's mouth she knew she meant them. Tameka's death had been one more time she'd glimpsed a better way, only to have it snatched away so she'd remember her place in life. She smiled and accepted Shawana's hug. "Let's get ready for tonight, and I'll give you the number of my friend Sept in case something goes wrong. She's a cop but she's cool."

"Let's get dressed, then, and I'll let Brandi know we'll take tonight and the rest of the week. There's some convention in town and the guys are ready to spend money."

"They'll be here all week?" Erica tried to shake off the gloom as she got up.

"Arrived last night and should be in town till Friday. With any luck we'll find two guys who want company until then." Shawana waved before she left for her room down the hall. No one had taken Tameka's room, and Erica didn't know if she could stand to see anyone in it yet.

Sitting in Tameka's room every so often and touching her things comforted her. That would probably seem weird to anyone else, but it made her feel close to her murdered friend.

"If you're not busy tonight, keep an eye on us, okay?" Erica whispered toward the ceiling at Tameka before she opened the closet and flipped through her clothes in search of something to wear.

An hour later she and Shawana met downstairs, and Shawana squeezed her hand as she left with an orthopedic surgeon from Canada. His buddy, who was waiting in the front room with Brandi, smiled when Erica stepped in. Their date started like any other, with dinner and drinks, before he took her back to his room for what amounted to straight by-the-numbers sex, and then he fell asleep. He'd already paid Erica in full and told her she could either wait until morning or go when they were done.

As much as Erica craved the comfort of another person, she wasn't desperate enough to take it from a stranger, even if she'd just had sex with him. In the elevator to the lobby she thought about what Tameka had said about sex and retirement. When that day came, like Tameka, she wouldn't have sex with another person she wasn't interested in, no matter the lure of the money.

She was almost to the door where the cabs lined up outside when the police officer walked up to her and put his hand on her elbow. At first her blood ran cold. She thought he was going to take her in for prostitution, but he smiled and his green eyes softened.

"Thank God I caught you before you left." He led her through the door toward his car. "Sept talked to your boss and heard you would be here, so she sent me to meet you."

"Why did she do that?" Erica tried to slow them down when she noticed his car wasn't a police unit but an older sedan.

"Her main suspect may be in the area, and she wanted to make sure the people she cares about are covered. She panicked when she heard you were down here." He opened the door for her and let her go. "I'm supposed to drive you home and see you to that famous red door."

"She said to call her if anything was out of the ordinary." Erica laughed and pointed to the car. "This is definitely out of the ordinary."

"She's busy trying to catch a killer, but if you don't trust a guy in a uniform, then go ahead." He shrugged and stepped back.

Erica reached for her phone but hesitated. If Sept really cared about her, calling her would seem like she didn't trust her, so she sat in the passenger seat and put her seat belt on. "That's okay. It'd be great if you'd take me home."

As the officer walked around to the driver's side, she breathed through her mouth in an attempt to block out the stale smell of the vehicle. Probably from the piles of food wrappers and empty cans in the backseat. She laughed to herself that, for a cop, this guy wasn't very neat except for his uniform, which was pressed with precision.

"What's your name?" Erica asked him when he put the key into the ignition and pulled slowly away from the hotel.

"My name is Novice," he said as they turned to the dark side of the area between the aquarium and the hotel. The Westin was one of the only places open downtown, but even it still needed repairs to restore it to pre-storm conditions.

"Novice?" Erica pushed as close as she could to the door. Something about the guy was off. "That's an interesting name. Is it an old family tradition?"

"I've got no family, and my teacher gave me the name." He turned in the right place for the house, but before they made it all the way down Bourbon Street, he turned again and headed for the ravaged part of the neighborhood past the Faubourg Marigny.

"Teacher?" Erica looked out the window, her pulse picking up, but she wasn't scared yet. Maybe the street was closed ahead and they were detouring. "What teacher?"

"The one who showed me how to make sacrifices to the gods," Novice said. It was the last thing Erica remembered before the probes of his Taser hit her in the chest.

❖

When she woke up, she stopped imagining what Tameka had gone through in her final moments, since she figured they'd be able to talk about it once this guy killed her. She was tied spread-eagle outside in a neighborhood where the only sound was her own breathing and the only light was the stars overhead. She could still move her head, so she looked around.

The sight of Novice kneeling about twenty feet away naked and holding a big hunting knife made her want to scream, but that was probably what he expected. She was scared, but her will to live made her pull on her bindings to see if they would give.

"Is this what you wanted?" Novice said, and Erica lay still.

He didn't turn around or repeat the question, so he didn't seem to be talking to her.

"Of course I know who this needs to be in honor of. Since I want to keep using the knife and receive protection as a warrior, I have to call on Ogun, the god of iron."

When he turned around, Erica could see the knife silhouetted against his pale skin. He dropped to his knees again, next to her, and cut her right above her left breast. Then he dipped his fingers into the blood he held cupped in his hand and wrote something on her forehead. It was either the letter *T* or the number *7*. As he wet his fingers again he pressed harder into the wound. "You can scream if you want to. It's a good way to wake the gods."

Erica bit her tongue until she tasted blood, but for now she wouldn't give him the satisfaction. She tried to close her legs when he leaned over her to reach the bottom of her foot and his penis dragged along her thigh, but the rope wouldn't allow her the dignity of moving away from him. There he drew something else that felt like a question mark, which was appropriate since Erica wanted to know why the hell he was doing this.

"Elegua, open the door and tell Ogun I'm giving him the blood he wants," Novice said, then put his fingers in his mouth and sucked them. "I'll give you what you want, and I'll get to see Sept's face when she finds you." He ran his finger from Erica's abdomen to her throat, touching both nipples along the way. "You fucked her, didn't you?" he asked Erica.

She stared at him, trying to place him, but she had no memory of him. She should've known him since he had so much information about her. Her hesitation cost her, though, because he cut her forearm.

"I asked you a question," he said, and put his face close to hers.

"Not really," Erica said, and closed her eyes, not to keep from looking at him but to try to disregard the pain. The quick swipe had gone deep.

"You have to be pure for this to matter, so don't lie to me, bitch. Did you fuck her?"

He was talking loud and breathing on her eyelids.

"I touched her because she was nice to me. Are you satisfied?"

"Not yet, but I will be." Novice moved away from her again, and she could tell he was getting things out of the car. From somewhere above her, he struck a match and lit a green candle that he momentarily held over her head. He repeated the actions and this time held a black candle over her.

"If you're only killing me to get to Sept, wouldn't it be better if you called her and let her listen in?" Erica suggested as she frantically concocted scenarios of how to get away. "And I can see that you need me to touch you as much as Sept did the night we spent together."

Novice lowered his eyes to his groin as if he'd just noticed his erection. "Why would you do that?" he asked, sounding suspicious.

"I don't have any choice, do I, so I might as well do something good for someone so my soul will go to heaven." Obviously this guy had some hang-up about religion, even if it was twisted. It was the only thing she could exploit.

"You aren't going to heaven. I'm going to release you to live with Ogun, the brother of Chango, and in return I want you to do something for me."

Erica did her best to relax, her arms and legs coming to rest on the cool ground under her. "Name it."

"Look for my wife." He took a picture of a woman out of the bag next to him. "Tell her it's time to come home where she belongs. I never gave her permission to leave."

"I will, but I want to make you feel good now. That way I can tell her not only how much you miss her, but how good you felt in my hand."

He hesitated, but Erica could see in the candlelight the little part of his brain controlled by his dick working overtime as his eyes roamed her body like a glutton in front of a feast.

"Just untie one of my hands. Where's the harm in that?" she asked. "If you don't like it, you can tie me up again."

His expression told her it was the last thing he expected her to say, and he bent closer as if to see if she would recoil. She only smiled and moistened her lips like she couldn't wait to get started. That's all it took for him to untie her right hand, and despite the cut that was still bleeding she took his cock in her hand and started a steady up-and-down motion.

He dropped his head back and the knife fell from his hand as he let himself enjoy Erica's offering. She was disgusted by what she was doing, but the need to survive overrode the overwhelming compulsion to stop, though she did slow her hand.

"Why are you stopping? I'm so close." He looked down at her again and she ran her tongue slowly around her mouth.

"A warrior like you deserves everything I gave Sept."

"What are you talking about?" He put his hand over hers.

"If you want all of what I gave her, I need to put my mouth on you."

He paused, but then he moved so fast she almost laughed. He situated himself and moaned when she took him in and swirled her tongue on the tip.

"That's so good. If my wife had been that good she'd still be here," he said, then put his hand on the back of her head.

Erica maneuvered her loose hand until her fingers were wrapped around his testicles. When he started to move his hips, she bit down as hard as she could and squeezed and pulled at the same time. She tasted blood again, but this time it wasn't hers. As he fell back in a fetal position, holding his genitals, she picked up his knife and stabbed him in the side before cutting herself loose. Then she ran.

She had no idea where she was or how long Novice would be incapacitated, so she put as much distance between them as possible. The debris still in the street cut the bottom of her feet, but she didn't stop. When she heard him screaming behind her, she moved toward the backyards of the abandoned houses. She was a least a couple of blocks over but had to deal with fences and downed trees that cut into her skin as she tried to find help.

After what felt like an eternity she saw a beautiful sight—a Humvee full of National Guardsmen on patrol. They were moving down the street slowly and stopped when she screamed. "Please, I need to get out of here," she told the first guy who reached her.

"What happened to you?" he asked. His partner came up behind him and removed his jacket for her to put on.

"Can I use your phone?" Erica had an idea. "And we need to get back to where this guy took me before he leaves. He's the killer the police are looking for." The guys glanced at each other and didn't move. "I'm not crazy, and once you talk to Detective Sept Savoie you'll know what I'm talking about."

"Here, you can use my phone," the first guy said.

"Sept, please, you have to help me," Erica screamed into the phone when Sept answered. Once she heard Sept's voice, the horror of what had almost happened fell on her like a cold bucket of water, and she became hysterical.

"Who's on the line, please?" the guardsman asked.

Once Sept finished screaming at him for not taking Erica seriously, they put her in the vehicle and she pointed them to where she thought she'd come from. In the darkness and in her condition she had no idea of the exact location, so they waited for the police reinforcements before driving Erica to a temporary military base to see a doctor.

It took a few hours, but they finally found what Novice had left behind—the candles still burning in the yard and the ropes he'd tied Erica with. But this time the ghost had left footprints. His blood was on the ground, along with Erica's, and Erica still had his knife.

"You won't be able to hide forever now, you son of a bitch," Sept said as George took samples of everything in sight.

"They have Erica patched up and the doctor gave her a sedative. If you're ready, we can go over there," Nathan said. They were both in jeans since the call had come after they'd both taken off for the night. "I phoned the artist too, so maybe we can get a sketch of this asshole."

"Hopefully we can, since George said DNA will take a few days, and we'll only get lucky if he's in the system."

The drive out of the area was slow, with all the police units cruising through the neighborhood with their floodlights on, but Sept knew the killer had slipped through the net before it was in place. Erica had said he'd driven her there, and when the first units arrived any sign of a car was long gone.

"We're the good guys, so luck has to eventually swing back our way, right?" Nathan said.

"We'll see, kid, but for now I'll be happy with a hint of who I'm looking for. Once I find him, you'll have to hold me back from putting a bullet in his head for all the crap he's put us and these victims through."

"Who said I'd hold you back," Nathan said, and he sounded serious.

## CHAPTER FORTY

Y ou idiot," Teacher screamed at Novice as he tried to bandage his side to stop the bleeding. He had to concentrate and kept blinking from the pain in his groin, which he'd bandaged first. "This was never about sex, but you're so weak you couldn't help yourself, could you?"

"She offered," Novice said weakly, sweat dripping into his eyes despite the cool temperatures. He peeled off the mustache he'd glued on before going out that night and threw it on the bathroom floor. He'd wash out the stuff he'd used to lighten his hair later.

"It was a test and you failed, you piece of shit."

"How was I supposed to know that?" Novice finally reached the part of his back where Erica had wounded him.

"Because this has all been a test, and you've passed very few of them. So don't bitch and whine when you don't get your reward. Tonight you can go to sleep and pretend your wife is coming back to you, but I hope you have a good imagination, because pretending is all it'll be."

"You promised," Novice said, and started crying.

"Save it, weakling. I promised you something in exchange for another heart for Ogun. Instead, you chose to put your dick in the mouth of a girl you were about to kill. What exactly did you think would happen, you fucking idiot?"

"She seemed so sincere."

"She's a hooker." Teacher sounded exasperated. "What about that concept don't you understand? You should be proud of yourself for what that brief moment of pleasure cost you."

"I know all that already. I lost my knife and the kill."

"You don't understand, do you?" Teacher whispered so close to Novice's ear that, if he closed his eyes, he could almost feel Teacher against his back. "Right now the true warrior is holding your weapon of choice, and she's talking to your prey. Only this time she's telling the story, not you, by what you leave behind at the sacrifices. She's describing the moron who caught her and how brilliant she was to get away. You're done, because instead of leaving a cold trail, you've left the warrior a map right to your door."

"Sept's not that good," Novice said, but even he wasn't convinced by the way he said it.

"We'll see which of you is a better hunter."

"Only one of us will walk away from this alive, and it'll be me. Sept's too weak not to give in to my demands when I threaten to drive a stake through someone she feels so strongly about. She'll be here and alone whenever I want her to be."

"Tall talk from a little man, but remember, this is your last chance."

"Don't worry, I'm not about to waste it."

❖

"You coming home soon, Seven?" Keegan asked.

"Keep my side warm, but I'm afraid this will be a long night." Sept stood outside the medical tent and stared up at the sky as she told Keegan what had happened.

"He left one alive?"

"Not by choice, I'm sure, but Erica's a friend of mine, so I'm praying she got a good enough look at him to make a difference."

"Oh, honey, I'm sorry. Can I do anything?"

Sept held her finger up to Nathan for one more minute. "She's one of Brandi's girls that I actually took there before she died on the streets or her abusive boyfriend killed her. We're not best friends, but she's way too young to throw her life away for twenty dollars a trick."

"Don't blame yourself. I can hear in your voice that you're trying to."

"I'll do my best, and don't let anyone in until I get back."

"Love you, and be careful."

"Love you too."

When they walked in, Erica was sitting on a cot rocking back and forth, still wearing the jacket the guardsman had given her on the street. Her wounds had been treated, but the decorations Novice had made were still in place. When she saw Sept she started crying, and Sept sat and held her until Erica was finally able to talk.

With Sept's gentle questions and Nathan taking notes out of Erica's sight, Erica told them the entire story, including how she got away. That made her cry harder, and Sept stopped talking until she calmed down. Then Erica handed Sept the knife she'd refused to give anyone else.

"If I show you a picture, can you tell me if he's the one who did this?" Sept asked.

"I think so." Erica took the picture Sept held out and studied it so long that Sept felt her heart slow and sink in her chest. "This guy's hair's too dark, and I can't tell if his eyes are green. The guy who did this to me had green eyes, a well-trimmed mustache, and light sandy brown hair. I can't describe his face well, but I know for sure it's not this guy," Erica said as she gave Sept back her copy of Damien's official police ID picture.

"You're positive?" Sept needed the reassurance.

"I'm positive. From what I remember of his face, it's not him."

"And the picture he showed you of his wife, was this her?" Sept held up the picture of Noel and Sophie she kept in her wallet.

"That's not the woman he showed me. That I'm sure about." Erica gazed up with an expression that begged for reassurance. "Can I take a shower now?"

"In a little while, but we have to process you first. I know it sounds degrading, but it'll help us catch this guy."

"You'll take me home afterward, right?"

"I'll call ahead and have Wilson make you some hot chocolate. I'm sorry this happened to you, Erica, but I'm glad you survived."

"I only wish Tameka had been as lucky."

"Don't worry, he'll pay for that."

Sept stood aside when the female officer from George's office arrived and took her kit out. She swabbed the inside of Erica's mouth for any remaining trace of Novice, then took pictures of the number seven on her head and the bottom of her foot, where only a small hint of the shepherd's hook was left—at least, that's what Sept thought it was when Erica had described it to her.

"One more thing, Erica," Sept said as the woman took her last set of photos. "He told you his name was Novice and he was taking orders from someone named Teacher?"

"That I'll never forget, because he was talking to this Teacher guy."

"Was someone else there?"

"I guess." When the woman finished photographing her wounds, Erica put the jacket back over her hospital gown. "I didn't see him, though, sorry."

"That gives us more to go on, so don't be sorry. As much as I hate what happened to you, you've proven what I've known all along. You're a survivor who's going to make it, and you're the break I've been waiting for."

"Thank you." When Sept put her arm around Erica to walk her out to the car, she fell against Sept. She let Nathan drive them to the Red Door while she sat in the back with Erica.

Once Erica was in her bed, with Brandi on one side of her and Shawana on the other, Sept said, "I'll be back tomorrow with some more pictures for you to look through, and the artist will be here shortly to try and sketch something from what you remember of your attacker. Brandi and Wilson will be here with you so there's nothing to worry about, but call me if you need anything."

"Can you stay longer?" Erica asked her.

"I'll be back later, but I have to go to work." Sept kissed her forehead. "Try to get some sleep after the police artist finishes."

Outside, Sept called her father and asked for the complete file of police department employees who had access to a uniform during the last ten years.

"I don't know how easy that'll be to put together, Sept," Sebastian said.

"Put as many people as you have on it, and I need a car with people you trust outside Brandi Parish's house. He finally screwed up, and I have a survivor who saw his face."

"He left one alive?"

Sept smiled at the excitement in her father's voice. "Not

intentionally, but I learned a few things tonight. He's dressed like a cop because he most probably *is* one, and he doesn't hide his face because he doesn't intend to leave any of them alive. And he's making sacrifices to these gods to see his wife again, who, most important, isn't Noel. This guy is definitely not Damien, so if he calls, make sure you tell him he needs to come home."

"You got it. Hopefully someone won't shoot him on sight for what we thought before."

"Whoever it is planted evidence at his place. Call the patrolmen you had sitting in front of Damien's the other day in for a talk so they can describe in detail this crime scene guy who stopped by there."

"Where are you headed next?"

"Over to give George the probable murder weapon to see if we get any fresh prints off it." Sept had dropped it in a pillowcase, since they didn't have any evidence bags big enough in the car. "I'll either be at the lab or at the scene, depending on when George finishes."

"Good. Keep me updated. I'm on my way to the office and will stop by and give Fritz the good news."

"You got it, Dad, and get me those pictures as soon as you can."

George was still at the crime scene and searched the knife for prints immediately, so Sept wouldn't have to wait any longer than necessary. He found only a pair that most probably belonged to Erica.

"He was smart," George said as he showed her the grip that had been added to the blade. "He used this, and there's no way to lift prints off this material. He was also careful to keep his fingers to himself when it came to the blade. The only chance we might have had was when Erica stabbed him. Most people would grab the blade, but supposedly she stabbed him in a spot where it would've been awkward for him to do that."

"Thanks, Uncle George. I'll check with you later." Sept took the knife with her and waved to Nathan to get going. "I'll be at the office."

"Did he find anything?" Nathan asked.

"Not yet, but let's get to the office and start on the pictures we'll need to show Erica, because who she described isn't anyone who comes to mind."

"You really think he's on the job now?"

Sept slammed her door closed and rested her hands on the steering wheel. "As much as I'd like to say no, I can't. Since he's one of us, he's been able to hide within plain sight and knows what areas aren't heavily patrolled. That arrogance is getting ready to bite him in the ass."

"Only if Erica can pick him out."

"Erica won't let us down. From what little she saw of him, and because of what he did to her, his face is carved into her memory, whether she wants to accept that or not."

Nathan nodded and sighed. "Let's hope you're right."

"Let's hope."

❖

When Sept and Nathan arrived at the precinct, Royce was there with all the pictures from their house and from two other nearby precincts. About half of them had mustaches, but a smaller number had the right hair and color eyes. Hopefully the short list wouldn't overwhelm Erica into being uncertain.

By the time they were done it was light outside, but the rain was coming down in heavy sheets, with no let-up in sight. Being up for so many hours was starting to catch up with them, and Sept looked forward to spending a rainy day inside, if only for a little while, when she could.

Royce came in and forced them both to go home for at least six hours to get some sleep. "Even if you find this guy today, he'll have the upper hand on you in this condition," he said when Sept wanted to stay longer.

When she got home, Al was sitting in the kitchen having coffee and reading the paper, looking as beat as she felt. "Thanks for staying this long, Al," Sept said after he unlocked the dead bolt, and she took off her soggy shoes by the door.

"Not a problem, and thanks for clearing it with my captain. I wanted to be here, and it's nice to get paid too, you know." Al shook hands with her and went to gather his things. "If you'll be here for a bit, I'll go catch a nap and be back later."

"I'm not moving until this afternoon, so take your time. I'll wait for you to get back." She locked up behind him and slumped against the edge of the glass door trying to erase the images of Erica tied spread-eagle. Erica's survival was the most important thing to focus on, but all

Sept could think about were the ropes tied to the fence and pieces of lawn equipment and how Novice had lured her there in the first place.

Novice had used her friendship with Erica to lead her to her death. What had started as some sick fantasy on his part had turned personal. Day after day she put herself on the line for the good of the city and the people who called it home, but that was her choice, and she made it freely because she could accept the consequences of what could go wrong.

"If you turn around, I'll make you feel better than you do right now."

Sept laughed at Keegan's words, and no matter what she had left to do to close this case, it wasn't a concern right now. "I feel better already," she replied.

"You know something, Seven?" Keegan put her arms around her waist.

"I know a lot of things, but why you're still here isn't one of them."

"You think after the night you had last night, I'd just run off without seeing you?" Keegan pinched her stomach as hard as she could through Sept's jacket. "Shame on you, Seven. What kind of partner do you think I am?"

"The best one I could hope to find, since no matter how horrible my night was, having you here is just what I need." Sept turned around and embraced Keegan. "I know that sounds so sappy I should be embarrassed, but it's true. So tell me what else I don't know."

"I was going to tell you the same thing. Every time you leave I go a little crazy, but when I see you standing here, something in me rejoices. That's equally sappy, but I've never felt like that." Keegan was still in her robe and slippers.

"So what do you have in mind to make me feel good?"

"Don't get any ideas, Detective." Keegan took her hand. "You'll feel great once I get you upstairs so you can shower and take a long nap. If I know you just a bit, I know you'll leave for work as soon as your eyes open again."

"I have to, sweetheart. We're getting close but we're not there yet."

"I'm not complaining, but I want you on those cute toes of yours and not falling asleep while you're chasing some crazed killer. Call *me* crazy, but I want you around long enough that I can eventually pick out china."

"Does that mean you've added one more thing to your Christmas list?"

Keegan stopped on the stairs when she was higher than Sept and turned so she could kiss her since their heads were level. "All I want is to have you around safe and in one piece. That's all I need, and the rest, whatever that is, is like meringue."

"Don't people usually say icing?"

"Meringue is a type of icing, and it tastes better than regular icing."

"Do you have time for a nap?"

"For a shower, nap, and a good meal before you go back."

With the shades down in the room, Sept was able to sleep until noon, and when she woke up Keegan was rubbing her stomach in soft circles that went lower as Sept got more awake. Over lunch she told Keegan what had happened the night before, and if Sept expected more talk about Brandi and her girls, Keegan only expressed concern over Erica and what she would have to face.

"Can you do me one more favor?" Keegan asked as Sept strapped on her gun.

"Sure." Sept finished and kissed Keegan's forehead. "What can I do for you?"

"It's a two-part favor," Keegan said, and softened it with another kiss. "First, don't go anywhere without Nathan backing you up. I know you think he's a rookie, but I don't want you out there alone."

"That's simple enough, since Nathan acts like we're Velcroed together. What else?"

"Will you be in the office for most of the afternoon?"

"Probably. I have a lot of evidence to go over from last night." Sept put her jacket on and slipped her cell phone in the front pocket.

"Can you take Mike with you for a while?" Keegan held up his lead. "Mom has been babysitting for us, but she has an appointment with a new seafood vendor for lobster, and Gran is picking up Jacqueline's slack while she's out of town."

"What about Carla?" Sept asked, but took the leash anyway.

"If you can't, I could call her, but I'm not ready to ask favors of her just yet. Though my mother would probably be thrilled."

"Don't worry about it, I'll take him."

"What if you have to go somewhere?"

"We'll let him ride in the car and I'll put the windows down. I'm sure he'll love it."

"Are you sure? Now that I ask, I sound like I'm five years old."

"Honey, seeing your mom with someone new can't be easy, so don't worry about it. If something happened to my father and my mother started seeing someone else, I'd be asking you to drive me to therapy."

"Thanks, Seven, I owe you one."

"If I'm lucky I can get Mike to pick this guy out of a mug book."

"That promise of being careful goes for the dog too."

As soon as Sept put Mike in the backseat he stuck his head out the window, and Keegan stood outside and waved until she reached the corner. This level of domesticity wasn't something she'd hoped for, but all of a sudden picking out china sounded enticing. "You really are in love, Savoie," she said, and Mike barked in agreement.

## CHAPTER FORTY-ONE

Novice opened his eyes and closed them right away when the pain in his side and in his groin flared. He had taken all his pain pills, but they hadn't helped. He had been able to sleep the night before only after he'd decided how he'd eliminate Sept, then kill Erica.

"Isn't that wishful thinking?" Teacher asked.

"Last night was a temporary setback, but I have a plan to get this all done. I don't know why, though, since you haven't kept a promise yet."

"The strong receive rewards, and so far I haven't seen strength in you." Teacher's voice floated closer and settled next to him. "Chango is your last chance to make this right."

"You don't think I can, do you?"

"Since you can barely move, I have my doubts, but I won't discount you yet. You're certainly persistent."

"Even if you don't give me my reward, I'll kill Sept or die trying. No matter what happens, I come out a winner. But if I do kill Sept as my sacrifice to Chango and you don't deliver, I want you out of my life."

"If you don't succeed, Novice, that's exactly what'll happen." Novice felt Teacher's breath on the back of his neck. "You may not think you need me, but when you're all alone in Sept Savoie's crosshairs, you'll beg for me, and all there'll be is silence."

"That's just wishful thinking."

❖

Sept and Nathan sorted through all the photos of the latest crime scene and the prints that were lifted from different places in the yard. "Has the city informed us whose house this is?" Mike lay on the floor beside Sept with his head on his paws, eyeing her movements.

"They haven't been able to give us anything yet on the place we found Tameka," Nathan said. "That section of city hall partially flooded, so they're cleaning up. The woman I spoke with said they'll get back to us in about three weeks."

"Three weeks? They need to step it up. That might be a lead."

Nathan nodded and flipped to the front of his notebook. "I explained that to her, but I'll try again."

While Nathan was on the phone Sept picked up the pictures of the knots around Erica's ankles. They were the same ones used to tie Frieda Hearn down, and Sept tried to place where she'd seen something tied like that before. Nothing came to her so she Googled "intricate knots." The third entry on the list was the Boy Scouts, and when she clicked on it, she found a page on their Web site that dealt with knots and their related badges. Novice had used the most difficult one on the page.

Sept clicked on it and followed the directions to tie the knot. Even if the killer's victims were unconscious from the Taser gun, this particular knot took time unless it was second nature. "Who practices something like this?" she asked herself.

Even though this time Novice's ritual had completely fallen apart, he hadn't left behind one print that could identify him quicker than his DNA.

Nathan ended his phone call. "After the housing division got more than a few calls from their higher-ups and the police chief, the woman I talked to said they may have something by either this afternoon or tomorrow at the latest."

"How about the knife? Anything on that yet?" Sept stopped at the picture of Erica's forehead and the number seven Novice had put there in Erica's blood.

"The only true specialty knife store left in town is in the Riverwalk Shopping Mall, and the guy who runs it told the officer I sent over there that this model is mostly sold for display and not for hunting. The chrome finish isn't practical in the field."

"He's right." Sept put a picture of the knife next to the one she'd been looking at. "It's more like the finishes on swords you see in movies. Not practical for the field, but perfect for someone who thinks of himself as a warrior, don't you think?"

"I guess, and before I forget, Lourdes said her mom is available today if you want to finish the list you were working on the other day before Novice called."

Sept nodded but didn't raise her head. "Where are Lourdes and Bruce?"

"Helping George finish up at the scene, since he's shorthanded." Nathan dropped into the seat next to her and started to pet Mike. "Alex had to take a few days off because his little boy got sick, but he should be back by Monday."

"Tough break, but call Lourdes and tell her to pick her mother up before she comes back here. We can go through the last few names, and that'll give us enough time to run by Tulane for our next crazy religion class."

"You think the seven has to do with one of the gods or you?"

"I'm not that egotistical," Sept said, and laughed. "But like my mother, seven must be one of the Orishas' favorite number."

Mike got up when Sept did and went with them to the campus, where Julio reviewed the pictures and consulted a couple of books. He gave them the information they already had from Erica's statement as to what god Novice had picked and what he stood for.

"I was wrong," Julio said as he handed back all the pictures she'd brought with her.

"How so?" Sept asked.

"I really thought he'd pick Chango next, not his brother. At least that's what I speculated he was building up to."

"Why do you think he deviated?" Sept asked.

Julio shrugged and fingered his necklace. "I'm not really sure, but he may have more to prove than we realized."

"Can I ask you something, professor?" Nathan asked, and Julio nodded. "If you teach different beliefs from around the world, why did you decide to practice Santeria?"

"What faith are you, Detective?"

"Baptist, but I'm not the best one out there."

Julio laughed along with Sept. "Then you're one of the lucky few who get to pick what you believe and whether you want to follow what the church teaches you, since you had to agree to be baptized. I believe your partner is Catholic, and that set of beliefs is chosen for you at birth, when you're baptized without giving consent."

"Fascinating, but what does that have to do with his question?" Sept asked.

"Sometimes religion is chosen for you, and sometimes the religion chooses you. That's what happened to me the first time I went to a Santeria ritual."

Sept bent forward in her seat, now more curious than Nathan to hear what Julio had to say. "Who took you to this ritual?"

"I may appear white, but my grandmother is Matilda Rodriguez's sister. I grew up around Santeria, but the Orishas didn't take hold of my blood until I tried to turn away from it. No matter how far and hard we run, Sept, sometimes we can't outrun who we are."

"Then you aren't much different from me in that your religion was chosen for you," Sept said with a smile. "Some of us just take it more seriously than others."

"Do you mean me or you?" Julio asked.

"I'm not knocking what you believe, and I'm grateful for your help on this case, but I've never needed a priest or anyone else to show me what faith is about. So I'm talking about me when it comes to not taking the divine very seriously." She stood up and shook hands with him.

"I see my aunt has given you a present." Julio pointed to the necklace Sept wore. "You wear the warrior's colors well, Sept, but be careful when you find the guy you're looking for that he doesn't mistake you for a true believer."

"Why's that?"

"His last letter said he will kill the warrior who tries to stop him. The colors you wear around your neck mark you as the next sacrifice."

"If that happens, he'll get his wish to see his wife again, only he won't need a séance to get in touch with her," Sept said before she left.

❖

When they got back to the precinct, Sept had a hard time finding a parking place. Since the failed attempt on Erica's life, Fritz Jernigan had assigned new officers to follow any new leads. He had told Sebastian to find the guy as soon as possible so he could stay ahead of any bad press.

"This is about to become a nearly uncontrollable zoo," Sept said as she circled the block again. "That crowd can cover everything that's going on, so let's swing by the lab and see if George has anything."

"Are you sure we don't need to get in there?" Nathan glanced over his shoulder at the building as Sept turned the corner.

"Trust me, we won't be missed for a while."

A few newcomers were working in the lab, mostly watching computer screens as a series of prints flashed on the screen. George was swabbing the knife in different locations.

"Anything?" Sept asked as Mike sat at her feet.

"A few partials that could belong to the previous owners, but I want to be sure. As for this knife, I'll probably get DNA off the handle that'll match the blood at the scene, along with a good set of Erica's prints on the blade."

Sept saw the same frustration she felt. Mike started pulling on his lead as he started to growl. He was acting so uncharacteristically she almost took him back to the car, then realized what was upsetting him. Mike was the only survivor, aside from Erica, who'd seen the killer, but he could identify clues not only by sight but by smell. The handle of the knife held no prints but it had a scent, one that even Novice's injuries hadn't erased.

"It's okay, boy, you're okay," Sept told him when she got on her knees to comfort him, but he wasn't growling near the table where George was working.

"What's wrong with him?" George asked when Sept let the leash go and Mike walked to an office chair and bared his teeth.

"Who sits here?" Sept asked as Mike barked and glanced back at her.

"That's Alex's desk."

"Where is he again?"

"His wife called and their son is sick. He hated to go now, but his family's important to him." George stepped closer and stood next to Sept. "I put some stuff down there earlier while I set up another scan on his computer for prints. Think that's what he's picking up on?"

"It could be. I haven't had him very long, but this is the first time I've seen him act this way." Sept picked up the lead again and tried to get Mike to back away. "Come on, Nathan. Let's go to the office and I'll call Keegan to pick him up. Let me know if you find anything, Uncle George."

Mike wasn't moving, and he alternated from barking to looking back at Sept like he desperately wanted to tell her something. When Nathan opened the door and Sept didn't let up her gentle pressure, he finally relented.

"I thought we were going back to the office," Nathan said when Sept put Mike in the back seat, got in, flipped open her phone, but didn't start the car.

"We are, but I want to do something first." She spoke to the operator who answered at police headquarters and asked for Alex's home address. "There's no way I'm right, but this will bug me all day if I don't check it out."

Nathan took the note from her and shook his head. "If this is where he used to live, let's take off before dark. I doubt anyone's around, and there's no streetlights."

It was five past five, and Nathan was right. "I want a quick look, then we'll go back so we won't keep Lourdes's mother waiting." Sept glanced at Mike, who was still agitated and pacing in the backseat.

## CHAPTER FORTY-TWO

The house wasn't hard to find, even though it was in one of the most devastated areas in the city. About five blocks from the University of New Orleans, it was the only one for blocks with a FEMA trailer in front of it. On one side stood a line of dead shrubs, and on the other, half of a plastic playhouse that once resembled a medieval castle.

Out front was a pile of trash that had probably resulted from Alex's attempt to clean the inside of his house, but judging by its height it had been there for weeks. Sept saw no signs of regular trash pickups by contractors hired by FEMA. She stared at the place in the waning light and almost got back in the car, not wanting to walk through another mold-and-trash-filled house, but it would take only a minute to ease her overactive imagination.

She told Nathan, "Leave Mike in the car and check out back to see if you find anything out of the ordinary." Her car door sounded extra loud when she shut it in the deserted neighborhood.

"Holler if you do the same inside," Nathan said, accepting the flashlight Sept held out.

They knocked on the trailer door first, since what Sept assumed was Alex's car was parked alongside it. No answer, so Sept pointed to the backyard. "Come inside when you're done." She clicked on her light and walked to the front door of the house.

It was locked, and she was willing to buy Alex another one but she didn't want to come back here if she could help it, so she put her shoulder into it. One sweep with the flashlight and she reached for her gun before she stepped inside. The house had been cleared of its clutter, which wasn't strange, but the order Alex had left behind raised alarms in her head.

He had put the rotting furniture back in place, including the magazines that still had some shape, and the only thing recognizable was the picture sitting on the warped coffee table. It had obviously been taken in the yard next to the castle playhouse.

Alex stood next to the structure holding a little boy, who appeared to be about three, and next to them was a slight young woman, looking up at Alex instead of the camera. The pose was as surreal as the room it sat in, since the woman didn't seem to adore Alex.

"What the hell?" Sept said softly as she walked back to the kitchen and found the same order as in the front room. The table was covered in a thick layer of black and yellow mold, but it was still set for dinner, including a Spiderman plate and spoon. Upstairs, the bedrooms were in the same flooded but neat condition, except the master bedroom.

The bed linens were starting to tear, but they looked slept in. But that wasn't the strangest thing in the room. Two candles, one red and the other white, burned under the mirror, giving off a soft light that flickered and danced on the walls. Finally Sept stepped in to examine the undamaged, handwritten book laid out and open on the dresser.

A beautifully drawn sketch of Saint Barbara dominated the top of the left page, followed by a recipe of what needed to be done to sacrifice to Chango. Sept staggered back a step. Novice wasn't just a cop. He was part of her team. "Holy mother of God," she said softly, but hesitated to call Nathan or any kind of backup.

"The mother of God has no place here," Alex said as he shot the probes of his Taser into Sept's back. He laughed as she fell to the floor and twitched. "You're early, but I'm sure Chango won't mind that this isn't Friday."

"Don't even think of waiting until then," Teacher warned.

"Why would I do that when the 'great warrior' made this so easy?" From the nightstand he retrieved a set of handcuffs and leg shackles and put them on Sept, not wanting to take any chances she'd come to quickly.

Alex held his side as Sept's chest rose and fell, still shocked that he was looking at her. At first the closing car doors had panicked him from the one place his son had always said was the best spot on the property. From the castle outside he'd watched Sept do her usual scan of an area before she took her first step, and when she turned away from him, Alex had looked to the sky and sent a silent thank-you to his son. He'd been in the castle with the spirit of his child, trying to think of his next move.

"He was thanking me for setting him free of the bitch who was his mother," Alex said, trying to decide how to get Sept downstairs. With his injury he couldn't even drag her the whole way.

"Let her do all the heavy lifting," Teacher said, and he finally materialized in front of him in the form of his late grandfather, but just as quickly morphed into the shape of his late wife. "We're so close now that you don't want anything to go wrong."

"We'll see if death has made you any smarter," Alex said in disgust. "I hope so, because it's your fault I'm in this mess."

"I'm sorry," the image of Sonia Perlis said from where she hovered near the mirror.

"Not as much as you're going to be."

❖

Sept kept her body relaxed as she listened to Alex talk to someone who seemed to be across the room. The stun gun had left her with a wicked headache and a body as sore as the first time she'd been Tasered, part of her police training. With her eyes closed and from what little she remembered of the room, she tried to place him. The creaking indicated he was sitting on the bed, most probably rocking, to make the springs move like that.

The conversation Erica had described about Teacher didn't sound like what she was hearing now. In that short time Alex had apparently gone from the underling to the aggressor, since his accomplice was somewhere in the room taking the abuse Alex was dishing out.

"You've slept long enough," Alex said, and kicked Sept's rib cage.

No matter how much longer she wanted to play possum, the gasp she let out at the sudden attack gave her up. "Relax, Alex, I won't hurt you," she said, and almost laughed, since she could feel the cold metal encircling her hands and ankles.

"You're a riot," Alex said, and kicked her again. "Get up and don't make me wait too long, or I'll kill you up here and be done with the whole thing."

"Where are we going?" Sept asked as she sat up and saw he had his uniform on. The crime scene guys wore it only for official occasions since they usually preferred dark pants and a polo shirt underneath a vest with enough pockets to carry all their equipment. "And why can't we talk here?"

"Do I need to cut you to prove who's in charge?"

Since the knife he'd used for the other murders was sitting in George's lab, Alex had replaced it with what looked like a regular kitchen knife with a rusty blade, probably from one of the drawers downstairs. Sept glanced at it but stayed focused on Alex.

"Why are you doing this, Alex?" Sept got on her knees, still wobbly from the Taser shot. "Think about your family."

"I'm doing this for my family, so don't talk about things you don't understand." With Sept's gun in his other hand, he started walking backward toward the stairs. "Don't make any sudden moves or you won't get your surprise."

"You've murdered six people and you've got nothing to say? I find that hard to believe." Sept decided that she might have a better chance to try to free herself out in the open, so she shuffled along.

"You call it murder, but I did what was necessary. Besides, most of them were a waste of humanity." When Alex reached the bottom of the stairs, he disappeared for a moment but was back quickly with the picture she'd seen on the coffee table. "I needed to make the sacrifices to get my family back."

"Like I told you on the phone, if they died in the storm it's not your fault, and all you need is help to accept their loss."

Alex pushed her toward the back door, causing Sept to stumble into the small table and bring the dishes down with a crash. "Shut up and move."

It was now fully dark outside, but Alex had set up three spotlights that shone on an area near a swing set that measured about five feet by five feet. The rest of the yard was covered with weeds and dead grass, but there the dirt was level and as black as the night sky. As strange as that was to Sept, it wasn't what captured her attention.

Two silhouettes were up in the air under the swing set. One of them had to be Nathan, which destroyed any chance that he'd gotten away to call for backup.

"And like I told you on the phone, you'll do everything I ask. If you don't, you'll die anyway, but with the blood of those you care about staining your hands," Alex said, and swiveled one of the lights so Sept could see what he was talking about.

Nathan and Damien were standing on tiny footstools. Around their necks were nooses short enough to guarantee death if the stools were kicked away. "See, I told you I had someone you cared about."

Damien appeared so weak that Sept was afraid he'd fall without any help from Alex. "I'm who you want, so cut them down. The notes, the crimes, and all the phone calls were all for me, so let them go and we'll settle whatever you like."

"So noble." Alex took the light away from the two men and put it back on the patch of dirt. "But they're going to stay put until we finish what needs to be done." Alex pointed the knife at the ground. "Lie down."

The little clues, from his interest in the case to his constant, careful study of the pictures, came back to Sept as she pressed her back to the ground. They made sense now, but Alex would be long gone before anyone else, from her father down to George, figured things out.

"Tell me about your family, Alex."

"They're gone, so what does it matter?" He looped a rope around one of her wrists and tied the knot she'd become familiar with, muttering the steps. The other end he tied to the stake he'd driven in one corner and pulled tight, which forced Sept to twist her body in that direction. From that angle she saw his family picture. "But if you're dying to know." He laughed.

"I could tell from the picture that you loved them."

He tied another piece around the other wrist and walked the end out of sight. When he came back, the key clicked in the cuffs as he unlocked the side he needed to tie next.

"I loved them to a fault, but that stupid bitch I married couldn't take what was coming to her, so I punished her the only way I knew how."

Overhead the sky turned darker as rainclouds moved in, and the temperature dropped. For once the weather forecasters had been right.

"What does that mean?" Sept asked as he repeated his process at her feet.

"When I told her to stay put, for once in her miserable life she tried to grow a backbone and leave with my son." He cut Sept's coat off and made a slit at the base of her shirt so he could rip it off. "She kept crying about the storm and how she needed to take him away, and the more she cried the more she packed. I kept telling her not to put another goddamn thing in that suitcase, but all of a sudden she acted like she had the right to do whatever she wanted."

The cold raised goose bumps on Sept's skin, but she ignored the discomfort since the story he was telling made him pay less attention to her. His story and his movements engrossed him. She could've been anyone lying there.

"What happened?"

"What happened? Ha," he said with so much venom that he drove the knife into the ground right by her head. "I took away the reason for her wanting to leave." Alex screamed and wrapped his hands around her throat like he didn't realize what he was doing, then started to squeeze. "I took the life right out of him, but it wasn't wrong. My boy needed to get away from that bitch before she turned him against me."

Sept tried to bring her hands up to stop him before he killed her. At first the ropes wouldn't let her move much, but the harder he squeezed, the harder she pulled. The recent rain made the stakes in the ground move enough for her to notice. She still couldn't rip them out, and as her vision started to go black, she inanely thought of not having to face disembowelment.

The rain eventually brought her back to consciousness. When she opened her eyes again, she felt the soreness around her throat. Alex was pacing beside her and hitting himself on the head and repeating, "I'm not stupid."

When Alex finally stopped walking, he whispered, "I said I was sorry, so you can shut up now. I didn't lose complete control again, so stop your bitching."

The rain started to come down in a steady stream, the cold droplets making Sept feel more alert. She raised her head, hoping Damien and Nathan weren't hanging by their necks.

"See, she's awake," Alex said to someone she couldn't see.

"Finish your story," Sept rasped when he dropped to his knees close to her. "Please, I want to know."

"Why?" Alex's face was so close to hers that she could smell his breath.

Everything Julio Munez had told her came back to Sept, and she tried to frame her words so they'd have some impact on him. "Because you are the better warrior and I want to learn from you."

"You're about to die, Warrior, so why's it important to learn anything at all?"

"I might have failed in this life, but I want the knowledge of your strength in the next. If you don't share it with me, once I'm dead I'll keep your wife and son from returning," she said, and dropped her head and turned her face away from him like what he did next didn't matter.

"That's not fair," he shouted, sounding like a petulant child, but Sept wouldn't answer him. "All right," he said, talking louder over the rain. "While she packed, our son walked into our room, and the only thing I could think of was to keep him with me. I picked him up, and when I came to, my hands were around his throat and he was dead. I don't remember exactly what happened, so I blamed it on my wife. She had to pay, so I killed her."

That had to be when he went insane, Sept thought as she started to shiver, and Alex started to cry. "Once they were gone I had to get them back, and I was willing to try anything."

Before Sept could speak, Alex jumped again and started arguing with someone near the swing set. With any luck he would keep screaming and she could try to tip the scales. She closed her eyes and pulled down as hard as she could, not stopping when the ropes bit into her wrists. The stakes were driven in a foot deep, but they were no match for the rich delta mud that made up the foundation of most of the city.

Her right hand came loose first, but Alex noticed her before she could free her left, and instead of coming after her, he kicked Nathan and Damien down. She screamed as she used her free hand to pull the other stake out and reached for the knife to cut her feet free.

When she came up and wiped her hair out of her eyes, Alex was running for the house, probably for his gun. But she didn't have time to go after him before she saved Nathan, who, unlike Damien, was twitching.

She ran to the swing set and positioned Nathan on her shoulders so she could bear his weight and reach behind him and cut his hands free. He was still conscious enough to stop fighting and reach up for the bar long enough for Sept to put his stool back in place.

"Hurry up before the nut comes back," Sept yelled as she handed him the knife and moved to hold Damien up. She didn't want to think about the fact that he was swinging and putting up no fight for air.

Nathan cut himself down, then Damien, whom Sept lowered in place. "Where's your gun?" she asked Nathan, who was rubbing his neck as if trying to make the pain go away.

"He took it," Nathan gasped.

"Never mind. I see it," Sept said as she stared at Alex by the house, holding both her and Nathan's weapons. He opened fire, and Sept pushed Nathan to the ground.

She conjured up a picture of Keegan before she took a deep breath and started to run toward Alex. If she was destined to die, that's what she wanted to remember, she thought, as she moved closer to him. If she had learned one lesson while trapped after the storm in the Superdome with some trigger-happy idiots, it was that aggressiveness made for a lousy target.

Someone running at you instead of cowering in one spot was harder to hit, and Sept gambled that would ring true now. As she got closer he hit her left forearm and her leg, but she kept going, and when she ran into him, they fell with her on top.

Sept's arm felt broken, but she refused to stop and was able to hold his left hand down so he couldn't fire. As he raised his other hand to shoot her in the head, she imitated Erica and bit him.

Alex screamed and pounded the side of Sept's head with the gun, but she refused to release the bridge of his nose. He stopped hitting and got a deafening shot off.

It took Sept a few seconds to realize she was still alive and Alex was yelling again, only this time Mike was biting him in the bicep, and he wasn't letting up no matter how many swipes Alex took at him. Sept rolled off and grabbed her gun.

"Mike, no," she screamed when he moved from Alex's arm to his neck. She cracked Alex in the head with the butt of her gun and touched Mike's back to stop him from ripping out Alex's throat. "No, boy." Mike growled and lifted his head, but he didn't bite down.

Nathan got there as Sept sat up and cradled her left arm against her chest, making Mike finally quit. "Get the cuffs he used on me," she told Nathan.

"Are you sure?" Nathan whispered.

"I'm too tired and hurt too much to play God today, so yes, I'm sure," Sept said as she kept her eyes on Alex for any movements to make her change her mind.

The rain continued as Nathan cuffed Alex and rolled him onto his stomach, then called for backup and an ambulance for Damien.

"I don't understand any of this," Nathan said as he sat next to Sept and pressed his shirt into the bullet hole in her leg. "How did we miss Alex as the killer, and why is Damien here?"

"I don't know, but I guess even crazy killers have moments of lucidity." She looked in the direction of Damien's body and shook her head. "I don't have any explanation for Damien, but this explains why we couldn't find him. Evidently Alex was going to use him as a way to get me here so he could kill me." The sound of sirens in the distance made Sept close her eyes in relief.

"You were right," Nathan said. "There's no such thing as ghosts."

"The closest we'll ever find is a crime scene investigator who becomes a murderer, then investigates his own crimes. If he left clues or made mistakes, he could certainly take care of them."

The first person to make it to the yard as Sept finished talking was her brother Gustave. "Check on Damien first," she told him when he ran to her. "I need to know I wasn't too late." Then she gave in to the pain and welcomed the darkness that brought numbness.

## CHAPTER FORTY-THREE

Is she awake?" Sept heard her father ask Keegan. They'd kept her in the hospital for a couple of days and she'd been home ever since, everyone from Royce to Fritz ordering her to stay there until the bullet wounds healed enough that she was walking without crutches and her arm was out of a sling. According to her doctor, that would take at least a month and a half.

"Come in, Dad," Sept called out to him. With the restaurant closed for renovations, Keegan and Jacqueline had been content to stay home and dote on her, which was nice, but they didn't have news about the case.

"Hey, kid, I brought some company," Sebastian said as Nathan followed him in.

"I was wondering what happened to you, partner," Sept said, and held her hand up to him. When Nathan ignored it and hugged her instead and started sniffling, she rolled her eyes at her father. "Nathan, I know you think you could've done more, but we're both here and we're alive to tell the tale and testify."

"I'm sorry, but I feel guilty for letting this happen." Nathan let go and wiped his eyes.

"Granted, it was dark out there, but I don't remember you shooting me. If you did, don't tell me. I don't want to have to waste time planning my revenge on you," Sept said. "Anything new?" she asked both men, since Nathan had been cleared for duty when the swelling in his neck went down.

"It's too early to tell, but the district attorney's office thinks Alex is too far gone to be found competent to stand trial," Sebastian said. "They have him locked in isolation in St. Charles Parish since the jail here isn't open yet."

"Did he add anything else to what he said that night?"

"He hasn't uttered a word since we took him into custody, but he holds his hands to his ears like he's trying to drown something out all the time," Nathan said. "The best we can tell is that Teacher was someone Alex made up, not a real person. The doctor monitoring him said it was like a pressure valve his head made up to keep him somewhat tethered to reality."

"Reality? Is he kidding?" Sept said.

"Not yours and mine by comparison, but it did help him blend in and do his job. On the flip side, it also helped him plan and execute the murders," Sebastian said. "We need him to talk some more if we're going to find out why he had it in for you."

"I'll give it a try," Sept said.

Keegan broke in. "Don't even think about it, Seven. You're not going anywhere until I get a note from three doctors that it's all right for you to leave the house."

"It might be best if we do let her talk to this guy before she recovers," Sebastian told Keegan. "According to the same shrink, if Alex sees Sept in a position of weakness, he might open up."

After some more convincing, Nathan and Sebastian left with Sept for the thirty-minute drive to the neighboring parish. The jail was small compared to the one off Broad Street in New Orleans, but there were plenty of deputies on duty talking to the one Fritz had assigned from the NOPD.

Sept waited in an interview room in a wheelchair the jail had lent her, leaning on her right elbow since her broken arm was still sore. She'd been waiting to have this conversation since the moment she woke up in the ambulance.

The door opened and Alex shuffled in with a blank expression. He never lifted his head as the guards pushed him down in the chair opposite Sept's, but he moved a few feet back. Before she said anything, she noticed that he now looked as mad as he acted.

His hair was uncombed, he'd stopped shaving, and he hadn't wiped away the drool marks on the sides of his mouth. A row of scratches littered his arms, and the red streaks clashed with his orange jumpsuit. Those, Sebastian had told Sept, were self-inflicted, as were the bruises on his forehead where he beat his head against the bars of his cell until they sedated him.

The only wound she could identify was the set of teeth marks at the bridge of his nose, which she recognized as her contribution to his look. "Hello, Alex," she said, and watched as the fog lifted and he sat forward and raised his head.

"You," Alex said, and slammed his cuffed hands on the table that separated them. "I killed you."

"We found them," Sept said, ignoring the delusional talk. "And you'll have to answer for them as well."

"You found who?"

"Your wife Sonia and your son. It wasn't hard, since you kept that part of the yard so spotless." Sept shook her head at the guard when he stepped closer as Alex slammed his hands down again. "As it turns out, you're not blessed by any gods, you're just a damn wife beater who went a little crazy when he lost his punching bag."

"You don't know anything," Alex screamed, and pointed at her with both his index fingers. "She was mine, and I didn't say she could go anywhere. Those others were only human garbage."

"You can act crazy all you want, but you aren't walking away from what you did."

"How did you find me, anyway?" The more Alex talked, the more lucid he became.

"It would've taken me a few more hours if I'd had the chance to talk to Lourdes's mother, so I can't take the credit."

"Ha." He laughed and knocked on the surface of the table this time. "I knew you were more lucky than good."

"My dog found you, so what does that say about you?"

"The dog," Alex said, and spit on the floor. "That was my first mistake. I should've buried my knife into him, but I didn't have time. Someone was coming. What did Maria have to say about me? We never met."

"She knew Sonia, though. Your wife was related to her sister's husband and was an only child. I might have had a lot going on, but I remembered your story of where she was. I might not have put together that you were the killer from that, but I would've taken the same drive to your house. Her brother-in-law's name was second to last on the list, so you had a few more days' reprieve, but how this ended wouldn't have changed. One step into that freak show at the house would've blown your cover."

"At least I took one of yours before I was done," Alex said, and laughed. "That pathetic brother-in-law of yours is more of a screwup than you are." He laughed harder. "All of you out looking for him, and I'm the one who finds him, headed for your family's place on Sunday."

"I know what happened to Damien and how he ended up with you."

"How do you know that? Did you get Matilda Rodriguez to contact him on the other side?"

This time Sept laughed at his attempt at sarcasm. "What amazes me is how you got away with it as long as you did, because in the end you're not very smart. Six bodies to your credit, and it was you who was more lucky than good."

"I know you don't care about the others, but why do you keep saying six bodies? Did you put Damien in another category?" Alex glanced up at the two-way mirror, but not for long. His eyes came back to Sept's and his eyebrows rose.

"I can't count Damien because he's alive. You managed to sprain his neck, which will limit his job to a desk for months, but he's alive and talking," Sept said, and took pleasure in watching his face twist in anger.

During the story Damien had told her as they shared a hospital room, Sept felt compassion for him, and all the resentment she didn't realize had built to a boiling point concerning Noel and Sophie melted away. The only thing she saw when she'd looked at Damien was a man beaten down by the tragedy that would forever define his life, and his grief that he'd failed again because his life hadn't ended. She'd told him she was glad he'd survived and that she'd had the chance to help him find some peace, no matter what the past had been.

"Damien might not share my name, but he's a part of my family." Alex sat in his seat as if Sept's words had been nails that pinned him there. "So tell me, Alex, what did you get out of all this? You were calling the dead and they weren't interested."

Slowly, as if she'd given Alex a tranquilizer, he deflated, became silent, his face expressionless. He had finished talking to her, but whoever was sharing his head was back. Sept could tell by the way he put his hands to his ears. He was taken out, and at the door he glanced back and a little of his anger shone through, but Sept didn't give him the satisfaction of another word.

It was over and her part of the job was done. The DA's office would finish taking Alex through the system so he wouldn't be a problem to anyone else. She waited until the door closed again before she signaled her father to come wheel her out and take her home. Nathan and her father talked on the way back, but Sept stayed quiet as she thought of Sonia Perlis's hellish life with Alex. She couldn't conceive of a mother having to witness her husband kill her child right before she died.

He was crazy, but also extremely lucky, because a day after he killed his family, Katrina covered up his mess. The total evacuation of his neighborhood and the police enforcement that kept people out for days gave Alex the opportunity to bury both Sonia and his son in their yard.

He'd gotten the idea for the ritual killings from listening to Sonia's family, who were Santeria practitioners. But Julio, Maria, and Matilda had been correct in that faith had nothing to do with what Alex had done. His victims had merely replaced the role Sonia had played in his life.

Keegan was waiting for her outside, and Sept accepted her help into the wheelchair she was using around the house. Instead of taking her inside, Keegan wheeled her to the yard and to the table she'd set under one of the oaks. The time had gotten away from Sept, and when she saw the poinsettia plant at the center and the gift at one of the places, she remembered it was Christmas Eve, or close to it.

"Can I wait to open that?" Sept asked.

Keegan put her arms around her neck from behind and rested her chin on the top of Sept's head. "Sure, but can I ask why?"

"I don't have anything for you." Saying that hurt Sept more than Alex's bullets.

"The gift isn't from me, honey, so you can open it if you want." Keegan kissed her temple. "And you did get me something. Considering there weren't many places to shop this year, your gift was something no one else could've given me."

Sept lifted her good hand to touch Keegan's arm. "I don't remember buying anything, so give me a hint."

"I asked you for a day without a phone, gun, or work, and I'll get more than one of those," Keegan said, and sat next to her. "I asked for a vacation, and home is always as good a destination as any. Later on, I'll model my bathing suits for you."

Sept laughed and kissed the back of her hand. "You have a good outlook on life."

"I know, but I'm not finished. I also got a call from Mercy Alderson today."

Sept gazed at her with confusion, trying to place the name.

"Gym owner Alderson?" Sept finally asked. "Should I be jealous?"

"Mercy called me to complain about the traffic stop she endured yesterday," Keegan said with a smile so wide her cheeks should have hurt. "She called right after they released her from custody and discovered that the pills she had in her purse really were vitamins. Funny, she thought I was somehow responsible for her almost being strip-searched on the side of the road."

"You're telling me this because you think I had something to do with it?" Sept asked, but couldn't help smiling back. "Sounds like an unfortunate accident."

"Uh-huh," Keegan said. "There's one more thing."

"I can't wait." Sept closed her eyes when Keegan pressed her hand to the side of her face.

"You kept your promises and you came back. The best gift you gave me is that you belong to me. I love you."

"I love you too." Sept accepted Keegan's kiss. "If the present's not from you, who's it from?" she asked when they broke apart.

"Della." Keegan pushed it closer to Sept and helped her open it. They both laughed when Keegan lifted a new BlackBerry out of the box. The note read: *To replace the one you lost recently, only don't bring it to brunch. Love, Della.*

"I think you're in, Seven." Keegan put the phone back on the plate. "And you can count on us to love you along with your family."

On the other side of her, Mike barked in what sounded like agreement.

"I'm looking forward to it," Sept said.

Alex was now squarely in her "done" column. It was time to move forward, only now the future held more than just the next adventure and, more important, no more nightmares.

# About the Author

Ali lives right outside New Orleans with her partner of many years. As a writer, she couldn't ask for a better more beautiful place—so full of real-life characters to fuel the imagination. When she isn't writing, working in the yard, cheering for the LSU Tigers, or riding her bicycle, she makes a living in the nonprofit sector.

Ali has written *The Devil Inside*, *The Devil Unleashed*, *Deal With the Devil*, *Carly's Sound*, *Second Season*, *Calling the Dead*, and *Blue Skies* (available in 2009).

# Books Available From Bold Strokes Books

**Dreams of Bali** by C.J. Harte. Madison Barnes worships work, power, and success, and she's never allowed anyone to interfere—that is, until she runs into Karlie Henderson Stockard. Eclipse EBook (978-1-60282-070-8)

**The Limits of Justice** by John Morgan Wilson. Benjamin Justice and reporter Alexandra Templeton search for a killer in a mysterious compound in the remote California desert. (978-1-60282-060-9)

**Designed for Love** by Erin Dutton. Jillian Sealy and Wil Johnson don't much like each other, but they do have to work together—and what they desire most is not what either of them had planned. (978-1-60282-038-8)

**Calling the Dead** by Ali Vali. Six months after Hurricane Katrina, NOLA Detective Sept Savoie is a cop who thinks making a relationship work is harder than catching a serial killer—but her current case may prove her wrong. (978-1-60282-037-1)

**Dark Garden** by Jennifer Fulton. Vienna Blake and Mason Cavender are sworn enemies—who can't resist each other. Something has to give. (978-1-60282-036-4)

**Shots Fired** by MJ Williamz. Kyla and Echo seem to have the perfect relationship and the perfect life until someone shoots at Kyla—and Echo is the most likely suspect. (978-1-60282-035-7)

**truelesbianlove.com** by Carsen Taite. Mackenzie Lewis and Dr. Jordan Wagner have very different ideas about love, but they discover that truelesbianlove is closer than a click away. Eclipse EBook (978-1-60282-069-2)

**Justice at Risk** by John Morgan Wilson. Benjamin Justice's blind date leads to a rare opportunity for legitimate work, but a reckless risk changes his life forever. (978-1-60282-059-3)

**Run to Me** by Lisa Girolami. Burned by the four-letter word called love, the only thing Beth Standish wants to do is run for—or maybe from—her life. (978-1-60282-034-0)

**Split the Aces** by Jove Belle. In the neon glare of Sin City, two women ride a wave of passion that threatens to consume them in a world of fast money and fast times. (978-1-60282-033-3)

**Uncharted Passage** by Julie Cannon. Two women on a vacation that turns deadly face down one of nature's most ruthless killers—and find themselves falling in love. (978-1-60282-032-6)

**Night Call** by Radclyffe. All medevac helicopter pilot Jett McNally wants to do is fly and forget about the horror and heartbreak she left behind in the Middle East, but anesthesiologist Tristan Holmes has other plans. (978-1-60282-031-9)

**Lake Effect Snow** by C.P. Rowlands. News correspondent Annie T. Booker and FBI Agent Sarah Moore struggle to stay one step ahead of disaster as Annie's life becomes the war zone she once reported on. Eclipse EBook (978-1-60282-068-5)

**Revision of Justice** by John Morgan Wilson. Murder shifts into high gear, propelling Benjamin Justice into a raging fire that consumes the Hollywood Hills, burning steadily toward the famous Hollywood Sign—and the identity of a cold-blooded killer. (978-1-60282-058-6)

**I Dare You** by Larkin Rose. Stripper by night, corporate raider by day, Kelsey's only looking for sex and power, until she meets a woman who stirs her heart and her body. (978-1-60282-030-2)

**Truth Behind the Mask** by Lesley Davis. Erith Baylor is drawn to Sentinel Pagan Osborne's quiet strength, but the secrets between them strain duty and family ties. (978-1-60282-029-6)

**Cooper's Deale** by KI Thompson. Two would-be lovers and a decidedly inopportune murder spell trouble for Addy Cooper, no matter which way the cards fall. (978-1-60282-028-9)

**Romantic Interludes 1: Discovery** ed. by Radclyffe and Stacia Seaman. An anthology of sensual, erotic contemporary love stories from the best-selling Bold Strokes authors. (978-1-60282-027-2)

**A Guarded Heart** by Jennifer Fulton. The last place FBI Special Agent Pat Roussel expects to find herself is assigned to an illicit private security gig baby-sitting a celebrity. (Ebook) (978-1-60282-067-8)

**Saving Grace** by Jennifer Fulton. Champion swimmer Dawn Beaumont, injured in a car crash she caused, flees to Moon Island, where scientist Grace Ramsay welcomes her. (Ebook) (978-1-60282-066-1)

**The Sacred Shore** by Jennifer Fulton. Successful tech industry survivor Merris Randall does not believe in love at first sight until she meets Olivia Pearce. (Ebook) (978-1-60282-065-4)

**Passion Bay** by Jennifer Fulton. Two women from different ends of the earth meet in paradise. Author's expanded edition. (Ebook) (978-1-60282-064-7)

**Never Wake** by Gabrielle Goldsby. After a brutal attack, Emma Webster becomes a self-sentenced prisoner inside her condo—until the world outside her window goes silent. (Ebook) (978-1-60282-063-0)

**The Caretaker's Daughter** by Gabrielle Goldsby. Against the backdrop of a nineteenth-century English country estate, two women struggle to find love. (Ebook) (978-1-60282-062-3)

**Simple Justice** by John Morgan Wilson. When a pretty-boy cokehead is murdered, former LA reporter Benjamin Justice and his reluctant new partner, Alexandra Templeton, must unveil the real killer. (978-1-60282-057-9)

**Remember Tomorrow** by Gabrielle Goldsby. Cees Bannigan and Arieanna Simon find that a successful relationship rests in remembering the mistakes of the past. (978-1-60282-026-5)

**Put Away Wet** by Susan Smith. Jocelyn "Joey" Fellows has just been savagely dumped—when she posts an online personal ad, she discovers more than just the great sex she expected. (978-1-60282-025-8)

**Homecoming** by Nell Stark. Sarah Storm loses everything that matters—family, future dreams, and love—will her new "straight" roommate cause Sarah to take a chance at happiness? (978-1-60282-024-1)

**The Three** by Meghan O'Brien. A daring, provocative exploration of love and sexuality. Two lovers, Elin and Kael, struggle to survive in a postapocalyptic world. (Ebook) (978-1-60282-056-2)

**Falling Star** by Gill McKnight. Solley Rayner hopes a few weeks with her family will help heal her shattered dreams, but she hasn't counted on meeting a woman who stirs her heart. ( 978-1-60282-023-4)

**Lethal Affairs** by Kim Baldwin and Xenia Alexiou. Elite operative Domino is no stranger to peril, but her investigation of journalist Hayley Ward will test more than her skills. (978-1-60282-022-7)

**A Place to Rest** by Erin Dutton. Sawyer Drake doesn't know what she wants from life until she meets Jori Diamantina—only trouble is, Jori doesn't seem to share her desire. (978-1-60282-021-0)

**Warrior's Valor** by Gun Brooke. Dwyn Izsontro and Emeron D'Artansis must put aside personal animosity and unwelcome attraction to defeat an enemy of the Protector of the Realm. (978-1-60282-020-3)

**Finding Home** by Georgia Beers. Take two polar-opposite women with an attraction for one another they're trying desperately to ignore, throw in a far-too-observant dog, and then sit back and enjoy the romance. (978-1-60282-019-7)

**Word of Honor** by Radclyffe. All Secret Service Agent Cameron Roberts and First Daughter Blair Powell want is a small intimate wedding, but the paparazzi and a domestic terrorist have other plans. (978-1-60282-018-0)

**Hotel Liaison** by JLee Meyer. Two women searching through a secret past discover that their brief hotel liaison is only the beginning. Will they risk their careers—and their hearts—to follow through on their desires? (978-1-60282-017-3)

**Love on Location** by Lisa Girolami. Hollywood film producer Kate Nyland and artist Dawn Brock discover that love doesn't always follow the script. (978-1-60282-016-6)

**Edge of Darkness** by Jove Belle. Investigator Diana Collins charges at life with an irreverent comment and a right hook, but even those may not protect her heart from a charming villain. (978-1-60282-015-9)

**Thirteen Hours** by Meghan O'Brien. Workaholic Dana Watts's life takes a sudden turn when an unexpected interruption arrives in the form of the most beautiful breasts she has ever seen—stripper Laurel Stanley's. (978-1-60282-014-2)

**In Deep Waters 2** by Radclyffe and Karin Kallmaker. All bets are off when two award winning-authors deal the cards of love and passion… and every hand is a winner. (978-1-60282-013-5)

**Pink** by Jennifer Harris. An irrepressible heroine frolics, frets, and navigates through the "what ifs" of her life: all the unexpected turns of fortune, fame, and karma. (978-1-60282-043-2)

**Deal with the Devil** by Ali Vali. New Orleans crime boss Cain Casey brings her fury down on the men who threatened her family, and blood and bullets fly. (978-1-60282-012-8)

**Naked Heart** by Jennifer Fulton. When a sexy ex-CIA agent sets out to seduce and entrap a powerful CEO, there's more to this plan than meets the eye…or the flogger. (978-1-60282-011-1)

**Heart of the Matter** by KI Thompson. TV newscaster Kate Foster is Professor Ellen Webster's dream girl, but Kate doesn't know Ellen exists…until an accident changes everything. (978-1-60282-010-4)

**Heartland** by Julie Cannon. When political strategist Rachel Stanton and dude ranch owner Shivley McCoy collide on an empty country road, fate intervenes. (978-1-60282-009-8)

**Shadow of the Knife** by Jane Fletcher. Militia Rookie Ellen Mittal has no idea just how complex and dangerous her life is about to become. A Celaeno series adventure romance. (978-1-60282-008-1)

**To Protect and Serve** by VK Powell. Lieutenant Alex Troy is caught in the paradox of her life—to hold steadfast to her professional oath or to protect the woman she loves. (978-1-60282-007-4)

**Deeper** by Ronica Black. Former homicide detective Erin McKenzie and her fiancée Elizabeth Adams couldn't be happier until the not-so-distant past comes knocking at the door. (978-1-60282-006-7)

**The Lonely Hearts Club** by Radclyffe. Take three friends, add two ex-lovers and several new ones, and the result is a recipe for explosive rivalries and incendiary romance. (978-1-60282-005-0)

**Venus Besieged** by Andrews & Austin. Teague Richfield heads for Sedona and the sensual arms of psychic astrologer Callie Rivers for a much-needed romantic reunion. (978-1-60282-004-3)

**Branded Ann** by Merry Shannon. Pirate Branded Ann raids a merchant vessel to obtain a treasure map and gets more than she bargained for with the widow Violet. (978-1-60282-003-6)

**American Goth** by JD Glass. Trapped by an unsuspected inheritance and guided only by the guardian who holds the secret to her future, Samantha Cray fights to fulfill her destiny. (978-1-60282-002-9)

**Learning Curve** by Rachel Spangler. Ashton Clarke is perfectly content with her life until she meets the intriguing Professor Carrie Fletcher, who isn't looking for a relationship with anyone. (978-1-60282-001-2)

**Place of Exile** by Rose Beecham. Sheriff's detective Jude Devine struggles with ghosts of her past and an ex-lover who still haunts her dreams. (978-1-933110-98-1)

**Fully Involved** by Erin Dutton. A love that has smoldered for years ignites when two women and one little boy come together in the aftermath of tragedy. (978-1-933110-99-8)

# *Bold Strokes*

## B O O K S

# WEBSTORE

## PRINT AND EBOOKS

Romance
Mystery
Intrigue

Adventure
Erotica
Fantasy    Sci-Fi

MATINEE BOOKS

LIBERTY
EDITION

BS
BOLD
STROKES
BOOKS

victory
EDITIONS

ECLIPSE
e

http://www.boldstrokesbooks.com